Midnight in Oz

Also by Roger Helm

ISLAND GAMES

Midnight in Oz

ROGER HELM

Liberty Tree Publishing

Liberty Tree Publishing
1713 Persimmon Lane, Suite 300
Knoxville, Tennessee 37922

All of the events and characters in this book are fictitious, and any resemblance to actual persons, living or dead, is purely coincidental.

Library of Congress Cataloging-in-Publication Data

Helm, Roger.
Midnight in Oz / Roger Helm.
p. cm.
ISBN 0-9720767-3-5
LCCN: 2004094119

Printed in the United States of America
First Edition

This book is printed on acid free paper.

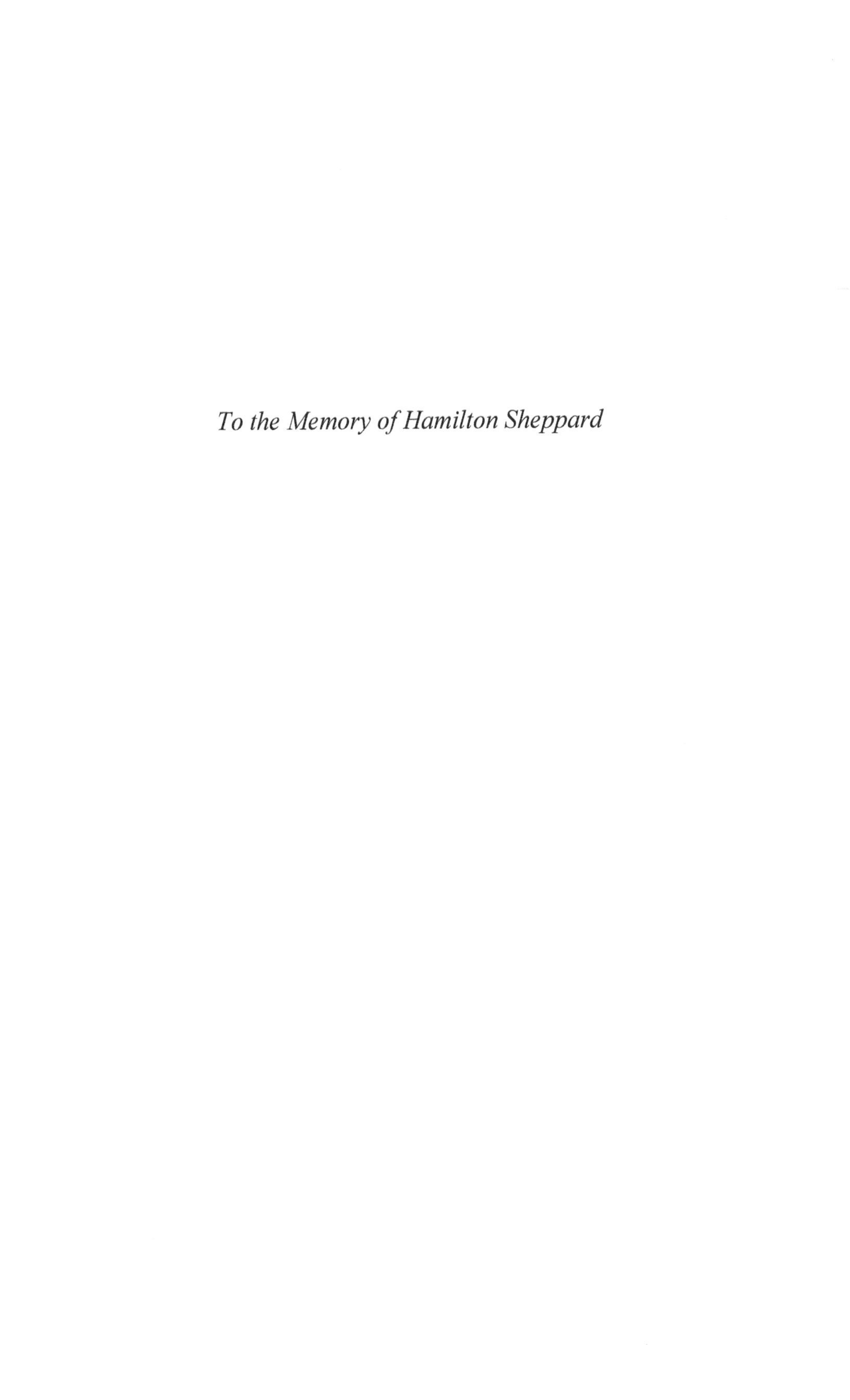

To the Memory of Hamilton Sheppard

Special Thanks To:

Virginia Sheppard
Mary Linn Roby
And my wonderful wife

PROLOGUE

Like a lamb to the slaughter, that's what she was. She seemed confident now, with her stoic posture, pursed lips, and determined eyes. But so had all the others. Soon she'd be transformed, coming out of the master's chamber like a blubbering baby. It didn't matter how good the money was: no compensation would cover what this poor woman was about to be subjected to.

Randal Belstrom knew all of this, but he didn't have the heart to tell her. She appeared happy and ready to serve, ready to take her new position seriously. Randal let her bathe in self-confidence while life remained as she knew it, before the Viper destroyed her little bubble. Why try to warn her? What would be the point? Nothing could ease the inevitably brutal blow to her psyche.

"Just remember, he needs to take his medication, even though he won't want to," Randal said, feeling a tinge of guilt for setting the woman up. "Be firm. Don't take any guff. He'll be sure to dish it out."

"No worries," she told him, while using a hand to make sure her perm was in order. "I'll have him eating out of my hand before I get back."

Randal wished it were so, wished Patricia Porter or someone like her could march into the man's chamber and put him in his place. Unfortunately, that never happened during the fourteen years he had been the head servant at the Guerridelli Estate in Palm Springs, California. He'd been kept on staff because he somehow managed to find a speck of favor with the man and now it appeared that he would be at the don's beck-and-call until the ole geezer finally gave up the spirit. What Randal wanted didn't matter anymore. His life now belonged to Devon "The Viper" Guerridelli.

Once, he had tried desperately to find a way out, convinced that Guerridelli was evil incarnate. But one of the man's demonic spawns had sat him down and told him in no uncertain terms that he could never quit now unless The Viper wished him to. To drive the point home, Guerridelli's son had left a present for Randal on his dining room table, along with a note, explaining what would happen if he didn't obey his father's every wish. Randal still became nauseous thinking about his pet, the Doberman's eyes staring at him from a severed head.

Going to the police would have been pointless since the Guerridellis owned most of the higher-ups. Besides, in spite of serving in the devil's own home, there *were* fringe benefits. While at the estate, Randal lived like a king, served by other staff performing peripheral duties. Not only that: Guerridelli had drafted a letter stating Randal would receive two million tax-free dollars on his death, provided it could be proved he wasn't responsible for any untimely departures.

The family, over the past few years, finally recognized Randal's faithful service and tolerance, and had agreed he could hire an assistant. Randal had interviewed dozens of potentials and selected some he thought might work. He had tried gentlemen with backgrounds similar to his own, sticky-sweet old ladies, and fresh young women. When none of those worked out he even tried pretty boys, thinking the old man had alternative tastes.

But all the trials had ended the same. As this one would. He was sure of it.

Randal tried to smile encouragingly as Patricia marched, chin first, into Guerridelli's quarters. And for a brief moment he considered stopping her, to spare her from the sadist within.

᯽

Patricia Porter's last job, attending to the former CEO of a fortune 500 company – a crotchety old man who was used to having his own way – had ended three years ago. Raised a staunch Baptist, she didn't intimidate easily. Although the man had tried desperately to get the upper hand, and despite the fact that she was younger, she assumed the role of his mother, providing him so successfully with a healthy regimen that, in the end, she had become his only confidant. When he died, her reward had been substantial, although not enough to live on for the rest of her life.

She'd looked halfheartedly for other work, but the cushion of cash had made it too easy to wait for the right opportunity to come along. Now, with her windfall running low, she needed to find work. She'd seen the Guerridelli estate with its high surrounding wall, but the name Guerridelli had meant nothing to her, even when Randal had interviewed her. Now as she entered the man's room she had no clue he'd been one of the modern-day crime bosses, or that the twisted fingers gripping the armrests of his wheelchair had often wrapped tightly around the neck of a rival, while all life drained from his flailing body. She might have fallen to her knees and prayed for protection had she seen how he personally cut off every last finger of an employee accused of skimming off the profits. And had she known the truth, Patricia certainly would not have so much as contemplated serving a man who had destroyed the lives and businesses of so many in order to build his own dark empire.

No.

Patricia was here to serve and prove she was the best person for the job. And somewhere in the back of her mind, she knew that if she did her job well, Mr. Guerridelli would one day thank her and reward her for her dedication, the way her previous employer had.

The suite was spacious and held everything an aged man might need while awaiting the remainder of his days. There was a massive bed and marble bathroom. In the center of the suite, eight pillars surrounded a small pool, while French doors opened onto a balcony overlooking the immaculately manicured gardens.

The sound of an Italian opera drifted though the suite. Passing beneath massive paintings of men she believed must be Guerridelli ancestors, she approached the man in the wheelchair, medicine in hand. He sat with his profile to her, his pure white hair straight and long enough to stretch halfway down his back.

His face was tan, leathery with age, his frame draped in a dressing gown, frail. He stared expressionlessly ahead, listless, unresponsive to her presence in the room.

A chill ran up her back as the music peaked to a full crescendo and then ceased. Shaking off a sense of dread, she bent over him to speak. "My name is Patricia Porter," she said. "I'll be helping out from now on. I have your medication."

There was no response. The old man continued to stare blindly ahead.

"Here's your medication and something to take it with," she said crisply, holding out a glass of water and three small pills.

"Where's Randal?"

His voice startled her. It was raspy and harsh.

"Like I said, I'll be helping out from now on," she told him patiently. "Randal will still be here, but –"

"I want to see him *now*," Guerridelli said with such force that it made her pause.

"Right now you need to take your medication," she said. "You can see Randal later. We have to see that you're properly taken care of."

The muscles in the man's face tightened. His eyebrows furled, his jawbone clenched. A muscle near his nose twitched as he turned to look at Patricia.

Having lived for well over fifty years, Patricia had seen her share of folks giving a wicked eye. But nothing prepared her for the glaring malevolence pouring from Mr. Guerridelli's gaze. It's been said that the eyes are windows into a man's soul and Patricia was staring into a house full of evil. Seconds passed during which she felt as though she could not breathe.

She dropped the glass. It shattered on the tile floor, the sound shaking the man's hold on her. Stooping to pick up a few of the larger pieces she said, "Oh dear! I'm terribly sorry."

As she bent over, the man grabbed a fistful of hair and pulled her face, with the foul stench of his decaying breath, to within an inch of his own. "You will leave me and have Randal return," he said. "Do you understand?"

Patricia quivered with fear, her scalp burning with pain. Hyperventilating, she tried desperately to avoid those eyes.

Those wicked eyes.

She couldn't speak but attempted her best effort at a nod.

Guerridelli loosened his arm slightly, but the grip on her hair remained. Suddenly he yanked her face back even closer to his. "Pray that I never see you again," he snarled, "because if I do, someone will pay you a visit in the middle of the night. I'll tell them to slice the eyelids from your face, leaving your peepers to dry up in their sockets like prunes. Have I made myself perfectly clear?"

Patricia's legs gave way and she fell to her knees on the broken shards. "Yes," she whimpered. "Yes."

❧

Another dust-biter, a tragic waste of a perfectly acceptable employee. Randal watched as Patricia grabbed her purse and staggered toward the door, knees dripping with blood, her eyes wet with terror.

"I'm sorry," was all he could muster before she disappeared out the door and back into her own world, a world that he suspected would never be the same.

Randal swallowed hard and entered the don's chamber. Before he could say anything, the old man spoke. "Clean up this mess before I cut myself," he said. "It stinks. I think the damn woman peed. I've told you I don't want anyone else. I can barely tolerate you."

"But your son thought an assistant would be a good idea, sir," Randal reminded him, beginning the process of cleaning up.

"I don't trust them," Guerridelli grumbled under his breath. "Damn woman was trying to poison me. Probably sent by the Savino brothers."

"Sir?" Randal said. "I thought they were all dead."

"Don't believe it. Nowadays, being dead isn't what it used to be. The bastards are probably still trying to get even, fending off the worms with one hand and plotting to do me in with the other."

"I dare say you needn't worry about enemies that are dead, sir," Randal suggested. "Even their families have all been – disposed of."

"Little man, you have no idea what kind of power men like me possess. Even when our lives seem over."

"Yes, sir." Although Randal had no idea what he meant. He had always found it the better part of wisdom to simply agree.

As he finished mopping up the floor, Randal reflected that Guerridelli was treating him with respect, which made it a good day, indeed. Had the old man been in one of his sour moods, the poor woman might not have gotten out of the room alive. It had happened once before and Randal had gone to great pains to cover up the mess after Guerridelli had strangled one of the applicants with his viselike hands.

"Roll me over to the balcony," Guerridelli said. "And turn on the music. Have you ever been to Bootleg Hill, Nevada? I had a nephew who lived there. I ever tell you that?"

Even though Randal had heard the story several dozen times, he told Guerridelli that he didn't recall it. It pleased him to speak of such things. And anything that pleased him made him easier to tolerate.

"Helluva kid. He stood up to me and said he didn't want to be in the family business. Can you believe that?" Guerridelli said and chuckled. "The little shit stood there and threw it back in my face. Thought he was too good for that, thought he could make it on his own. I should've finished him on the spot but didn't. *Give the kid a break*, somethin' inside told me. So I did. I watched him kinda like an experiment. See what happened when he came groveling back to the family."

"Never did. Moved to Bootleg Hill, Nevada," he continued. "I always wanted to go see him, see what kind of life was so much better than the family. Know what I mean?"

"Yes, sir," Randal said, waiting patiently for Guirridelli to finish.

"Maybe the kid had the right idea. Tough life, the business."

"Yes, sir."

"I wondered sometimes what it would be like if I'd moved to Bootleg Hill, Nevada. What if I'd stood up to my old man like that?"

"I'm sure you would be respected no matter what you chose to do, sir," Randal said.

Guerridelli stared out at the swaying palms. "I coulda done more, you know. If I'd wanted to."

"Sir?"

"The business world was my own private playground. If I were young again – hell, I could own the whole damn world. Give me fifty more years…"

Randal shuddered at the man's words. The scariest part was he believed it. Being young again and given enough time, Guerridelli could probably strong-arm his way into the political arena, launching himself into a position to wield enormous power.

"Sir, you *do* need to take your medication," Randal said. "I've made sure, myself, that it came straight from the bottle I have locked in the safe."

When he handed the pills to Guerridelli, the old man seized Randal's neck and squeezed.

"If you've poisoned me, so help me, you'll be sorry," he growled. "Pathetic little man. I'll have you by the balls long after I'm dead. You'll see. Just try me."

Randal was having trouble breathing, let alone answering. Yet, he knew better than to fight. Released at last, Randal took several deep breaths and stood, rubbing his neck, waiting for the don to make the next move.

Miraculously, Guerridelli reached out for the pills and took them.

Later that afternoon while the desert temperature rose, straining the air-conditioner, Guerridelli attempted the transition from wheelchair to wading pool by himself. Locking the wheels, he struggled to lift himself out of the chair and onto his weak legs. Turning around and gripping the chair, he descended the steps into cool water, whereupon the old man's failing heart simply tried to keep up, each valve gulping blood as fast as possible to distribute the meager oxygen sucked in by frail lungs.

All at once, having served the man for eighty-three years, the machine stopped as his heart repaid him for all the hatred he had harbored there. His feet slipped from under him and his frail bones crashed against the side of the pool. He cried out, but he was alone, the way he had been for his entire life. No matter that he had had several wives, children, grandchildren, and even two great-grandchildren. No matter that he easily commanded anyone within the long reach of his empire. The man had always been alone.

With one hand he flailed for the call button on the wheelchair. By the time Randal appeared, the old man was unaware of anything other than the pain wracking his chest.

As for Randal, he stood with mouth agape at the sight, unable to move. Considering the two million he would receive – a paltry reward for the hell he'd paid the past fourteen years – he should turn around and walk out the door. Morally, it was a no-brainer. Whatever ethics, humanitarianism, or good-heartedness he had possessed before working for Guerridelli had long been extinguished. Now he had grown cold and greedy, having learned how to look out for *numero uno*, regardless of who got hurt.

Sure. He would walk back out the door and close it, go to the kitchen to see how the cook was doing with dinner, thus establishing an alibi. No sense in taking any chances and risk being blamed. Guerridelli could wallow in his own pool of blood as far as Randal was concerned.

But just as he turned to leave, he pictured Vincent, the old man's son, questioning him about where he was while The Viper was dying, asking why he hadn't been there to call for help, probing and twisting everything into a pretzel until he could prove that it was actually Randal's fault that his father was dead. And then, at best, he would be able to walk away without any cash. At worst, he'd be at the unmerciful hands of the Guerridelli brothers for leaving their father unattended.

Randal screamed for one of the servants to call the paramedics.

As Guerridelli aged, the estate had been equipped with a hospital room adjacent to the man's suite. Now the old man's son, Vincent, stood over him, gripping his father's hand with thumbs locked.

"Doc says your hip is broken," Vincent said, tears forming in his eyes. "I can't believe this happened. Where the hell was Randal?"

Guerridelli had oxygen tubes in his nose, heart monitors on his chest, and an IV dripping fluid into his arm. The don waved his free hand; wire attached to his index finger with a clip. "It's my own fault," he said, waving his free hand. "I could've called him to help me into the pool but didn't."

"Has he been giving you your blood thinner?" Vincent asked. "He didn't, did he? You just leave it –"

"Listen, Vinny," the old man said. "He gave me the pills. When you get to be my age, when you've had the kind of life I have, you don't trust nobody. I think to myself, what if someone put the wrong pills in the bottle without Randal knowing? What if someone paid him off to do me in? Know what I mean?"

"What are you saying?" Vincent asked.

"I never took the damn pills. Flushed 'em down the toilet, dropped 'em down the sink. Whatever. But I never took them."

Vincent sighed. "Why didn't you tell me? I coulda made sure for you. You'll die if you don't take the pills. What good's avoiding a hit if you die anyway?"

Suddenly one of the machines sounded an alarm. Vincent's eyes grew wide as he stared at the equipment as though the very life of his father was held inside their cold circuits.

"What's wrong?" he demanded. "I'll get the nurse."

"It's nothing," Guerridelli told him, gripping his hand even tighter. "The clip fell off my finger."

With the clip reattached, the beeping stopped.

Vincent walked to the window. "I've been thinking about something," he said, speaking softly now. "Doctor said hip injuries at your age aren't good. You're not going to have much of a life anymore even if you recover. I think it's time."

The old man considered. "And how can we trust this company? How do we know they won't let something go wrong?"

"They're scientists, not the mob. I paid 'em a visit and they're secure, trust me. Maybe more than you are here."

"I don't know if I'm ready."

"If you wait any longer it may be too late," Vincent said. "Besides, I've made some special arrangements. I think you'll be pleased."

"What arrangements?"

The old man listened as Vincent explained how he'd secured the services of one of Guerridelli's grandsons, a kid who knew how to hack into computers to change people's records for the family business, usually for his own benefit at someone else's expense. Such activity was foreign to the don. But he recognized that like all forms of business, times change and so do the methods.

"Okay," the old man said finally after careful consideration. "Might as well get on with it. Now get me some damn food. I'm starving."

When Vincent emerged from the room, Randal was waiting. "How does he appear?" he asked. "I've been worried."

"Save the act," Vincent told him. "We won't be needing your services any longer. I'm prepared to offer you a quarter million to walk away right now."

A quarter million was a far cry from two. Yet Randal was afraid to protest. "That's very generous," he said, "but the arrangement…"

"Screw the arrangement. You want to stick to the arrangement, fine. But I better warn you that it's going to be a very, very long time till The Viper croaks. Capeesh?"

CHAPTER 1

Jack Stuart stared at himself in the mirror, something he frequently did, studying his brown eyes roaming over his reflection, the wavy hair, sun-darkened skin and lean body, as though searching for a minute flaw, almost begging for the tiniest hint of something wrong, but not finding any. And, often, those eyes would meet with the man standing opposite and plead the same question over again.

Since it was after hours on Friday evening he should have been packing it in and heading home, should have been eager to have Maggie and the kids welcome him for an enjoyable weekend together. She would likely kick things off by cooking a favorite dish and doing up the table with china and flatware, inviting candles waiting to be lit in the center. Soft music would be playing from the family-room stereo while Justin and Amanda would sit quietly at the table looking sweet as buttons. It was a ritual Maggie enjoyed on Friday nights.

He'd discuss his day and she'd discuss hers. Justin might offer one of his tall tales about a safari he'd taken in the backyard, while Amanda would roll her precious eyes at her little brother's imagination. When the meal was finished, Maggie would clear the plates and sit the children in the living room to recite one of their favorite poems. If their delivery met with her approval, she'd say, they could each have a reward, which almost always meant they'd get a slice of whatever dessert she'd prepared. Simply opening their mouths and making a sound was enough to please, but Maggie had a way of making a big deal of the occasion, making them feel as if they'd just delivered their Pulitzer winning poetry to a crowd full of culture.

After that, Jack would receive two kisses from little lips and Maggie would usher them off to their rooms, tucking in tight for some much-needed sleep and, at the same time, allowing her quality time with her man. She'd find him waiting in the living room where she'd bring a shared glass of wine for them to loosen up with. One thing would lead to another and, voila, the perfect evening in the Stuart household would be crowned with a glorious union of passion, unrivaled by any they'd previously experienced.

Who could ask for anything more?

It was too good to be true and yet Jack couldn't put a finger on a feeling that had been seeping up through the contentment, literally starting to ooze over the placid bliss of his life as though something altogether nasty were rotting underneath. Every time the feeling began to overwhelm him, he stared in the mirror; stared until he had memorized every contour of his perfect face and each speckle in his eyes. And every time he stared, the question screamed at him from behind the glass.

Who are you?

For though he could see his reflection and watch the exact command he wielded over every facial muscle, something was altogether amiss. Those eyes staring back seemed more alien than those that had somehow managed to traverse the galaxy and land within his body, uninvited. He felt out of place, as if he shouldn't be here; maybe shouldn't be anywhere at all, let alone living in a postcard life.

Finally, having exhausted his patience, he switched off the bathroom light and returned to his private office. Before grabbing his jacket, he stuffed his paycheck in a pocket, but not before looking at the name on the front.

Jack Stuart.

Even his name seemed wrong. He'd now received dozens of these things and every time the name of the payee, his name, looked as though the check belonged to someone else. He wasn't sure to whom they *should* be made out. Just not Jack Stuart. His salary was always more than the Stuarts needed to live on, a salary that afforded them a healthy savings account and frequent vacations to their luxury condo in Destin, Florida.

He made his way to the bay of elevators, dreading the drive home, anticipating another one of Maggie's "evenings" which sometimes seemed unbearably concocted. And for just a moment, he wondered what would happen if he never showed; wondered how she'd respond if he merely got in his car and started driving somewhere he'd never been before; maybe not coming home all weekend. Always the understanding wife, Maggie never got mad for any reason and he wondered if the woman was capable of anything so unruly.

As incredible as it seemed, he could picture her behavior down to the last detail as he would walk in the door on Sunday evening. She'd run to him and hug him desperately, asking where he'd been, was he all right. Upon learning he'd merely wigged out and taken off to parts unknown, she'd probably just tell him it was okay and that he needed some time away.

Jack decided that the idea that she could respond in such a way was a little bit comforting and also more than a little nauseating.

The elevator stopped in the lower-level garage and Jack exited to find his Porsche Carrera, one of the few remaining cars in the structure. As he approached and gazed at the sleek black lines of the automotive marvel, he wished he could remember purchasing it. For most men his age, buying a new Porsche would certainly rank in the top ten events of their life, but he'd managed to miss it completely. Now, the car merely haunted him like the rest of his life.

Sliding into the gray leather seats – the fresh smell of new car still lingering – he brought the machine under the hood to life, purring with contentment, ready to growl with power at his command. As he motored out of the garage past the empty guard shack, he seriously considered not going home…*ever*.

He didn't belong there. No matter what his life had been like before the accident – a life he could no longer remember – it didn't suit him now. How did one simply pick up from where he'd left off when he couldn't even remember the most important things of his life: falling in love and getting married, the birth of his children, buying his first house, becoming V.P. of Marketing and a partner in a prestigious technology firm?

Buying a Porsche.

It was as though he'd woken up one day with someone else's life, one which he hadn't worked for. And the most frustrating part was that he couldn't remember anything. Every once in a while at night, when his mind drifted between consciousness and sleep, vague sensations of the past would float by like eerie ships, taunting and daring him to remember. But the effort of trying was pointless. It now seemed buried so deep he'd be left to go on faith, simply believing that he'd been a certain person, living a certain way, and this was where he'd ended up.

Unless...

Unless he just went away and never came back. He could start his own life somewhere else, one in which he could remember all the choices he'd made, good or bad. But they'd be his, by God, not some phantom's that haunted him from the other side of a mirror.

He felt like reaching into his pocket and pulling out a coin to flip and determine if he'd go home or not, leaving it to chance if he'd stay put or finally give up trying. Instead he pulled into Timmy's Food Shack and ordered a double burger, fries, and a large Coke to wash it down.

"That'll be five-twenty-three," the girl at the window said. She was a young blonde and had on too much makeup, creating a disconcerting plastic effect. "Are you all right this evening?" she asked as Jack handed her a twenty.

He sighed and said, "Guess I've been better."

When she gave him his change and handed over the bag, she said, "Don't you worry. We've made it extra special for you. I promise it'll make you feel better."

"Thanks," he said and pulled into a parking space to wolf it down.

He wasn't sure what he'd do after that. Being a responsible husband he knew he should have called to tell Maggie he'd be home late; lied, at least, and said he'd been stuck working on some project or caught up in traffic. Yet he'd stopped doing that months ago since it never seemed to matter. He was convinced he could stumble in the door just before dawn with tattered hair and lipstick on his collar and she'd merely choose to ignore it; tell him he needed to sleep in since he was up so late.

In his previous life – before the accident – he'd somehow managed to marry the perfect woman, something men have been striving for through the ages. That, or she was crazy and didn't know the truth from fiction. Either way, it was a novelty for awhile but he feared he could never come to respect the woman, to truly revere her the way one spouse comes to revere another with a deep love from many years of trust.

Oh, he was sure Maggie would always be there. But she'd merely smile and think everything was all right no matter what turmoil was going on inside. He'd even tried to tell her once but she'd kissed him and said, "It'll all get better. Don't you worry," in much the same way the plastic girl at the drive-through had promised him that his burger was made extra special. And to Jack, it meant about as much, fluff with no substance.

As he munched on fries, he could still remember seeing her face for the first time. He'd woken up in a hospital bed and there she was, this gorgeous woman with shoulder-length hair, gentle brown eyes, and infectious smile. Patiently, she explained he'd been in an automobile accident and was lucky to be alive, that he'd been in a coma for several weeks. At first, Jack thought she was a nurse, but when she said she was his wife, he had suddenly realized he couldn't remember anything.

When he was discharged, she'd brought him home to see his children.

His children.

Little people he'd never met ran to greet him with tears in their eyes. The first few weeks of recovery were nothing short of surreal, speaking to old friends and business associates he didn't know, all the while grappling with the fact that he was living in the house of someone who had claimed him for their own as if he were a puppy picked from a litter.

Jack choked down the rest of the fries and took several gulps of Coke before starting the car and driving out of the lot. He could swear he actually *was* feeling better. Sometimes he just needed to let his mind vent, to let his emotions go with the flow. Then he'd usually come around and realize how ridiculous it would be to leave Maggie and the kids. Even though she wasn't deep, she was a good woman and he couldn't complain about that.

And the kids. How could he leave Amanda and Justin with their perfect dispositions?

No. This was, indeed, a good life. He had a great job and a loving family that any man would be proud of. And his own black Porsche.

He sighed and sunk into the leather seat, motoring toward the I-75 and home. Suddenly life didn't seem so bad after all. Everything was a little bit nicer, more pleasant than it had seemed earlier, from the feel of the car beneath him to the tidy businesses that lined the street with their immaculate signs and polished glass windows. It came as a surprise to him that he actually felt like going home and spending the evening with Maggie. She wasn't so bad. At least she cared for him. And from behind the newfound contentment another feeling was welling up, one that made the thought of spending an evening with Maggie altogether inviting.

Yet as he approached the onramp to head north on I-75 another voice spoke softly in the back of his mind, telling him to pass it by. It was the same voice that had been screaming at him before but now had become a whisper.

Pass it by. This is all wrong.

And with barely another thought, he shifted to the left lane and sped onto the ramp to I-75. Only instead of going north, he went south.

CHAPTER 2

Driving through the center of Atlanta two hours earlier would have been a stop-and-go ordeal. But now the cars moved along at a respectable pace, even if slightly slower than the posted speed. Most of the traffic consisted of trucks passing through and heading south like a flock of birds for the winter, folks heading into the city for some Friday nightlife, and stragglers coming home late from work. Jack wondered how many other husbands, disillusioned with life, were heading in the opposite direction of home as fast as the traffic would allow, not knowing quite where they'd end up.

Probably not many. Maybe only one.

He knew his unrest would come back like it always did – next week, next month, next time he looked in the mirror. The accident had taken far more from him than mere memories. It had taken his very identity.

Up until this point, each time the unsettled feelings had arisen, he had always managed to come around and give up any notions of escape. At one time he had thought they would eventually go away as he grew accustomed to the idea of Maggie, the kids, his job. But they never had. In fact, they were growing worse. Somewhere he'd heard that in cultures in which they still practiced arranged marriages the divorce rates were paltry compared to America's fifty-percent. As far as he was concerned, that had to be proof that two people – just about any two random souls – should be able to learn to love each other, or to at least live with.

Yet as Jack considered his own circumstances, he wasn't sure that was possible for Maggie and him; in fact he was convinced it was not. Still, simply divorcing her wouldn't be fair. He'd never thought it through logically, but the idea of having papers served to her after she'd nursed him back to health was repugnant to him. To her, he was still the Jack she'd fallen in love with and married. Somehow, it seemed to him that if he disappeared, it would be less abrasive, more humane.

An eighteen-wheeler blew by on the left, causing a gust to make the Porsche rock and Jack to realize how slow he was going. He was still trying to recover from the peaceful haze that had taken control of his mind, making him keep questioning why he wasn't going home to make love to his wife, instead of fleeing like a convict.

Where was he headed, after all?

And then a sign gave him the answer as though he had asked the cosmos and it had fixed the answer to an underpass on his behalf.

Hartsfield Atlanta International Airport.

That was it. He'd been thinking of going to Europe but Maggie had explained they'd already been – before the accident. She'd said the food hadn't agreed with them and their experience hadn't been a pleasant one. It was one of the few things she'd ever said that caused them to disagree. It was as though she had closed the door to something he might have enjoyed if only he could remember. Instead he had to take her word for everything.

Now he'd get his chance. He could use his plastic to buy himself a new life somewhere else, perhaps discovering and exploiting some hidden talent in the process. Perhaps he'd find himself in Paris, painting on street corners, or performing in a theatre in London. Perhaps he'd be a chef in Rome or a clockmaker in the Black Forest, but he'd find himself, all right.

The second he exited at Montgomery, a wave of nausea passed over him like a sickening breeze. Sticking two fingers between collar and neck, in an attempt to alleviate the noose-like grip, he began questioning his decision to stop at the shack to pick up a bite, wondering if perhaps the meat hadn't been up to standards. Food poisoning was the last thing he needed right now, given his newfound courage to finally break free from his superficial life.

And suddenly the mental haze was gone, replaced by a new conviction that this was the best thing he could be doing. Sick or not, he'd get on the next flight to Europe, no matter where it was headed. The plane would have lavatories and little bags for any unpleasantries that happened along the way. He could live with that.

But by the time he turned onto Camp Creek Parkway, just seconds from entering the airport, the nausea had grown so much worse that he felt like vomiting. He ripped open the knot to his tie and pulled it from his neck, unbuttoned the top button of his shirt, and rolled down the window.

The urgency was fierce. He headed for the short-term parking structure, not caring about the cost since he'd probably never be back to pick up the car – Porsche or not. Pulling into the first space he could find, he bumped into the tire stop and spilled out of the car while beads of sweat ran down his forehead. Leaving the keys in the ignition and the door ajar, he stumbled toward a waste barrel he spotted in the distance.

A couple walking their suitcases – complete with leashes – stared at him as he made for the can. When he finally reached the barrel he bent over it, heaving. All remains of Timmy's Food Shack purged from his system, he slumped to the ground on his knees.

The nausea subsided, but the weakness remained. And along with it, he felt mildly feverish.

Damn.

He must have picked up the flu somewhere. Traveling after having eaten bad meat was one thing, but the flu would make for a very long trip. Still, the alternative of simply returning home would be all too easy. Maggie would tuck him in bed and spoon-feed him chicken soup. But the result would be a complete surrender of his personal identity. The urgency he felt was real. So much so, that he never even considered postponing the trip for the future to give him time to plan more carefully. The truth was that he didn't trust himself. One minute he could be a brooding pot of angst, and the next as content as a lazy hound on Valium.

Jack found his legs as he made his way toward the terminal. The departure lanes were crowded with cars filled with stressed-out travelers. A little girl gazed at him with mouth agape while her parents unload suitcases from their car's trunk.

Realizing he must look the spectacle, he stopped just inside at a drinking fountain, where he rinsed his mouth, splashed cold water on his face, ran a hand through his hair, and adjusted his shirt. Though he figured it helped with outward appearances, it did little for the way he was feeling. Inside the air conditioning seemed to be barely functioning. He made his way to the carrier with the shortest line while his head pounded with each step. The few minutes it took to make it to the counter seemed like an hour. A perky young girl with short, lively hair greeted him.

"Hi there!" she said. "And how can we help you today?"

Jack gagged on his dry throat. "I need to get to Europe. Just get me on your next flight to anywhere in Europe."

"I'm sorry," she told him. "I'll need to have a destination in order to help you, sir."

"Look, just check any flights to Europe," he told her. "I'll take any one-way ticket."

Looking down at her computer, the girl tapped on a keyboard. "I've got a direct flight to London in the morning at 6:30 AM."

"Tomorrow?" Jack groaned. "Nothing sooner?"

"That's the soonest I see," she said. "Oh, that won't do."

"What?" Jack asked.

"It's completely booked. I can put your name down for stand-by."

"What else have you got?"

The overhead lights were torturing him with their fiery heat. He wiped the perspiration from his face, at the same time shivering as though standing knee deep in ice water. This girl was taking forever.

"Well…I can get you on a flight to J.F.K. International in New York.," she told him finally. "It's leaving in the next hour. From there I can transfer you to an international flight to Paris at 7:15 in the morning."

"Okay. That'll do," he said and pulled out his wallet.

"Ouch," she said. "I'm afraid this won't be cheap. We're looking at over three thousand for a one-way and coach class."

"Do it," Jack said, and handed her a Platinum Visa.

"I'll need to see some I.D.," she said, but Jack had already pulled out his driver's license.

"Are you all right, sir?" she asked him as he continued to mop his face.

"Fine. Let's get on with it."

She handed the license back. “Have your bags been with you at all times since you entered the airport?”

“I have no bags.”

She stopped and peered over the counter as if she didn’t believe him.

“Miss,” Jack said. “I don’t mean to be disrespectful, and I know you’re only trying to do your job. But I have no bags; no one has approached me for anything. So could we hurry?”

“Okay, sir. It will just take a minute.”

Jack waited. He was starting to feel nauseous again. He put his head down on the counter and listened to her computer’s keyboard clicking, feeling worse by the moment.

“Please wait here,” the girl said. “I’ll only be a moment.”

With that she disappeared into the back, leaving Jack, hanging onto the counter for support. When she returned, a large man in a security uniform was with her.

“I need you to come this way for a routine security search, sir,” he said.

Jack could barely stand anymore. He clutched the counter and tried to breathe.

“I don’t think I can,” Jack groaned.

“Are you all right?” the man asked him, frowning. Suddenly Jack realized that he’d become an object of general curiosity.

Picking up his credit card, Jack stumbled away to find a bench. Slumped on one of the standard airport seats, somewhere between consciousness and delirium, he couldn’t help wondering what had possessed him to be so adamant about leaving while feeling this way. The idea of climbing aboard a cramped jet for hours would be a nightmare.

Now the busy terminal seemed to be rotating slowly as though the whole place had been fixed to a revolving platter. He still felt hot and his mouth dry. Suddenly, all he wanted was to be at home and in bed. He felt foolish for having come to the airport for no good reason.

Pulling himself to his feet, Jack walked lopsided toward the exit. By the time he reached the outside, his vision was becoming straight again and the nausea was subsiding. He stopped himself before crossing the arrival lanes and looked back at the terminal, stuck between a kind of surreal juncture of two paths, one that would cause him to die a slow death, and another that appeared to be just out of reach.

The little voice inside suddenly screamed at him to fight. In that moment he knew that getting on the next flight was his only option, so he turned around, purposing to crawl onto the plane if need be.

CHAPTER 3

As he stood at the Delta ticket counter for the second time, Jack couldn't avoid considering the possibility that his symptoms were psychosomatic. The minute he had reentered the building, the nausea had returned and now he was feeling chilled again. It was becoming sickeningly obvious that every attempt at taking this flight was somehow causing – or at least aggravating – his illness. Was it guilt over the fact he was leaving Maggie, the kids? He wasn't sure. He could never remember such an obvious display of self-infliction from a merciless conscience. Yet somehow he was convinced that if he merely turned around and walked out the door he would instantly feel better.

"Sure you don't want to go to Hawaii instead?" the girl beamed. "I've got a flight I could put you on within the hour."

Hawaii?

What was this? People didn't just go to the airport and spin a dial to pick their destination. The fact the clerk offered it in all sincerity made it seem even stranger. Had he been feeling better he might have responded with some degree of incredulity.

He shook his head.

"So, you want the next flight to New York and then on to Paris," she commented, working the keyboard feverishly. "Do you have some I.D.?"

Jack's stomach was at his throat. The counter in front of him seemed to be moving, while a cold chill swept over him.

"Look, I went through all this a few minutes ago," Jack said.

"I'm very sorry, sir. But I can't sell you tickets without an ID."

He pulled it out and showed her. Once again she looked from him to the picture and back again. "Are you all right, sir?" she said.

Jack felt exasperated. The girl *had* to be a robot. There was no other explanation. It apparently didn't matter that she'd gone through the identical exchange with him just moments earlier. When he told her he had no bags, she would peer suspiciously over the counter; he was sure of it. The only difference in their exchange so far had been the suggestion that Hawaii might be his destination instead of London, which wasn't enough to assure him he was dealing with a warm body.

He considered flirting with comic repetition. "I'm okay. And I have no bags."

Once again she looked over the counter to be sure.

"No one has given me anything to take on the aircraft and since I don't have any bags, no one could have planted a bomb in them," Jack said sarcastically.

The girl stared blankly at him, his response no doubt frying a circuit in her meticulously prepared responses.

"It will just take a moment." She said it cheerfully, returning her attention to the computer.

Right on cue, the big security guard stepped out from the back.

"I need you to come this way for a routine security search, sir," he said.

~

Fortunately for Jack, he was presently only suffering from a cold sweat. And the cold was very real, since he was sitting on a chair wearing nothing but his underwear in an air-conditioned office, security having asked him to remove all his clothing and his shoes. Having searched his belongings thoroughly, they had had him stand in front of a scanner, apparently to make sure that he hadn't tucked something into some orifice; perhaps looking for a plastic explosive that would be none too pleasant had it gone off while he was being seated.

But Jack was clean. He pulled on his socks while the burly guard stood in the corner trying to act as though he wasn't watching, a revolver perched on his hip. He rapped the side of a desk with thick fingers as he waited for Jack to dress.

"How do you guys determine who to search?" Jack asked as he pulled on and zipped up his pants.

"We're required to make random searches."

"So, I was a random search?" Jack asked.

"That's right." The guard's voice was monotone and uncompromising.

A dark-haired woman in a Delta uniform walked in, holding Jack's credit card. "I'm terribly sorry," she said, "but your card has been rejected."

"But that's impossible," he told her. He always paid the balance of all his cards off each month and he was sure there was a $20,000 limit with this particular piece of plastic. "What reason did they give?"

"They couldn't give me one, but just told me there was a problem and that they were looking into it."

Jack sighed. As if his subconscious now knew he wouldn't be traveling, the fever subsided. The invasive search had been for nothing. All the confidence he had mustered to leave had been for naught.

He walked out of the room without saying a word and headed for the exit. Whatever was keeping him from leaving had won again. This time when he walked out the door into the cooling night air, he didn't stop to decide if he should try another carrier; perhaps find an ATM to withdraw cash, or figure another way to get on the flight. He'd had enough.

As he walked through the arrival lanes, another small girl stared up at him exactly the way the other child had looked at him when he'd arrived. Jack shivered but this time not because he was chilled. He felt as if he were in a time loop where everything kept happening over and over; first the clerk at the counter, then the security guard, and now the girl waiting for her parents. And as he found his car – keys still in the ignition – he questioned whether or not his whole life weren't spinning round and round like a record; the monotony passing him by with each sickening revolution until the needle wound toward the center, ultimately leaving him with nothing but the raspy wisps of white noise.

He shifted into first and hit the gas, squealing around corners to find his way through the concrete labyrinth. When he found the exit, he grabbed the ticket stub from the dashboard and slid it into the slot. It wound up being three bucks, but he wished it had been infinitely more – and that he'd never been back to pay.

Had he managed to get on a flight to Europe, he'd have certainly bounced the needle and made a big scratch. But at least he'd have broken free. If there *were* such a thing as destiny, Jack decided she was a dutiful old prude.

As he rolled to a stoplight, Jack considered his options – if, in fact, he had any left. The obvious choice would be to drive straight home, forgetting the notion of attempting anything foolish, and concentrating instead on reaching a compromising level of happiness while learning to accept who the world said he was.

Or he could continue to fight it, running away to find himself.

Or perhaps something in between was in order. He had to find out if his inklings about Maggie were right. If he disappeared for the weekend, how would she react? Would she be like a normal wife and become hysterical with worry, or would she simply brush it off as if he could do no wrong? Though he felt he knew the answer, he had to prove it. Not only that, but disappearing for a few days would also give him some time to himself. Think things through.

The light turned green and he headed for the Interstate. Before getting on he pulled into a gas station. Since he had no way of knowing for sure where he'd end up, a full tank wouldn't hurt. Even though signs on all aisles read self-service, a gentleman was at his window before he had rolled to a complete stop. Startled, Jack thought for a second he was being carjacked.

"This is some fine car you have here, mister," the attendant said. He sounded like Gomer Pyle with his lazy drawl.

"I thought this was self service," Jack said.

"It is. Call me stupid or bored, but I like juicin' the wheels. Makes the time go faster. Especially when I have the nightshift. It can drag on forever."

"I guess I can appreciate that," Jack said. "Just top it with the cheapest you got."

"Ya sure? Car like this should have nothin' but the best."

"It'll be fine," Jack said.

The attendant brushed the wet sponge vigorously across the windshield. "So where you headed on a fine night like tonight?" he said. "Home to the family?"

Jack didn't reply. If there was anything he didn't need tonight, it was a reminder of his family.

Destiny.

"Sorry, mister. I'll be straight up, I'm a nosy person. But I bet you figured that one out on your own. My momma always told me that curiosity done killed the cat and jumped on *my* back."

Jack chuckled. There was no need to take this fellow too seriously, even if he was a bit nosey. "Your momma must have been some lady."

"Oh, she was a mountain in the eye of a storm, a battleship in a pond, if you know what I mean. Some lady, indeed."

"I'm taking a weekend break, that's all," Jack said. He wasn't the type to offer information where it didn't belong, but it just came out. And now that it had, it actually felt good to tell someone something, anything.

"Excuse me?"

"You married?" Jack asked.

Gomer stopped wiping and looked through the glass. "Why? You got someone nice to set me up with? Maybe someone like momma?"

Jack laughed again. That felt good, too. "No," he chuckled. "Sounds as if someone like your momma would be hard to find. No, it's just not always easy."

"Oh, I hear you," he said as he switched sides and continued washing. "Marriage is a little confining, so I hear."

"I guess you could say it that way."

Gomer came around to Jack's window. "I bet she's pretty, your wife."

"Oh yeah. Gorgeous," Jack said, handing the attendant his credit card.

"Little ones?" He slipped the card into the pump and selected credit on the button choices.

"Two of the cutest, most well-behaved little tikes you've ever seen," Jack told him. He decided not to think too much about this for fear of becoming wracked with guilt for having nearly left them.

"Sounds to me like you shouldn't take too long a break," the attendant said when he handed Jack his card. "Family like you describe is hard to come by."

"You're probably right," Jack admitted.

"Well, it's a fine evening for a drive, anyway," the man said abruptly. "Goin' anywhere in particular?"

"To be honest, I hadn't really thought that far ahead."

"Well, good luck – with everything," he said and waved as Jack pulled away.

As he settled against the leather seat and motored onto the street, Jack considered the irony that someone pumping gas had more common sense than a V.P. of Marketing who couldn't be satisfied. The premise of his little breather from home *was* ludicrous. The fact he actually *wanted* Maggie to get mad, a bizarre notion.

Just the same, he motored onto the Interstate and continued south, passing a massive lighted billboard featuring a picture with a man and woman on a white sandy beach, holding hands, standing in the surf. "Florida," it read, "always a nice place to be.

Of course!

He could drive down to their condo in Destin. It would only take six or seven hours and he'd have the place to himself. Yet even as he throttled up, settled into his seat, and set the cruise control, a realization nearly lambasted him to mid-lane.

The credit card he had handed the station attendant had been the same one that had just been rejected by the airline. And yet it had gone through. Why? Had there been a credit limit problem? Or had there been some glitch in the system that had finally been resolved. Because if the latter were the case, he could take a flight, after all.

But Jack stopped himself. No more airport. No more déjà vu all over again. Destin it was. At least the universe didn't seem to be fighting him on this one. Perhaps throwing in a frivolous weekend occasionally was all right. Certainly it was nothing as life-changing as an escape to Europe.

And then Jack realized how fitting the name of the town where he was headed.

CHAPTER 4

The space was suffocatingly tight. No light, whatsoever. Kristen could hcar the grains of dirt as they seeped relentlessly through cracks in the rotting wooden slats, cascading around her like tiny waterfalls, stealing what little space she had left to move in, what little air she had left to breathe. The smell was that of musty earth and her nose rubbed against rough wood when she shuddered. No doubt a lid that had been nailed securely in place. But worst of all, there was no room to move. Even her arms and legs were held fast against the sides.

The only sound louder than the falling dirt was the pounding of her heart. She shivered and tried to stay the panic creeping up through her body. Though she could try to push the lid of the coffin-like box in which she was entombed, she knew the effort would be pointless. Even if she managed to loosen the nails, several feet of earth lay between her and sunlight.

Somewhere in the distance she could hear the faint sound of breathing, an inhuman, mechanical sound.

She was trying to keep the panic from spreading, inhaling what little oxygen remained, still clinging to a shallow ledge within her mind, when she finally faced the truth.

Buried alive!

She screamed and flailed, abandoning all rational thought. And then, in the very throes of despair, she was suddenly aware that it was The Dream.

Kristen Bandy popped open her eyes and felt the ground beneath her. Her heart was still pounding while she shivered uncontrollably. She rolled to one side and brushed against a cluster of ferns. The dream had left her disoriented, confused. There was trickling water nearby and the ground beneath her felt loose, like soil.

Then she remembered where she'd fallen asleep and sat up, hoping she hadn't overslept. Crawling a few feet toward the stream, she splashed a handful of water over her face, trying to ignore the strong smell of chlorine before pushing herself to her feet and climbing over a railing onto the tile floor.

Shoppers would soon be filtering into the place, security guards roaming the corridors, and iron grids retreating up into their homes in the ceiling.

She found a clock and realized it was still early. Heading for the public restrooms, she couldn't help thinking how different her life was now compared to a month ago. She considered her two years at Harvard Law School, thankful she'd finally managed to escape. It was ironic that some folks would do anything short of killing to get into that particular university and yet she'd thrown it away as if it were nothing more than a local junior college. And the funny thing was, she hadn't even *tried* to get in. Admission had been handed to her without her ever breaking a sweat. Looking back now she felt she'd wasted two perfectly good years of her life.

She thought of Adrian, the French lover she'd been living with in Boston while going to school. She could still see his sad eyes as she had finally told him it was over, that she had to leave. His perfectly sculpted body and long, free-spirited hair were the crowning touches to his puppy dog eyes and playful banter. But that hadn't stopped her from seeing that he was a complete and utter idiot, shallower than a wading pool for amebas. She could still remember the frustration she had felt whenever she had tried to talk to him about anything intelligent, how his eyes would glaze over. And even though she'd probably never again enjoy the kind of sack sessions he had provided her with, she had realized her intelligence had been melting from the heat he generated. Not the kind of intelligence you get from pounding the books at Harvard Law School. The kind that made you realize who you were and who you wanted to become, the kind of awareness that makes you wonder why the sun comes up every morning and how it is that you're still alive to feel its warmth on your cheeks.

It all had to do with *being alive*, the antithesis of her dream in the wooden box. It was as if all the people she'd been thrown into relationships with were like the suffocating confines that haunted her dreams.

Sedatives, that's all they were. Some people found them in their opiate for success, some with sex or drugs, others with popcorn and movies, but they all accomplished the same thing: make you forget about living – *really living*. For most, it seemed far easier to simply lie still while earth filled around them until no room was left to move, no air to breathe.

Not Kristen. She'd shake herself awake even if it meant leaving everything she'd ever known to push up through the soil and find the warmth of the sun, roaming freely among the living. And so her quest had begun as she had abandoned her plastic life, a mold more restrictive than the wooden box of her dreams.

Kristen found the mall's restrooms and she was grateful to learn they hadn't been locked for the evening. She turned on the light, used a stall and then rinsed the chlorine off her face with tap water – a compromising level of chlorine instead of the algae-annihilating proportions that had been fed into the mall's fabricated eco system. Staring briefly into the mirror, she brushed her wispy black hair.

Once she was finished getting ready, she walked through the empty corridors for a bit of morning exercise until the doors were unlocked and people started wandering in, contributing to the carnival-like atmosphere that would soon reign. For most the mall was a place to buy more stuff they didn't need. For Kristen, it was merely a place to meet a few basic needs; like getting a good sleep in a dry place.

Just before nine o'clock a man in gray overalls made his way around unlocking the doors, passing Kristen at least twice without noticing her. Clearly, when people expected things to be a certain way – such as there should not be anyone in the mall when it's locked – they usually didn't go out of their way to see the exception to the rule.

Finally, after five or ten minutes, the public started moseying in; grazing on a diet of windows filled with clothing, jewelry, and whatever else they happened to fancy. It had been Kristen's observation that middle-aged women and mothers with strollers were usually the first to arrive along with the occasional elderly couple, looking for something to do. Later the teenage girls would stampede through the corridors in herds. By late afternoon, the place would finally be swarming with all types, including bored husbands who didn't want to be there and crying toddlers – one, not entirely unlike the other.

But now it was nine-thirty and the metal grids were being lifted, time for Kristen to head for the food court where one or two of the vendors would be setting up.

Only one place had opened: a small walk-up café named Daphne's, offering cappuccino, bottled juices, and various baked goods. A small, dark man who looked like he might have come from India was setting up behind the counter. Kristen pressed against the counter, her bag out of sight and open.

With her right hand she pointed to the breakfast pastries in a transparent enclosure behind him. "What kind of roll is that one?" she asked. "No, no. The one with mauve filling."

The man turned just long enough for her to remove a bottle of orange drink and a muffin sitting in baskets on the counter and slip both into her bag.

The man turned back to her frowning. "I'm sorry, miss. I don't understand."

"Mauve is a kind of strong purple. It's the one just to the right of where you pointed."

"Aha," the man said. "Terribly sorry. It looked red to me."

"Don't mind me. I'm probably colorblind," Kristen said.

"It's raspberry."

"I'll take one, please."

"Would you like something to drink with that?" he asked as he removed one with a sanitary paper and placed it in a bag.

"No thank – Oh dear," she added, staring into the depths of her bag with disbelieving eyes. "I must have forgot to put my wallet back when I took it out last night. I needed it to look up the number to the children's hospital where my son is staying."

"Tell you what," the man said after studying her face for a moment. "You pay me next time you're here. Deal?"

"Oh, I couldn't. That's so kind."

"Please, miss. It's my pleasure," he said and handed her the bag.

Kristen sat at a table with her back to the café while eating her raspberry pastry and sipping the bottle of warm orange drink. It would have been better cold, but lukewarm was better than nothing. The muffin would come in handy later when she needed a snack.

After breakfast, she made her way to one of the large department stores where they always keep the cosmetics up front.

At the Estée Lauder counter, she picked up a new bottle of beach colored foundation, ignoring the store samples. Twisting off the cap, she peeled back the little cardboard seal with a fingernail and, glancing around to make sure nobody was watching, applied some to her cheeks and worked it around her face until she was satisfied, with her reflection in the small mirror obligingly provided.

Fixing the cardboard to the top, she screwed on the lid and placed it back on the shelf. Who was she hurting? Certainly Estée Lauder would never know the difference. And so she continued her morning makeover, borrowing a bit of blush here, eye shadow and mascara there.

The finishing touch was a tube of black wine lipstick – the darkest color she could find – which she applied generously to her pouty lips. Sometimes she felt guilty about using the lipstick. It was one thing to purchase a bottle of foundation that someone had stuck their finger on, or mascara that someone had used on their own lashes. But running a soft stick across your lips seemed a bit unsanitary for the next user. Still, as far as Kristen knew she didn't have any diseases and nobody would be the wiser.

She was just placing the tube back on the shelf and kissed a piece of tissue she'd stuffed in her purse while in the bathroom when a voice from behind her said, "May I help you?"

Most girls in her position would have panicked and considered sprinting toward the nearest exit, but not Kristen. She turned around boldly and smiled with her freshly made, black wine lips and said, "Actually, yes you can. You see, I used up the last of my lipstick this morning and need to purchase more. Silly me, I left the empty tube at home and can't remember the name." She held up the tissue for the clerk to see. "This is the color, and I'm quite sure it was Estée Lauder."

The woman smiled broadly. "It's a lovely color on you. Let's see if we can't just find it." She took the tissue from Kristen and held it up near the color strip. "Oh, it has to be black wine. It's the only one close." The clerk removed the very tube Kristen had borrowed a moment earlier and handed it to her.

Kristen pulled off the top, rolled up the stick and examined it closely. "It's close," she said, "but this one's a tad darker. "Maybe it was L'Oréal, after all."

"Oh, I don't think –"

"You know what? I just remembered that I bought it from my neighbor who sells Mary Kay. How silly of me. Well, sorry to bother you," she said and then walked away, dropping the lipstick into her purse.

Kristen headed toward the interior where inviting clothes hung on racks, begging to be tried on. She looked them over quickly to see if there were any she couldn't live without, before settling on a black shirt to replace the one she was wearing. Stopping by the undergarments for a fresh change, she made for the fitting rooms, where she was able to change in comfort, discarding yesterday's models in a waste can on the way out.

Now she felt refreshed and ready to face the day.

Ready to really live.

CHAPTER 5

When she stepped outside, the air was far muggier than it had been two days ago when she had first arrived at her home away from home. And the sky was cloudy. Clearly rain was a possibility. She considered turning around and going back inside, but she'd already wasted enough time. She should keep moving if she hoped to make it to Panama City.

She started as she heard a crash. But then she saw that it had only been a woman slamming closed the back of a minivan.

Stepping to the edge of the sidewalk, Kristen gasped and jumped back as a yellow Volkswagen darted around the corner. Clearly, this was going to be harder than she'd imagined. On the days she traveled, some were good and some were scary. This was going to be one of the latter and she had to muster all the courage she could find to not turn around and find safe haven back in the big comfortable mall. It would have been far easier to just spend the day in the theater, nabbing buttered popcorn from the concession stand without paying.

But getting to someplace that would remain warm all year was her goal. And besides that, she loved the beach. Panama City would be just the place and she'd heard there were lots of tourists to pilfer from. She'd stay there for the winter, doing nothing but enjoying the warmth, water, and other people's suntan lotion.

She hurried across the road and into the lines of cars beginning to pile up side by side in the large lot, big ugly beasts, staring at her with their crystal eyes. The things were a menace, noisy creatures rolling around, honking at each other and spewing their toxins into the air. She'd ride in one when she had to, as she planned to today, while traveling great distances. But the idea of getting behind the wheel made her cringe as though fingernails were being dragged across the blackboard of her mind. It hadn't always been this way. And if anyone cared to differ, she could produce a Massachusetts driver's license in earnest to prove it.

She couldn't explain how something like a fever could change a person so dramatically. She'd once been able to drive, but afterwards she could no longer get behind the wheel. It was the same way with law school. Gerty, her grandmother, had tried to remind her again and again of how badly she'd wanted to be an attorney since she was a youngster.

But what Gerty hadn't understood was that her dreams had disappeared along with her ability to drive. When she'd tried to explain her decision to quit to one of her advisors, he'd merely put a hand on Kristen's arm and told her that whatever she wanted would be best and that he would fully support any decision she made. It seemed odd to her that he'd respond this way. It was easier that he had, but not altogether gratifying. Shouldn't he at least have tried to change her mind? Even a little? Then again, that was more or less the way the whole college experience had been. She had realized after her fever that she just didn't belong there.

Gerty had wanted her to stay for selfish reasons anyway. Though the family was singularly lacking in blue blood, Gerty had always fancied herself that way and hobnobbed with the old money around Boston whenever possible. Having a real Harvard lawyer as a granddaughter would certainly have supported the illusion famously. Though Kristen loved her grandma, the woman was starting to grow senile. Every once in a while she'd say something strange, like telling James – an imaginary servant – that they would take their afternoon tea on the veranda, or that the President would be up next weekend to visit. It had all been a bit unnerving. She'd begun to wonder if she would ever have another coherent, meaningful relationship.

Adrian had been her lover, although scarcely a friend. He existed in the world as an ornament for women to admire, but nothing more. His response to her leaving Harvard? "Whatever you want is what I want, babe." That was it. That's all there was. He hadn't even had the intelligence to encourage her to stay for selfish reasons. Had she finished and become a prosperous attorney, he might have been able to stay with her as her own private boy toy to be indulged without ever lifting a finger to work. But, "Whatever you want is what I want, babe," was the deepest he could offer.

She'd got up one morning and left without ever bothering to kiss Adrian goodbye. She wasn't exactly sure why she had done this, but it just felt right. Taking a cab to Gerty's over on Huntington, she had shared a bagel with cream cheese with the old woman. And then she just left. Picked up and started hitching it south toward the sandy beaches of Florida.

So here she was, about to cross a major intersection in Atlanta, on her way to Panama City. Fortunately, it was still somewhat early and the traffic could have been worse, but to Kristen, the street might just as well have been the Red Sea waiting for Moses to part it. *Lord Almighty*, she thought, *is there any other way?*

Too late!

She pressed the walk button for the second time and waited for the next cycle. This time she was ready, but the tide of traffic had increased. She could feel them watching her as she stepped into the street and started walking, making sure to keep her eye on the other side like a tightrope walker might keep from looking down. She made it past one lane, uncomfortably aware of the hot breath of the mechanical monsters panting. Panic bled into her feet. The light suddenly changed to red and Kristen started to run. It was either that or fall to the mercy of the roaring beasts around her. But as she sprinted across one of the lanes, a growling Lexus rolled across her path. She screamed and flung herself to the sidewalk where she slumped to the ground. Holding her knees tight to her chest, she rocked back and forth, comforting herself.

It took her a full half hour to recover, until she found herself at an onramp with a thumb pointing south, standing as far back from the road as she could and still be seen by those entering the Interstate.

The branches of a large hickory tree near the ramp suddenly shook violently and stretched unnaturally to one side as a gust of wind set the leaves vibrating and dancing amongst themselves. Kristen looked up at the sky, now growing thicker with gray clouds.

Realizing it was about to storm, she considered her options, eyeing the underpass through which she'd just come. It could provide some protection, but she'd still feel exposed, vulnerable.

The only buildings in the area were of the professional type and didn't look like they'd be opened on weekends.

A distant rumble, sounding like a faraway air-show – Thunderbirds screaming around the skies doing things jets weren't made to do – came louder this time and lasted for at least ten seconds. This was turning into a really bad day and she'd barely even started.

The wind kicked up in random gusts and a few droplets hit her face. Kristen bit her nails and looked around with eyes full of terror. She was petrified of electricity. Wall sockets were bad enough; plugging things in and hoping a surge didn't decide to arc and zap her a good one for the devil of it. But at least that electricity was confined. You simply needn't go near it. But the loose kind that roamed menacingly around the skies, free from power lines, was altogether nerve wracking.

An eighteen-wheeler pulled slowly to the corner and turned wide onto the entrance ramp. It rolled far enough to clear the turn and then pulled to one side. Large brake lights lit up Kristen's face, as the sky grew darker from the glut of clouds. The only reason the huge truck hadn't scared her was the fact she was already facing a greater danger.

The cab door flew open. Inside a jolly looking fellow peered down at her. He was nearly bald, with a rounded face and red bulbous nose. He wore blue jeans, a white, button-up shirt that could use a washing, over an undershirt that was even dirtier and his belly slumped into a pile on his lap. "Where you headed, missy?" he called, smiling.

Kristen's eyes widened as she looked took in the size of the cab. In her opinion, people were harmless. It was machines that gave her the willies. So far she'd always managed to get rides in cars. This would be her first ride in one of the really big monsters.

But at that moment, she saw the vein-like spikes shoot out of the sky behind the cab, followed seconds after by a sharp crack and rolling rumble. Shivering, she made a quick decision to take her chances.

"Florida," she said and grabbed a chrome bar to hoist her onto the step and then up into the seat. From up there, she felt a mile high and far above the rest of the world.

"This is your lucky day, missy," the truck driver said. "That's just where I'm a headin'."

Suddenly sheets of water fell across the hood in giant drops and a gust hit the side, rocking the cab. As the truck began to move, the man said, "Looks like you just made it. I wouldn't wanta be standin' out there."

"Thank you for stopping," she said.

He glanced over at her. "My pleasure, missy."

As the driver throttled up, Kristen shivered and hugged herself, but not because of the rain.

CHAPTER 6

He'd made it to the condo by five in the morning and fallen asleep in the master bedroom, dozing soundly until he woke to see the little clock on his nightstand read 10:23 AM. The room was warm since he hadn't turned up the air and the sheets were moist from Jack's perspiration. He got up and moved the thermostat down to seventy-two degrees and immediately heard a muted purr kick on and fresh air poured into the room.

Pulling open the drapes partway, he looked out at the Gulf; still right there where it belonged, the emerald green water sparkling in the morning sunlight. Just the other side of the condo's small patio, a sandy white beach stretched away from the building, a million footsteps having made a mess of things.

Numerous beach lovers were already gathering for their morning ablutions. Children romped in the surf. A couple of men cast lines from the shallower water, and seminude teenage girls lay about as still as death, soaking up the sun. Jack knew that by one o'clock there would be three times as many beach lovers, coming to douse themselves in the Gulf's bath-like water.

Jack could see Maggie and the kids out there, as he had on so many occasions. They'd usually take a bamboo mat within twenty feet of the water's edge, stuffing an umbrella in the sand to provide some shade from the beating sunlight. Then Maggie would lather up the kids with suntan lotion and lay back on a lounge, adjusting her sunglasses, her long legs, tan body, and shapely figure drawing glances from men and women alike.

For just a moment, he tried to imagine her now, fretting over the fact he hadn't come home last night, calling hospitals and police stations, worried sick and praying he was all right; or maybe seething at him because he might be having an affair. But the fantasy was simply that. He couldn't imagine Maggie upset. The best his mind could conjure was that she'd be getting on with her Saturday, thinking there was a perfectly good explanation why he never showed.

The vision of his family blurred as a hunger pang shot through his stomach. Whatever flu symptoms he'd had at the airport were now completely gone and his empty stomach seemed bent on reminding him that it occasionally needed food to keep the unit running. He looked in the cupboards and refrigerator, but knew he wouldn't find anything but supplementary condiments like ketchup, mustard, salt, and the like. When they came down for the weekend, they'd always stop at the grocery store, only selecting enough for the stay. If they happened to have any left over, they'd pitch it, since coming back to rotting food was the last thing they wanted.

Jack showered and put on some beach attire he kept in the condo, white shorts, a tropical shirt, and the flip-flops from Hilo Hattie that he'd picked up while in Hawaii last Christmas. He skipped shaving – even though he kept a separate shaver for their frequent trips south – to give him that beach bum look, another way to rebel against providence, if only for a weekend. When he went out to the one-car garage, the air was already hot and muggier than it had been in Atlanta.

He drove to the nearby grocery store where he picked out a few items for his stay. Again he revolted and chose the antithesis of Maggie's health conscious selections. Barbeque potato chips would be his staple along with nacho chips. He picked no less than three kinds of dip to accompany the feast, including ranch, spicy bean, and a synthetic guacamole that had been pumped full of enough preservatives to remain on the shelves through the next holocaust, along with a six-pack of Coke and a can of peanuts, a big bag of candy corn, and finally the family sized box of Goobers. And even though he wasn't normally a beer drinker, he couldn't resist nabbing a six-pack of cool ones, just for the hell of it.

Once he felt that he'd proven his point, he wheeled the buggy to the register as proud as a mugger after a good day on the streets. Except that for Jack, his biggest crime was getting away with living as he damn well pleased without anyone or any *thing* to tell him otherwise.

The cashier rang up the items without ever eyeing him suspiciously or commenting how unhealthy his choices were. In fact, when the total popped up, she said, "Congratulations! You just won fifty dollars."

Already removing his wallet, Jack looked surprised. "Excuse me?"

"This year is our fiftieth anniversary. Everyday, we give away fifty dollars to the fiftieth customer. And you're it," she said with a smile.

Instead of spending about thirty bucks, Jack was handed nineteen dollars and change after his purchases.

A woman walked by, wearing flip-flops, her tan legs even longer than Maggie's. She wore a green T-shirt and bathing suit underneath. Long, sun-bleached hair fell down the center of her back. "This must be your lucky day," she said, sizing him up and down in a way that told Jack just how lucky he might be very soon.

Jack picked up his two sacks and was surprised to find Long Legs waiting out front. He suddenly felt awkward and wondered how he could get past her without making contact.

"Down here for the weekend, or do you live here?" she inquired.

"Just the weekend," Jack told her.

"Me too. I've been lying out on the beach all morning and I'm getting bored. Know what I mean?" she said. Her sultry voice was slightly on the rough side.

"Actually, I just woke up," Jack said and chuckled.

"Mmm," she murmured. "Sounds nice."

"Look," Jack said, deciding to be frank. "I find you very attractive. But I'm a married man."

"I already saw the ring," she said. "It makes things more interesting, don't you think?"

"Complicated, is the better way to put it," he said, starting toward his car. "I'm sorry, but I'm really not interested."

"What exactly *do* you want?" she said in a very different tone.

Jack stopped in the middle of the roadway, halfway between the store and his car, halfway between the life he couldn't remember and whatever the future held. "I just want the world to make sense again. That's all," he said. And with that, he hopped in the Porsche and drove out of the lot, not looking back to see if the woman watched him leave or found another catch for her long, hot afternoon.

He'd meant it with all sincerity. Maybe it was a condition of his amnesia, but nothing in his life felt like it belonged. He'd belabored the issue in his mind and was tired of thinking about it. In some ways, he'd wanted this weekend to be a break from the dilemma. He'd wanted to feel like a regular guy: watching a game, scarfing down munchies after getting a good buzz off a six-pack of beer. And yet how quickly a strange woman had forced him to revisit his haunting dilemma.

What exactly do *you want?*

A good enough question, indeed. If he could remember anything before the accident – the way he felt about Maggie and the kids, his passion to work and get ahead, his goals and ambitions – maybe the answer would be obvious. Maybe he'd already have exactly what he wanted. But now, his family and career merely served as a constant reminder that he was leading someone else's life. Someone that existed before an auto accident.

The accident.

After coming to in the hospital after the coma, he'd discovered that the accident had happened while he'd been on a road trip with one of the sales staff, Steve Buckley. He'd come along on a hard sell since nobody was better than Jack at closing a deal – or so he'd been told. They had been on their way home when they encountered road construction, causing traffic to slow. An eighteen-wheeler had rammed the back of the car, sending it careening off the road and into a ditch. Steve had been dead when the paramedics arrived, while he had been unconscious.

Later Jack had returned to the scene where skid marks still painted the highway. But it didn't help to jog anything loose in his memory. He had stared at where the car left the road and walked down into the concrete ditch where the Buick had flipped over onto its back. The most unnerving part about the experience was that he couldn't feel anything. A man he'd worked with, a subordinate and friend, had lost his life on that very spot, yet the knowledge of it did nothing to fracture his emotionless heart. He'd sent flowers to Steve's wife. He'd thought about paying her a visit to speak to her in hopes he could remember something. But she had moved away.

With no other connections to the accident and no hope of finding further enlightenment Jack had been stuck in a state of limbo, hoping that in time his memory would return. In just over eighteen months, it hadn't.

Before returning to the condo, Jack stopped by a video store and picked out a movie, an old Schwarzenegger flick about a guy who'd unknowingly been cloned. At the counter he handed the clerk a rental card he'd acquired for trips to Destin when they grew bored of the beach. Usually they were ones the whole family could enjoy. Renting a guy movie was another way to break from the norm. Any little thing felt good. His own choices felt good.

He returned to the condo, kicked back, tore open the bags of chips, and tossed back a couple of suds while watching a poor guy in worse shape than himself, struggling with his own identity. By the end of the movie, a full stomach and a light buzz on, the fanciful thought crossed his mind that if he'd actually been cloned, that would have been why he couldn't remember his life before the accident. In the movie, the hero's memory loss had been overcome by performing an almost instantaneous download of past memories through the retina. Suddenly the clone knew everything about the original host's life as though he'd lived it.

The idea that he'd participated in such a conspiracy was a novel idea, making substantially more sense after a few beers.

If only it were true, he could at least have an answer. The reality of his amnesia was a bigger, more painful pill to swallow. Suddenly Jack laughed out loud at the thought of himself being created in a lab alongside a bunch of sheep. That was rich. He popped open another beer and took a few sips while imagining what would happen if he'd really been the first human clone, all his contemporaries sheep. He'd no doubt be like the ugly duckling among the group, crawling around, bleating and carrying on, wondering why he had skin instead of a thick coat of wool.

Sheep Boy, they'd call him. There would be no better fodder for the tabloids for months on end. If nothing else, he'd be able to have a promising career in the circus.

Jack left the living room a mess just because he could, and went out to the patio where he cranked open a large umbrella mounted in the middle of a wrought-iron table. Sitting in one of the white plastic chairs with a beer in hand, he watched the clutter of people sunbathing up and down the beach. The water lapped gently at the shoreline where children and adults played: dogs catching Frisbees, teenagers floating lazily in inner tubes, dads launching children into the air, warm bodies soaking up the sun. And he began to categorize.

First there were the families, units of three or four, five at the most, with the mom as home base. Sometimes the husband would be lying next to her but not for very long. More often, he'd be helping the kids dig in the sand or playing with them in the water, being a big kid himself. Every once in a while, Mom would call out to the family or mosey down to the water to cool off. But the family would never stray far from her as though she had an invisible tether tied to each one.

Then there were the bathing beauties, often alone. These would be like the woman Jack had met at the grocery store – maybe younger – here for the day to perpetuate their tans. Occasionally they'd come in pairs, or perhaps one would have a boyfriend, usually antsy, tossing and turning, offering to apply more lotion, hoping the long exercise of patience would eventually pay off.

There were the jocks with their tight abdomens, often accompanied by dogs. There were sometimes kids who looked lost. Once every several hundred feet would be an elderly couple looking out of place amongst the younger set.

At two, Jack went back inside for an afternoon nap to make up for the prior night's lost sleep, and he dreamed he stood in front of a mirror. Only instead of seeing his own reflection, he found himself looking at a short, unattractive man. When the man spoke, his voice was crude and raspy.

He woke to the phone ringing and hesitated to answer for fear it was Maggie. Then again, that wouldn't be a bad thing, he decided. Maybe she'd finally be angry, which would be something. He answered before the forth ring. But it was only a wrong number. Now fully awake, he noticed it was well after five and that he was hungry. He decided to treat himself with some decent food at a nice restaurant.

Just because he had left his wife and children didn't mean that he had to go without a good meal.

CHAPTER 7

Coming back from Petrov's office, Mark Sweeney hesitated before descending into the pit. He'd just learned that Albatross's medical staff was in OR and prepping for Guerridelli's procedure, something his team needed to brace themselves for once the man recovered. Mark held a folder, filled with psychological and physiological data extracted from days of exhaustive testing. He was glad his position allowed him to avoid the ordeal. He'd heard the rumors: Guerridelli had broken down the medical interrogators, being interrogated, themselves, by the old man's scrutiny. They'd had to prevent his son from interfering while keeping him appeased long enough to conduct their tests. Mark had heard that the staff psychologist was quite disturbed after the last session and Mark suspected it was because Guerridelli didn't fit the mold of any standard diagnosis they taught in psych classes, even at graduate levels.

Watching the monitors from a raised catwalk, his eyes were drawn toward Erin's station. Slouched in her swivel chair, wearing well-fitting jeans, she was facing Zack, clearly amused at what her coworker was saying. Her dirty-blond hair pressed against the chair's back as if she were a little girl, eyes sparkling, fully engaged in the playful banter. Being the only female in the pit got her lots of attention from the other monitors. They watched, listened, captivated by her every word.

Instead of acting the part of a boss, settling idle chitchat and refocusing the group, Mark opened the folder and pretended to look over Guerridelli's profile, all the time surreptitiously observing. Watching her alluring mouth form words made strong feelings well up inside Mark, inappropriate feelings that shouldn't be present in the mind of a supervisor. The girl was a seductress without even knowing it with her childlike posture in a woman's body, innocent ambition, and an infectious, upbeat personality.

Mark took a deep breath and shook his eyes loose. There was work to be done and the folder in his hand proved it. Just behind the medical data was a packet of stapled papers. This was the information his group needed, an outline of everything Guerridelli wanted, no doubt a circus of fantasies. The trick would be assigning a monitor who could separate relevancy from all the rest of the chaff.

Mark considered his options.

Zack was well meaning and intelligent. But he struggled with a lack of intuitiveness, a desirable trait in situations such as this. He was too smart for his own good, extremely analytical, but not so much so that he couldn't make Erin laugh.

Erin.

Her giggle blew through Mark, tinkling the wind chimes of his obsession.

Back to business!

None of the others stood out as possible candidates. Ridley was the best, but he was handling too many cases as it was. Jared was the new guy. While he seemed competent, Mark feared that letting him handle this case would be a mistake. He wasn't experienced, especially with someone like Guerridelli.

Then there was the seductress. Given what Mark knew of her personal life, combined with her gutsy flair, it could make for a dicey situation, in spite of the way he felt about her other attributes. She wrote screenplays in her spare time, but had yet to gain the attention of anyone in Hollywood. She'd confessed to taking the job at Albatross because it was a good place to observe, possibly even a way to refine her eye for the dramatic. Mark cringed while thinking about how she'd handled some sticky situations. She was a firecracker waiting to go off. No good. He'd need to give it more consideration.

"Here's the man," Zack said as Mark descended into the pit. "Got the scoop on the big bad gangsta?"

Erin giggled.

Mark held up the folder and gave a thin smile. "Right here."

"So who gets him?" Zack asked. "I'm in pretty good shape."

"I haven't decided yet."

Erin clasped both hands, eyes pleading. "Please, please," she said. "I won't screw it up. I promise. Please?"

Having her beg that way almost undid Mark. "Whoever I choose is going to have their hands full," he said with as much disinterest as he could muster. "This gentleman is one colorful character. How are things going, here? Subjects content this morning?"

Zack help up a hand, tilting it side-to-side. "So-so. But I'm workin' on it."

"Anything I should know about?"

"Nah! Same old stuff."

"Mine are doing *great*," Erin quipped. "So great, in fact, I could handle another. Maybe even a colorful character." She smiled up at Mark dreamily.

The girl was a relentless flirt.

"That's not what you just told *me*," Zack said.

Erin stared Zack down. "Shut up!"

Mark might have wondered what Zack had meant had he not been so amused by Erin's childish glare. Catching himself, he cleared his throat to sober the atmosphere. "Listen," he said, addressing the whole group. "Petrov just informed me the board hired some analyst types to storm the place, figure out how the company can turn a profit. They'll be looking at things like efficiency, seeing if there are ways to cut back or make better use of our existing resources. Don't lose any sleep over it. I don't think they're looking to eliminate positions – especially not in this department – but we need to get our house in order. That means staying focused and working on keeping clients happy, if you know what I'm saying. And, as you know, keeping happy clients is our department. Are there any questions?"

"When does this shakedown occur?" Zack asked.

"Anytime in the next several weeks. They'll show up unannounced."

Several, including Zack and Erin groaned.

"Do you know what they'll be doing?" Erin asked, sounding mildly concerned.

"I'm guessing it involves looking over shoulders, seeing how we operate. Then again, I don't know for sure. Try to keep in mind that they're just consultants. All they can do is make recommendations to the board. But we *would* like them to say nice things about us."

The pit area was uncharacteristically quiet while the monitors digested this information.

"Okay, then. If there isn't anything else, I'll be in my office. Let me know if anything comes up. We'll need to take care of situations as quickly as possible if we intend to look good."

Mark headed across the pit toward a hallway leading to his office. "Onward and upward," he said, just before disappearing to his office.

The consultants didn't worry him. What could they do? After all, this wasn't your typical biotechnology company. They would need the monitors and technicians' help, just to understand the business model, let alone to determine if the company was operating efficiently. It was Guerridelli that had him mildly concerned. From the moment when he'd first learned of the man, Mark had been hesitant. Now he wished that Petrov had reconsidered taking him on as a client. After all, the procedure they were offering was still relatively new and having someone with such a violent background might disrupt the delicate balance his group tried so desperately to maintain.

He closed his office door, ready to take on Guerridelli's folder.

Jared kept quiet. Listening. Watching. Waiting for an opportunity. Until now, he hadn't found one. The clock was running, gramps was about to go under the knife, and he still didn't know how to pull it off, how to become the ole man's watchdog. Sweeney'd probably try to give old man Guerridelli to one of the other, "more experienced" assholes. Jared consoled himself that he was probably smarter than the others. He ran a hand though his black, oily hair, while having a hard time ignoring the girl-talk going on behind him. The socialites were at it again, only quieter since Sweeney had come and gone. Zack was foaming at the mouth over Erin, as usual, and the teasing bitch was leading him on like she always did. He considered, again, why he'd agreed to lie his way into a job at Albatross. But it didn't take long to come up with an answer. And he certainly couldn't complain about two paychecks for the same day's work.

"He'll be on my leash in no time," Erin was saying.

"Who? Cochran or Sweeney?" Zack said. "Funny how you failed to mention your current dilemma."

"Hey, I want Guerridelli and I'll do whatever it takes to get him," she replied.

"Anything?" Zack asked, raising his eyebrows.

"You know what I mean. Besides, I can handle Cochran. It's no big deal."

Zack sighed. "Yeah, well, maybe that's true. But I've got problems of my own."

Jared had heard enough. He put headphones on, attached to a CD player and pressed play. Even though Sweeney-the-weenie would probably disapprove, what the hell? He had to do something to mask Zack's annoying voice. It was getting on his nerves and he couldn't concentrate.

Out of the corner of his eye he saw Erin roll her chair over to Zack's station. She moved in close and, for a second, Jared thought Zack would finally get some. But they both gazed at Zack's computer screen, her hand reaching for the mouse. Two love-nerds diddling with their high-tech gear. *Id'nat special.*

At the end of the workday, Jared's brain was sore from working on an under-the-table project while pretending to learn the position. Hacking into computers had been his gift since high school – which he'd attended, but from which he had never actually graduated – and that skill came in handy now in order to break into Albatross's mainframe for a snoop around. Though their security was unusually tight, Jared was able to navigate past the firewall that held "supposedly" secure accounts shrouded in mystery to anyone who didn't belong.

He discovered that they'd changed the standard port number for access through a secure shell – a program that encrypts all communication between client and server – and was able to determine the new port number. Then it was just a matter of tripping the password.

Some systems were set up to timeout after a certain number of failed login attempts issued by the same user. But Jared had found a way around that. He'd written a program that utilized every computer in the company outside of the protected mainframe, by uploading a ghost process. Every hour, each of these processes would receive a batch of potential passwords from the main program on Jared's machine. They would use this list to attempt a series of logins. The processes would never attempt more than three logins within a ten-minute period, and never under the same user's name. With so many processes trying to logon from so many different locations and users, the mainframe wouldn't grow suspicious in spite the constant bombardment of suspect logon attempts.

One of the processes had just found a usable password and Jared was jazzed. He walked confidently toward the break room, knowing that nobody would ever discover the background processes, never learn he'd been up to no good. As soon as the password was discovered, he'd issued a kill order through the main program, which systematically shutdown all ghost processes and removed them from their hosts. Then he deleted the main program. It could never be traced and now he could login and take a stroll through the mainframe whenever he damn well pleased.

As he approached the break room, he could hear some of his fellow monitors clucking about the new client, Guerridelli. There was Erin and of course, Zack and Ridley. He'd been concentrating so much that he hadn't noticed they'd left the pit. Now he realized that's probably why he'd been able to get as much done as he had. He stood near the entry, just out of sight, listening.

"God, I hope he lets me have Guerridelli," Erin was pining. "How often do you get an opportunity like this?"

Another voice spoke. It sounded like the brown-noser, Ridley. "Realistically, Sweeney'll pick someone with more experince."

"Like you?" Erin said sarcastically.

"Maybe like me."

"Well, I'll just take him over," Erin quipped.

"Like you did my subject?" Jared heard Zack join in.

"You were having trouble, so I helped."

"Yeah, well, we'll see how it turns out," Zack said. "I'm still a skeptic."

"Whatever Sweeney decides for Guerridelli, we stick by it. You know how it is with the mob," Ridley said. Suddenly his voice sounded tight and unnatural, as if someone were squeezing his neck. "My name is Don Vito Corleone. And I only have one thing to say. Never go against the family."

A round of careless laughter broke out while Jared nearly came undone. They were all morons and it was so typical of what people thought of organized crime. Gramps had been a businessman much like any other, if only a little more persuasive in his dealings. It wasn't as if his family dealt drugs or acted like terrorists. They were God-fearing, America-loving, salt-of-the-earth people who knew how to make a shady buck. That's all. The Viper had explained to Jared at a young age that the economy was better off, having people like the Guerridellis to keep things in check. A kind of Robin Hood calling, he'd said.

Zack began suggesting they accommodate Guerridelli by arranging for him to live in Chicago where he could spend his afternoons in the dark corner of a seedy Italian café, giving orders through a mouth full of marbles. This only brought more laughter until Jared had just about had enough.

He was just about to storm through the door, punching, when something stopped him. Maybe it was the realization that doing so would blow his cover, or perhaps it was a sudden burst of the creative reasoning that so often eluded him.

Suddenly it was clear. Capturing the careless spirit in that break room could solve his dilemma. If done properly, he was certain he would have the chance to take on gramps, Albatross's new client.

Painting his own nose brown, Jared headed for Sweeney's office.

CHAPTER 8

When she woke up, Kristen could hear the sounds of highway and feel the vibration beneath her. The driver had been kind enough to let her rest in the back where she'd fallen asleep. Now awake, she reached into her purse and removed the muffin she had saved for later. Biting the edge of the cellophane wrapper, she tore it open.

"You find the accommodations acceptable, back there?" the driver called from the front.

"Very much so," she told him, gobbling down the muffin in several large bites.

"It does me a good sleep, that's for sure," he said.

Kristen climbed out of the back and into the passenger seat, straightening her punk leather jacket.

"Name's Randy Longfellow," he said, grinning, and stuck out a pudgy hand. "Ancestors must have been taller'n me. It's the only explanation I can think of for havin' a name like Longfellow. Either that or they were makin' up for somethin' lacking."

Kristen laughed. "Pleased to meet you," she said and shook his hand. "My name's Kristen Bandy from Boston."

"Glad to know you, Kristen Bandy from Boston. What brings you south?"

"Insanity, I suppose," she told him flippantly. "Life up north was choking me and I needed a change. Florida sounded as good as anyplace."

"I hear you. Sometimes these roads seem so long it feels like they're never gonna end. But what the hell. What else've I got to do?" he said with a chuckle. "Anywhere in particular in Florida?"

"Panama City."

"Panama City," he said, stretching out the words as if he were analyzing each syllable for phonetically correctness. "I can drop you within fifty-six miles," he suddenly said, matter-of-fact like.

"That'd be great," she said, peering suspiciously through the windshield at the sky. "Storm all cleared away?"

"Reckon so," he said. "They come and go so fast when you're on the road you start to ignore 'em."

Kristen shivered. "They scare me."

"What's that, hon?"

"Electrical storms. Just the thought of electricity up there in the sky is terrifying."

Randy paused and glanced over at her. "You have family in Boston?"

"Just Gerty. She's my grandmother. She's been going senile, lately."

"No parents?"

"No. They tell me my dad left when I was little and my mom died of cancer. I lived with Gerty until I got a place of my own," Kristen said.

"Not that it's any of my business," the driver said, "but a pretty thing like you shouldn't be hitchhiking. Don't you have a car or something?"

"I don't drive," she told him. "Besides, when I was going to school, I didn't need to."

Randy downshifted as the traffic slowed.

"I thought everybody drove. It's not hard to learn," he said. "If not, you could always take a bus or somethin'."

"Cars…well, vehicles in general give me the creeps. Besides that, I don't have much cash. Look, could we talk about something else?"

"No problem. But I expect everyone's scared of somethin'. Being afraid of vehicles isn't any worse than anything else. No one's passin' judgment. And as for being short on cash, hell, that's me on any day of the week. I spend money like a drunken sailor."

Kristen hated exposing her fears to a perfect stranger. It was one thing to live with them everyday, occupying the same space with demons that regularly caused her fingernails to remain short.

"So, Mr. Longfellow," she said, trying to divert attention away from herself. "What scares you?"

"Well, not a whole lot I suppose," he confessed. "There's only one time I remember being really scared."

"Tell me about it," Kristen said.

He glanced over at her without speaking, making Kristen wonder if he was afraid of damaging his macho reputation as a trucker.

"I probably shouldn't," he finally said.

"Why not? I won't pass judgment, either."

Randy chuckled at having his own words thrown back in his face. "It's not that, hon. It's just somethin' I shouldn't be talkin' about. That's all."

"Scared?" Kristen asked. "Maybe there're more things than you thought."

Randy sighed. "I suppose it's a long trip and you won't ever talk about it, will you?"

"I'll never mention it," she said and then made a zipper motion across her black wine lips.

"Well," he said. "It was a tight spot I got into once in Vegas. That used to be my home base, Vegas. I was a little younger and a lot stupider. A friend of mine got us into a poker game in the penthouse of one of them big hotels. Said he thought we were good enough to play with the big boys. Hell, we used to play any chance we got. Sometimes if we had a really big job – cross country and such – we'd team up, share the driving and split the profits. We'd play with truckers at stops and beat 'em nine times out of ten. It was all low bills – fives and tens, never more'n twenties – so we couldn't rake in the big bucks. Ever once in a while we'd have a little run-in in the parking lot and have to pull a baseball bat from the cab. But for the most part we got on okay and made a little extra on the side.

"One day he tells me 'bout this game he'd heard of where the minimum bet was a hundred bucks. 'Sign me up,' I say, clueless to what I was gettin' myself into. We show up on the top floor of this place on a Saturday night around eight o'clock with several grand each in C notes. We get off the elevator and there're guys in suits to frisk us. I ain't never been frisked in all my life. It made me kinda nervous, if you know what I mean."

"Is that what scares you?" Kristen asked with a grin. "Getting frisked?"

Randy looked out of the corner of his eye at her. "Funny girl," he said. "I said it made me nervous, not scared. That part comes later."

He continued. "They take us into a place like I ain't never seen. Everything is marble or gold or ivory – other stuff I didn't even know existed. Anything but regular material places are supposed to be made of. They show us a room with a round table; I'm thinkin' must be where we play. But the damn table looked like it was worth more'n all the money in both our pockets. Hell, the walls might as well have been in the Taj Mahal. They sit us in chairs that look like they'll break and I don't want to have to pay for 'em.

"There we stay with a couple other guys and nobody says nothin'. A few more chairs are empty and we figure we'll start when they get filled. Finally, in walk these three business types with their three-piece suits. These guys are different than the ones who frisked us. You know the kind: deep pockets and no brains – at least when it comes to poker. About then I start feelin' pretty confident and think to myself, this'll be a cinch. The money'll be flyin' and I'll be catching."

Randy paused to take a swig from a bottle of water. "Before we knowed it we're all anteing up with C notes. It's a little weird watching that much cash goin' down. Just as I figure, the suits are terrible and don't know their ass from a hole in the ground. For one solid hour they lose more'n I make in a year. My friend and I come out on top. Hell, everyone at the table comes out on top except Curly, Moe, and Larry.

"But then somethin' changes. One of the suits says he wants to raise the stakes; says they want the minimum bet to be a thousand instead of a hundred. I tell 'em it's time for me and my buddy to go, but guys at the door say we can't till the game's over. We can sit out if we want, but nobody leaves. That's when I start gettin' real nervous. Not scared, just nervous."

"I know," Kristen quipped with a smile. "That part comes later."

"Boy does it," Randy said. "Me and my buddy sit there watchin'; too damn rich for our blood. They lose a couple costly rounds and then one of 'em finally wins. They lose a couple more rounds and then another one wins. Pretty soon the game turns in their favor and it starts to come clear there's more to those morons than meets the eye. Within another hour, they make back their losses several times over. Whatever the hell kinda system they had goin' was like nothin' I ever saw.

"I start lookin' around at the ones in charge and see 'em glancing at each other. Never said a word, but more information was passin' between 'em than the Sunday paper. I seen one give a nod to another. They switch out the deck and Curly, Moe, and Larry stop winning. Just like that."

Randy took another swig of water. "So there they are, losin' worse than before. One of 'em suddenly says he's got to take a leak. He and a big guy near the door disappear in the back while we wait. Longest five minutes of my life. Nobody says nothin'. When the suit finally comes back, he's holdin' a little gun. Hell, he must've tucked the thing into someplace the sun don't shine for 'em not to find it when they frisked him, and I'm thinkin' better him holdin' it than me."

Kristen laughed. "You're kidding?"

"No joke, missy. Either that or he found it somewhere in the back. But with the guard that went with him, I don't see how. Anyway, the guard isn't with him and we figure he's either dead or tied up in the back. Besides the gun, the guy's carryin' somethin' else. It's a black notebook-like thing. He tells a guy at the table to stuff all the cash into a bag and I'm thinkin' this guy's crazy if he thinks he and his buddies are gonna just walk out with no problems. Funny thing is, they did. Last thing they say is that if anyone tries to find 'em, they turn over the books to the police. I'm thinkin' it's a funny thing to say from a bunch of guys robbin' the place. But then later I figure out that we were in the presence of none other than the mob. I figure that black notebook has lots of incriminating stuff or something; all the things they've become so good at hiding."

"Yeah, I guess I'd be scared too," Kristen said.

Randy gave a nervous chuckle. He waited a long time before finally finishing. "I still wasn't that scared. Not yet. Curly, Moe, and Larry left with the cash. They question the rest of us for over an hour to make sure we aren't working with 'em as some kind of setup. Then this little guy I never seen during the game comes into the room. He has this air about him the others don't, like he's the boss. He takes each of us out separately into another room…"

Kristen could tell Randy was starting to have trouble at this point, the memory obviously a disturbing one.

"I was scared. Real scared," he said.

"What happened?"

Somehow Randy seemed smaller than he had when she'd climbed into the truck.

"He threatened us in ways I never knowed a man could be threatened. When he was finished, he explained that if we ever repeat any of what happened to another soul, he'd have us hunted down and body parts would be removed from the inside out. Comin' from someone else it would seem like an empty threat. But I'd just experienced what the man was capable of and I can tell you it weren't no empty threat."

Kristen wondered what the man had done to terrify Randy so. But something told her not to push it simply to satisfy her curiosity.

"Wow, that doesn't sound too pleasant," Kristen said.

"Missy, that's like sayin' a major heart attack is a bit uncomfortable. Damn near peed my pants. I was finally scared, all right."

Randy eased the rig into the next lane to pass a slower moving truck. "Funny thing is," he finally said, "you're the first person I've told. My buddy and I never talked about it. I lost touch with him and that was that. It's been four or five years now, but it still gives me the willies just thinkin' about it."

"Did you ever find out who the Three Stooges were? Ever hear about it on the news or anything?"

"Not the news. I'll tell you what. They weren't no dummies. They knew exactly what they were doin'. Some balls, walkin' into the mob and walkin' out with their cash. Guys were either geniuses or the stupidest people alive. Kinda like the real Three Stooges, I reckon; actin' like idiots and carryin' on…laughin' all the way to the bank."

Randy chuckled. "Couple nights later I seen one of 'em in a bar just outside Vegas. Shocked as hell he was still in this country, let alone within the mob's easy reach. He was pretty tanked, like maybe he was either celebrating or real scared. Curiosity gets the better of me and I sit down next to him; ask him if he remembers me from the game.

"Getting a better look up close, the kid couldn't of been thirty years old. Being pretty well saturated, he opens up and tells me he and his buddies ain't really the gamblin' types. Apparently one of 'em came up with this hair-brained idea to screw the mob out of enough cash for some business thing. It was either that or they'd have to borrow it from a bank or get investors and such. This way, they wouldn't have to pay it back. 'Like pullin' money out of the air,' he said. I'm thinkin' air doesn't come after you with guns when you screw it.

"Helluva thing," Randy concluded.

"What about the mob? They ever come after you? Ever hear from them again?"

"Fortunately not. Guess I'll never know if they got their book back or not. In some ways I hope they did so they never have to worry about it; never have to think about me or anyone else at the game that night."

Kristen looked out the window. Far to the west she saw dark clouds that suddenly lit up from behind as though someone were turning on and off a lamp.

"Don't feel too bad about being scared," she said. "I don't know anyone who wouldn't be, in that situation. But you never know. Sometimes it helps to get it off your chest."

The cab grew silent as Kristen decided she might not be the best person to give such advice.

CHAPTER 9

They made such good time that Kristen figured she'd get to Panama City early the next morning. Randy explained that the lack of eighteen-wheeler friendly routes meant he'd have to take Interstate 65 to Mobile and then cut in toward Pensacola. From there he'd drive along the Gulf cost until reaching the warehouse for delivery at which point she'd be within his promised fifty-six miles of Panama City. Her only request was that he drop her off near a mall and Randy told her he knew of one they'd drive right by.

"Why a mall?" he asked. "Need to do some shopping?"

"In a way," Kristen said. "Malls are great places because they have just about everything you need. It's especially useful if you don't drive."

They found a service station just outside Pensacola and Randy made one last stop to stretch and take a potty break before driving another forty or fifty miles to the warehouse. Kristen offered to pick up some snacks in the store while he did his business, so he handed her a twenty, asking for some peanuts, a candy bar, and a can of Coke.

It felt good to stretch, having been cooped up in the cab for so long, and Kristen breathed in the fresh air-conditioned smell of the tiny store. She nodded to an older gentleman at the counter who was about to service a customer and made her way around the miniature aisles to find Randy's snacks. Three packages of peanuts went into her bag, followed by beef jerky, several candy bars, and from the cooler in the back, two cold cans of Coke. She held her bag low as she approached the front of the store.

The clerk was watching a small T.V. behind the counter.

"Excuse me," Kristen said. "Do you sell molasses? My recipe says it has to be black strap or nothing at all."

"Sorry, ma'am. There's a grocery store up the road about four miles," he said.

"Oh really? Which direction?"

He pointed and told her to turn right when she came to the third light.

"Thank you, so much. I've got this party I'm going to tomorrow and don't know the area…actually," she said, interrupting herself, "There is one more thing you could do for me. Could you break a twenty, and let me have a small paper sack?"

"No problem," he said.

"A ten, a five, four ones, and change."

"Quarters?" he asked.

"Mmm…better make it three quarters, two dimes, and a nickel."

"Sorry about the molasses," he said as she headed for the door.

"Oh, you've helped more than enough," Kristen told him. "Trust me."

Tucking two one-dollar bills and fifteen cents from Randy's money into a snapped coin purse, she returned to the truck, leaving the remainder of the cash in her hand.

Randy had already returned and was waiting for her patiently in the driver's seat, the big rig purring contentedly. She opened the passenger side door and pulled herself up into the massive vehicle, barely thinking anymore about her fears. Since she knew the operator, the beast wouldn't bother her.

"Got your stuff," she said and reached in the bag, pulling out the can of Coke.

When she did, she noticed something shiny lying at her feet.

It was a large hunting knife. Not only that, but half of it had been painted red. Except that, when she picked it up, she saw that it wasn't paint but blood, still dripping.

"What in the world is this?" she asked, turning to look at Randy who was slumped unnaturally in the seat. His button-up shirt had a large dark stain in the middle.

"My God! What happened?" She looked around the cab as though the beast had somehow turned on its master while she was in the store. Her hands began to shake.

The knife slipped from her hand as Randy reached over and grabbed her by the jacket, pulling her in close. "They'll be after you now." His voice was a thin rasp. "Shouldn't have said anything." Stuffing a scrap of paper in her hand, he forced her fist to close around it. "Go. The police are useless. This person can help," he said. "Don't think about me, Kristen Bandy, because I'm not scared no more."

And then with one last breath and all the strength he could muster, he shouted, "GO!"

ஓ

Whoever had stabbed Randy might kill her as well. That was the first thing that crossed her mind. Yet she couldn't just leave him there to die. There was a pay phone at the front of the store, so with shaking fingers, Kristen dialed 911. "A man's been stabbed," she told the dispatcher who answered. "He's in a truck parked in front of…" She strained to look at the tall sign out front, take in her surroundings. "At the Pilot station on route 90, right across from the Texas Roadhouse."

She slammed the phone down before the questions began. She had to get out of here before the police arrived. She was a hitchhiker Randy had picked up. She'd be the first person they'd suspect. But there was something else to consider. Someone around here had stabbed him and she might be next. There was safety in numbers.

Going into the store, she went to the end of the first aisle and pressed up against a display of 2-liter jugs of soda. Two men had come into the store behind her, one wearing a tropical shirt, the other a beefy looking fellow in faded blue jeans. As she slipped to the back and out of sight, she watched them as they craned their necks, looking for something. No doubt looking for her. Ducking down, she came back up the far aisle behind them, slipping out the side door unnoticed. In the distance she could hear the scream of a siren.

She had to get away. The police would be here any moment. She tried the door to one car but it was locked. Going to the next – a dated Chevy Impala – she tried again. This time the door opened and she scrambled inside, ducking down on the floor in the back. Agonizing minutes passed until the last wails of the siren grew silent somewhere nearby, while a faint pulse of light continued to reflect through the car's interior.

Then there was a different sound. Footsteps on pavement and getting closer. Before she had time to react, a door opened and someone got in, put a key in the ignition and started up. When the car pulled away, Kristen couldn't tell which direction it was headed. Acceleration plus momentum equaled a swaying car and immediately she felt lightheaded and woozy. Kristen held her stomach and tried to keep still. After several minutes the car found a straightaway and she lifted her head for a peek. The driver's hair was black and glossy. When she looked at the rearview mirror, her heart jumped. Staring back at her was one of the men from the store.

The look on his face, as he saw her in the mirror, was one of amusement.

CHAPTER 10

Jack found himself seated in a booth at a seafood restaurant called The Crazy Lobster. He'd ordered the Shrimp-Fest, which included everything from batter-fried to scampi in garlic sauce. During his meal he had two glasses of white wine and concluded the meal with a number of gin and tonics, as he sat looking at lapping water along the shoreline.

He turned his attention to the waitresses, carrying loaded trays, as well as the patrons, rolling themselves out of their booths and walking with a fat-dumb-and-happy look out the door. And somehow it seemed to him that the place was really nothing more than a refueling station. Cars needed gas and people needed food. But humans demanded they be humored and waited on, hand and foot.

From purely a necessity standpoint, Jack speculated, there was no reason there couldn't be food-stations where people pull up, wrap their lips around a nozzle, pull the lever, and consumed a nutritionally balanced blend of glop. It might not do much for the taste buds, but it would certainly be one heck of an efficient way to eat. The whole process could take place in two minutes, tops. He could see a whole family rolling down their windows and sucking nourishment by the mouthfuls until satisfied. Dad would slide a credit card into the pump and off they'd go. No muss, no fuss.

Jack shook his head. He must be far drunker than he'd realized. Some people got wild or sleepy when they drank. For some reason, Jack always became philosophical. He wondered if it were that way before the accident. He couldn't remember. Maybe some new part of his brain had clicked on and the old rules of merely accepting the way things were had turned off. Maybe when he drank, the new part of his brain would go to work, analyzing everything to a fault.

Yet, whether drinking or not, Jack always seemed to struggle with his amnesia. He'd asked the doctor why he could remember much from before the accident, such as how to drive, talk, and eat, sometimes even places and major social events. But when it came to personal items, like remembering his wife and kids, his position at CareSoft, such memories left him as void as the way he felt when staring into a mirror. The doctor had explained there were two categories of amnesia: retrograde, when the victim has no recollection of memories before a traumatic event, and anterograde, where the victim sporadically loses recent memories.

Jack's was clearly retrograde, but within that category, the doctor had said there were many types and an unlimited number of manifestations, which basically, was a doctor's educated way of saying, "How the hell should I know?" The man had rambled on, mentioning conditions like Dissociative Identity Disorder and other equally unpleasant terms until Jack had finally tuned it all out and never asked again.

One more drink and Jack was on the road in his Porsche, weaving down the road and cursing himself for driving under the influence when he knew better. Somehow he found his way back to the condo where he used the remote to open the single car garage and pulled in as carefully as his numbed abilities allowed. When the car bumped into the wall, he shut it off before he could do further damage.

Pressing a button on the wall to shut the roll top, he exited through the side door, which placed him just outside the front of the condo. Whether out of habit or conscious thought, he managed to lock the garage before pulling his keys out to unlock the front door to the condo. Yet when he made a feeble attempt to push the key into the slot, the door swung open.

Jack stood there in a stupor, wondering how he'd managed to leave without locking up, without, in fact, latching the door. Locking and latching it behind him, he stumbled down the short hall singing to himself *Who Are You* by The Who, and reaching the master bedroom, dropped onto the bed and immediately fell asleep.

He saw the short guy from his earlier dream, the one with a face only a mother could love. "You fool," he said, taunting Jack from the other side of a mirror. "Don't you even know who I am? I'm you." And then he tipped back his head and laughed uproariously.

ஒ

When Jack opened his eyes, the brightness of the room gave him an instant headache. His throat was dry and the room didn't look too steady. He pulled himself onto one elbow and sat up carefully. Something that made you feel this way should be outlawed, he decided, knowing that he could safely change his mind later.

Suddenly he heard a noise in the other room. It sounded like the clank of a plate. And for just a moment, he wondered if he'd somehow been dreaming. Perhaps he was here with the family, after all.

No. It wasn't possible.

Jack stood and walked carefully to the door, and into the hallway. All was quiet now but he sensed he wasn't alone. When he walked into the living room he half expected to see Maggie in the kitchen making breakfast while the kids sat quietly watching cartoons.

But the TV wasn't on and Maggie wasn't in the kitchen. However, what he did see was a young woman sitting at the dining room table, helping herself to his bag of chips and dip.

She looked up and said, "Oh. Hi."

Jack glanced around the room as if to find the one responsible for letting a complete stranger into the condo, but none of the furniture fessed up. She wore a black leather jacket, slit vertically from top to bottom all the way around, over a black T-shirt. The girl had short, midnight black hair, strands randomly jutting out in all directions. Her face was made up in gothic fashion and a small ring pierced her nose. She wore black gloves cut short with fingers stabbing through, exposing a number of peculiar rings, including one featuring a skull and crossbones. To complete the ensemble, a chrome chain was wrapped several times around her neck and held with a small padlock.

"How did you get in here?" Jack demanded.

"The door was open so I came in," she said with a shrug. "I thought it would be all right if I waited in here. Sorry if I startled you."

"Wait?" Jack demanded. "Wait for what?"

She pulled a small piece of paper from a pocket in the shredded leather jacket and placed it on the table. "Here," she said.

The scrap of paper had his name and address scribbled on it in pencil.

"What's this?"

"You tell me," the girl said. "Randy Long – I think his name was Longfellow, gave it to me; said you could help."

"Who? Help with what? I don't know what you're talking about. You better leave or I'm calling the police."

"Somebody got up on the wrong side of the bed this morning," the girl said. "Chill for a second, would you? I'll leave if there was a misunderstanding. Perhaps *you* could explain why a dying man would give me your name and address?"

Jack filled a glass with water, gulping it down in a single tip-back, and braced himself with the counter. His headache was starting to subside and he could feel the liquid working its way through his system like oil through the cylinders of an engine.

Once his motor was running properly again, he said, "What do you mean, a dying man?"

"I'm sorry you have to find out like this, but Randy was stabbed to death. At least I'm pretty sure he's dead."

Jack shook his head. "Find out like what? I've never heard of him."

"He's a truck driver," she said, agitated. "You *have* to know him. He obviously knew you."

Jack felt his life was spiraling out of control. After the accident, he had often been completely disoriented, but over time he had managed to grow accustomed to a sane level of confusion. He'd had to live with a family he didn't know and act like he was the V.P. of a company, when he felt entirely inadequate at the position. But he'd somehow managed. Now he felt everything caving in around him again. Who was this girl? Who was this truck driver who supposedly knew him, a man who had been stabbed?

And then it dawned on him as he looked at the girl with her death-like getup. She was playing him. She'd found his name in the phone book – no, that wasn't right. They weren't listed in the Destin directory. Okay, so she'd somehow managed to get hold of his name and the condo's address and broken in. Maybe the story was a cover up in case she got caught. Maybe she'd been living here for some time now, since their last trip down several weeks ago.

The girl popped another dip-laden chip in her mouth and munched away as if nothing could worry her.

"I see what's going on here," Jack suddenly said.

"Good. I was beginning to think you were really going to call the cops or something."

Jack picked up the phone. "I am." He punched 9-1-1 on the keypad.

"Wait!" the girl exclaimed, leaping to her feet. "You can't. Randy said they wouldn't be able to help. Besides, they'll throw me in jail. I swear! I'll do anything you say. Just don't call the cops."

Now that she was standing, Jack could see her shirt was a midriff and that even her bellybutton was pierced with a small silver ring.

Jack hung up the phone. "Okay. Here's how it's going to work, then. You walk out the door and never come back. Understand? If I ever catch you again, you're going to jail. And don't try to come back, because I'm having a security system installed."

"Are you sure you don't know Randy Longfellow?" she asked him. "He said you could help."

"It's a made-up name, I'm sure. Don't bother with your story. Just get out."

The girl's face looked incredulous. "You think I'm lying? Just look in the paper. You'll see that a guy by the name of Randy Longfellow was stabbed yesterday outside a gas station near Pensacola."

"I don't have a paper," Jack said. "And even if this man *was* murdered, what's it to me?"

The girl threw up her hands in disbelief. She plopped onto the sofa in the living room. "I've never met anyone like you," she told him. "You don't believe anything I say, do you? If you'd been here last night when I arrived –"

"What?" Jack demanded. "You've been here all night?" Taking a quick glance in his kid's room, he saw that one of the twin beds was in a disheveled mess.

"How long have you been here?" he said, storming back to the living room.

"Just since last night. I told you, already. If you'd listen…"

Jack was baffled, seeing the way the girl planted herself on the sofa as if she owned the place. There was no point in arguing with her. He had the authority to demand that she leave then and there. But despite himself, Jack was humored by the girl's insistence on her fabricated story. Rather than calling the police, he came up with a better idea.

"I'll make you a deal," he said, picking up the remote. "I'll turn on this TV and make a pass over each channel. If there's nothing about someone named Randy Longfellow getting stabbed, you walk out that door and never come back. Do you understand?"

"But what if the news isn't on right now? Even if it is, what are the chances of them talking about the story this minute?"

"That's my offer. Take it, or I call the cops."

The girl held up her hands. "Okay, wait. What if you do find something on TV about the stabbing? Then what?"

"Right. Okay, I'll give you no more than five minutes to explain everything you know about it and why you think I shouldn't turn you in. Deal?"

"I don't know."

"Deal?" Jack said, starting to move toward the phone.

"Okay. Okay," she told him. "You're sure some kind of jerk, aren't you?"

Ten seconds later, both their mouths dropped open when the first image that appeared on the screen was a reporter standing near a gas station, an eighteen-wheeler in the background. "Randy Longfellow, a truck driver from Knoxville, Tennessee, was found stabbed to death just outside Pensacola yesterday," she announced. This was followed by a brief interview with the store attendant who had seen a distressed girl use the pay phone shortly before the police arrived. A grainy video taken by the store security camera followed and Jack heard the girl on his sofa gasp when she saw herself appear, walking down an aisle. The anchorwoman completed the sequence by saying the police were asking for information surrounding the murder or the whereabouts of the girl caught on the store's security camera."

"So," the girl demanded, almost triumphantly. "Do you believe me now or what?"

~

Zack and Erin were up to something. Mark could tell the moment he returned with his morning coffee. Presently, however, he wasn't as interested in what mischief they might be planning, since he was studying Erin's backside moving slowly up and down, as she bent over, elbows propped on Zack's desk, chin resting on her hands. Her thick hair was tossed to one side and she wore black, strapless sandals, as her heels raised and lowered. Up and down. Up and down.

Intent on the view, Mark took a swallow and nearly choked from the scalding coffee. He cursed, sticking his hand under his mouth to catch some drips. It served him right for staring at Erin's ass. She was easily ten years his junior and he felt foolish for behaving so unprofessionally.

Mark knew he had to gain control of himself and cut the adolescent-like crush he had on Erin. He hadn't felt like this in years, but the fact such feelings were still inside made him wonder if he'd ever grow up.

Descending into the pit area, he walked to where Zack sat and Erin was bobbing slowly up and down. "What's all the fuss?" he asked, averting his eyes with an effort.

Immediately, Erin stood upright – rescuing him from temptation – and wheeled around to face him. "Nothing," she said too quickly. "I was just reviewing one of Zack's subjects. No big deal."

Mark studied her face for just a moment without speaking. Her lively blue eyes. Her alluring lips. That perfectly sculpted nose and beautiful matching eyebrows. And an impish smile that endeared her to him all the more.

"You're sure everything's all right?" he said. "No major hiccups?"

"Everything's fine," she assured him. She reached out and Mark reeled back as if contact would complete her power over him. "There's something on your chin," she said.

"Thanks, uh," he stammered, rubbing at his face so furiously that what was left of his coffee slopped on the floor. "I'll be, um, in my office if you need me."

Why was he behaving this way? He hadn't spent all these years working his way up the food chain merely to come unglued by a pretty face. Or had he? It was simply ridiculous. And yet he couldn't help the hypnotic control she seemed to wield over him.

Sitting at his desk, trying to put her out of his mind, his eyes fell on Guerridelli's folder. He'd just learned that the medical staff had successfully completed the procedure after eleven hours in OR. It had been one of the more difficult cases, but everything had turned out all right. Soon it would be his group's turn to take over and he still had a decision to make.

Which led him to Jared. The new guy had stopped by his office last night before leaving, an impromptu visit that had puzzled Mark. He'd had his reservations about hiring Jared although he was extremely intelligent. The fact that he was unkempt and socially immature didn't bother him since this was common for highly technical people. But this young man seemed barely able to carry on a conversation, and had spent his interview awkwardly fidgeting and spewing random bursts of copious knowledge. Mark had been quite impressed with his resume and had rationalized his behavior as being somehow the result of Jared's extraordinarily high IQ.

Mark sat back and took a sip of coffee. A vision of Erin suddenly filled his mind. Leaning on Zack's desk. Moving up and down, up and down.

Back to business, he scolded himself.

Jared had knocked tentatively on his open door, apparently afraid to barge in uninvited. It was clear that he'd had something on his mind, something that was apparently taking lots of courage for the kid to bring up.

"I've been noticing something about other monitors you should know," he'd said, and gone on to explain how they were cracking jokes about the new client because of his affiliation with organized crime. He felt like they were stereotyping the man and that he was worried it might cloud their judgment. And even though he was new, Jared pointed out that he was ready for his own subject, particularly since he felt he could be more objective when dealing with Guerridelli.

The kid had actually made a lot of sense, even though Mark had been taken back by Jared's sudden display of tolerance and altruistic concern. Your typical, everyday nerd didn't think squat about fairness or consider other people's feelings. The kid was certainly one of a kind.

He'd heard the jokes, himself, and knew that what Jared was telling him was true. If the analysts got a whiff of that kind of humor, it could get back to the board and then his department would have some explaining to do.

Mark's mind began to drift again. *Erin.* Leaning over Zack's desk

He opened the folder and studied the assignment sheet with Devon Guerridelli's name listed at the top. Even though he would have never considered it a day ago, and in spite of the fact his department would soon come under the scrutiny of efficiency consultants, Mark filled in the name of the monitor responsible for the new client, before signing his own name authorizing approval at the bottom.

Jared Stephens.

CHAPTER 11

The word *murder* stuck in Kristen's head from the moment the anchorwoman said it. And the worst part about the dreadful word was that she was now implicated as possibly the one to drive the shiny blade into poor Randy's gut.

The weekend had turned bizarre, from the moment she'd hitched a ride with Randy and he'd told her about the poker game. Now she was riding a wave of confusion, hoping it wouldn't crash her to shore where she'd be locked up for murder.

Things could have been worse. For one thing, the grim fellow she'd thought was after her could have been a member of the mob prepared to finish the job he'd started. But in fact, he'd wound up being as harmless as a stuffed animal. He was even heading toward Destin – the location of the address on the paper – and since he knew the area well, he had been kind enough to drop her in front of the condo at around dusk, to the accompaniment of her profuse thanks.

When no one had answered the door, Kristen had found it unlocked. Exhausted and certain that this Jack Stuart would sympathize with her position once he'd learned what happened to Randy, she had wandered into a bedroom as though she were Goldilocks, finding the bed *just right*. She'd slept sounder than she had in weeks, straight through until morning, in fact.

Now the man she had seen earlier, sprawled fully clothed on the top of the covers in the other bedroom, had turned out to be a tall, good-looking fellow who seemed about as harmless as the guy who'd given her a ride, someone who was apparently willing to listen to her explanation of how she'd been hitching south and been picked up by Randy in Atlanta. She went on to give him a nutshell version of the poker game Randy had told her about, the stop for a break and snacks, and then finding him stabbed. Jack looked perplexed when she came to the part about Randy telling her that he could help.

"Even if he'd pulled my name out of a hat, how could he possibly know I'd be here in Destin now?" Jack said. "Nobody knows. I live in Atlanta and just happened to come down for the weekend without anyone's knowledge. Not even my wife knew."

"Maybe he didn't know," Kristen offered. "Maybe it was just a coincidence you were here."

Jack shook his head. "I just don't get it. Besides, that doesn't even begin to explain the fact I've never met the man."

Kristen tried to think of a plausible explanation. She grasped at a slippery straw. "Maybe you have a mutual friend, or something. You know. Maybe he knew *of* you, without necessarily knowing you."

"At this point, I suppose anything is possible."

Kristen was just as baffled over the fact Randy had given her Jack's name and address. She'd been certain that he would have known the trucker. Now she wasn't so sure. Even though Jack seemed a bit possessive about his precious condo, she didn't think the guy was lying.

"Even though I have no idea why the man aimed you in my direction," Jack told her, "I guess I owe it to you to let you stay here for the day. I'll be heading back to Atlanta this afternoon. Then I'm afraid you'll have to find somewhere else to go."

"Don't want to take me home to the family, eh?" Kristen said.

Jack looked perturbed. "No. Although it probably wouldn't make any difference."

Kristen studied his face. "You never did say why you're down here all by yourself. Having some trouble at home, are we?"

"That's really none of your business," Jack told her.

It was written all over his face. The man was clearly midlife crisis bound. Why else would he have come down here for the weekend without telling his family? Maybe he was looking for a way out of his failing marriage. Maybe he was looking for a little fun on the side. Something she, herself, wasn't the least bit interested in. Whatever his situation, Kristen found Jack's enigmatic personal life an entertaining theme.

"Maybe you need to lighten up. I wouldn't want to live with someone as uptight as you," Kristen said.

Jack glared at her. "Keep your observations to yourself. And try to remember that I'm letting you stay here temporarily."

"Out of the goodness of your heart, no doubt," Kristen said, feet now propped on the coffee table. "I've never met a man like you, but I've heard a lot about your type. I know what you want. Don't think for a minute you'll get it."

Jack looked shocked she would imply such a thing. "Don't flatter yourself," he said. "Try to remember that *you* came to *me* for help, help which I'm attempting to give you, probably something I'll live to regret."

"Yeah, but isn't it convenient I'm here," Kristen said sarcastically.

"I'll show you how interested I am," he said, going to the door and throwing it open wide. "Get the hell out of my condo. Now!"

"I'm just playing," Kristen said. "Can't you take a joke?"

"I don't play games, Miss Bandy. You want to fool around: you'll have to find someone else. On top of that, I'm a happily married man."

"I'm sure you are," Kristen said, keeping the sarcasm out of her voice with an effort. "Look, I'm sorry. All right?"

"All right," he said and shut the door.

Kristen was grateful she'd been able to calm him down. She'd been right on the mark about his midlife crisis.

❧

There was something about this girl that appealed to him. Perhaps it was the fact Maggie and his kids never gave him anything to get riled about. Even the good folks he worked with seemed all too eager to please, perhaps because of his position in the company or perhaps because of the accident. But here was someone who knew nothing about him. She had no reason to treat him specially, except that he was helping her. But the fact that she was treating him as she would anyone somehow made the experience all the more real.

"Do I make you nervous?" she asked, having watched him wipe down the counters, wash the dishes, clean out the refrigerator, and buzz around the condo like a Merry Maid.

"Me?" he said.

"I was actually speaking to the beef jerky, but I just realized it's already dead. Of course I was talking to you."

Jack finally sat down, watching Kristen chomp on a leathery piece of jerky. "Okay," he said. "You want to get personal? Why were you hitchhiking?"

"None of your business."

"Where were you headed?"

"Ditto."

"How do I know *you* didn't kill this guy? How do I know you're not going to kill me when you get half a chance?"

"You don't," she said, without missing a beat.

Jack sighed. "I can see that with your copious information and my sleuthing genius, we'll be able to solve this mystery in no time."

"Well put, Sherlock," she said. "Why should I bother answering any of your questions when you aren't being honest, yourself?"

"I am being honest."

"And I'm Mother Teresa."

"Ask me anything and I swear I'll tell you the truth," Jack said.

"Really?" Kristen said and looked carefully at his face to make sure he wasn't lying.

"Really."

She gnawed on the jerky like a dog nursing its bone. "Okay. How many times a week do you and your wife have sex?"

Jack's face flushed. "That's none of your damn business!"

"Uh, huh. See what I mean?" she said.

He gritted his teeth, but said, "Twice. Three sometimes."

"I'm impressed," she said. "Okay. Then why are you here without the fam?"

"You've had your question. Now it's my turn. Why were you hitchhiking? Where were you going?"

"That's two questions. But I'm feeling generous. Because I don't drive and I wanted to get to Panama City."

"Couldn't you find another way? Plane? Bus?"

"How many questions does that make?" she asked. "I think it's my turn. You know the one."

Jack leaned back in his chair and looked out the window at the beach. "I just needed a break; some time to myself."

"See, that wasn't so hard, was it? So how's your marriage, really?" she asked.

"Splendid!"

"Splendid? Really?"

"It's outstanding. Certainly nothing I should complain about."

"But you do, don't you?"

Jack looked down and sighed. "Look, this honesty stuff is fine, but we're not getting any closer to the truth. Since we're being so honest, why didn't you wait and talk to the police?"

"I have my reasons," she said. "Besides, if it *was* the mob, it probably wouldn't do any good. The trucker said so, himself."

"But we don't know that for sure, either that it was the mob or that it wouldn't do any good. I think we need to call the police. I can do it."

"NO!" Kristen exclaimed. "I'm out of here if you even try."

"I understand you're in some kind of trouble, but you don't want to be a fugitive running from murder, do you? Whatever you've done can't be that bad."

"We're not going to the police."

"Once I leave here, I have no choice. I'll give you plenty of time before I make the call. I could be charged with accessory if I don't."

"No, you can't. I'm not a principal," she said.

"A principal?"

"You know. One fulfilling the elements of substantive offense. *Actus reus* and *mens rea*. Since I'm only a witness, they can't charge you with accessory."

"Huh?" Jack said, looking confused.

"Trust me."

He studied her carefully. How was this apparent vagrant able to speak so fluently about the law, and with such confidence? Perhaps she was a law student, although she certainly didn't appear to fit the mold. It was either that or she'd spent lots of time around attorneys, possibly as a defendant. The last thing Jack needed to add to his own identity crisis would be to hook up with someone like Kristen, whose picture would probably soon be hanging in post offices around the country.

"How do you know so much about law?" he asked her.

"It's not important."

"Well then, what about this. How do I know you didn't do it? If so, I could still be charged with accessory."

"You know I didn't," she said.

"And how do you figure that?"

"Because if you believed for one second I really killed him, you wouldn't be sitting here with me."

The girl could easily be on a debate team. "That's an interesting observation," Jack admitted. "But a jury might not find it so convincing."

"It happened just like I told you," she insisted, the dark mascara around her eyes making Jack feel like he was conversing with a corpse.

"You said you picked up the knife. Right? Suppose the killer wore gloves, which he probably did. That means the only prints will be yours."

"Crap!" she said. "This is just great."

"Like I said all along: we need to call the police. If you turn yourself in and tell them the truth…"

"Forget it. You've just convinced me there's no way I'm going to the police. I can always disappear. I've been doing it for weeks."

"But did you have detectives looking for you? For murder?" Jack asked. "It may not be so easy to disappear now."

"Let me stay here."

Jack laughed unconvincingly. "I don't think so."

"If I'm caught I'll just say I broke in. You're going back today anyway. Well, even if you kick me out, I'll just break in after you leave."

"Like hell you will," he said. "I already told you I'm calling the police. They'll be all over this place searching for you."

Kristen was fuming. Jack could tell she was no upstanding citizen and considered the wisdom of pushing her too far. He honestly didn't believe she'd committed the murder, but who knew what she was capable of, especially when threatened?

"Look," he said. "This has all been very interesting, but I've got a long drive home and you need to leave. I'll wait several hours to give you plenty of time for a head start before I pull off and call the police. Deal?"

Kristen crossed her arms and remained silent.

"The sooner you go, the more time you'll have," he said. "I'm going to batten down the place, but you'll need to leave. In fact, I want you gone by the time I've finished changing my clothes."

As he changed into the pants and shirt he'd driven down in, he wished he'd never come. His time away had turned into nothing more than a complicated mess. Maybe if he hadn't been here, the girl would have tried the bell and moved on. Now she'd dug her heels in and it might be difficult to pry her loose. Somehow the idea of going home to face Maggie and the kids should seem more appealing.

Suddenly, he heard shattering glass from the other room, followed by something hitting the floor. *Great!* He'd pushed her too far and now she'd gone and done something rash. He hurried to the living room where Kristen stood, staring at a rock with a strip of paper wrapped around it. Bits of glass from the shattered window covered the kitchen floor.

"What is it?" Kristen asked apprehensively.

"What is this?" he demanded, reading the paper. "Some kind of joke?"

"What does it say?"

"It says: Men are coming. Leave through the back. You don't know what you're dealing with."

"Oh, God," Kristen said, unlocking the sliding door.

"What are you doing?" he asked.

"Getting out of here."

"It has to be some kind of prank," Jack said.

"You weren't there," Kristen wailed. "You didn't see what they did to Randy."

It was at that precise moment that they both heard the sound of a car squeal to a stop out front.

CHAPTER 12

Sharp pain. Deep, deep pain.

His temples throbbed with an excruciating headache.

Where am I? What's happening?

He opened his eyes but the glare only made his head ache worse. As he desperately attempted to remember his last conscious thought, his hand touched something cold and hard. He gripped it and held on as if the alternative would be to slip perilously into unending darkness.

Though all memory was gone like the cold sea, silently disappearing over the edge of a flat world, there were still impressions that bubbled up from great depths. One was that if he were about to die, he wouldn't be admitted into Heaven on moral merit. Certainly he was not there now. No angelic creatures swarmed the air and no harps played melodious refrains. In fact, instead of harps, he could hear a strange puffing sound, accompanied by the faint, regular beep of a device somewhere above his head. His body felt separate, as though it was somehow detached from his mind. For some time he lay in this state, not knowing what would come next, drifting sleepily in and out of consciousness, aware of little beyond the fact that he was at someone else's mercy for the first time in his life.

And then suddenly, for no apparent reason, he became alert, his mind able to focus. All at once, the pain was replaced with a sense of well-being. He opened his eyes and saw that he was in a hospital bed. Slowly he began to make a routine check of his limbs, hands, feet. Everything seemed to be working. There was an I.V. station holding a bag of liquid, attached to his neck with plastic tubing. More plastic tubing came from somewhere above the bed and covered his nose, while an array of wires disappeared beneath his gown where they monitored his heartbeat.

He sat straight up and could feel strength surging though his veins as though the vessels were delivering pure intoxicating adrenaline. Whatever pain he'd had was now gone. He looked over the mess of tubes and wires, feeling like he was half machine. The thought of lying there while others had hooked him up was humiliating. He needed to break free from the vine-like tubing that tethered his body or risk going mad.

He began ripping them away, kicking off blue boots, pulling off the monitors, jerking the oxygen tube from his nose. When he yanked the central line from his neck, blood squirted everywhere. And yet he felt no pain. Could it be the result of having been so heavily medicated?

Tearing off a piece of sheet, he tied it around his neck, creating a makeshift tourniquet.

Machine alarms were sounding, while the medical equipment tried to rediscover his pulse. He stood, walked to the sink and stared at himself in the mirror. He was looking at a man who appeared to be around thirty and of medium height with thick black hair and glowing olive skin. His biceps well defined, the muscles were of a man in excellent physical condition. Grabbing the hospital gown, he ripped it off and saw that his chest and abdomen were taut with muscles, chiseled lines running around his chest and down the center into the leaf-like spines of his abs. He wore nothing below the waist. He looked up and down over the unfamiliar body. Not a bad specimen if he'd say so himself.

But still he couldn't remember. Who was he? Why was he here?

The plastic band around his wrist read "Jed Pope", a name with which he was completely unfamiliar, yet willing to accept for the moment. He snapped the band off just as a nurse, dressed in a white nylon pantsuit, sauntered in to see what the machine's fuss was all about. "What are you doing Mr. Pope?" she demanded, her eyes huge with disbelief. "Get back in bed this instant."

Pushing past the woman without answering her, he went to the window. She gasped and fled the room.

Outside, the wind was kicking up and pushing against the pane, causing it to flex and moan. He stared into a desert wasteland where tumbleweed blew wildly across the sandy landscape, wondering how he had wound up in this godforsaken place. There had to be an explanation.

Naked, he left the window in search of something to wear. In the closet was a pair of jeans, so he slipped them quickly on and was relieved to find they fit.

As he made his way into the hallway, the nurse returned with two men. One was short with thinning hair and had on wire-rimmed glasses. He wore a white lab coat and had "doctor" written all over him. The other, young and burly, standing well over six feet, was stuffed into blue overalls, several sizes too small.

"Mr. Pope," the short man said. "It's so good to see you've come around. We do need to get you back in bed, though. You'll be shipshape in no time. We'll have nurse Parker ring up Loretta, let her know you're conscious." The nurse scurried away, obviously relieved she wouldn't need to be involved.

Ignoring the doctor, Jed looked around like a commando attempting to determine the building's vulnerability. His blue-gray eyes were cold and calculating. He said nothing.

"Mr. Pope. Let's get you back to your room now," the doctor said, giving the orderly a nod. The men moved in to guide Jed back to his room. When the orderly touched his arm, Jed reached out to push him away, surprised to see the result. The large man flew backwards, crashing through a door on the other side of the hall.

The doctor's mouth dropped open.

Jed stared at his hand and flexed it curiously. How was that possible? He turned and looked at the doctor who shrank away, clearly terrified.

"Mr. Pope," the doctor said. "Please. I'm only trying to do my job."

Jed walked down the short hall into an open room that appeared to be a waiting area and reception desk.

The wind was howling around the edge of heavy glass doors. The nurse, who was huddled in the corner, followed him with huge eyes as he pushed open the doors and walked outside. The air was hot and dry. Wind pushed hard against him as he made his way across a small parking lot and into the street. The sun's heat on his shoulders and back became more intense as the wind subsided. Then the wind kicked up and the heat was held in check in the midst of hot and heavy gusts. The pavement should have been sizzling his feet like steaks on a grill, but he felt nothing but warm pavement.

An old pickup was racing up the street toward him and drew to a halt. The door opened and a vision stepped out. Long hair blew loosely in the wind. Smooth brown skin glistened with perspiration. Her face was beautiful and inviting, while a flowered dress fluttered and pulled against her shapely figure. She ran to greet him, her eyes moist, lips swollen with passion, and began to kiss him with feverish compulsion, while her breasts squeezed against his chest.

He felt nothing. Finally, after several minutes that would have been enough to raise a man from the dead, she stopped and looked into his eyes, her arms still around his neck.

"Jed," she said. "I've missed you so much. I didn't think you were going to make it. I came the minute they called. I've been so lonely without you."

Breaking free from her grasp, he stared at the building from which he'd just emerged, where he could see the nurse, the doctor, and the orderly, gawking at them from behind the glass doors. A fading sign, long battered by the desert sand, read, "Bootleg Hill Medical Clinic."

"Jed, honey. Are you okay?" the woman asked.

"Who are you?" he asked her.

"I'm whoever you want me to be," she said, throwing her arms around him again.

Pushing her away, he began walking up the street toward what looked like downtown, consisting of an intersection with several aging clapboard buildings.

"Jed? Honey?" she called after him. "Don't you know me? I'm Loretta. Come home with me, baby."

He ignored her and kept walking.

A smallish weathered sign by the side of the road declared the population of Bootleg Hill to be 283. No more. No less.

Loretta followed but kept her distance. The desert threw hot blasts at them from across an endless sea of sand and the road shimmered with heat waves, making it look like the town was floating on water. It might well have been, for no cars seemed to be on the road, nobody in sight. Jed stopped in the middle of the intersection. A small tumbleweed bounced by to one side, ignoring the stop sign.

A flapping screen door banged against the doorjamb of a market, its windows coated with dust. A gas station sat on one corner with pumps so old it appeared they might crumble to pieces with the next heavy gust. Several other buildings lined the street, looking very rundown.

"Jed?" Loretta asked.

Having studied the town at length, he turned to her and said, "Where the hell am I?" But even as he said it, he spotted a small building with a sign that read "Dude, Drop In – A pub for the hot and bothered."

"This is where we live," she began, but Jed was off again, headed toward the pub.

Inside, the contrast from bright desert sun to the dimness inside, forced him to stand at the entrance, peering into darkness until his eyes adjusted. Heavy-metal music was jamming somewhere inside, but it wasn't loud. Loretta followed him in.

Slowly, he began to make out small round tables with chairs. At the front was a bar where an old man sat hunched on a stool. The place smelled musty, while the sound of a swamp cooler blew futilely into the large room.

"Jed?" a voice asked. "Is that you? I'll be damned. Didn't recognize you, man. 'Tween you and me, I thought you were a goner after – well, you know. Loretta, always a pleasure."

The man behind the bar appeared to be in his forties and clearly a throwback from the sixties. He wore wire-rimmed glasses and a tie-dye rag around his forehead. His hair was long and stringy, while his body was thin, an Iron Maiden T-shirt hanging limply over his frame.

"Pull up and take a load off. Dang, dude! What happened?" he said as he looked at the bloodstained rag around Jed's neck.

Jed studied the place but couldn't remember ever being here. A strained riff from an electric guitar wailed through scratchy speakers, sounding nearly like a cat being tortured. Various stemmed glasses hung from a crude rack above the bar as though they'd been that way for a thousand years. The bartender clearly considered him to be an old pal, yet none of this seemed the slightest bit familiar.

"Who are you? What is this place?" Jed asked.

"I'm Stan," the bartender said, and then smiled curiously. "What? Don't you remember me, man?"

The old man turned lazily and looked at Jed from several stools down. His chin sprouted gray whiskers while watery eyes, deep set in his pudgy face, appeared almost innocent.

"You really don't remember, do you?" the bartender exclaimed. "Dang! Well, don't feel too bad. Ain't nothin' much around here worth remembering anyway. Except maybe Loretta." Stan grinned at the woman, holding Jed's arm. "I see you got that one under control. The rest of it ain't worth shit. Know what I mean?"

Stan poured a shot of whisky and scooted it in front of Jed.

"What's this for?" Jed asked.

"On the house. They say drinkin' makes you forget. Hell, you done forgot and you didn't even do it while enjoying the virtues of alcohol. Might as well make up for lost time. Who knows? Maybe it'll have the reverse effect and make you remember. Resurrect some of them brain cells instead of killin' 'em."

Jed ignored the drink. "Why don't you just tell me where I am? How I got here?"

"Ask Loretta," Stan said. "She knows more about you than anyone else around here. *Intimate* knowledge, if you know what I mean."

"I'm asking you," Jed said. "You can start by telling me what happened."

"The wreck? All I know is you flipped a bike doin' about fifty down the ravine. Hit your head. Never would wear a helmet, would you? Damn good thing Carl saw it or you'd probably still be layin' out there, bird food, if you know what I'm sayin'."

"I hit my head while riding a motorcycle?"

"You're on the edge, man," Stan told him. "It's what I always liked about you. I love the way you strap the CD player to the bike, wrapped in headphones, racing up and down them hills with metal scratchin' your ears. It's an inspiration, man. Don't you remember? You're the one who turned me on to Iron Maiden." Stan nodded toward the jukebox.

"Baby? Can we go home now?" Loretta moaned.

Jed ignored her.

It was all very strange. Somehow he knew things. Like what it meant to ride a motorcycle, though he wasn't sure he knew how. Being in a bar seemed oddly familiar, but not this pathetic little place. And the music. It was all he could do to keep from finding the source and putting it out of its misery with the swift swing of a blunt object. It was as though he were Rip Van Winkle who'd suddenly awoken after twenty years to find the world had changed. Only his world of the future – if that's what it was – was somehow cruder, more unrefined. He somehow remembered the faint taste of caviar, certain he'd eaten it on countless occasions. Certainly not in this town. He couldn't help feeling that he didn't belong here; had never really met these people.

But why would they be lying to him? What purpose would it serve?

He thought about asking what year it was, but decided knowing the answer wouldn't do any good since he couldn't remember what year it was supposed to be.

Instead, he asked, "How long have I been out?"

"Almost three weeks, baby. Could we *please* go home now?" Loretta said.

"And how long have I lived here? In this town?"

"You're a newbie, man," Stan said and poured himself a shot of whisky before downing it in one gulp. "Most of us have been here longer'n elephant crap. Know what I'm sayin'? Place like this has a way of grabbin' you by the balls and won't let go."

"How long?" Jed repeated.

"Mmm. I'd say 'bout a year and a half. Maybe two," Stan said. "What do you think, Loretta?"

"I don't know. We can talk about it later, baby. I want to go home." She nuzzled her face to the side of his head.

Stan grinned. "I wouldn't keep the lady waiting. If I was you, I'd listen to wisdom," he said and winked.

Jed pushed her away. "Not until I get answers. Where did I move here from?"

Loretta looked injured but hopeful as she struggled to keep her distance.

"Look, man. I think you better get going. We can talk about this later," Stan said and reached for the shot he'd poured Jed.

With the quickness of a striking viper, Jed seized Stan's arm. "Where did I move from?" he demanded.

"I don't know, man. Lighten up."

Jed suddenly realized that this man honestly didn't know. He was wasting his time asking the bartender questions, yet he was unsure how he'd come by this information. It was more than merely intuition or anything as logical as reason. It was as though he'd been able to look into the man's mind and see that the information didn't exist.

Then he realized something else. He knew a good deal about Stan, that he was forty-seven, born on July 26, that his family tree was filled with generations of losers, that car he drove; an old beat up Honda Accord that had once been navy blue, now a lovely shade of desert yuck; that his residence was a single-wide at the edge of town, and that his disposition was easy going, if a tad eccentric. He even knew of the man's sordid fantasies involving Loretta.

But he learned more about his relationship to the bartender by what he couldn't sense than by what he could. It didn't exist. There had been some vague idea of mutual friendship, but nothing tangible. Someone was trying to deceive him. He didn't belong here. In this town. This was all nothing more than an elaborate façade.

Jed pulled Stan's arm toward a gap in the counter, where a hinged section was flipped up to one side. Forcing the bartender's fingers over the edge, he continued to hold his arm in place while closing the panel on Stan's fingers.

Stan screamed in pain.

Jed bore down on the panel. "I don't know what the hell's going on," he said, "but you're going to tell me. Do you understand?"

Tears were forming in Stan's eyes while he nodded his head.

Loretta had backed up and looked horrified. "What are you doing, baby?"

The old man watched but was clearly content not to get involved.

"Who brought me here? Who do you work for? *Why the hell can't I remember anything?*"

"I don't know, man. You gotta believe me," Stan cried.

Jed watched Loretta as she edged away from him. The woman who was supposedly his lover lived a block away in a small house left to her by her grandmother, a house full of religious relics because her grandmother had been a devout Catholic. But there were no memories of them together. She had to be lying.

As for the drunk at the end of the bar, he was an empty warehouse with sketchy and useless information, having mostly been in a catatonic state for the last twenty-three years since he'd lost his job and his wife had left him.

Something had happened to him, Jed realized, and he would find out who was responsible if it were the last act of his dying breath.

Releasing Stan's fingers, he pushed the man backward into a shelf of bottles, causing it to give way and send them crashing to the floor in a heap of broken glass. Stan rolled to one side, trying desperately to avoid being cut by shards.

Loretta held a hand to her mouth, nervously chewing her fingernails.

"I hope it was worth it," Jed told them as he turned to leave. "Enjoy what they paid you while you can. Because after I find out who did this to me, I'm coming back to pay this town a visit."

CHAPTER 13

This couldn't be happening. Jack didn't remember the last time he'd felt scared about anything. Sometimes when life appears to be going along smoothly, you get it in your mind that nothing bad – nothing really bad – can happen. It was that way for Jack. Even though he regularly wrestled with his identity and the amnesia that set it off, he was always in control.

Even his boss gave him a lot of leeway in the company operations – marketing or otherwise – and nearly always consulted him when approaching a big decision. Peter Lynchman was the President of CareSoft, Inc. and Jack's business partner. After the accident, Peter had gone to great lengths to make Jack feel comfortable with his position. He'd explained that the two of them had started the company together; forged a path into the world of medical software where they'd managed to carve a niche in the industry. The company had grown to eighty employees and they had only good things to look forward to.

But now, as he peeked through the condo's shuttered living room window, his position at CareSoft seemed as far away as another planet in another century. His already unsettled life was now turning completely upside down and backwards, as though he were riding the latest attraction at the fair.

Questions were forming in his mind faster than he could sort, let alone answer. And these questions were in addition to the ones already baffling him, like, "Who am I?" These were brand new, but no less perplexing.

Who was the truck driver? Someone who knew me before the accident? And why was he murdered?

He wondered also about Kristen. What role did she play?

And what, in heavens name, did any of this have to do with him?

But the single biggest question he faced at the moment was perhaps the most disturbing.

Who the hell are these men walking toward the front door with stone-cold faces, one hand tucked into their suit coats?

None of the questions had any answers. But there was no longer time to stand around contemplating them. It was clear that these men wouldn't want to spend an afternoon over tea and crumpets, discussing the peculiarity of his situation. They were here to complete some business that somebody had started, and he'd managed to get his thumbs stuck in the middle.

He glanced at the front door and was relieved to find it was still locked, the deadbolt firmly in place. Stuffing the strange message into his pocket, he raced to the back door where Kristen was already scurrying across the lanai toward the sandy ground on the other side. Just as he slipped out the back and slid the glass door closed as fast, yet as silently, as possible, the doorbell rang, followed immediately by a sharp rap.

Once the glass door was secure, Jack followed after Kristen who was running parallel to the condos that crowded the top of the beach. Several people in bathing suits turned to stare at them as they ran past. It certainly wouldn't help if the thugs decided to follow, handing out big bills to anyone who'd seen them. "Sure," he could hear one of them say. "There was this punk chick wearing leather, being chased by a guy in slacks. They went that-a-way."

With a little effort he caught up to her and struggled to tell her they needed to get off the beach. He was winded and kept turning to see if the men had followed. So far he didn't see them.

A gap in the buildings appeared with wooden stairs ascending to the road above. Across the street were more condos that offered hedges for concealment and observation. Once there, they ducked behind a row of trimmed oleanders. Jack could see two late-model sedans parked in front of his condo, several hundred feet to his right.

"I want to get a closer look," Jack said as he began moving along behind bushes toward the parked cars.

"Wait," Kristen said. "Are you sure? What if they see you?"

"Stay put if you want," he called back.

They got within a hundred feet and Jack decided that was all the closer he cared to venture. Two of the men were in clear sight, looking up and down the road. They wore dark suits and there was a roughness about them that seemed to eliminate the possibility that they were law enforcement officers. One was lean and tall with sad, dark eyes, as if years of the underworld had squeezed the life from his soul. The other man was stocky, had a thick neck, and shook his head agitatedly as he spoke to his companion.

"You think they're the mob?" Kristen whispered.

"If I had to guess, I'd say so," Jack told her.

The two other men joined them and the conversation became even more animated. Jack hoped they hadn't broken in, since if they had it would be obvious he'd been there recently. Not to mention the broken glass from the kitchen window.

Three of the men climbed into one car and drove off in the opposite direction. The fourth man got in the other car, circled around and parked at the side of the road about thirty feet from them, facing the condo, apparently prepared to wait for something to happen.

Great!

Jack had been hoping to return to get the Porsche once their visitors left. Now they'd have to find another way or risk being seen.

ൟ

The grocery store, the nearest place where there might be a pay phone, was within walking distance at around a mile, mile-and-a-half. At the very least they'd need to call a cab to get somewhere safe. Exactly where, he wasn't sure. They could have circled around and gone back into the condo to use the phone, but Jack felt that was far too risky.

Kristen heartily agreed.

As they headed toward the store, Jack couldn't help wondering why this was happening. The girl had clearly brought trouble and his very life was now in danger. Trying to understand it all, he glanced over at Kristen. She was strolling along, uncaring, while baking in her leather jacket.

"Aren't you hot in that getup?" Jack asked.

"What getup?" Kristen asked indignantly. "You don't like it?"

Sweat was forming on her face. "It suits you. However, I just think it's a little much to be wearing in this heat."

Kristen pulled off her shredded leather jacket and dropped it on the ground.

"Happy?" she asked.

"You're just going to leave it there?"

She stopped and turned toward him. "What is it with you?" she asked. "First you think I'm crazy for wearing it. Then you think I'm crazy for getting rid of it. Maybe I *am* crazy. I don't know." She continued walking, leaving Jack following several paces behind.

"I never said you were crazy," Jack said as he caught up. "Look. Forget it. I'm sorry I said anything."

"And what do you mean by, 'It suits you?'" she asked. "You mean because I'm crazy? On someone else it would look stupid, is that it?"

Frustrated. Jack kicked a small rock ahead, making it bounce off a curb and into the middle of the street. "Just forget it," he told her. "I didn't mean anything by it…really. I just thought you looked hot."

Kristen grinned and caught his eye out of the corner of her own. "Thanks, Mr. Nimble. You're not so bad yourself."

"Mr. Nimble?" Jack questioned, ignoring her comment.

"You know. Jack be nimble, Jack be quick…the nursery rhyme."

They continued walking in silence. Jack couldn't help enjoying Kristen's company even though he would never have admitted it to anyone outside of the space between his ears. She seemed to test him with every conversation, constantly keeping him off balance. This was the way relationships were supposed to be, he realized. He hadn't thought of it before, but in comparison, his relationship with Maggie hardly seemed like a relationship at all. Some things in life were supposed to be consistent, like turning on a light or starting up the car, or even the concept of working hard to get ahead. Those things were stable, predictable.

But relationships weren't supposed to be like that, especially relationships with women. He suspected that men had tried for centuries to make their relationships predictable, without success.

"If you're angry, just tell me, damn it!" Men were like dogs, up front and in your face. Licking or barking, but never indifferent. Whereas women were different animals altogether, always keeping life a mystery, keeping you guessing, pussy-footing around – entirely inconsistent by design.

At least they were supposed to be that way.

Maggie wasn't like that at all. She was predictable. When she was angry – *wait a minute.* Maggie never got angry. Nor did she sulk about, acting like she wasn't when she was.

The perfect woman. Always consistent.

In some strange way, Jack's interaction with Kristen seemed to plug a hole in his unfulfilling life. He only wished he'd met her under different circumstances.

"What are you thinking about?" Kristen asked.

"Uh…I don't know," Jack said.

"That's deep."

"I guess it's just that none of this makes any sense."

"What do you mean?"

"Let's go over the facts. Five years ago a poker game in Las Vegas gets ugly when a few guys wind up stealing the mob's books and walking off with their cash, threatening to turn over the information to the authorities if the mob comes after them. Someone at the game – your trucker friend – is a witness so the mob warns him to never tell anyone about it or they'll kill him. He stays quiet for all these years and then decides to tell a hitchhiker he picks up."

"I have a name, you know," Kristen said.

"Right," Jack said. "You stop at a gas station for a break and someone stabs him. You don't think it's coincidental because he tells you they'll be after *you* now, and hands you a piece of paper with my name and address on it, the address to my vacation condo where I happened to be for the weekend. And I never told anyone about it and had no idea I was even coming there before I headed down.

"Now one of the things that doesn't make sense is how they knew the trucker told you about the poker game. They would have had to monitor everything he said. How long was it after he told you before you stopped at the gas station?"

Kristen thought about it. "I'd say about an hour."

"So, not only that, they would have had to get somebody there within an hour. And you're certainly not going to tell me they followed him everywhere he went? And if that isn't enough of a stretch, you say there's no way they could have known where you went since nobody followed you, and yet they were able to find the condo inside of a day's time. And who the heck threw a note through the kitchen window? Like I said: none of it makes any sense. And the worst part of it is I don't even know this trucker friend of yours. How did he have my name? My address?"

"Oh no," Kristen said. "I just thought of something."

"What?"

"I may have led them right to your place without even knowing it. The man who gave me the ride dropped me out front. I thought he was okay."

"But even that doesn't make sense. They already had you. Why wait until you meet up with me?"

"Unless it's you they're after and they didn't know how to find you," Kristen said.

Jack suddenly got a terrible feeling that maybe she was right. After all, he couldn't remember his life before the accident. What if he'd somehow been involved with the mob? What if it really *was* him they were after? What would they do to him if they caught him? He supposed that all depended on *how* he'd been involved. As he and Kristen came within sight of the grocery store, he decided that even though he wanted to know the truth, it might be more than he bargained for.

"Oh, I don't believe this," Jack suddenly said and stopped.

"What is it?"

"I just had a thought. Didn't you say that the trucker –"

"Randy."

"Whatever. Randy. Didn't you say Randy happened to meet up with one of the three guys who stole the money?"

"Yeah. A few days later in a bar. Why?"

"What did the guy tell him?" Jack asked, sounding urgent.

"He said they weren't normally gamblers or something like that."

"Anything else? Did he tell Randy what they needed the money for?"

"Something about a business deal or project or something. Why?"

"*No!* It can't be. I have an idea, but I need to make a call."

"Tell me," Kristen said.

"It would take too long and I've got to know right now," Jack said and walked toward the store where there were two payphones at the front.

If his suspicions were correct, Jack's life was more complicated than he realized.

CHAPTER 14

Kristen asked Jack if he wanted anything from the store, but that was the last thing on his mind. She disappeared through the automatic sliding doors while Jack thought about his hunch. It was the only thing that made a splinter of sense in a forest of strange circumstances, and yet he was having difficulty conceiving that such a thing could be true.

Reluctantly, he picked up the receiver and punched in his long-distance access number followed by that of Peter Lynchman's.

The phone pulsed in his ear as he waited for someone to answer. Finally, after the third ring, a woman picked up. It was the voice of Frances Lynchman, Peter's wife.

"Frances," he said. "This is Jack. Is Peter in?"

"Jack?" Frances exclaimed. "Are you all right? Maggie called, wondering where you were. She said you never came home after work on Friday."

Curiously enough, it made him feel a little bit better to know that Maggie had been worried. "I'm fine," he said, "but it's really complicated. Is Peter in?"

"Yes. Sure. I'll get him. Have you called Maggie? Does she know where you are?"

"Not yet," Jack confessed.

"Promise you'll call the minute you finish with Peter?" Frances said.

"Okay," he told her. "I promise."

What would he say to the man, Jack wondered. "Just curious. Did we happen to steal a bunch of money from the mob to start our business?" It sounded ludicrous, and yet at this point, strangely like a possibility. CareSoft had a silent partner by the name of Charles Hasselbaum, whom Jack had never met – at least not since the accident or that he could remember.

Three partners.

Curley, Moe, and Larry, three stooges.

It was too obvious to overlook. Hasselbaum was someone Peter had known in college and Jack knew little about the man other than he was an investor who, although he didn't live in the area, had helped open the doors at CareSoft. After that, he'd pursued other interests and kept loose tabs on the company. But Jack didn't even know where the man lived.

"Jack? Where the hell have you been, buddy? Maggie's worried sick." Peter's strong, gregarious voice boomed over the line.

"Peter, I've got to discuss something with you. I drove down to the condo for the weekend without telling Maggie. I'll call her to say I'm all right, but I need to ask you something about CareSoft."

"I should have figured you'd gone to Destin. What's up? Everything all right?"

Jack took in a deep breath, not quite sure where to begin. "You may have explained this to me already, but where did we get the money to start CareSoft? Hasselbaum's our only investor and we don't owe the bank."

There was a pause. "What's this all about? Can't we discuss it tomorrow, buddy?"

"Please, Peter. Just answer the question."

"Okay," Peter said, obviously reluctant to continue. "It's true that much of the money came from Hasselbaum. You and I each kicked in a little. It wasn't much compared to Hasselbaum's portion, but enough to get us going. We were the ones working the business, anyway. He agreed to a three-way, equal partnership since it was our idea and we were the ones doing the work. Beyond that, we've taken out a few business loans here and there for cash flow, but they were all short-term and we always paid them back reasonably fast. We had to do some bootstrapping in the early days since we didn't have much, but we managed. Why is this so important right now?"

Jack fidgeted the cord, wondering how to drop the bomb. "Do you know anything about a poker game in Las Vegas?" he asked. It was as safe a question as he dared ask at this point.

This time the pause seemed endless. "Who told you?" Peter said finally.

Jack groaned. "Why, Peter? How could you do this?"

"Wait a minute, buddy. Hold up. How could *I* do this?" Peter said in a low voice. "It was *you* who concocted the damn plan. Hasselbaum and I thought it was too risky, but you convinced us it would work. We went along because you refused to get other investors. Frankly, I'm glad you did, because now we don't have to answer to anyone. It was brilliant."

Jack felt a lump forming in his esophagus and a darkness closing around his heart. So *he* had been the one to formulate the plan. No wonder he couldn't relate to the man in the mirror. After hearing this, it was obvious he really didn't know him. What kind of person had he been before the accident? Nobody he'd care to trust, that's for sure.

"Hey. Your memory's starting to come back," Peter said. "Congratulations, buddy!"

"No. It hasn't come back," Jack told him. "I can't explain. It's too complicated. All I know is they're after me now. Why did you think – I mean, we – why did we think they wouldn't track us down?"

"You can't be serious," Peter said. "They're after you? It was the perfect plan and that's why it's worked so well. Hasselbaum goes underground with the books. Changes his identity so they can't find him. He never wanted to work the business anyway. If they give us any grief, he releases it to the feds. Why would they come after you now?"

"When was the last time you spoke with Hasselbaum?" Jack asked him. "Maybe they found him." He couldn't believe he was discussing this rationally.

"I talked to him yesterday, as a matter of fact. They don't know where he is. I'm sure of it."

"Well, they know where *I* am."

"Of course they do. That's the whole point. You and I aren't trying to hide. They know we have them over a barrel. Just sit tight. If they try anything, they know what we'll do. Trust me on this one. I trusted you five years ago."

Jack would have gladly given up the use of at least one limb and thrown in his hearing for good measure simply to be able to remember the diabolical frame of mind he'd somehow harbored before the accident. Peter had trusted him five years ago. That was just swell.

"Peter, why didn't you tell me?" was all he could manage to say.

"I thought it might be better if you didn't know," Peter said. "In some ways, I thought your amnesia was a blessing in disguise. How the hell did you find out?"

"A blessing in disguise? You don't know what it's like…never mind. Look. All I know is a bunch of thugs showed up at my condo and looked like they wanted to have a motivational chat."

"Are you serious? You okay?"

"They never got the chance. Fortunately, I slipped out the back before they could get to me. What do we do now?"

Peter was quiet and Jack gave him a moment to digest the information. He saw Kristen come out of the store.

"If they're coming after you then maybe we should keep our promise," Peter finally said. "What good is a threat if we have no intention of backing it up? But are you sure it was the mob?"

"Peter, I have no idea what's going on anymore. A homeless girl breaks into my condo and tells me about our scheme. Somebody throws a rock through my window with a message telling me they're coming for me. And then they show up. With all that, on top of my amnesia, I feel like I've just been teleported to another dimension. No, I can't be sure of anything other than the fact I'm standing outside a grocery store in Destin, speaking on the phone with someone who's supposed to be my business partner."

"Buddy…" Peter said but trailed off; clearly no words would suffice. "You need to get back here right away. We'll work it out, I promise. When can you get here?"

"You said it was the perfect plan. Hell, maybe I said it. I don't even know. You said that without investors we don't have to answer to anyone. Well, guess what? We apparently have to answer to the mob. I dare say that answering to a bunch of investors would be a lot more constructive to our health.

"Look," Jack said. "I can't race back there right now. I need to sort things out. Besides, I can't get to my car. They're watching the condo. I feel like I've just been told I have three months to live. Maybe less. Just tell me one more thing. Where can I find Hasselbaum?"

ꕥ

Kristen pulled open the tab to an individual-sized can of tuna, used a finger to scoop it out onto a slice of bread – one of several pieces she'd managed to take from a full loaf – and then screwed off the top to a jar of grape jelly. The lid popped as the vacuum seal surrendered to the influx of oxygen. She licked her tuna finger and then dug in for a generous dollop of jelly. Spreading it and mixing it together on the bread, her mouth watered in anticipation of the flavor extravaganza she was about to enjoy. Most meals were boring and uninteresting. She always liked trying new combinations and rarely found them disagreeable.

"*Uggg...*" Jack said as he approached. "What are you doing?"

"Want some?" she asked.

"No…thanks."

"So, what was the big call?" she said and then pinched two halves of bread together and stuffed a large bite in her mouth.

"Well," Jack said. "I think we're getting closer to understanding what's going on, even though I don't like it."

Kristen popped open a can of Sprite and drowned the bite, putting it out of its misery. "Really?" she said. "Tell me."

Jack sighed. "It would seem that I know the three stooges your trucker friend, Randy, told you about."

"Oh, yeah? Who?" she asked, then took another bite of tuna-and-jelly sandwich.

"Try yours truly."

She chewed slowly and peered up at him suspiciously. After swallowing, she said, "Right. It just somehow slipped your mind? I mean it's not something you'd tend to forget. Oh, by the way, I just remembered something *I* did a couple months ago. I robbed the First National Bank of Boston. Just remembered where I stashed the loot. Silly me."

"It's true," Jack said and watched as Kristen eyed the last bit of sandwich. "I can't remember anything over a year-and-a-half ago. I was in an accident and have amnesia."

She was raising the last of the sandwich toward her mouth when her arm suddenly froze halfway to her lips, which remained parted in suspended animation. She couldn't believe what he'd just told her. It couldn't possibly be true. Life was sometimes littered with strange coincidences, but this one was too much to fathom. She looked up at him in astonishment.

"I know it's hard to believe, but supposedly I was the one who came up with the plan," Jack said, unaware of the shock Kristen placed on his last statement. "It's just so incredible."

"What did you say?"

Jack looked down at her. "About what? You mean that I was the one who came up with the plan?"

"No. Before that."

"You mean my amnesia?"

"That's it."

"It's true. I don't remember getting married, the birth of my kids, the poker game in Las Vegas – anything."

Kristen dropped the rest of the sandwich. Suddenly she felt nauseous. She wiped the sweat from her forehead and bent her head down in her hands.

"You all right?" Jack asked.

"Four years ago…" she said and then stopped.

"What? What happened four years ago?"

"I caught a virus and became deathly ill. They didn't think I was going to make it. They say I had a fever of over a hundred and six."

"I'm sorry," Jack said. "And I certainly don't mean to be insensitive. But I'm not sure what that has to do with anything."

"When I finally pulled through, I couldn't remember anything before the fever. My doctor told me I might never remember."

She turned and looked into Jack's shocked face. "I have amnesia, too."

CHAPTER 15

Marilyn Monroe sat in the casino, waiting for Mr. Prescott to return. She'd madc hcrsclf up real nice before going out. There were no smudges of lipstick around her mouth and she'd managed to do her hair just like her famous counterpart. She stared with lazy eyes into the jumbled mess of jingling machines, lips slightly parted revealing white, straight teeth. Even the beauty mark on her left cheek was real, an added touch, which made her look exactly like the American pop culture icon.

She noticed a man at the end of the bar, nursing a drink, gawking. Right now, she felt pretty and wanted, unlike the many occasions when she'd felt lonely, ugly, and unloved. As she looked around the bar, she could see that nearly every man was glancing her way.

Toying with a straw against her lips, she tried to ignore the attention, blushing and taking tentative sips from her soda. But her nervous fidgeting only seemed to make matters worse. Her fans were growing more restless by the second.

Marilyn was unaware of their true motives. To her, they thought she was pretty and that made her feel nice, flattered, like they were schoolboys, thinking enough of her to share a swing instead of a bed.

As her bright red lips puckered around the straw, one of the men who'd been watching lurched from his chair and came to sit on a stool next to her.

"Hey, Doll," he said. "Anyone ever tell you you're the spitting image of Marilyn Monroe?"

She ignored him, still toying with her straw. Mr. Prescott – Drew – always warned her not to speak to anyone, especially men, while they were in places like this. She wasn't sure why he had said it, but she didn't question him. He was good to her and wouldn't tell her anything like that unless it was very, very important. She was sure of it.

She and Drew didn't come to places like this very often. But when they did, Marilyn liked the attention and listening to the funny sounds that those gazillions of machines made when people put money in them. The jangling, ringing, dinging, and donging made her feel like she was in a happy place where people came when they wanted to celebrate. Every once in a while she'd see someone stomping their feet or hitting a machine. It didn't happen too often. When it did, she figured they'd got up on the wrong side of the bad. That's what Miss Reynolds used to say when someone was grouchy.

What she really liked to see – which didn't happen very often – was when one of the machines would spill lots of coins out its silver mouth and make an extra loud siren sound. Then the player would almost always jump up and down and up and down like a kangaroo. Sometimes they would even scream like something really bad was happening. Only this wasn't something bad, but very, very good. It was funny and made her laugh.

"You here alone?" the man asked.

She kept her head down but glanced at him from the corner of her eye. From what she could see, he wore a pretty blue shirt with strange white buttons. His hair was slicked back and looked a little like the man she'd seen in a movie they'd rented called *As Good As It Gets*. She pinched her eyes closed in embarrassment. She had always had this funny idea that if she couldn't see someone, they couldn't see her.

"Now, I would ask you if a cat got your tongue, but I've seen it and know that ain't so," the man said as he put his hand on her leg.

It wasn't like Mr. Prescott putting a hand on her back when he wanted to give her attention. Somehow, this didn't feel nice. And somehow she started getting the idea that this man wasn't a very nice man, after all, though she couldn't explain why. Maybe he was like the man in the movie. He always seemed like he'd got up on the wrong side of the bad. Very grouchy all the time. But the man in the movie wasn't really a bad man. He just needed someone else to care about. Maybe this man was just like that. Yes. He needed someone to care about and then he'd be okay.

She pushed his hand off her leg, smiling.

"Well now, isn't that a pretty smile. I knew you had it in you, Doll," he said. "I like the shy ones."

He put his hand back on her leg again and she pushed it away in a manner that seemed like a game children play. He put it back and she pushed it off. *"Can too." "Can not." "Can so." "Will not." "Oh yeah." "Yeah."*

And as if to say, *"Watch me"*, the man slid an arm low around her back at the same time his other hand was finding its way up her leg. A creeping chill ran down her spine.

"Leave me alone," she said. But her voice didn't sound like that of a seductive woman.

The man quickly removed his roaming hands and frowned.

"What are you?" he said. "Some kind of idiot or something?"

"Mr. Prescott says I'm smart," she said, sounding as if she strained to pronounce each syllable.

The man now looked flustered and not sure what to do. "Frick'n moron," he mumbled as he turned to go back to his seat.

Other men in the area were starting to chuckle. Staring and laughing. She felt them drilling into her with their eyes. This time it didn't feel nice like before. They were making her feel stupid and unloved. She wished Mr. Prescott would hurry up. She felt weak and dizzy from the multi-colored lights, the smoke, and the sounds that had begun to rattle through her head.

"How was I supposed to know she's a freakin' moron," the man shouted over the casino noise and pointed in her direction.

Marilyn slid off the bar stool and stumbled out into the crowd of machines. She knew Mr. Prescott was out there somewhere. She just needed to find him. He was the only one who could make the bad go away, like he'd done when he came and took her out of that home with people who didn't really love her. They were nice to her and all. But she could tell they only kept her because somebody told them they had to.

As she walked down a row of the machines, people turned to watch her as she went. Watching. Peering. Staring. Gawking. That's all people ever did. And tonight, what started out nice had quickly turned into yuckiness. The hot lights and hysteria of sounds made her feel disoriented, confused. She had to get out of there.

Pushing through a crowd of people, she came upon a long table surrounded by folks who were watching a man at the end throwing dimples into the middle and calling out numbers. She called them dimples because when Mr. Prescott had told her they were *dice* and that only one was called a *die*, she had decided that was a bad name, so she made up the name dimple, for when they played board games. When she passed, everyone turned to stare.

Marilyn began to run frantically from table to machine, from one end of the carnival-like room to the other, desperately trying to find the only person who could make it all go away. Finally tripping on an empty stool, she spilled to the floor, out of breath and hyperventilating. Now everyone was watching. Watching and laughing!

Make it go away.

Make it go away.

Please, please. Make it go away.

ஒ

Cautiously approaching the table that supported a large roulette wheel, Drew Prescott dug down inside of himself to conjure up an attitude, one that he'd rehearsed while standing in front of a mirror. But even though he'd acted it out dozens of times before a live audience, it still felt unnatural: to cast off the person he was twenty-four, seven. He hated it. Yet in some strange way, this was God's plan to provide for them. To say the Lord worked in mysterious ways was a dire understatement because, as often as he'd done this, he'd never been able to come fully to grips with something so blatantly at odds with what he had taught his small congregation.

But the money was getting low again and yesterday he'd received The Word. It started in the form of a newspaper headline, "19 Car Pileup Near Los Angeles." The number stuck in his head and when he was frying up a pan of bacon and discovered there were nineteen strips in the package, which took nineteen minutes to cook, he had been put on alert.

Marilyn had watched cable channel 19 most of the day where they had broadcast a marathon of nineteen episodes of her favorite show – *Gilligan's Island* – clapping each time her favorite character, Ginger, said something funny. When he'd gone into his office to study The Word, he'd opened directly to Psalm 19, and when he'd listened to the radio that afternoon while pulling weeds in the yard, the Dodgers beat the Diamondbacks, ten to nine, a total of nineteen runs during the game.

By evening, after he'd come across the number nineteen more times than he could count, he'd finally gotten the message and acknowledged this fact in prayer.

I get it, already.

Not that he was being disrespectful. But God seemed to have a sense of humor about these things, sometimes making Himself so obvious that it brought Drew to laughter.

Sometimes he wondered if it had been this way for Elijah in the Old Testament when God had provided for him during a famine. Only in the case of Elijah, instead of telling him to put every last penny he owned on a table at a casino in Las Vegas, God had sent ravens to bring him bread and meat each morning and evening. Elijah's provision seemed immensely more spiritual than his own, but who was he to question how the Lord had decided to provide for Marilyn and him. These were far different times, after all. He suspected that ravens probably wouldn't get within ten miles of the bright lights of Vegas, let alone drop loaves of bread, steaks, and possibly even a bottle of wine for special occasions on their doorstep. In his case, the roulette wheel would have to suffice.

He approached the roulette table, with his five twenty-dollar chips, as though he were David with his five smooth stones approaching Goliath. And Drew felt about as intimidated as David should have, standing here in the company of so many gambling giants, people who knew exactly what they were doing. Then again, each time he'd taken such a step of faith it had paid off, keeping Marilyn and him from having to give up his modest house for another month, keeping the refrigerator full and gasoline in the tank and the utilities paid with a little cash left over for spending.

Sauntering up to the table with a feigned air of confidence, he ran a hand through his hair, pressed a tongue against his upper teeth and sucked air through to make a *nish* sound. He'd studied gamblers before ever placing a bet and this was one of many little nuances he wanted to get down so he wouldn't draw attention to himself as anything other than a lucky spinner, which would keep him from winding up in a back room being questioned by security. It was the same reason he always chose a different casino when God gave him insider information.

"I'm feeling lucky today, my friends," he said aloud, eyes on the checkered board, as he slid his five chips into the middle of the square. "Straight up on number nineteen. Bring it home, baby." He rubbed his palms together as though they were sticks with which he hoped to start a campfire.

All the while, he struggled with a really sick feeling. What if he'd been wrong this time? His seed money would be gone. He'd have to find a regular job and Marilyn would have to go back to a home. Even though he'd watched God's miracle occur time and time again – literally turning a hundred bucks into thirty-five times that amount in seconds – it always gave him the willies to watch the ball being tossed around the spinning wheel on the way to determining his fate. What if God was going to be wrong this once? Logically, he knew God was omniscient and that he didn't make mistakes. But on a more emotional level he was ready to consider a kind of glitch in the cosmos that would land him in the poor house, giving the devil a good laugh.

Faith. You must have faith, Drew Prescott. He's brought you this far. He'll provide today like He has on countless other occasions.

The other possibility he dreaded was that one of his congregation would see their former pastor here, flirting with sin. It wouldn't matter that he had told them that he no longer felt called to the pulpit and had turned in his robes for a quiet life of reflection and taking care of Marilyn.

He still remembered the phone call he'd received while wallowing in the depths of self-doubt. He'd just given up his position as pastor of New Life Fellowship – a tiny church at the south end of town – and was wrestling with his heartlessness towards the people of God. How could a man of God pastor a church when he felt nothing for the members? Something somewhere had been a big mistake. And there he was at age forty-five, unskilled in anything but preaching The Word, without work and on his own.

The call had been from Candy Reynolds, the housemother at a large foster care facility downtown. She'd been given his name by someone, who had explained that he was the pastor of a small church, and she wanted to see if something could be done about a girl who was extremely disruptive to the other guests at the home, especially to the males. When she insisted upon seeing him, despite the fact that he had tried to explain that he no longer pastored New Life Fellowship, he had left it in the Lord's able hands and went to see if he could do anything about the problem girl.

Nothing had prepared him for Marilyn Monroe. It was immediately obvious why she was causing such a disruption in the home filled mostly with young men. With as shy and innocent as she was, Candy Reynolds admitted to Drew that it was just a matter of time before something unfortunate was bound to happen.

Drew thought it odd that Ms. Reynolds would suggest Marilyn go home with a man, even though he was a former pastor. What would make her think she wasn't scooping Marilyn out of the pan and dropping her into another fire?

Fortunately, Drew had never thought of Marilyn as anything other than a big girl with a little mind. Oddly enough, he felt more protective of her than he had of all the members of his former congregation combined. It took just one more logical step to decide that the Lord had brought Marilyn into his life for a purpose. What that purpose was he would no doubt discover in God's good time.

Within a week he'd decided to apply for permanent custody of Marilyn and found his cold heart beginning to melt with new purpose and direction. If his place in the world were nothing more than to give Marilyn a loving home where people couldn't take advantage of her, then that would be something. Maybe even enough.

And then, as his meager savings began to dwindle, he started to receive strange messages and see odd coincidences in everything he did until finally realizing that it was none other than the Lord trying to get his attention. The first time, God had used the number seven. For days everything seemed to come in sevens until he had the heavenly number coming out his blessed ears. And since gambling was the bedrock of his community and a tip was a tip, no matter what the source, it came to him that it might be God's intention that he visit a casino. Backed into a financial corner, he finally decided that an isolated spin of the roulette wheel wouldn't drag him into greed's bottomless pit.

And it had worked, by God! *Literally,* by God. He'd put every last dime he owned on number seven in an act of faith rivaled only by Abraham willing to sacrifice his son as a test of obedience and faith. Only Drew's altar had been his stubborn conviction that God only worked in certain ways – ways that *Drew Prescott* must approve of – and he would keep the Lord safely in this little box if it were the last thing he did.

Right. And he was also the master of the universe.

But Drew wasn't perfect. The very thing he feared began to infect his heart. Maintaining his uprightness, he reasoned that it would be God's will to make as few trips as possible to the worldly casinos. Placing a few more bets using the anointed number could allow them to live on reserves for months, possibly years. But he should have shoved a comment card into the suggestion box that he so enjoyed keeping God in, telling Him as much. Because when he tried the spin at a different table, he lost.

Fortunately, he'd had the presence of mind to test his theory with a small portion of his winnings, rather than giving it all back to the devil. Among other things, the experience taught him that it exercised faith to rely daily on the Lord for his provision.

Drew bit the underside of his lip while watching the blurry ball, waiting to see if God would be good to his word as he had in the past.

Please, please, please, he prayed, not unlike a thousand other gamblers at that very moment. Except that Drew was making it a literal request of the divine eyes watching over him.

The wheel slowed until he could almost see the numbers as they flew by. His heart thumped in anticipation, his eyes focused on the spinning wheel, ever realizing that if he truly believed, he'd stand nonchalantly by, unemotional, waiting to collect his winnings.

Now he could see the numbers as they passed, the heavy smooth wheel gliding almost to a stop. His heart nearly seized as the ball tried to settle in slot thirty-two and then thankfully bounced over and came to rest at nineteen.

"Yesss!" he said and punched the air with one clenched fist, adding a little dance to make the performance complete. As a matter of fact, he was genuinely rejoicing in God's faithfulness to a promise made.

Suddenly, something stopped him cold. He could feel the fine hairs on the back of his neck stand up and a shudder waft though him. It was that sixth sense that something was terribly wrong, as though he had an identical twin that was in desperate need of help. He tried to play out his routine but cut it short.

She needed him. Though he couldn't explain, somehow he knew that Marilyn was in trouble.

CHAPTER 16

True to his promise to Frances Lynchman, Jack had made a call to Maggie, leaving Kristen sitting on the curb still mulling over the amazing fact that they were both victims of amnesia. As for Jack, he'd written it off as one of life's mysteries. It was all he could do to make it coherently from one moment to the next, without thinking about Kristen and her amnesia.

Maggie had sounded uncharacteristically concerned. Had he been in an accident or was he in some kind of trouble? *If she only knew.* Yet he'd spared her the disturbing details and told her that he had come to Florida to give himself time to think. "I've still never gotten over the accident," he told her, "and felt I needed time alone." Once that had been taken care of, she had returned to life as usual. She'd told him about Justin's T-ball game, Amanda's sleepover. Everything was perfect and he wondered why they even needed him, save for the fact he brought home a V.P.'s salary. Never once did she say, "I miss you" or "please hurry home". In fact, she told him to take all the time he needed. She understood. She'd hold down the fort.

She certainly hadn't become angry like he had hoped. Instead, she was energetic and full of enthusiasm, coldly dismissing Jack's problem as if she were nothing more that one of those block ice carvings. Pretty to look at, but relationally too frigid to touch. Maybe he'd even loved her at one time. Who knew?

Clearly he'd been a different person before the accident, the person who had been involved in – even planned, no less – something he couldn't conceive of now. It seemed to be becoming increasingly apparent that amnesia could change a person's personality, their make-up. Once he'd seen a movie about a ruthless, uncaring lawyer who'd been shot and lost all memory of his past. The man had to reacquaint himself with his wife and daughter. Only in his case, the man found out they hadn't cared much for him before the shooting, and he soon discovered he used to be somebody he didn't much care for either. Even though that had been a Hollywood invention, maybe amnesia did have the ability to change a person's basic ideals. It was the only way to account for the fact he'd planned and stolen a great deal of money. Never mind that he had helped steal it from the mob.

At one time he had seen something in Maggie that he now no longer did. It was a little scary, wondering what his future with her would bring. In some ways it was more daunting than the predicament he found himself in at the moment.

"Earth to Jack. Anybody home," Kristen said, waving a hand in front of his face. "You still haven't told me what the plan is. Who'd you call after you called your wife?"

"A cab."

"Where're we going?"

"Don't you think that's a bit presumptuous of you," he asked, "automatically thinking you're going with me."

Kristen looked injured. "After all this you're still trying to get rid of me?" she demanded, jumping to her feet. "Fine, then. I don't need you anyway."

"Relax," Jack said. "I didn't say you weren't coming. I just said it was presumptuous of you to think so. That's all."

After a long, martyring pause, Kristen sat back down again, perspiration forming on her face.

"Lynchman told me where Hasselbaum lives," he told her. "He's the third partner and the one who has the stolen book from the poker game. I want to pay him a visit and see what he has to say. Make sure they haven't got to him yet. Because it's the only reason I can think of why the mob would suddenly come after me. Lynchman assured me they haven't got to him, but I want to see for myself."

"Sounds like a plan," she said.

A thought suddenly occurred to Jack. What if Kristen wasn't the person she said she was? What if she was really a member of the mob, perhaps one of the crime boss's daughters, here to flush out the location of Hasselbaum so they could get their book back? Maybe this was all part of some clever scheme, which would account for the sudden interest the mob was showing in him. He wondered how far back they would have planned it.

Could they have somehow had a hand in his decision to come to Florida unexpectedly? No. That had been his own idea. But then he remembered the strange illness he'd been stricken with at the airport. Could people make you sick, at will, to keep you from escaping the country? He wasn't sure.

This new theory made more sense, given Kristen's sudden appearance at his condo. It could also explain the rock through his window. That could all be part of the plan to get them on the run together to make him confide in her. He realized he might need to ditch her before heading to Hasselbaum's place. Certainly he couldn't let her know where the man lived until he was sure she wasn't part of some grand plan to squeeze it out of him.

"You need me now, you know," Kristen quipped.

"And how do you figure that?"

"I'm obviously key to this thing. Without me you might never figure it out. I'm sure of it."

"Oh yeah?"

"Yeah. What are the odds we'd both have amnesia? Answer me that."

"Coincidence." *You probably made it up.*

"My foot."

"What possible bearing could our amnesia have on the poker game, the mob, your trucker friend getting stabbed?"

"Do you believe in God?" Kristen asked.

The question took Jack off guard, a regular occurrence while interacting with Kristen. "I don't know. I've never really thought much about it. Why?"

"I don't know. Maybe he put us together. You know. To help us."

Jack stood up and brushed off his seat as a cab pulled into the parking lot. "If there is a God," he said. "I'd think he has better things to do than giving a couple people like you and me emotional support. He should be up to things like keeping the world from war. Then if he had time left over, he might keep auto accidents from happening and young girls from getting viruses and fevers of a hundred and six."

"Maybe he does. Or at least maybe he makes the best of it when things like that do happen. You didn't die, did you? Neither did I."

"No. But the guy I was with did."

"Maybe it was his time to go."

She had an answer for everything. He found himself wishing that he did too.

Drew felt his way through the crowded casino, certain that Marilyn was hurt or in trouble. He hadn't bothered to collect his winnings but that didn't matter. He could retrieve them later or not. At the moment, he didn't care. Marilyn's entry into his life had been a gift and he felt he'd no longer have purpose if she were gone. He'd been given the task of protecting and taking care of her – a task that was both simple and monumental – and she was in trouble.

He cursed himself for having brought Marilyn here. If the jingling sound of machines, the myriad of voices, smoky haze emanating from the bar, and drunk-filled laughter caused him to be dizzy and confused, how must Marilyn feel with her child-like mind? If they made it safely back to the house, the Lord would simply have to find another way to provide for them, for he would never step foot in one of these places again. That was that.

He turned down a row and suddenly felt certain he was going the wrong way. Something was guiding him. Whether it was the paternal love he felt for Marilyn or a sovereign and divine hand, he wasn't sure. Immediately he turned and went back the other way until his internal compass approved. Yes. This was right. After several such corrections, he came upon a small crowd surrounding Marilyn, who was curled into a fetal position on the floor, her eyes squeezed shut and her hands clasped firmly across her ears, her blouse now wrinkled and twisted awkwardly around her body. As Drew squatted next to her he could hear her humming; apparently to make it all go away.

"It's all right, sweetie," he said, smoothing her tangled blond hair. "Let's get out of here."

ঔ

A salesman, sporting a colorful Hawaiian shirt, approached Jack and Kristen as they stood outside Sam's Cars for Less. "Never accept 'no' for an answer," was all but imprinted on his forehead. Salesmen were the reason Jack hated purchasing cars. Though he couldn't remember doing so before the accident, the general distasteful idea had somehow made it through the crash.

"What can I do you for," the man said, reaching into his bag of annoying clichés.

His name was Les, and he and Jack went several rounds together, Jack explaining that he wanted the cheapest car in the lot so long as it ran, and Les pointing out bargains in the ten thousand dollar range. "I've just got some vehicles in that the boss will be willing to let me push for real cheap," he said repeatedly. "You just tell me which one you're interested in and I'll go to bat for you, man."

"I'm not interested in a good deal," Jack told him. "I want the absolute cheapest car you've got. My only real criteria is that it has to be less than two thousand bucks. And it has to run."

The man grinned at Jack shamelessly. "Right."

Having lost another round, Les finally sent for backup help. "Tell you what. I'll let you talk to the lot manager and see if *he* can help you."

When he was gone, Kristen said, "You have enough money to just buy a car cause you can't get to your other one?"

"It's only two thousand. And I won't spend a penny more," Jack assured her. I can put it on my Visa, but I want to make sure I have plenty of credit left. Who knows what else we'll need to charge before this is over."

"I take it Hasselbaum lives somewhere within driving distance," she said. "How long a drive are we talking here?"

"You know, I've been thinking," Jack said, ignoring the question. "Maybe it was Hasselbaum who threw the rock through the window. Maybe he somehow knew they'd be after us."

He wasn't sure if he really believed it. But it kept him from having to tell her where Hasselbaum lived.

The manager was an older man wearing a getup that wasn't all that different from Jack's.

"Les tells me you need something on the economical side," he said. "Says you don't want to spend much. I'll do whatever I can to find something for you."

"I don't want to spend over two thousand, including taxes," Jack said.

"Uh, huh. Well, unfortunately, the cheapest thing I've got is a Toyota Tercel for thirty-four, fifty. I've got a little room to maneuver, but not fifteen hundred dollars."

"Sorry," Jack said. "I guess we'll have to look elsewhere."

"Hold up a minute," the manager said when Jack turned to leave. "I may have something. I just remembered."

Surprise, surprise, Jack thought.

An ancient Pinto hatchback sat parked next to a trash bin behind the office building. Dust covered the hood and windows, looking as though it hadn't been driven in years. The color was a nauseating shade of green and what had once been chrome bumpers were now rusted over, clinging for life.

"She isn't much to look at, but she recently had her engine replaced. I promised it to a friend for his son who just got his driver's license. For the right price, I'm sure he'd let it go."

"How much?" Jack asked, even though he already knew that the answer would be exactly two thousand, once the taxes and registration had been paid. It was severely overpriced, but there wasn't much he could do about it.

"Just don't get rear-ended," the manager told them as he handed Jack the keys. "That's all I've got to say."

"Cute," Kristen said as she studied the vehicle. "A self-destructing car. As if the things aren't evil enough to begin with."

By the time they were heading east on US-98, Jack had sketched out a rough plan, which included a backup. There was no way he was going to chauffeur Kristen to the front door of the only man who knew where the mob's book was. If she were who he was beginning to think she was, his life – as disoriented as it was – would be over with a single phone call. Once the book was safely in their hands, there would be nothing left to stop them.

The car sputtered along with the air-conditioner cranked up all the way, making feeble attempts to overcome the late-afternoon heat, and failing miserably.

"You never told me where this guy lives," Kristen said. "How far is it?"

"Right. Ironically, he lives just outside of Tallahassee," Jack lied. "Not too far."

"What's the plan? We going to show up and make sure he has the book? I'm still not sure what this will accomplish."

"Actually, I had another idea. Didn't you say you were originally headed for Panama City?"

"Yeah. But plans have changed," she told him. "Haven't they?"

"I'm going right through there on the way. I can drop you before continuing on to Tallahassee. You're not really involved in this, anyway. It would be safer for you."

"No!" Kristen said. "I *am* involved now, whether you like it or not. I'm coming with you. Like I already said, you need me."

Jack sighed. "Anyone ever tell you you're incredibly stubborn?"

He'd have to go with plan B now.

When they pulled into Panama City, evening was quickly approaching and dusk was settling on the horizon. Jack turned into a gas station with a convenience store and motored up to a pump. Removing his wallet, he folded a hundred inside of a five-dollar bill and handed it to Kristen.

"I'm going to fill up," he told her. "Could you run in and pick me up something to drink. Bottled water will be fine. Get something for yourself if you want."

She looked at him with fearful eyes. "I don't know," she said.

"What's wrong?"

"The last time someone asked me to pick up something from one of these places, he wound up dead."

"Relax," Jack said. "Nobody's going to kill me. They can't possibly know where we are." *Unless you've already told them,* he thought.

As soon as Kristen was inside the store, he jumped in the car, started up and zipped out of the parking lot without looking back.

As he did it, he felt a tinge of guilt. What if he'd been wrong about her? The poor girl would come out of the store to find him gone. Instead of being stabbed to death like her trucker friend, he would have vanished into thin air. He supposed that was why he'd slipped her the hundred. It was a kind of insurance premium in case he'd got his wires crossed and she really knew nothing.

Jack followed Lynchman's directions from memory until he pulled onto Persimmon Lane, a shady neighborhood several miles from where he dropped Kristen, where he immediately pulled to the side of the road. Directly ahead, right about where Hasselbaum's house should be, lights flashed on the tops of parked police cruisers, an ambulance, and a paramedic's truck.

"Oh no," he said. "This can't be happening."

Jack suddenly sensed that he was too late.

⁂

Even though things weren't going well with Erin's latest attempts at tampering with Zack and her assignments, her optimism and misguided self-assurance prevented her from realizing her failures. In her mind, obstacles were merely steppingstones of opportunity that led to richer experiences and a need for more creative energy. Although she had a vague sense that Zack was beginning to feel uncomfortable with her shenanigans, she barely gave it a second thought. Eventually he'd realize that she knew what she was doing, see the logic of it, the artistic finesse.

Even though the new guy had been assigned the crime boss, Erin barely had time to be bummed. Besides, it wasn't her style to mope around. It was her way to grab whatever was within reach and squeeze every last drop of satisfaction from it before moving on. And she had the uncanny ability to improvise. Which is why, if she couldn't be party to observing a real live Godfather, she'd create her own. That was that.

Yet little did she know, things were slowly getting worse.

Cochran had now abandoned Kate, the actress – only a minor problem in Erin's mind – and she was quickly formulating a new plan. Get them back together. So far, everything she'd attempted had backfired to some degree, but she knew she'd eventually get it right. Besides, she was having a blast.

"Okay, okay," she mumbled to herself. "You wanna play that way? We'll see about that." Using Zack's station, she rattled away at his keyboard, completely immersed in what she was doing.

"What are you doing?" a voice behind her said. She swiveled around and stared up at Zack's frowning face. He stood with hands propped on his sides.

"I just thought, you know, since we'd been working together…it wasn't a big deal."

Zack glanced over her shoulder. "What are you up to *now*?" he asked, sounding more perplexed than angry.

"Don't be so anal," she said flippantly and wheeled around to continue.

Zack sighed. "You know we're going to have to tell Sweeney. He'll kill us if he finds out what you've done, without hearing a reasonable explanation."

"So now it's, what *I've* done, huh?" she said. "He'll thank us when he sees the end result. That's all that really matters. We'll probably get promoted. Unless, of course, you insist that it was all my idea." She tipped her head back now and smiled up at Zack.

He shook his head and sighed. "You are one crazy broad. You know that?"

"Sit down and get with the program or go away. I'm trying to work here," Erin said, studying the screen. "See! Cochran is leaving. Take a wild guess where he's going. I know what I'm doing."

"Okay, but if one more thing goes wrong, we're going to Sweeney," he told her, lowering his voice and looking furtively around the pit.

"Nonsense," Erin said, confident she was in complete control of the situation.

CHAPTER 17

Jack's fears were realized when he joined a small group of bystanders outside the small house with a rock façade front. Stephens, who they all agreed was a quiet man and kept to himself, had been found dead. As a chopper flew overhead with a spotlight, searching the shadows, Jack confirmed the address on the side of the mailbox. It was definitely the same address Lynchman had given him.

Back in the car, he kept thinking about how he'd left Kristen alone at the gas station, vulnerable to anyone lurking about or who might have followed them. Since they'd managed to get to Hasselbaum without her help, it seemed clear that she wasn't part of the conspiracy.

When he arrived back at the gas station, he was relieved not to see any police cars or other emergency vehicles. He estimated he'd only been gone for fifteen minutes and hoped Kristen was still there.

Then he saw her standing at the far end by the corner of the building looking suitably dismal in her black attire, no doubt mourning the death of their new friendship, simply cut off before it reached maturity. He'd betrayed her and now he had to come up with a plausible explanation.

It wasn't too difficult.

Pulling up beside her, he leaned over and opened the door. She got in but didn't speak, merely staring blankly out the grimy window, gnawing on what appeared to be a mouth full of gum.

"Look," Jack said. "I'm sorry. I didn't think it would be safe for you. Hasselbaum really lives – lived – here in Panama City and I wanted to check it out, first."

"Whatever," she said and tossed a wad of money into Jack's lap.

"Do you even care to know what I found?" he asked her.

"If it will make you feel better," she said. "You're going to do whatever you want anyway."

"I was wrong, Kristen. I'm really sorry. Can't you understand I was just trying to look out for your safety," he lied.

"Okay," she said. "What did you find?"

"They got to him. When I showed up, there was a bunch of police swarming the place. Apparently, he'd been murdered."

"And this is the guy who supposedly had the book from the poker game?" she asked.

"The same."

Jack could sense a new fear in her voice.

"What are we going to do?" she asked, as much to the cosmos as to Jack.

He motored the car around to the side of the building to get out of sight. "I've got to make a call to Lynchman; tell him what's happened. Warn him. Then we'll play it by ear."

"This is so messed up," she said as Jack opened the door to get out.

At the phone he dialed Lynchman's residence, certain that on Sunday evening he'd be in, only to hear the robotic voice announce, *"We're sorry. The number you have dialed has been disconnected. If you feel you have reached this message in error, please check the number and try dialing again."*

Jack wondered why the phone number would be out of order. To think Peter hadn't paid his phone bill was laughable. Even if that were the case, would they turn it off on a Sunday? He doubted it. It was more likely that someone had tampered with his line and what he had just heard was the stock message the phone company gave, whether the line had been disconnected, or the equipment had failed.

Jack's heart began beating rapidly as he tried to analyze the implications. If the mob now had the book, they'd probably begun tidying up, removing the remaining flies from their carefully cooked ointment. Hasselbuam would be first. Then Lynchman.

Jack froze and his hands began to shake. He dialed his home number, half expecting to hear the same canned voice informing him that what little life he'd had in Atlanta, Georgia, had now been disconnected. It rang three times before someone picked up. And then he heard the click of the receiver being put back in its cradle.

Jack's mouth went dry and his throat felt tight. How could this be happening? He might have forced himself to believe that Maggie was angry, after all. Too angry to speak. But since he hadn't said anything, she couldn't know it was him. The truth might be far more terrible and frightening. He dared not think of how far things had gone in his absence, the result of a frivolous trip to get away.

Dialing operator assistance, he was put through to the Atlanta city police department, where he explained that his family might be in danger. Jack didn't carry a cell phone so he arranged to check back with them. He was assured that a cruiser would be dispatched immediately.

When Jack hung up the phone he didn't feel any better. But the thing that bothered him the most wasn't the fact the mob had probably pushed through the front door to his home and done who knew what to his wife and children. Best case scenario, his family was tied up in the back room while meaty fellows sat around on *his* couch, watching *his* TV, eating food from *his* refrigerator, while they waited for him to return so they could plant a smooth round slug into the fleshy soil of his forehead.

At worst case…

For sanity's sake, he dared not go there. Although he was far from being as apprehensive as he should have been, there was a worm of guilt. What was he doing in Florida? Why wasn't he leaving Kristen and racing back to Atlanta? Was he fit to be a husband and father anymore? All evidence pointed to the contrary.

Time stood still as he pondered what his life meant if he could feel nothing for Maggie and the kids at a time like this. Suddenly, he felt a hand on his back.

"Are you all right?"

Kristen's voice was like medicine in Jack's ears. This strange girl who'd showed up at his condo. As quirky as she was, he felt a connection with her at this moment. He wanted to embrace her, if for no other reason than to be comforted. Instead, he took in a deep breath and said, "I'm okay."

It was what men were supposed to say when everything around them was falling apart, including their legitimacy as a human being.

ᘐᘛ

While Jack was phoning home, Kristen had been thinking that he was somehow different than all the walking dead that had previously filled her life. Having spent the day with Jack, she could tell he was different. There was a connection that hadn't existed with anyone else since the fever raided her memories. Strangely enough, she wanted to cling to this new relationship for all she was worth. The man was truly alive. She could feel it.

So why had he driven off and left her? Regardless of how he tried to console her, assuring her he was merely looking out for her best interest, one simple fact remained that she couldn't overlook. She'd have been able to let it go except for the hundred-dollar bill. Why couldn't he have just given her the five and been done with it. That bill, wrapped secretly inside the five said, "You're on your own now, kid. It's been real and it's been fun. But it hasn't been *real* fun." It revealed his true intentions: a pat on the back and a boot to the ass. Sure, he'd thought enough of her to want to help. He was probably a good guy, after all. But the first chance he'd had, he'd tried to ditch her.

Knowing full well that she was already vulnerable from the hitchhiking experience, she found she wanted to strike back. She decided to tell him off the minute he returned. But as she sat bathing in anger, contemplating how she'd lay into Jack, she slowly began to realize how long he was taking. What if he had left her again?

No. That wasn't possible. Why would he come back only to leave again? It wouldn't make sense. Kristen craned her neck but couldn't see the phones. To stay the nervous tension, she applied some lipstick and tried not to think about worst-case scenarios. Jack would be back in a moment and they'd be on their way.

Unless…

What if he'd *really* wanted to help her – more than just a hundred bucks – and had decided to give her the car? She glanced over at the keys dangling from the ignition. She'd told him she didn't drive, so that couldn't be it. Unless he'd forgotten.

Unable to sit still any longer, she had left the car to see if her fears were warranted. When she came around the front of the building and saw him clinging to the side of the phone housing as though it were his only friend, her heart collapsed with empathy.

That was when she put her hand on his back to comfort him. It was a meager gesture, but anything more intrusive would violate his space. She was virtually a stranger, after all.

The two were silent as Jack pulled away from the gas station, not entirely sure where they were headed.

"What happened?" Kristen asked him.

"When I called Lynchman, the phone company said the line was disconnected," he told her grimly. "Then I called my house. Someone answered but didn't say anything."

"You think…"

"No question," Jack said.

"God, I'm so sorry."

Kristen felt helplessly inadequate in the presence of such tragedy. So much so that it made her feel sick to her stomach. How does one console a person in a situation like this?

"I called the police. They said they'd send someone over to check it out," Jack said. After a long pause, he said, "Maybe I'm wrong. But what else can I do? I told them I'd call back in the morning. Until then, we need to figure out what we're going to do."

"This is where you were heading, right? Panama City?" Jack asked.

"Yeah."

"I'll get us a couple of hotel rooms and head back to Atlanta in the morning. Tomorrow I can drop you wherever you want. I'm sorry I can't do more. But it's best this way. You got in the middle of this thing by accident. It's me they want, not you. You should be okay. Just lay low for awhile."

"I don't blame you for going back," Kristen said. "But what if they are there waiting for you. There's probably nothing you can do now anyway."

"You're right," Jack said. "The truth be told? They'll find me no matter what I do. There was probably nothing I could have done if I'd been there. Hell, I wouldn't have even known why guys were coming into my house with guns, shooting up the place. I'd have thought they were terrorists or something. At least now I can die knowing it was my own damn fault."

"It's not your fault," Kristen said.

"And how do you figure that? I was the one who planned the poker game scheme. Remember?"

"It wasn't you."

"Of course it was. What are you talking about?"

Kristen pondered this for a moment and then turned to look at Jack. "You wanted to know how I knew so much about law. You know, when I was explaining why you couldn't be charged with accessory."

"I remember."

"I dropped out of Harvard Law School."

Jack looked over at Kristen, apparently trying to decide if such a thing were possible.

"I can't even remember applying. Gerty, my grandmother, says it was my dream from when I was a little girl. I was supposed to be a lawyer. But it isn't true."

"I don't understand," Jack said.

"Whoever I was before the fever took my memory, I'm not that person anymore and neither are you."

Jack was silent.

"It's so messed up," she said. "It's like we don't belong or something. Can't you feel it? Losing my memory, I can understand. But it's like – I don't know. How can a fever make you totally different? Shouldn't something deep down, some unconscious desire, still be there to make me want to go to law school; be all the other things I used to be? It isn't there. I promise. I've looked and it just isn't there."

"So you really do have amnesia," Jack said.

"What? You thought I was lying?"

"I don't know. It just seemed too incredible. I mean, what are the odds? But now that I've heard you describe it, you couldn't possibly be making it up."

Jack turned off the highway at a roadside motel and pulled up outside the office where a vacancy sign glowed in the window. He looked over at Kristen and said, "That's exactly the way it is." Then he got out of the car and went to register two rooms, putting an end to the day's harrowing events.

CHAPTER 18

He found the pickup right where Loretta had abandoned it earlier. Finding the door slightly ajar, Jed pulled it open and climbed in. Smelling the aging vinyl, Jed reflected that the old pickup had weathered many lonely roads before ending up in a nothing place called Bootleg Hill, the same place he had woken up, confused. A wooden cross hung from the rearview mirror and a plastic cactus dangled from the keys still in the ignition.

Pushing in the clutch, Jed turned the key and gave it the right amount of gas to bring the pickup's engine to sputtering life, as the sad sound of country wailed at him from a tinny-sounding radio and the broken heart of a cowboy bled into the airwaves.

He considered stopping at the clinic to interrogate the doctor, asking why the man hadn't transferred him to a real hospital. But he knew, via his new intuitive abilities, that the weasel would have no more information than the bartender had.

As he drove out of town, he passed a sign that read, "Las Vegas, 88 miles." Though he couldn't remember ever going there, he seemed to know all about it. It was the country's gambling hotspot jammed packed with commercialized glitz and glitter. For lack of knowing where else to begin his search for his identity, Jed decided Las Vegas would be as good as any. The fuel gauge showed the tank was three-quarters full. That should be plenty – assuming the thing still gave an accurate reading. He tapped the glass several times to be sure. When the needle remained fixed, his confidence in the crude device grew enough to chance 88 miles of open desert.

As he drove, Jed wondered what all of this meant. He couldn't be sure that he'd been in an accident-induced coma or if he'd become the victim of something far more sinister. Stan, the bartender, had told him that he'd flipped a bike while going down a ravine. He'd supposedly hit his head at fifty miles-an-hour. If it were anywhere close to the truth, Jed should be happy to be alive. But the reality of taking such a spill should have left his skull mush, let alone allow him to walk out of a clinic three weeks later in excellent health, which wasn't possible. Even if he had been involved in such an accident, it would no doubt be months – possibly years – before he could function normally, let alone be in the superior condition he found himself.

That meant something else was going on. The people in Bootleg Hill honestly believed he was Jed Pope, Loretta's boyfriend. He could feel it. And yet as he scanned their minds, the actual experiences of their supposed acquaintance were missing. The only plausible explanation was that they'd somehow been brainwashed. The same people who'd orchestrated the accident had made the folks in Bootleg Hill believe he'd been a part of their community. But a whole town brainwashed? It was hard to fathom.

Jed considered various possibilities, such as: he'd been given a new identity for some reason for protection; the identity being so complete that he himself wouldn't know the truth. If there were others who had this ability to read minds, maybe they'd be scouring the country to find him. Perhaps his lack of memory was necessary to keep him safe.

If it were true, the only sensible thing would be to wheel the truck around and head back to Bootleg Hill where he would remain safe from whatever evil lurked in his past.

The hell with that!

Safe or not, he had to find the truth.

~

The desert terrain between Bootleg Hill and Las Vegas was nothing but a sea of sand, an occasional knoll making it impossible to see oncoming traffic. Even though Jed drove on the right side of the road, it wouldn't matter if he'd occupied the center since he could tell if oncoming cars were approaching simply by *feeling* them.

The aging truck had its limit and he decided not to push it, keeping at a healthy pace that hopefully wouldn't wear its cylinders thin or cause it to fall to pieces in the middle of the road. Anything above sixty-five and the body would start to rattle uncontrollably, the tires singing as they met the coarse, hot pavement. Amazingly, the old pickup had a respectable air conditioner that managed to keep the cab cool in spite of the blazing heat so intense as to cause the road ahead to shimmer.

Jed pondered how he'd begin the search for his true identity in Las Vegas. With a little luck, who he was, where he belonged, and why he'd woken up in Bootleg Hill, would come back to him. But he couldn't count on it. He decided that if his suspicions were correct, it would catch up to him sooner than he could uncover the truth. He was counting on it, since his present options were more akin to finding a needle in a haystack. Only this haystack was as big as the whole country. Maybe bigger.

An odd sound like someone kicking the floor came from the passenger side of the cab. Jed hoped the steel underbelly – probably rusting and ready to give way – would hold until he could make it to a civilized area with payphones and gas stations. He looked over at the floor but saw nothing out of the ordinary. A torque wrench and screwdriver lay toward the front where he suspected they'd sat in that spot for countless years, probably coming as permanent fixtures when the truck had last traded owners.

As beads of sweat from the sweltering sun formed on his face, he reflected on his name, Jed Pope. It didn't feel right and he suspected it had been fabricated along with everything else. Searching for his identity based on this name would no doubt yield little fruit. The inhabitants of Bootleg Hill were probably the only people that could vouch for its questionable authenticity.

The thumping on the floorboard sounded again, this time fainter, but no less apparent. Ignoring it, Jed kept to the matter at hand. He listened to the endless sound of rubber against pavement and reflected on the fact that he'd need cash if he intended to get anywhere.

Robbing a liquor store wasn't out of the question, but it probably wouldn't give him more than a few hundred bucks. Better than nothing. Not nearly enough. Where most people robbed stores with guns, he'd have to improvise. Maybe he'd stop off for a stick to tuck under a shirt. Problem was, he wasn't even wearing a shirt. That was no good.

He held the wheel with one hand and felt in pockets to see if there was a wallet or any lose bills. But unfortunately there was nothing there but lint. He'd have to start from scratch. Work his way up the food chain until he had the resources to go on his quest.

Then a thought occurred to him. Certainly there would be *something* in the glove box. Anything. With a little luck there would be some cash. With a lot of luck there would be a weapon of some kind, maybe a knife. *"Give a man a fish and feed him today. Teach him to fish and feed him for a lifetime."* The words came to him out of nowhere. That would be true if he found a weapon. Cash would be great to grab a bite or fill up the tank with. But fishing for cash while holding a knife to some poor clerk would be better. Staying one step ahead of the law should be easy, especially with his mind reading ability.

He reached for the glove box, pushed the silver button and flipped open the door. When he did this, Jed suddenly sensed he was not alone. There was a presence in the cab with him, an entity that instantly made the hair on the nape of his neck stand up. At the same moment that he saw that the glove box was empty, he turned and saw the rattlesnake slithering along the top of the backrest toward him, its skin detailed with stencil-like diamonds.

Jed slammed the brakes hard, not bothering to engage the clutch or gear down, launching the snake forward from its perch. It landed on the dashboard, with part of its tail hanging down over the side. It writhed while the pickup screeched to a halt in the middle of the road. He pawed desperately at the door handle and pulled but it was loose, broken.

Meanwhile, the snake's long body twisted and convulsed, vigorously battling with gravity. Sliding from the dashboard it plopped to the floor with a thud. Immediately, the flex-sectioned tail started vibrating and the rattler coiled into a mass, its neck and head hovering over the body, cocked back like a spring.

As he watched the black, forked tongue flipping slowly up and down in a menacing dance, Jed braced himself for the worst. He sat completely still, now clinging to his only hope of blending into the fabric and somehow conveying the possibility to the snake he was no more a threat than the worn vinyl seat. Time stood still as the two stared hypnotically at each other, each waiting for the other to move.

In that moment, in spite of his fear, Jed identified with the snake. The creature was out of its element, placed in a vinyl environment instead of sand, rocks and blue sky stretching for as far as its beady eyes could see. It had just been tossed forcefully around and was probably more terrified than he was. Why wouldn't it strike at the first thing that moved? And in some deep recess of his mind there was another connection with the snake, almost at a primitive level. Somehow he was just like that snake, yet here they were, mortal enemies.

Breaking his gaze, he slowly turned his head to assess his options. There weren't many. With the door latch broken there would be no way to exit the driver's side unless he rolled down the window and climbed out, an acrobatic activity he doubted his new friend would allow. Crawling across the seat to the other door would be equally disrupting and draw a certain strike.

He spotted a rag on the floor near his feet and slowly reached down to take it, not making any sudden movements, while the rattler remained ready to strike, hissing, tail vibrating. As he wrapped the rag around his fist, the snake repositioned itself for a cleaner strike. Jed froze, thinking he'd pushed too far, too fast.

The idea that something so small and insignificant as a snake could terrify him made him angry with himself. He wanted nothing to do with fear, a trait best left to the weak. It no more suited him than the name, Jed Pope.

"The hell with it," he said and shoved his fist forward, taunting the snake. "Let's see what you got."

The serpent lurched and spat.

"What's wrong?" he asked. "You ain't got the guts to take a bite?"

He jabbed his fist at the snake, causing it to flex back and hiss.

The rattler suddenly sprang toward the exposed part of Jed's arm, sinking its fangs into his flesh. He flailed while the snake hung on, knocking against the dashboard and seat. Using his other hand, he grabbed its neck just as the rattler released.

"Son of a bitch!" Jed screamed. He struggled the snake to the glove box and forced its head inside. Then he used his right foot and kicked the metal door closed, over and over until the rattler's writhing body went limp.

"Son of a bitch!" he said again as he threw the dead serpent against the passenger side door and began to study the four tiny holes in his arm. Curiously, it didn't hurt and hadn't even when its fangs had sunk in. It was the idea of being bitten that made him scream.

Sinking back against the door, Jed waited for the venom to take affect. There was little he could do now. Even though he couldn't feel any change – no hot poison traveling through veins or internal organs starting to seize – he knew it was only a matter of time. When the onslaught of fatal toxins reached his liver, the vital organ would be unable to deal with it. For just a moment, he wondered how it would feel.

As he leaned against the door, Jed closed his eyes and tried to comprehend what had happened. His was a consciousness that had appeared out of nowhere – not understanding or perceiving his origins – and yet was about to disappear into oblivion before he had been able to make any sense out of what had happened.

Still feeling fine, he decided to drive for as long as he could before passing out. The closer he could make it, the more likely it would be that someone could help. If he even had that much time left.

But he slowly began to realize that nothing was going to happen. Strangely enough, he still felt fine. Touching the bite marks, he wondered why they didn't hurt. He should have been hunched over the steering column by now, lifeless. But fit as a fiddle, he was apparently immune to the snake's poisonous venom.

"I hate to be the one to tell you this, buddy," he said to the limp body of the snake. "But you're impotent. All that trouble and you couldn't deliver. Don't worry, I won't tell anyone."

Suddenly, out of the corner of his eyes, Jed caught sight of the shiny barrel of a revolver inside the glove box, which he was certain had previously been empty. He picked it up and studied it. It was a nickel-plated, snub-nosed .357 magnum with a wood grip. He released the cylinder, which flipped out to the side, and spun it slowly to reveal 5 occupied chambers.

"Son…of…a…bitch!" he said. "How the hell did that get in there?"

The dim yellow light of the radio blinked on and white noise came through the tinny-speakers. A faint, static signal came from the truck's radio, pulsating through the cab.

"What the…" Jed said. "What's going on here?"

That's when he realized that the strange sounds emanating from the speakers weren't just random noises drifting through the lifeless desert airwaves, but the voice of someone or some *thing* trying to give him an answer.

CHAPTER 19

Kristen had set the alarm to get up early. Even though Jack would be leaving today she wanted to make sure he didn't sneak off like he'd done at the gas station. She'd miss his company and wished he would take her advice and not go back to Atlanta, although she couldn't blame him. If she were in his shoes and thought that Gerty was in trouble, she'd do the same thing, regardless of her own safety.

It's just that she'd come to see Jack as more than a friend. Perhaps it was that common awareness that life could never be right when you're the victim of amnesia. Or maybe his discontent mimicked her own, giving him a clearer understanding than anybody she'd ever met. Whatever it was, he was alive, and the thought of breaking up their little team sickened her. However, she'd just have to buck up and be brave. She'd made it to Panama City on her own and that was something.

For more than an hour she sat there, watching out the window, waiting until he finally emerged from his room at just before eight o'clock, looking like he'd barely slept, tucking a wrinkled shirt into his pants. He looked as disheveled as she felt. It was no joke, wearing the same clothes day after day without a change. It was a good thing everything she had on was black, Kristen told herself.

She was relieved when he walked directly to her room and knocked. She opened the door. "Sleep well?" she asked.

"I've fared better, but it isn't important. If you're hungry, I think they have coffee and donuts in the lobby. I don't know if I can stomach anything at the moment."

"Same here," Kristen said. "You leaving right away?"

"Pretty much. If you're ready to check out, I'll run the keys back to the office. Think about where you'd like me to take you, or…" Jack hesitated. "I could prepay a few days here if you want, long enough to get you on your feet. I'll give you some cash –"

"Thanks. But no thanks," Kristen said with a slight edge. "I can make it on my own."

She handed him the card-like key, then closed the door behind her as they left.

"I'll be right back," Jack said as he headed toward the office.

The memory of trying to pay her off with the hundred-dollar bill was fresh in her mind. How dare he try to give her money like he was paying her to simply go away, and at the same time, ease his conscience? She knew she was overreacting, that he was only trying to help, but his earlier betrayal still hurt.

Kristen leaned against the dirty Pinto, not caring if the grime rubbed off on her skirt. She stared at an eighteen-wheeler parked along the street and thought of Randy, how he'd confided in her before he'd been stabbed. Had it all just been a coincidence? Was she really just an innocent victim who'd stumbled into the middle of Jack's poker game ordeal, or was she somehow more a part of it than she knew? The fact that both she and Jack had lost their memories was enough in itself to make her question if she played a bigger role.

A man wearing a bolo tie came out of a room several doors down, carrying a small overnight bag and heading toward the office. As he approached, Kristen realized that he looked incredibly like Randy. The only difference was that this man had a thick head of hair where as Randy had been balding on top. Her heart beat faster as he came closer.

This is ridiculous, she told herself. *He can't possibly be Randy. Randy is dead.*

When he passed her with a nod, a frightening quiver ran up Kristen's spine. Those eyes. That same beer belly. That face. As impossible as it seemed, this man was Randy. He had to be. By the time he passed Jack who was coming out of the office, she was taking frequent, shallow breaths to keep from hyperventilating.

Kristen grabbed Jack's arm with one hand and pointed with the other. "That man that just walked by you," she stammered. "He was Randy! The truck driver! The one who told me about the poker game. He just walked past you into the motel office."

"But he was stabbed to death," Jack said, frowning. "We heard it on the news. It can't be him. Must be someone who looks like him."

"No! It's him! I swear it," Kristen cried.

"Okay. Let's find out," Jack said, taking her by the hand and leading her to the office door. "We'll have a chat with him when he comes out."

"I know you think I'm crazy," she said, "but I'm not. That face. It was him."

"Excuse me," Jack said when the man appeared. "Your name wouldn't happen to be Randy by any chance, would it?"

"Can't say that it is," the fellow said good-naturedly. "Name's Gus."

Kristen squeezed Jack's hand. The voice was exactly the same as Randy's.

"You're Randy Longfellow," Kristen said. "A truck driver. Don't lie to us."

The man chuckled and reached around to scratch the back of his neck. "Well…it's true I'm a trucker," he said and pointed to the rig sitting at the side of the road. "But I promise my name isn't Randy. Must be another good lookin' guy you got me confused with."

"Is that the same truck?" Jack asked Kristen.

"No," she admitted. "The one he was driving the other day was dark blue. But it's him. I know it."

"Missy, I don't know what you're talkin' about," the man said.

"I'm sorry to bother you," Jack said.

"I don't get it," Kristen said in a low voice as the trucker swung himself up into the cab. "I know it's him."

She suddenly felt disoriented and confused. The still, humid air made her feel claustrophobic and dizzy. Closing her eyes she tried to think things through, make sense of it all. She knew it was Randy. At least she *thought* it was.

Suddenly she was engulfed in her dream again. The dirt spilling around her ankles. Fighting to stay above ground. Trying to stay in the sunlight where it was warm and safe.

Someone was shaking her. She opened her eyes and looked into the face of Jack Stuart. The nightmare faded and she was back; at least for a while.

"Are you all right?" he was saying. "What happened?"

"Sorry, I…" she said but didn't know for sure. It was the first time her dream had happened while she was awake.

"I think you'd better sit down. Let's get you to the car," Jack said.

Kristen dropped herself into the Pinto's seat, wondering what had just happened to her.

Jack had called the Atlanta Police when he first woke up, learning that officers had rung the doorbell to his home and checked the yard, but couldn't detect any foul play. Without a search warrant they wouldn't be able to enter unless there was stronger evidence, such as a broken window or forced entry. It appeared to the officers that the house was secure. They offered to send another cruiser by in the afternoon to see if anything had changed.

As he sat in the car with Kristen, hoping she'd recover from whatever had caused her to zone out, he couldn't help wondering if all this business about the trucker weren't some elaborate scheme she had cooked up to get him to stay. Yet the notion that she'd actually seen Randy was preposterous, even delusional. His main concern was to find a safe place for her before making his way back to Atlanta.

"Are you okay?" Jack asked. "You didn't look too good for a minute there."

"Thanks a lot," she said.

"You know what I meant."

"Something weird is going on," Kristen said. "It's like a bizarre dream that makes perfect sense when you're sleeping but seems ridiculous when you wake up."

"Want me to pinch you?" Jack asked.

"Ha, ha…I mean it," she said. "I swear to you that was Randy. I know it doesn't make any sense. I know he didn't admit it and this guy had hair. But in some strange way, I know it was him. He even called me Missy. Did you notice that?"

"Uh huh. And what's that supposed to prove?"

"Randy called me Missy. Just like this guy did. And his voice was exactly the same. Not just similar. Exactly."

Jack sighed. "I'd like to believe you," he said. "I really would. But look at it this way. Let's say he really *was* Randy. That means that the stabbing would have had to be faked. In fact, so much so that it would have fooled the police and reporters who showed up at the scene. And then, he'd go on his merry way and would have just happened to meet us here in Panama City at this very motel."

"I never said it made sense. I just know it was him. That's all. What if they used him? Paid him to act like he'd been stabbed. Suppose the mob actually set this whole thing up to find the book. Then, what if Randy – or Gus, or whatever his name really is – accidentally happened to see me here? Wouldn't he try to deny the whole thing?"

"Hmmm," Jack mused. "I suppose anything's possible. But think for a second about when he first saw you just a few minutes ago. Were you looking at him at that moment?"

"Yeah. Why?"

"Did you see any look of shock or surprise on his face? Any shred of recognition?"

"Well…no," Kristen admitted.

"If he happened to suddenly see you, don't you think he'd look surprised?"

"What if he saw me through the window before he came out of his room?" Kristen said with renewed conviction. "Maybe he wasn't surprised because he was ready for me."

"Please!" Jack said. "You think he would have come out if you were standing there? I don't think so. Besides, I've been thinking about the whole book thing. If this was all a setup to find it, then how come they got to Hasselbaum *before* we led them there? Unless…"

Suddenly it hit Jack with the force of a locomotive. How stupid of him not to consider it earlier. Wouldn't they have bugged Lynchman's phone? Probably his own phone was tapped as well. When he'd spoken to Lynchman they probably heard every word. That would have given them plenty of time – especially if they suspected Hasselbaum's general location – to get to him, get the book back and kill Hasselbaum. Then the remainder of the cleanup had begun.

"Unless what?" Kristen asked.

"Oh God. I don't believe this."

"What? Tell me," Kristen demanded.

"When I spoke to Lynchman on the phone. They probably overheard it. His phone must have been bugged."

Jack started up the car and backed out of the space.

"Where are we going?"

Jack slammed on the brakes and turned to Kristen, looking directly into her dark eyes. "Tell me you weren't involved," he demanded. "Promise me right now you weren't behind any of this. Swear it on Gerty's life."

Kristen looked horrified. *"No…God, you think…no. Of course not!"*

"Okay," he said. "But you better not be lying."

Jack pulled out of the parking lot; unsure if Kristen hadn't really seen Randy, after all.

❧

Twenty minutes later, they pulled up two houses down from Hasselbaum's place, a little closer than where he'd parked the evening before. The neighborhood now seemed quiet and peaceful, the street shaded by giant oaks, lawns neatly maintained. It was an unlikely crime location but Jack was sure something violent had happened here, even if there had been nothing about it on the news this morning.

Jack had to know if they'd actually found the book. He doubted Hasselbaum would have been foolish enough to leave it lying around. Assuming he could get inside without anyone noticing, he might be able to find out. Then again, it might be futile.

"Where are we?" Kristen asked.

"That's Hasselbaum's house," Jack said, pointing. "I just want to poke around a bit. See if I can find out anything."

"What if the police are still hanging around? Won't there be people in there taking pictures? Removing fibers from the carpet and lifting every fingerprint in the place?"

"What do you think this is?" Jack asked her. "CSI? There aren't any cars out front. I doubt anyone's still here. I'll have a look."

"I'll come too," Kristen said.

"The hell you will. Stay put. I'll be back in a minute."

Jack slipped out of the car and walked casually toward the house. When he was even with it, he stopped, glanced around, and then walked quickly up one side of the yard toward a gate. He lifted a metal latch and made his way into the backyard. Drapes covered the windows preventing him from looking inside. He tried a sliding glass door, but it was secure. He tried another door but it was locked as well. He went all the way around, testing windows, considering breaking one as a last resort. But if there was a security system – surely something Hasselbaum would have installed – forced entry would surely set it off.

The opposite side of the house was narrow and he had to step over rocks to make his way along. After checking several locked windows, he decided there was likely no way in. When he returned to the backyard, movement caught the corner of his eye. Someone was standing at the door. Shock turned to anger as he recognized that it was only Kristen.

"What are you doing?" he demanded in a whisper and then noticed the door that he'd tried earlier was now open.

"How did you do that?" he hissed. "It was locked a second ago."

"Well, it's open now," she said and walked inside.

"Wait. What if there's motion sensors?"

"Doubt it," she said. "If Hasselbaum's dead, who would turn them on?"

Jack frowned and wondered why he hadn't thought of that. He followed her into a utility room where there was a new washer-and-dryer set. The white walls were free from marks and smudges, possibly from a recent coat of paint. This room exited to the kitchen. Again, there were all new appliances. The counters were clean and bare.

"He had to be the tidiest bachelor I've ever seen," Jack commented and opened a few cupboards to peer inside. They were sparsely filled with neat rows of glasses, plates, dishes and bowls, all matching, all looking as though they'd never been used. A drawer held a silverware tray with perfectly placed spoons, forks and knives. There were no dirty dishes in the sink or on the countertops.

Kristen opened the refrigerator. "You aren't kidding," she said. "I've never seen a refrigerator this organized."

Jack glanced over and saw a uniform row of bottles and drink containers. The second shelf held neatly stacked Tupperware containers and the bottom shelf had tidy stacks of various condiments.

She opened the freezer and a single, unopened carton of ice cream sat perfectly in the middle of the upper shelf. Rocky Road. Her favorite.

Jack disappeared through an arch and into the main living area, a large room with sofa and loveseat, a coffee table and end tables. Built-in bookshelves lined one wall where several hardback novels were propped up with metallic bookends, but the remaining shelves had little, if anything, on them.

"Shouldn't there be tape or chalk or something to show where the body was?" Kristen asked as she appeared at the archway.

"Maybe it happened in his bedroom."

"And what about the yellow tape stretched across doorways to the crime scene?"

"You've seen too many movies," Jack said. "Maybe they only do that in public places so people don't mess up the evidence."

"Something isn't right," Jack suddenly said.

"What do you mean?"

Ignoring her question, he headed down a hallway toward the bedrooms, of which there were three in all. One was completely empty and another was being used as a home office. The last was the master suite, which held a large, four-poster bed and a small TV on a dark wood dresser.

Jack investigated the dresser, which held a few socks and underwear, and that was all. The closet held a pair of dress shirts and pressed slacks hanging neatly to one side, while penny loafers sat on the floor just below them. He joined Kristen in the office where she was lifting the cover to a large, roll-top desk.

"I don't get it," she said.

"What?"

"There's nothing in it. Completely empty."

"That's what I mean," Jack said. "This isn't right. You're going to tell me a bachelor lives here? Only one small TV in the master bedroom. No stereo. No beer in the fridge. Flower covered sofas. I don't think so. He either has the tastes of an elderly woman or…"

"Or what?" Kristen asked.

"I don't know. It's almost as though this whole thing is a prop on a Hollywood set. Not real. Nobody could possibly live here. Unless he straightened up the place right before he was murdered. That might be admirably conscientious, but highly unlikely. And nobody I know keeps their house *this* neat."

Kristen studied the desk. She opened the drawers – also empty – and felt inside the dark cubbies for anything at all.

"You're right," she said. "Something about this isn't right."

CHAPTER 20

No matter how peculiar the circumstances, one fact remained plain to Kristen as they pulled away from the curb. Jack would be heading back to Atlanta today, leaving her in a state of complete confusion, and there was nothing she could do to stop him. It would be pointless to even try.

In order to maintain some shred of sanity, Kristen thought of better times in her life. There weren't many – ones that she could remember, anyway. The best she could come up with was hanging out in malls. She felt safe in malls. There were no cars around to scare her and people left her alone. Everything was clean and nice, and it was quiet after they locked the doors and turned out the lights. If only she had a comfortable place to sleep and a warm shower from time to time, the mall would be perfect. It had everything else she needed, from entertainment, to fresh clothes. And all the makeup she could use, to boot.

All right, then. She would have Jack drop her at a mall. That was the only sensible place to refocus on what she'd do next. An uncharacteristic sadness welled up as she thought about Jack leaving. He was all that had kept her from going completely bonkers during all this. She'd always felt like she wasn't assembled right, as though an emotional screw had jiggled loose when she'd suffered from the fever. And after seeing Randy stabbed, she had come dangerously close to dropping off the invisible ledge of sanity. And somehow, just as she was about to fall, Jack had grabbed her and pulled her back. If all this had happened while she had been on her own, she dared not think of what the outcome might have been.

To avoid the embarrassment of having Jack ask her what she was going to do again, Kristen brought up the obvious. "Do you know of any malls around here? If so, that's where you can drop me off."

"A mall? Really?"

"That's what I said."

"Well, yeah. Actually there's one not far from here. Sometimes when we come to the condo, we make it out to Panama City for dinner and I've seen it."

"That'll be fine," Kristen said, trying desperately not to let any sign of discouragement escape her voice.

"How will I get ahold of you – you know – if I need to?" Jack asked.

"You won't," Kristen said. "Besides, why would you need to?"

"I don't know. In case I find out more when I get to Atlanta."

"Like you said before, I just got caught in the middle of this by accident. I don't really need to know."

Jack paused. "I suppose you're right. But I just thought…"

"Look," Kristen said. "Do we have to go on about this? I just want to get to a mall and get on with my life."

As they drove toward the mall, Jack remained quiet.

Kristen was fuming. Even though she couldn't blame him for going back to Atlanta, did he really have to act like he wanted to keep up with her in his spare time? The next thing he might ask was if they could be pen pals or some other sentimental crap. It was unbecoming and made her want to puke.

As they approached the next intersection, the light turned red long before Jack could make it through on yellow.

"What's at the mall?" he asked her.

"Excuse me?" she replied.

"Why the mall? What's so important about going to the mall?"

"What's it to you?"

"I was just curious," Jack said.

"Don't worry. In a few minutes you'll be rid of me. The mall is air-conditioned and a great place to work out my game plan. That's all. Does that meet with your approval?"

The light turned green and the car stalled.

"Great!" Jack said and tried desperately to turn over the aging engine. A car behind them honked three times before it finally changed lanes and pulled around. Jack made several more attempts, but the engine merely responded with wheezing chuckles.

"This is just great!" he said. "How am I supposed to get back to Destin?"

"I thought you were going to Atlanta."

"I am. But first I want to see if our friends have left so I can pick up my other car. This one exhausted my patience long ago."

He tried again with no luck. By now he'd turned on his hazard lights and cars were going around them. The light turned yellow again and then red, bringing several cars to a stop around the Pinto as equals. Here at a red light, it was just one of the pack.

"Isn't there a mall in Destin?" Kristen asked.

"I don't know. Yeah. I guess," Jack said, flustered. "Nearby anyway. Why?"

"Panama City's more crowded than I thought. If you wouldn't mind, since you're heading back there…"

"Oh, I don't mind," Jack said sarcastically. "It's this damn Pinto that may have other plans. At this rate, we aren't going anywhere." He smacked both hands on the steering wheel in frustration.

The light finally turned green and he turned the key one more time. The engine started right up without any sign that there had been a problem a moment earlier.

As much as Kristen hated cars, this one was beginning to grow on her. If she didn't know better, she might have imagined that the old dusty thing was actually looking out for her. If it hadn't stalled, she wouldn't have known Jack was going back to Destin. In the long run it may not make much difference, but it *would* give her one more hour off the lonely streets and in the company of a kindred spirit. She smiled to herself and petted the seat as though stroking old Spot for a job well done.

They made their way back toward Destin on the Emerald Coast Highway after picking up some burgers, fries, and drinks at Wendy's. They spoke little during the trip, but as they grew closer to their destination, Kristen asked, "What do you really think about Hasselbaum? You know, how his house didn't even look lived in? No blood on the carpet. Makes you wonder where they offed him."

Jack glanced over at her, taken back by her choice of words. It was a good thing he couldn't remember the man from Adam.

"Maybe he was a compulsive cleaner; an organization freak, or something," Jack said. But knew it had to be more than that. Clean was one thing. Organized was another. The house was both of those, but something else.

Sparse.

It hadn't even had the ordinary things a person needed to live in a modern society. There had been no soap in the bathroom, no towels or toothpaste, no detergent in the laundry room. The place was a fabricated illusion if he'd ever seen one. But for whose benefit, he didn't know.

"I suppose it's possible," she said. "I still doubt it, though."

"Actually," Jack said, "so do I. But since I can't begin to imagine another explanation, it's the best I can come up with."

"I know," Kristen said, sounding hopeful. "What if he didn't really live there? You know, maybe he just told the other guy –"

"– Lynchman –"

"Right. Lynchman. What if he only told Lynchman that he lived there, knowing that he might be found out? What if he really lived somewhere else and that house was a front?"

Jack smiled. The girl was no dummy. But the theory had holes, which he promptly proceeded to punch a fist through. "Then why did they find him murdered there?"

"How do we know they did?"

"I was there. Remember? There were police cars and ambulances. Someone said he'd been murdered."

"Did you see the body? I thought Randy was dead until I saw him at the motel."

"But you don't know for sure it was Randy, do you?"

Kristen sighed. "I told you. I know it was him."

"This is insane," Jack said. "People dying that aren't really dead. It's making me crazy."

"What if Hasselbaum set the whole thing up to make it look like he'd been murdered," Kristen said, sounding excited now. "It makes perfect sense. After you spoke to Lynchman, he probably got ahold of Hasselbaum. Hasselbaum probably used his front – that house – to make people believe he'd been killed.

You'd lead them right to his front door. A fake front door. But when they get there, he's already dead. They can check him off their list. But they probably still didn't get hold of the book. It's actually quite brilliant."

"And how did he fake his own death? Find a body and plant it in the house? Change his dental records?"

"Of course not. We didn't see any blood for good reason. There wasn't any. He probably paid some cop to say there was a murder. Either that or he was in the crowd and slipped a busybody some juicy gossip. If I had to guess, I'd say he's probably healthy as a horse, living in a condo in South Florida, untouched by any of this. Probably has the book stashed safely in a locker at the airport."

"If that's the case, why would the mob go after Lynchman. Or me," Jack said as he was reminded again that Maggie and the kids may have become victims at the expense of his plan for an independent life. He'd tried to put it out of his mind, but now it came back in waves of guilt.

"If they thought Hasselbaum was dead, who would there be to turn the book in?"

Jack thought of the implications. "If that's the case, then Hasselbaum is an idiot."

"Maybe he never thought that far ahead. He was just looking out for himself and the book, not realizing what they would do if they thought he was dead."

"I suppose it's possible," Jack said. "I'm still not convinced."

"When you come up with a better explanation, let me know."

"How can I, if I can't find you?" Jack said.

"Touché."

They pulled into Destin and turned left on Gulf Shore Drive. Stopping at the grocery store, Jack picked up the Monday edition of *The News Herald*, Panama City's local paper. Certainly there would be an article about a murder if such an event had taken place. But there was nothing about it. Just like earlier when he'd turned on the TV to see if it had made the morning news.

Maybe Kristen was right, after all. But the way things looked to Jack the night before – numerous police cars, an ambulance and paramedics – you'd have thought some lunatic had gone on a rampage. How could the whole event go unnoticed by the media?

They turned right on Sandprint Circle, the street where Jack's condo was located. Easing the car forward, he hoped and prayed the shiny black sedan wasn't still parked out front.

"I have an idea," Jack said. "If the mob isn't around, why don't you stay at the condo? That way I can get ahold of you and you'll have a place to stay. That's what you wanted anyway."

"Thanks. But somehow I doubt they'll give up that easily," Kristen said.

"Well, we'll find out in a second. We're just about there."

As they got closer, Jack strained to see if any cars looked out of place. Pulling off to the side, he studied the beachfront activity. If his condo was still being watched, he suspected it wouldn't be difficult to spot them in this neighborhood. Amongst vacationing families – with their minivans, convertibles, bikinis, and kids lugging blown-up toys – a member of the mob would stick out like a sore thumb.

The dark sedan was now gone. While there were several other cars, none looked more conspicuous than those driven by beach-hungry vacationers. No silhouettes could be seen through windshields or rear windows.

"It looks clear to me," Jack said. "But just to be sure, let's go in through the back."

They abandoned the car – something Jack had been fantasizing about for some time – and descended the same wooden steps to the beach they'd used the day before. Here the beach was already a bustling stretch of sand. Pleasure seekers ignored them as they sauntered along toward the condo, looking as conspicuous as they had yesterday.

When they entered the condo through the sliding door, it was cool and quiet, the air-conditioner still rumbling softly. Jack stood in the living room, collecting his thoughts and staring at the broken glass still strewn over the kitchen counter and tile floor. The front door looked secure. Apparently there had been no forced entry.

"Where you goin'?" Kristen asked, as he headed down the hallway.

"To peel off these clothes. If I wear them another second, they're liable to crust over and I'll never get them off."

"*Ewww!* Gross," Kristen said.

"Yeah. How do you think I feel?" He disappeared into the back.

When he returned, he was wearing another tropical shirt and a pair of shorts, one of several such outfits here to make for light packing on last minute trips to the condo.

"Now what about you?" he asked her.

"What about me?" she replied.

"You might be able to fit into something of Maggie's. She's got some things in the closet and chest of drawers in the master suite. If you don't mind something a little brighter, that is."

"Thanks, but I'll wait until I can pick up some things at the mall that are more my style."

"You still want to go to the mall? Even though the place seems clear, unwatched?"

"We haven't determined that for sure," she said. "Besides, I know you really don't want me here. You're just being nice."

"It's okay. Really. But if you don't want to, then suit yourself."

He wanted to say something about how she was the only person he could relate to since the accident, including his own wife. He wanted to tell her that the only reason he was going back was to act like a responsible husband and stave off guilt for not cringing in horror over the possibility he'd lost his family.

Instead he called the office to see if by some chance Lynchman had shown up.

Isabel, the department secretary had offered to pick up sandwiches from a hole-in-the-wall deli down the street, and a stacked-pastrami on rye greeted Mark Sweeney when he popped open the Styrofoam lid. His mouth began to water as he tucked a napkin under his collar and then applied some spicy mustard.

So far, Mark was pleased with his decision to let Jared handle Guerridelli. The last time he'd checked, the new client had experienced some unusual manifestations, but Jared appeared confidant and more than able to handle things. In spite of some problems his department was facing, Mark felt with patience and careful thought, his group could turn things around. And having one more competent monitor was a step in the right direction.

Just as he was about to take a bite of his monster sandwich, someone knocked rapidly on his door and then opened it without waiting for a response.

It was Zack.

Mark was about to ask him to come back later, when he caught sight of Erin, as she came flying around the corner, apparently frantic, but gained some composure when she spotted Mark.

"We need to talk," Zack told him.

Mark eyed his sandwich and sighed. "What's going on?" He asked, aware that Erin was fidgeting nervously in the background.

"We have a little problem that you need to be aware of," Zack said frankly.

Mark leaned back and folded his hands. "How little?"

"I told Zack we didn't need to bother you," Erin chimed in. "It's no big deal."

"My subject, Kate, saw someone who's supposed to be dead," Zack said. "And she and Cochran entered a house they should have never seen the inside of. Now they're suspicious as hell."

Mark was confused. He held up a hand. "Wait. You better start from the beginning. I wasn't even aware they knew about each other."

Zack glanced at Erin, hesitating. "We thought it would help," he said.

Mark knew by the way Zack looked disapprovingly at Erin that bringing the subjects together had been her idea, and hers alone. Whether she intended to or not, she used her looks to get what she wanted and Mark didn't doubt for a second she'd reeled Zack in, hook, line, and sinker.

"You'd both better sit down and explain," Mark said, motioning for Erin to close the door.

What unfolded was a complex mess the two had concocted and, given the nature of it, Mark wasn't all that surprised, since Erin was involved. Had one of the other monitors pulled such a stunt he'd have sent them to collect their personal effects, immediately. But although he knew he shouldn't let it happen, Erin, with her sparkling eyes and bouncy enthusiasm, still had her hold over him.

When they were finished, Mark sat for some time without speaking, barely aware of Zack and Erin, glancing furtively at one another. Since they'd leveled with him, it was time he did the same.

"The analysts I mentioned earlier?" Mark began. "They aren't just coming to improve efficiency. I didn't want to say anything, but Albatross isn't doing so well. We all know the history, even though we all came aboard after the fact." Mark now questioned his wisdom in hiding Albatross's financial condition. He should have said something sooner.

"The investors feel they've been burned by Petrov and Hunter and their original plan. Now they're watching closely. If Albatross can't make a go of it at this point, they may dissolve the company, salvage what they can by selling off patents, technology, and so forth. Right now they're studying overhead costs. What they really need to charge clients. But they're concerned about client satisfaction. We can't keep getting new clients if things don't improve. In case you haven't noticed, our subjects aren't too happy. And pulling this kind of stunt…"

Mark stopped himself, keeping the anger from welling up.

"Look," he said. "We need to get this ironed out quickly or all of our jobs may be on the line. From now on, I call the shots. Neither of you do *anything* without my approval. Is that understood?"

Zack and Erin nodded in unison.

"Good. Now, one of you better have some suggestions about how we can fix this mess."

CHAPTER 21

In a penthouse far above the bustle of the Las Vegas strip, Eli Houston was waking up with another hangover from a night of partying and every manner of indulgence known to a reasonably attractive, middle-aged man with a taste for adventure and a propensity to push the extremes beyond their intended limit. Last night had been particularly brutal and his head pounded with each and every step as he walked into the kitchen.

"Come on boys. Kick in the juice," he called out, even though nobody else was there. His three female companions had already taken their departure long ago while the day was young and Eli still slept. Now well into the day, Eli simply needed to recover enough so he could start the merry-go-round all over again by the time the sun set. There was always that brief moment when he first woke up and got out of bed when he would question the wisdom of such a lifestyle. But then he'd feel better and go right back to his sense-numbing bliss.

"My head's killing me. You mind hurrying it up, folks," he said to his unseen audience as he downed a glass full of clear, thirst-quenching liquid.

Slowly. Finally. The throbbing in his temples subsided and his body began to feel normal again.

"It's about damn time," Eli said. Patience was not one if his primary virtues.

Walking over to the massive arched window, glass still in hand, he looked over the city – *his* city – and considered the life he'd chosen. He'd had enough of broken marriages and corporate ladders, a son who'd ran off to get brainwashed in a weird cult, committing suicide because of some damn religious freak. No more being responsible when everyone else could give a rat's ass. No. This was his life now. No matter how shallow and pathetic it seemed, what he had now was far better than all the crap his past life had dumped on him at each and every rung of supposed success. He'd been so naïve, thinking the view would be grand from the top.

Eli now only had one cardinal rule to live by, and it consisted of a single, solitary word.

Indulge!

Eat, drink, and be merry, was the expanded version in case he ever needed to explain it, which he never did. His philosophy was based on the fact that, by the time you finally arrive at the top, you're nearly already dead, either from a failing body or from life's relentless suffering. *Life's a bitch and ain't it grand!* This was now the only option that made any sense to Eli. It was his reward and probably the closest he'd ever get to Heaven, so he might as well enjoy it for all he was worth.

He was about to order champagne for breakfast, simply because he could, when "the phone" rang. He hated that damn little cell phone. It was the one thing that could interrupt his indulgent life and he nearly resisted the urge to answer. But he was instructed to keep it handy in case *they* needed to get ahold of him.

What did they want now? He doubted they were calling to chitchat about life on the edge or what it was like to sleep with three women at once. More likely, they wanted him to do some damn thing that wasn't in the original agreement, simply because they'd screwed up again. Why should he help them?

Yet somehow they always found a way to turn his screw, push his button, whatever the hell they did to make him be their little messenger of glad tidings. The whole thing was ludicrous. Why couldn't they just leave him alone? Let the poor bastards fend for themselves. They'd agreed to their predicaments. Let 'em suffer if they hadn't made their lives superficial enough not to care. That was their problem, not his.

Just because he could remember life before, shouldn't be reason to penalize him. It wasn't supposed to be this way. What he wouldn't give to have those horrid memories of his past erased forever, to keep them from confronting him whenever he happened to be sober for a lousy few minutes. Didn't it just figure that he was the one person in the project who had broken the mold and could still remember everything? It was an irony of fate that left him bitter whenever he considered it or happened to have half an abstemious mind to care.

He removed the phone from the mahogany desk and pressed the send button. It was Mark Sweeney, one of the project's leading geeks and a royal pain in the ass.

"Just checking to see how you're doing," he said, sounding every bit of the weasel that he was.

"Cut the crap, Sweeney. Or have you forgotten I know you don't need to call to see how I'm doing."

"Sorry, Mr. Houston. I…uh…need you to do me a favor."

"Why am I not surprised," Eli fumed. "When are you guys going to take care of your own problems and leave me the hell alone?"

"Well…it's just not that simple," Sweeney said, trying desperately not to break any eggshells that Eli put beneath his feet. "It's much better if these things are solved by someone on the inside."

"I know. I know. You've played your violin before. What is it this time? You got a cat on steroids you want down from a tree?"

Sweeney chuckled nervously. "We're going to be sending a couple of folks your way. We need you to…well just kind of talk them out of a mess they've got themselves into."

"Uh huh. I'm sure it was all their own doing," Eli said sarcastically. "What did you guys do to them this time? They see funny bright lights in the sky like the last one? Been abducted by aliens, have they? Or have you refined your abilities to make people go insane?"

"It's nothing like that," Sweeney assured him. "Something had to be done. One of them was caught trying to leave the country."

As unlikely as it was, Eli burst out laughing. "Hell, I'd have liked to been there to see that. That'd put a little cramp in the program, now, wouldn't it? What'd you do, crash the plane?"

"No! Of course not," Sweeney said, taking offense at the very idea. "One of our monitors…well, let's just say she got a little too creative."

"Uh huh."

"This couple thinks the mob's after them. We have a new client who's a genuine gangster and I guess it gave her the idea. It was a way to get them together. Like so many others, they weren't content. And we've found…"

"I know," Eli interjected. "I've heard this one before. When they interact with others in the project, things seem to smooth themselves out. Am I right?"

"Exactly. And they're together now. But…"

"The mob," Eli said evenly. "You guys have to be so damn dramatic, don't you?"

"Trust me, I didn't authorize it," Sweeney said. "I'm stepping in to help clean up the mess. If Petrov finds out, this monitor is history."

"So can her ass and be done with it. Why bother me?"

Sweeney paused. "She's actually very useful in some ways. She just got a little carried away. So, will you help, or not?"

"I'm listening. Not promising anything. Just listening."

"You won't have to go anywhere. We'll bring them to you. With a little luck we can have them there shortly. Don't go anywhere for the next few hours."

Eli sighed. "What do you want me to tell them?"

"I'll try to think of something and let you know. We'll come up with a way to tie everything together and send them on their way. Whatever you do, don't tell them the truth. It would be a breach of policy."

"God bless policy," Eli muttered.

"Like it or not, it's what we live by."

"*You* live by," Eli pointed out. "Not me. I don't understand why you can't just level with them. I have half a mind to call Petrov myself. No. Better. Give *them* his phone number so they can call him. Then they'd get to the bottom of things real quick, wouldn't they?"

"You can't do that," Sweeney said. "That would be in violation of the contract."

"I want you to hold the phone very closely to your ear so you can hear what I'm about to say," Eli sneered. "ASK ME IF I CARE!"

Sweeney was clearly shaken. Eli could practically see him sitting there with wide eyes, not knowing how to control his guinea pig who'd taken on a mind of its own.

"Now you listen to me, Mr. Houston," he said. "I didn't want to say anything, but all hell's breaking loose. This whole damn thing is falling apart. None of the candidates are happy. We've got some weirdness going on in a town near Vegas called Bootleg Hill – another monitor is handling that case – but now there's this thing with the mob. And I don't need to tell you what happens if investors pull the plug. Whatever life you think you have will be over. Contract or no. Understand?"

"Relax," Eli said. "I'll talk to them. I never said I wouldn't. I just think it's time you change your strategy. That's all. Preferably one that doesn't involve me."

There was a pause.

"They wouldn't do that?" Eli asked. "Would they?"

"Pull the plug?" Sweeney sighed. "Probably not. But if things don't get better, it's a remote possibility. Stay near the phone. I'll call you back when I have a coherent story to tell them."

The line turned into pure silence that characterized cell phone behavior.

Eli tossed the phone back on the desk, suppressing the urge to throw it against the wall. Not that it would have done any good. It had been his experience that, had he destroyed it, another would show up within twenty-four hours to replace it.

"Great!" Eli said, aggravated.

One more thing to keep him distracted from the important business of forgetting.

❧

It came as no surprise that Lynchman hadn't shown up for work and that he hadn't checked in by phone. Claire Wanamaker, the receptionist, didn't sound too concerned. Both Lynchman and Jack often showed up late for work. She knew they had important matters to attend to and sometimes they'd simply be at an early meeting or held over for the weekend on a business trip. Her job was to answer phones and pass messages, not be their personal secretary. They were big boys and could look out for themselves.

"Want me to have him call if he shows up?" she asked.

"No. I doubt he ever will."

"Excuse me?"

"Never mind. I'll try to stop by the office tomorrow, in case anyone wants to know."

"All rightie," she said and hung up.

Jack envied her, clearly clueless to what was going on. He'd been as oblivious a couple of days ago and in some ways wished he could go back. It would be a little while longer before she learned that her bosses had been the victims of the mob. The company would likely go under for lack of leadership and she would be out of a job. Yet for the time being she sat, answering phones, cheerful and unaware of any such calamity.

"Never came in?" Kristen asked.

Jack nodded.

"I guess there's little point in trying to persuade you not to go back."

"They could find me here as easily as they can kind find me in Atlanta. Although it does seem like they're no longer watching the place," Jack admitted.

"If you go back, you're as good as dead."

Jack knew she was right, but wasn't sure why the same wasn't true if he stayed. Unfortunately, his unappeasable sense of responsibility would never allow that. It was pointless to argue with her. But he had to go.

"I still think you should stay here," he said. "Even if they were watching the place, they'd never know – assuming you come and go through the back, by way of the beach. They obviously never came inside after we left. The worst that could happen is – well, let's just say it would probably be weeks before anyone ever got around to checking up on the place."

Kristen shook her head. "I can't believe you don't care if you die."

"It's not like I'm going to paint a target on my chest and spread my arms."

"Might as well, if you go back to Atlanta."

Jack looked at his watch. It was already past noon and he should have been on the road hours ago. "Look," he said. "If you want to stay, stay. I don't care. If I call here and you don't answer, I'll assume you've left."

He removed a set of keys from his pocket, unclipped the one to the front door and tossed it to her. She caught it with one hand. "I've got to go," he said. He thought about pulling out his wallet and giving her some money again, but decided it would only make her angry.

As he opened the front door to leave, Kristen said, "I hope you know what you're doing."

He stopped and looked back. "Enjoy the place. And…"

"What?"

"If I don't see you again, thank you."

But he had closed the door behind him just as he heard her saying, "For what?" Somehow he knew she wouldn't come after him to find out what he meant. He hoped he'd see her again; wanted desperately to go back inside, lock the door and spend the afternoon bickering with her. In the evening they could have gone walking through a mall, picking out a fresh set of funeral attire while continuing to argue. After that they could grab a bite to eat and come back to the condo and conjecture further about the mob.

It was tempting, but not enough to make him stay. Whether he liked it or not, he was a husband and a father – a life he'd chosen at another time – and he'd never be able to look himself in the mirror if he didn't go back. With keys in hand, he opened the garage door for the first time since Saturday night when returning from the seafood dinner. Little had he known at that time, Kristen had been sleeping soundly in the kid's bedroom.

As he was groping for the light switch, he heard a muted scream from inside the condo. And then an unnaturally soft hand was planted across his nose and mouth. He struggled to break free and nearly did. But the powerful arms that were now wrapped around him seemed to be growing stronger with each second. Soon he could no longer budge them even though it seemed as though he was flailing much more vigorously than he had moments earlier. The arms grew stronger and stronger.

Suddenly Jack realized he was moving slower and having a harder time breathing, and that the hand over his face was no hand at all, but a cloth. And it was not that his opponent was growing stronger. *He* was growing weaker, slower. His vision grew fuzzy, and peace descended on him as he fell back into the arms of his adversary.

৩০৫

When Kristen heard the sound of the glass door sliding open, she thought at once it was Jack returning for something. Then she saw a brute of a man dressed in black. He was holding a bottle in one hand and a cloth in the other.

As she screamed, the front door opened and another, equally intimidating man entered the house. With nowhere else to run, she headed down the hall toward the bedrooms, coming first to the bedroom she'd slept in. There was a window facing the back but she could hear the intruders coming and knew there wouldn't be time to climb out.

She slid open the closet and was grateful to find clothes hanging on hooks and a mount of toys and stuffed animals on the floor, not enough to bury her completely, but maybe enough to buy her a few extra seconds. Scrambling in, she slid the door closed and crouched in the back corner, pulling as much of the closet rubble toward her as possible.

She heard footsteps.

Ready or not, she told herself.

She could tell that at least one of them was searching the room. "Come on out," a man said in a rough voice. "I ain't gonna hurt you. We need to talk. That's all."

When Hell freezes over, Kristen thought.

She gripped one of the toys and recognized the shape. Perhaps somehow she could use it to buy her a few extra seconds. She lifted it and slipped a finger through a plastic ring. It would have to do.

"Come on out. We're just gonna have a chat. That's all," the man said. "You don't want Big Jake to lose his temper do you?"

Big Jake?

She wasn't sure if he'd meant the man in the other room or if he was referring to himself in the third person. If the latter were the case, it was almost laughable. What a goon. Kristen realized suddenly that she could do this. After all, she was a master of deception wasn't she? People didn't suspect you when you didn't act guilty. At least they hadn't in the mall. She'd have to muster up that same confidence if she hoped to get out of there alive.

As the closet door began to slide open, she pulled the toy's cord with as much force as if she were ripping a pin from a grenade. And just like a grenade, she tossed it to the other end of the closet to provide a distraction, as a scratchy voice said, "The rooster says." This was followed by the sound of a barnyard at sunrise.

The goon was stupid enough to buy it. He stopped opening her side and began opening the other end where she'd tossed the toy. At that same moment, Kristen slid open her side enough to squeeze through. With a push, she sent the man stumbling into a pile of toys.

She ran toward the living room, hoping she could make it to the front door. As she approached, she could see Jack sprawled out unconscious. The other man stepped from the side and grinned with yellow teeth. She nearly ran into him and he grabbed her. She clawed at his face until he yelped.

And then a cloth was pressed against her mouth by someone standing behind her and she realized that Big Jake must have recovered. She pawed at the hand in futility.

Strangely, the last thing that went through her mind was wondering which of them was Big Jake. Maybe both of them. They were probably brothers and their parents didn't have the sense to name them differently. To them, Big Jake was fine, so why let it go to waste on a single child.

Everything went dark.

CHAPTER 22

Drew Prescott was struggling to regain the faith he'd once so adamantly taught from a pulpit. The unfortunate incident at the casino, when he'd left his winnings to find Marilyn, had cost them his seed cash, not to mention their monthly expense money. He'd been deeply concerned about her at the time. But now that she was safe, back home and out of the devil's grasp – an easy reach in a place like the casino – he had something new to worry about. He was out of financial resources, save for a few dollars in change. Even that wouldn't be enough to make a faith-based turn of the roulette wheel to subsidize their income.

He knelt next to the bed while the sound of a sitcom Marilyn was watching made its way from the living room. She laughed with the audience while Drew wished he could be as carefree.

Lord, why did you choose to provide for us this way, he prayed. *You knew something like this would happen. Now I need to know what to do. You know how I hate asking for signs, but I need a little help.* "Please Lord," he said aloud. "What should I do?"

He kept quiet now, waiting for a word, waiting for an answer. But he felt prideful for putting the Lord on the spot. Was he so important that God should drop everything and do things his way? No. He would answer in His timing and in the way He chose.

Looking up now, he saw Marilyn standing in the doorway. She gave a bashful smile and he knew God had spoken.

"Come watch," she said.

Drew smiled. Her very presence restored his faith. "I'll be there in a moment."

"Promise?"

"I promise."

Drew looked at the ceiling and silently thanked the Lord for giving him Marilyn. But at the same time, he wondered how God would provide for them. More roulette numbers? No. He just couldn't bear the thought of going in one of those places again. He'd go back to the pulpit first, an idea he didn't relish.

As a pastor, he was supposed to have a heart for the congregation. But something had gone wrong. He hadn't lasted eighteen months since returning to the pulpit when he realized it simply wouldn't work. Maybe it was because the folks seemed superficial. Maybe it was because he'd changed after the illness. He wasn't sure, but nothing could bring back memories of his former life, a time when he'd been a shining example to the flock.

The deacons had been appalled at the thought he could leave his church; the one he'd created out of nothing – that is, until Drew reminded them that it wasn't *his* church, nor was he the one who had created it. Christ was fully capable of building his church whether Drew Prescott was at the pulpit or not.

At times he'd wondered what his life had been like before he'd been struck down with the fever. Certainly after his recovery, he'd felt incredibly alone and without purpose until Marilyn had appeared with her naive manner and tender heart.

Suddenly he could hear Marilyn laugh. She was watching I Love Lucy and Drew guessed the redhead must be in some kind of trouble. He got to his feet and went to go join her in the living room.

&

Navigating the dated pickup onto the Las Vegas strip, Jed gazed out the window at the ridiculously gaudy lights adorning every building he passed, certain that if he'd ever been here before he would have remembered it. There was something both sinister and enticing about the place, a kind of synergy of greed that made it easy to get caught up in the moment and a hope that the next chance would be a stepping-stone to fortune. Jed watched and *felt* the masses as they staggered around in a stupor, trying desperately to find their lucky break. For some it had simply become a lifestyle. They no longer anticipated the big win, but held to the faint flicker of hope growing slowly dimmer, never becoming fully extinguished.

Fortunately he would never be so naïve.

Jed pulled the pickup to a stop where the light had just turned red. An older woman made her way across in front of him with a purpose in her step that made him think she might be heading for a job she didn't dislike. She carried a large purse with a pair of straps lapped over her shoulder, pinning the bag under a stiff arm. It would take a considerable effort for a bag snatcher to struggle it away and he suspected it was the very reason she held it with such a passion.

He reached out to the woman with his mind and sensed she was on her way to the slot machines. Somehow he knew that she slept much of the day, getting up in the afternoon to have a bite to eat and watch talk shows before hitting the one-armed bandits, presumably playing the quarter slots, having figured out the odds could be beat if one were consistent. She'd sit in front of the same machine for hours as though mining for gold, certain that eventually the odds would turn in her favor and that the machine would cough up more than she'd fed it. And even though she was systematic and methodical about the process, she didn't discredit superstition just in case. Sometimes she'd kiss her finger and touch the machine, and other times she'd cross her heart, even though she wasn't Catholic. Never had been. She wasn't picky. She'd have chanted a verse from Confucius if she thought it would help. Eventually, when she felt she'd exhausted her luck, she'd go back home, fall asleep and start it all over again the next day.

As the woman finished her trek across the wide street, she disappeared onto a crowded sidewalk.

He reached down and felt the cool steel of the revolver to make sure it hadn't vanished into thin air as quickly as it had appeared.

"You and me buddy," Jed said, glancing over to the lifeless serpent. "Just a couple of snakes in the grass. We just need to find the right situation. No sense wasting all this talent on petty cash. You hearin' me, buddy? We need to be patient."

As he motored up the strip, searching and probing the minds of everyone he passed, he thought again of the strange voice he'd heard vibrating through the radio's static. Even a ham radio operator wouldn't have been able to turn the pickup's tuner into a two-way communication device. And nothing in his wildest imagination could explain how the revolver had appeared in the glove box. He shook his head, wondering again if perhaps it had been there the whole time and he'd somehow missed it.

Jed teeter-tottered back and forth, trying to decide if the gun had somehow materialized from thin air or not. But there were plenty of other oddities to occupy his mind, such as the fact he wasn't affected by the snake's venom, or the fact a voice had spoken to him over the radio.

The thing that disturbed him most wasn't what the voice had said, so much as what it hadn't said in response to his question.

Are there others?

Its lack of response was haunting. Finally, when he'd asked again, it spoke through quivering pulses, but the lack of conviction was obvious.

Jed was convinced there were others like him and that they could pose a problem. The very order of things was such that parallel powers grew together, coexisting in the same environment to keep things in balance. Seemingly, if one country grew all-powerful, another would spring up and strike back. It was the same in business, sports, crime, academics, and nearly every facet of life. He would be naïve to take the voice at its word and assume he was the only human alive to possess such abilities.

But keeping things equally balanced was better left to philosophers and politicians. Jed was no more interested in balance than he was in being a humanitarian. If others were like him, had somehow acquired his abilities, he would outsmart them. The one advantage he could count on was the ruthlessness that bubbled up from somewhere deep inside, from a past he could no longer remember.

He'd strike first when they didn't expect it, just like his snake-buddy had done when nailing his exposed arm. He'd hunt them down. If they knew he was coming, he'd find a way to sink his fangs into one of their other vulnerabilities.

As a dark blue Pontiac motored past in the right lane, Jed sensed something he'd been waiting patiently for, the presence of money. Plenty of money. As expected, the right situation had presented itself.

"Time to dance, buddy," he told his friend.

⁂

Jed let the Pontiac pass and then eased the pickup into the lane behind it. Getting too close wouldn't be a problem since he'd know if they became suspicious, a fringe benefit to his apparent psychic talents, he could simply track them with his mind instead of his eyes.

Finally, after several blocks, the car turned onto a side street, which led to the multilevel parking garage of a large casino, continuing past and into an older section of town where the streets were relatively abandoned.

The light turned yellow and the Pontiac rolled to a stop.

Securing the revolver, Jed leaped from the truck, approaching as the driver of the car turned his head. Jed pointed the gun at the back tire of the Pontiac and squeezed off a round, causing an ear-numbing *pop* to break crisply through the late afternoon air. Before the driver could do anything, Jed shot out a front tire as well, then used the butt of the handgun to smash in the front window on the driver's side. It exploded and splintered into a thousand tiny pieces, leaving only ragged fragments along the bottom.

The inside of the car was now alive with movement as three men – two in the front and one in the back – scrambled desperately to retrieve every manner of weapon stashed inside. Pushing the snub nose of the .357 against the head of the driver, Jed said, "Everyone relax."

Amazingly, it was as though he'd done it on countless occasions. In fact, it felt right, like he was meant to do such things.

"Bastard!" the man in the back seat was saying. "I knew we couldn't trust Ruckman."

"Shut up!" the man in the passenger-side seat told him. "You don't know nothin'."

"The hell I don't!"

"Like I said," Jed told them in a even voice, "Everybody calm down. Now. Give me the money."

"What'd I tell you," the man in the back said.

"Shut up!"

The driver said nothing, but his eyes looked as though they'd never close again.

Jed pulled the hammer back and said, "If you don't want the brains of your friend all over your clothes, I suggest you hand it over."

Two beads of sweat rolled down the face of the driver as he began to tremble. The man on the passenger side, a large Latino, held his hands out. "Okay, man," he said. "I'm just going to reach in my pocket to get my wallet. Okay?"

"You're funny," Jed said. "I like that. The world needs more humor. But you know what I mean. Cough up the briefcase."

"What briefcase? I don't know what –"

Jed moved the revolver to the left of the driver's head and squeezed a round, shattering the Latino's knee. The driver grabbed his ears. The Latino screamed in horror and pawed at a bloody leg. Though Jed had thought about simply pulling the trigger and finishing the driver to make a point, he'd decided that taking disciplinary action would be more appropriate. The Latino needed to be taught a lesson. It was as simple as that.

"Gentlemen," Jed said as though the encounter were nothing more than a business meeting. "My time is valuable and I'm sure yours is, too. Pass me the briefcase and we can avoid any further unpleasantness. Capeesh?"

The man in the back grabbed the briefcase from the floor and passed it across the seat to the driver, who took it stiffly and handed it to Jed. The Latino was making noises that sounded like a combination of groans and sobs.

"Thank you, gentlemen. You know, they probably would have stiffed you anyway. At least this way the money goes for a good cause. Plus, you should know by now that coke is bad for the kiddies. Shame on you."

"Go to Hell, you son of a bitch!" the Latino screamed.

Jed thought about doing his other kneecap for that outburst, but decided he'd probably be mad too if someone had disciplined him so severely. He wasn't an animal, after all.

"When was the last time you changed your shirt?" he asked the driver.

"Huh?" The driver looked confused.

"The shirt, Einstein. When did you last change it? I don't like the idea of wearing someone's B.O., if you know what I'm saying."

"This morning…I guess."

"Good. Take it off."

"Huh?"

"You're the bright one, aren't you? I said, 'Take. It. Off.'" Jed pulled back the hammer. The shirt was a bright red button-up, and fortunately, when the man handed it over, it didn't smell.

"Now everyone get out of the car, leave the hardware, and start walking that way," Jed said, pointing down the street.

"But what about him?" the driver said looking over at the Latino.

"He'll manage with a little help from you guys. Now move it."

"Bastard," the Latino mumbled under his breath.

The man in the back got out, opened the Latino's door and began helping him. He cried out while shifting his weight so Jed motioned for the driver to assist. Looking scared, the driver quickly made his way to the other side. Positioning himself to one side, they helped the Latino onto his good leg.

"Now start walking."

The Latino was at least six feet tall and clearly overweight. The other two were scrawny by comparison and it was a struggle to watch as they hobble-wobbled a few steps together, looking like they were in a strange five-legged race. The Latino groaned with each excruciating step and Jed watched until he was satisfied they couldn't easily make it back to the car for a weapon.

Jed took his time putting on the shirt and flipping open the briefcase to make sure he wasn't simply imagining the whole thing. Tidy stacks of one hundred dollar bills lined the interior.

He removed a couple of wads and thumbed through to make sure the dealers hadn't planned to stiff someone.

When he started up the pickup, he turned to the rattler and said, "See buddy. Much easier than the casinos. Things are looking up."

As he pulled away, his mind drifted back to the strange voice he'd heard on the radio. Now thinking about it, he realized that it had been attempting to tell him something about itself.

"Allow me to introduce myself."

When he'd asked it what had happened to him, the voice's answer was puzzling at best. *"You're here to do my bidding."* But regardless of his futile attempts to remember the past, he was nobody's servant. That was for damn sure.

Again, he wondered if there were others like him, as his mind stretched out searching. He could feel their presence now. There was a strong sensation that one of them was right here in Las Vegas. He'd need to be careful and probe with caution, unsure of how it worked. He suspected that if he could sense them with his mind, they could sense him as well.

As he took a chance and went deeper, trying to discover where the person was, the fuzzy notion divided, making him realize that there was more than one. Possibly three.

"Interesting," he said.

So far, nobody suspected Jared's tampering at Albatross, which he attributed to thoroughly covering his tracks. He'd created a process to remove his name from the mainframe listings each time he logged out. Nobody could know he'd been there. But he wasn't so naïve as to think he could go on forever, mucking about unchecked. It was only a matter of time until Sweeney called him on recent activities, possibly firing him if Sweeney suspected it was deliberate. For this reason Jared had begun to take precautionary measures, making the prospect of axing him less appealing. Stacking his deck with a few extra aces couldn't hurt, especially if they called his bluff.

So far, his extracurricular endeavors had gone unnoticed. Sweeney was busy with a mess Erin and Zack had gotten into, barely even acknowledging the other monitors. Jared didn't know what was going on and didn't care. He was having too much fun with gramps.

That is, until he heard the voice behind him and whipped his head around to see Sweeney standing over him.

"What the hell?"

Jared said the first thing that came into his mind. "He just started doing this stuff on his own," he said. "Really weird. I was about to come tell you."

But his boss didn't appear convinced.

CHAPTER 23

When he opened his eyes it reminded Jack of how he felt when he'd first come out of the coma. Confused. Disoriented. Where was he? Although the room was laid out similar to one in a hospital, it was decorated in quite a different manner with tan, textured walls and framed prints, and a television set in a richly carved, mahogany cabinet.

It was a hotel room.

Jack tried to climb up on one elbow to look around, only to fall back helplessly. Why was he here? He struggled to remember the last time he was awake and vaguely thought he'd been at the Destin condo for the weekend. And then slowly, painfully, as his body assimilated the surroundings, memories started to return, starting with Kristen's face: her round, pleasant features and lively eyes; her short, tasseled hair and the ornamental ring through her nose; her cocky, self-confident manner.

Then the events of the past few days started to unravel like the twine of a hideously tangled cat's cradle. Lynchman. Hasselbaum. *The mob.* Of course. The mob had caught up with him and that's why he was here. But why hadn't they simply killed him? Wasn't that what they did to people like him? Or had they kept him alive in order to watch him squirm when they sent a shiny steel slug through his forehead.

Whatever the reason, he was now at their mercy.

By the time he was able to prop himself up enough to look around, the door opened and in walked a man with a thick neck and the grim look of a mortician who seemed vaguely familiar.

"Let's go," were his guest's only words. From the look of him, Jack didn't think he'd take 'no' for an answer. Kristen stumbled into view in the hallway, being held by another thug.

They were led to an elevator, where a groggy Kristen looked apprehensive about entering in. She walked gingerly to the very center as though her hundred and twenty pounds would snap the cables.

The short ride to the next floor seemed painfully long. When Jack chanced a glance at Kristen, he could see the fear in her eyes. Jack felt fear, but the guilt hadn't left him. Who knew how many innocent lives were going to be lost over this ordeal, and apparently all because of his plan to start a business?

When the elevator doors rolled back, Jack half expected to witness a firing squad. Instead, they were led into a lavishly decorated room, thick velvet curtains, massive panoramic windows, and ridiculously high, vaulted ceilings. Seated on a black leather sofa, was a small man in his late forties, wearing slacks and a silk button-up shirt, together with enough rings and chains to rival any pimp. His hair was slicked down in a proper 50's fashion statement, while his arms were draped side to side across the back of the couch.

Jack and Kristen sat down hesitantly on a leather sofa opposite their host and looked across at the man who was about to dictate whether or not they lived. The two thugs left the room.

Jack didn't know what to expect but was taken aback when the man opened a case of cigars on the coffee table and offered him one.

"No thanks," he said.

"Pity," the man said as he snipped off the end and lit up for himself. "There's nothing like a good Cuban. Trust me."

He looked over at Kristen. "I'd ask the lady, but I've never met a woman who'd accept one of these bad boys."

Closing his eyes, he took a long ecstatic drag and blew out a perfectly sculptured ring, dissipating into a shapeless fog that reminded Jack of his own life.

"Name's Houston," he said. "Eli Houston. I already know your names. Glad you could join me. I'd ask how you like Vegas, but then…you've already been here, haven't you?"

"I don't remember."

"Oh, that's right," Eli said as he puffed on his Cuban. "Your little accident. I almost forgot. It's a damn shame, if you ask me. It would have been far more interesting if you could remember our last meeting. It would lend a certain poetic justice to the atmosphere. Don't you think?"

Neither Jack nor Kristen said anything. After all, what was the point?

"I'm not going to lie to you," Eli said. "What you did to me was unspeakable. If I could have gotten the book back quickly you wouldn't be sitting here right now. Are you following me?"

Jack nodded.

"Now that we have it back, I'm faced with the unpleasant task of determining what to do with you."

"She has nothing to do with this," Jack said. "Why don't you let her go?"

"*Au contraire*," Eli said as he stared Jack down with his beady eyes. "She knows as much as you do, which is far too much. It would be bad form if I didn't treat the lady with as much respect as I did you. I might get the feminists all over me if I'm not careful." He chuckled at his own cleverness, as though the whole confrontation was some sort of game and he was the star player.

"But she didn't do anything," Jack countered. "She just got caught in the middle because of the trucker. You can do what you want with me. Just let Kristen go."

At the mention of the trucker, Jack thought he saw the slightest bit of confusion enter the man's eyes. But it quickly melted into his former even stare.

"You don't seem to understand, Mr. Stuart. In case you haven't noticed, I'm in charge here. I can do what I want with either of you. How she came by her information is not important."

Yet somehow, Jack suspected that it *was* important. Immensely.

"I've worked long and hard to get where I am," Eli sounded sincere, but his eyes sparkled as though he were trying to suppress a smile. "I decide what happens to the girl, just like I decide what's going to happen to you."

Something wasn't right. Jack could sense it. Whether to kill time or see if he were only imagining things, he said, "I understand you have us where you want us. I also know you're ignoring the fact that I was the one who hurt you. Not Kristen. I just want to know one thing: How did your men get to the trucker so fast? How is that possible?"

There it was again. That look of confusion.

"You'd be surprised at how efficient our network is," Eli said without conviction.

"So, you overheard the conversation?" Jack asked, sensing that he touched a button that he might want to press long and hard.

"Well, yeah. We're always listening, you know. Watching."

"But how did you do it? I mean, within an hour you had someone there. Were you following him the whole time?"

Eli suddenly grew angry. "I ask the questions. Understand?"

"Of course," Jack said, glancing at Kristen for the first time since they'd sat down. She was wide-eyed, seemingly content to let Jack take the brunt of the conversation.

"Back to the matter at hand. Look," Eli said, mildly. "Between you and me, I'm getting too old for this crap. I'm willing to let bygones be bygones, cut our losses and move on. Now that we have the book, there's no way you can hurt us. Even if you went to the feds now, they'd want proof, which you no longer have. Besides, I know where you live."

Jack and Kristen looked at each other again for understanding.

"So, what exactly are you saying?" Jack asked.

Eli took a long drag on his cigar, only this time blew it straight across at Jack.

"I'm in a good mood today. You're free to go. Just don't screw me again or I won't hesitate to pay you an unfortunate visit. Am I making myself clear?"

Jack shook his head in bewilderment. "What about the money we stole. You're telling me you're just willing to forgive and forget? Because if you are, I don't believe it."

Eli ran a hand across his greased hair. "Pocket change," he said with a shrug. "Keep it. The family makes more money in a day than you stole. Don't push it or I may change my mind."

Jack looked disbelievingly at Kristen and found that she was glaring at Eli, her eyes narrowing as if she was about to zero in for the kill.

And she did.

"You're not the man Randy told me about," she steamed. "What is this? What are we doing here?"

Eli brushed his pant leg with one hand, avoiding her gaze. She was right, Jack realized. She'd pegged him and now he was squirming.

"You don't even know who Randy is, do you?" she demanded.

Eli stood up. "This meeting is over. If you don't want me to change my…" He stopped and put a hand to his chin, looking nearly like an Egyptian statue with his gold chains. "Look. I've been out of the loop lately. The business is mostly run by the young and ambitious. I'm nothing more than a spokesperson anymore."

"Bullshit!" Kristen snapped. "I'm not going anywhere until you tell us who you really are and what's going on?"

Eli looked around, as though hoping someone might come to his rescue.

Jack was baffled. He had thought her silence was a result of fear, but now, apparently, she was about to explode.

"What did you do to Jack's family? Huh? Lynchman?" Kristen was on a roll. "Explain to us how you got the book back? You probably have no idea what was *in* the book, do you? Or tell us about the poker game? Come on. We're waiting."

"I didn't hurt nobody," Eli told her defensively. "I don't know how the hell they got the book back. Like I said, the others do most…oh, hell, I don't need to put up with this crap. Why don't you just go?"

"You're nothing but a fraud," Kristen said, crossing her arms over her chest.

"What about my family?" Jack asked.

"Your family is fine," Eli snarled. "Don't you get it? Everything is like it should be. Nothing's wrong. Go back to your lives. And for God's sake, don't worry so damn much about it. That's how this whole mess got started in the first place. There *was* no poker game. There *is* no mob. Just get on with it. Tell them what you want and they'll give it to you. Don't you see?"

If Jack had been baffled before, he was totally lost now. Just when he thought he'd plumbed the depths of confusion, something happened to make him dive even deeper. First there was his amnesia. Then the revelation about the poker game and scheme to start a business. Now he was being told it had never even happened.

"Tell…who…what? What are you talking about?" she said.

"Somehow I know I'm going to regret this," Eli said, going to the desk to scribble something. "I've already said way too much, but I don't care anymore."

Jack stared at what appeared to be a phone number, complete with area code.

"What's this?" he demanded.

"I can't say any more," Eli told him. "Call that number. Maybe you'll get somewhere with it. It's all I can offer. Way more than I should have."

Eli was transformed. Instead of a powerful don, he now seemed like nothing more than a two-bit gambler, making excuses for himself, unable to look either of them square in the eye.

"I'm not leaving until you explain," Kristen declared.

"Suit yourself," the man said. "You can grow old sitting there as far as I'm concerned. Does Albatross Life Corporation in Scottsdale, Arizona, mean anything to you?"

"No. Why?" Jack said.

"I didn't think it would. With the amnesia and all. Just call the number."

"Let's get out of here," Jack told Kristen.

The man with the thick neck escorted them to the elevator. Within moments they found themselves in the middle of the casino and Jack could barely hear himself think over the noise.

"Let's get out of here," Jack said pushing his way toward the main exit.

Once outside, the two stood looking up and down the strip as though they were a pair of lost children, unsure of where their parents had gone.

"So what do we do now?" Kristen asked.

"I don't know," he said, checking to make sure he still had his wallet. "But at least they didn't leave us without resources. I don't know about you but I feel disoriented. I don't even know what day this is."

Jack studied his watch. "Same day. And I have a quarter to five. Last time I checked in Destin it was just after noon. Somehow they managed to get us here in a little over four hours."

"Isn't it a couple hours earlier here than in Florida?" Kristen asked.

"Yes, but my watch would still be on Florida time."

"Then how did we get here so fast?" Kristen asked.

"By plane, I imagine," Jack told her. "Even so, they made record time, must have been a private jet or something."

Kristen suddenly looked ill. He quickly put his arm around her as she began to sag.

"Don't zone out on me," Jack said. "I need your help, here. Remember? I need you."

"Isn't there some other way?" she asked him. "Did it have to be an airplane?"

It was the last thing she said before her knees buckled.

Scooping her up in his arms, Jack carried her to a nearby bench and put two fingers to her neck, hoping she didn't have something terribly wrong with her. He could feel the steady drumming of her pulse. Her chest rose and fell with each breath. Just as he was about to shout to someone to call for the paramedics, she opened her eyes and smiled. Jack jumped up, suddenly feeling awkward.

"You okay?" he asked.

"Better."

"Just glad to see you're still with us," Jack said. He was surprised at the extent of his concern for this girl who was, after all, a stranger to him. For all her quirks about cars and planes, and perhaps even elevators, she was spunky, an enigma of fear and confidence, wrapped up in a punk-like package. "I think we better get you to a doctor."

"Kristen sat up and adjusted her skirt. "No thanks," she said. "I'm okay."

"Maybe you need something to eat."

"I said I'm all right."

"It's been hours since we've eaten. If they flew us here…"

Kristen reached up and put an index finger over Jack's lips. "I'd rather not talk about anything that reminds me of…you know," she said and pointed up at the sky. "If you want to get something to eat, fine. Just let me believe we came by car. Okay?"

"I'll never mention it again. My lips are sealed," Jack said. "Now, let's get something to eat."

But the phone number that Eli Houston had given Jack began to tickle his curiosity.

CHAPTER 24

A casino in Las Vegas was one of the few places you could still get a steak dinner for under ten bucks. Earnings from casino restaurants were paltry compared to the card-dealing, dice-rolling, wheel-spinning industry that regularly paid cash to build huge edifices, attracting thick wallets, fat purses, and anyone with a greedy bent.

Suddenly ravenous, Jack and Kristen crossed the street to another hotel fronted by a huge volcano. The whole city seemed to be a fantasy of illusions. Certainly nobody driving the strip would believe the volcano were real. It was nothing more than a façade. Just like Eli Houston, the head of the mob he'd supposedly stole an incriminating book from. The man had turned out to be a fake. But for what purpose? The only hope of making sense of what was going on rested in a piece of paper folded in Jack's pocket. He reached in and touched it, afraid it might vanish. He was famished and would use it to make a call once he could think clearly again.

They made their way into the Mirage – a little city within a city, with its restaurants, shops, theaters, atrium, pools, and various other amenities – through the lobby, which was a replica of a rain forest with a massive aquarium, and past realistic looking tropical undergrowth. Casino sounds were never far, attempting to entice anyone within earshot.

They found a darkened restaurant with a South Sea theme where they were shown to a booth.

Jack felt exhausted, having never fully recovered from the forced nap. Every joint and muscle felt like jelly and it even took some effort to keep his lungs puffing air. As soon as they finished their meal and made some calls, he would secure a couple of rooms so they could rest up for whatever was still to come – something he dared not think about in his present state of weakness.

"So what's going on here?" Kristen asked him after they finished ordering.

Jack didn't answer. How could he? Even though the question was probably rhetorical, he wanted to be able to tell her exactly what was happening, why they'd been brought to this place, why she'd been told about a poker game that possibly never happened, why a man had been killed for telling her about the game, only to appear a couple days later at the same motel they'd stayed at. He wished he could make sense of the amnesia that haunted him when he stared at himself in the mirror, or answer the looming question as to why he was sitting in a restaurant booth in Las Vegas instead of at home with his family. And the thing that he wanted to understand the most was if his family was truly all right like Eli had said. If so, he'd be spared a ton of guilt mileage. But it wouldn't change the fact he didn't want to be there. For that, he feared, even the right information couldn't cure.

"Why would he – they – whoever, even bother to bring us here?" she asked. "It's just so confusing. And what do you think he meant when he said, 'Tell them what you want'? That *is* what he said isn't it? Who do you think he meant?"

Kristen wasn't helping. As much as the girl was growing on him, he just wanted to eat a nice dinner like a normal person; pretend for a few minutes that everything was all right. Instead she insisted on talking.

"Look," he said. "I don't know any more than you do. All right?"

"Sorry!" she said sarcastically. "I'm just trying to figure it out, unlike some people who'd rather stick their head up their ass and hope it all goes away."

"We'll talk about it," he assured her wearily. "But just not now. All I want is to enjoy a meal and not have to think. Is that too much to ask?"

Kristen shrugged. "It's your dime."

When the waitress brought Jack's New York strip, he carved it carefully and deliberately, savoring each bite as though it were his last, desperately trying not to think about anything except enjoying the buttery flavor of medium-rare beef. But Kristen's very presence, seated pretentiously across from him was a constant reminder that all was not right under the desert sun in

Las Vegas, Nevada; or for that matter, anywhere else in his mind-baffling life.

Kristen managed to respect his request by not speaking for the duration of the meal, which wasn't difficult since she was busily taking advantage of a roast beef sandwich while stuffing intermittent bites of chef's salad, drenched in blue cheese dressing, into her mouth. Jack found himself wondering how a girl of her size could scarf that way and maintain her figure. But he suspected the truth involved sleepless nights in the cold while her stomach growled in retaliation.

Tell them what you want.

It didn't make any sense. And Jack soon realized it was impossible not to try and analyze what Eli had said. Not only that, but the rum punch he was sipping was starting to turn him philosophical. Certainly the man hadn't been referring to some benevolent group of divine beings watching over everyone.

As Jack considered the only life he could remember, he thought again about how easy things had been for him. He was a V.P. and partner in a software company with a substantial salary. Unlike most people who hacked and slashed their way up the corporate ladder, he'd woken up and found himself perched safely on the second rung from the top. Not only that, but the position was really an easy one. Show up, make a few decisions, take as much time off as needed, and everyone was happy. There weren't any rivals nipping at his heels and he felt no need to conquer that last rung.

Then there was his home life with his plastic wife, mother to Amanda and Justin, the poster children for Better Homes and Gardens. Everything was – well, wonderful.

Tell them what you want.

But the antithesis of his own life sat directly across from him, eating salad like there was no tomorrow. How this Harvard dropout had ended up on the street. Perhaps Eli's statement didn't apply to her. Jack was the one at the center of the supposed poker game. Kristen might yet be an innocent bystander who'd managed to get caught in the middle.

As he savored the last bite of steak, Kristen having apparently reached her limit, put down her fork down and said, "Okay. Ready to talk?"

Miraculously, Jack, indeed, felt stronger. More coherent. Getting some nutrition in his system was just what he needed to feel reenergized. Things weren't as bad as they'd seemed twenty minutes ago and he was ready to face their dilemma head on.

"Before I do anything else…" Jack hesitated. "I need to find out if what Eli said was true."

"The phone number?"

"No. I mean my family."

"Oh," Kristen said.

Jack didn't want to read too much into the way she said it. She had to be tired. That was all.

He looked around. "There must be a phone around here. I'll be right back."

He found a payphone in the short hallway leading to the restrooms. When he dialed his home number he half expected to get the same hollow voice he'd received when last calling Lynchman's home. Instead, he heard Maggie's sleepy voice.

"Jack? Sweetie?" she said, pleasantly. "Are you all right? I tried to call the condo several times but you didn't answer."

He didn't know what to say. Whatever words he chose wouldn't matter, he was sure of it. Certainly he had no intention of trying to explain the whole mess.

"I'm in Vegas."

There was a long pause.

"Las Vegas? Nevada?"

"That's the one."

"What are you doing there, honey?"

"Actually," he said. "I really don't know."

There was another pause while she processed the information. Maggie had never been a quick study.

"Please come home," she said finally and now her voice was more serious. "We need to get you some help. We'll get through this, whatever it is you're going through."

"I'm here with a girl."

This time the silence was deafening. Jack's heart pattered into high gear. He hadn't meant to tell her, he told himself. It had just come out. He couldn't bear to hear her ramble on about how they'd get through a dilemma she couldn't possibly understand, when he knew that if he did go back to Atlanta, she'd be there to greet him with a picture-perfect smile and never say another word about what happened while he'd been gone.

"Jack?"

"What?"

Her voice seemed to quiver slightly when she said, "I don't understand."

Was her façade starting to crack? He wondered. For once, she sounded almost *genuine*.

"It's not what you think," he told her.

"Well, you don't have to worry about us," she told him. "We're holding up. The kids are fine. Please get whatever it is you're doing out of your system and then come home. But not a moment sooner. Understand?"

Clearly there were no cracks in Maggie's walls. He wondered how he could have been so silly as to even consider the possibility.

"I understand," he said.

"Fine then. We'll talk later." She might as well have been signing off with her interior decorator.

"Wait. I just have one question," Jack said. "Have you seen any strange vehicles parked out front; around the neighborhood? Anyone unexpected come to the door in the last couple of days? Any strange phone calls?"

"Get some help, honey," she told him. "Because I don't have a clue what you're talking about."

⁂

It was strange how you could be somewhere one minute and suddenly halfway across the country the next. Kristen deliberately avoided the implications for fear of going down again. The thought, the very idea, she could have been inside one of *those things* forced a chilly trek up her spine. Airplanes were the epitome of how deranged mechanical beasts could become, stretching out their horrid wings.

Kristen used her fork to play with the remainder of the chef's salad, shoving egg bits to one side, drenched lettuce leaves to the other. When the waitress dropped by to see if they needed anything else, the sudden thought that Jack might have deserted her again caused her apprehension. If he'd left her now she'd have no way to pay for the meal. No doubt be arrested and then they'd discover she was the one they were looking for in connection with the murder of Randy, the trucker. Then she relaxed, remembering again that Randy hadn't really been murdered, and Jack wouldn't leave her again. Not now, she mused.

The only thing she could be absolutely sure of at the moment was that her stomach was good and full, a state she'd lacked since she'd managed to cop a dinner the night before leaving Atlanta.

"Well?" she said when Jack finally returned.

"He was right. My wife answered. Everything appears to be fine. Not only that, but I phoned Lynchman. He'd stepped out, but his wife answered. The only thing I can figure is I must have dialed the wrong number before."

Kristen was now working on segregating the remaining ham pieces into another corner of the bowl. "Uh huh. Whatever."

"What's that supposed to mean?"

"Nothing."

"It's not nothing. What is it?"

"You're being played. That's all. For that matter, we're both being played. Nothing makes any sense."

"So what am I supposed to do?"

"How should I know? But I wouldn't be so quick to think everything's fine. That's all. For all we know Lynchman – hell, even your wife…Oh, never mind."

She watched how Jack would respond at the mention of his wife. Would he feel the need to defend the woman? But he didn't react.

"Well, I'll tell you what I'm going to do right now," Jack said. "Get us a couple of rooms. Sleep on it."

Kristen shook her head.

"What is it now?"

"Are you rich or something? Who has money to throw away?"

"What? You want us to curl up on a park bench? Spend the night on the streets?"

"It wouldn't be the first time," Kristen said.

Jack's expression suddenly changed. "Sorry. I didn't mean to…"

"Forget it. There's nothing to be sorry about," Kristen said. "It's not as bad as you think. But, you know, they *do* have rooms with two beds. You don't have to get us each a room?"

Jack fidgeted with his napkin, looking uncomfortable.

"What's the matter?" Kristen said. "Think I might bite? Don't flatter yourself."

Jack pulled the phone number from his pocket and unfolded it carefully.

Kristen wasn't trying to seduce him or anything. But having slept in malls while stealing food, the idea of getting *two* rooms seemed like overkill. Still, the notion of staying close while they slept was somehow comforting.

"What do you think?" Jack asked.

"About the phone number?"

"Yeah."

She studied him staring at the paper. "I think you're afraid to call."

"Not to call," he said. "Of what we'll find."

"*If* we find," Kristen countered.

"If we find," Jack agreed.

The waitress returned with his credit card and he signed the slip.

"No sense waiting," he said.

Jack slid out of the booth. This time Kristen followed him to the payphone.

"And the room?" Kristen asked.

"I'll get *two* rooms. Like I said."

CHAPTER 25

Right from the start there had been problems. Seemingly, one insurmountable obstacle led to another and this last one was an unspeakable mishap. The very thought caused Dr. Malcolm Petrov to grit his teeth so hard that he feared he might grind them to dust. Who would have done such a thing? Though he had made a point of overseeing the project from a distance, letting the monitors take their own initiative when a little nudging was required, he felt wholly responsible and now nearly considered turning in his resignation. The phone call had been the last thorn in his already wounded side, one more pain in his throbbing neck. It was no wonder he couldn't remember the last time he'd had a decent night's sleep.

It was odd to him that a future so bright had turned so dark. Sitting in this very office many years earlier, Dr. Hunter and he had been giddy with excitement at the prospect of building a scientific organization that might become a cornerstone of modern society. Between their combined knowledge of genetics and backed by research in The Human Genome Project – a massive undertaking sponsored by the U.S. Department of Energy and the National Institute of Health to identify the makeup of every human gene – they'd put together an ambitious business plan that included an ultimate goal that had been sought since the beginning of time. The only difference was that at this stage of human existence, the likelihood of success was altogether feasible, even probable.

A fountain of youth.

To live forever – or at least to live longer – was within reach, a tiptoe stretch away from reality. The only thing that had stood between them and possibly the single greatest contribution to the human race was to raise some needed venture capital, a trivial matter if they could make investors believe such an achievement as they had in mind were attainable. That had only been one of numerous obstacles. But after many heart-wrenching years of confronting tight fists and closed minds, nearly losing everything they'd worked for in the process, including family and friends, the pair of scientists had finally prevailed and Albatross Life Corporation had been born.

Basing their headquarters in Scottsdale, Arizona, they had begun preclinical testing of what they coined *Project Methuselah,* a project which, if the early stages were successful, might revolutionize gene therapy, bringing practical application to decades of theory and research. Up to that point, gene therapy had involved intense, costly testing and targeted the removal of disease-causing traits in individuals. As usual, insurance companies had been sluggish to cover such treatments, resulting in even higher costs for the isolated few that could afford it.

Project Methuselah had been a far different approach, directly attacking the issue of aging, therefore eliminating the need for expensive analysis. Only in rare instances where a show-stopping trait was involved, rendering Methuselah's gene therapy useless by virtue of a disease that blocked its positive affects, would the candidate need to seek more traditional therapy. But the percentage of people who would display this anomaly was estimated to be staggeringly low, in the neighborhood of one in two hundred thousand.

For years the scientific community had recognized the existence of longevity genes (primarily apoE, ACE, HLA-DR, and PAI-1), but it was Dr. Hunter and Dr. Petrov's intensive study of chromosome four while at Yale University that had led to the breakthrough idea that an ecumenical aging therapy was possible and could one day be harmlessly administered to the general population. Because of its widespread application, costs for such treatment would start high, but drop dramatically as methods were refined and pharmaceutical manufacturing increased. Since they were first of all scientists, it was their ultimate desire that every person alive have the opportunity to take advantage of the treatment, whether living on government-assisted income or the CEO at a major corporation. It would be a gift to the human race and no one should be denied. The only reason someone wouldn't benefit from the treatment was if they, themselves, chose not to for personal reasons.

But the theories were simply that. Theories. After Yale, it would be another nine years of floating on government grants before the doctors would have research results sufficient to validate their theories and prove the feasibility of an application. During this time there had been many obstacles blocking their progress. It was one thing to induce the longevity genes into a subject. Effective methods had even been devised that would deliver the genes to their target cells. The problem was activation, providing a condition whereby the modified cells could produce the proper protein rather than allowing the longevity genes lie dormant within the host.

The breakthrough finally came when Dr. Hunter had come down with a virus and was out sick for an entire week during their most crucial research. They'd successfully administered and delivered longevity genes in a test group of field mice that were known to have life spans of only nine months. At that time they'd spent over a year on the issue of activation and were in the middle of one of Dr. Petrov's latest hypotheses that candidates with certain blood types would be more likely to allow self-activation when the proper combination of genes was applied.

The hypothesis proved to be untrue. But when Dr. Hunter suddenly phoned from his sickbed, excited in spite of his illness, the two doctors knew they were on the right track. The solution seemed paradoxical in nature like so many things in science and medicine. Just like antibiotics – the administering of one form of bacteria to kill another, more virulent form – Hunter's illness had given him the idea that introducing a virus could actually agitate the genes, forcing the cells of a body's immune system to react. Within a few months they had discovered the perfect virus, one that gave them the most consistent results possible.

Once the longevity genes had been signed, sealed and delivered to the target cells, trace amounts of Eschericai coli (E. coli), administered to the candidates, would activate the genes in host cells in 97% of all cases. It was a brilliant bit of research, proving beyond doubt their thesis was correct when the field mice outlived their contemporaries by two to three times. Immediately they had begun creating the comprehensive business plan that would ultimately become Albatross Life Corporation.

Ironically enough, the same stubborn investors who had provided the initial obstacle were responsible for the second. The doctors had hoped to have free rein in the decision-making process, holding the majority vote. But the investors saw things differently. In spite of the doctor's determined efforts, they were only able to retain about twelve percent of the shares each, which when combined, failed to amount to one quarter of the company. They had justified the compromise by agreeing amongst themselves that, without their research, the company would be worthless. Surely the investors would see things their way when it came time to vote on important issues.

They were wrong.

The most vocal investors – those who had the most capital on the line – followed their progress carefully and injected yet another obstacle into the mix.

There were two approaches to gene therapy: *somatic* and *germ-line*. Somatic involved the modification of mature cells, which meant changes would not be passed on to future generations. Somatic was treatment for a single individual. Germ-line therapy, on the other hand, was directed at egg or sperm cells and intended to affect generations to come. Using germ-line, parents were no longer limited to passing on a monetary inheritance, but the potentially greater gift of a long, healthy life, a suitable exchange, given the fact monetary inheritances would become less frequent when people lived longer.

It only made sense to the good doctors that their efforts be used in the most globally beneficial manner and that meant germ-line. The investors would have nothing of it, however, insisting on the use of somatic therapy. Many were political activists and even sought to lobby for laws preventing the germ-line approach, justifying their positions by hiding behind a wall of moral indignation, claiming such treatments were inconceivable acts of playing God.

Dr. Petrov knew better. They were merely preserving revenues from future generations, an insurance policy to line their already cushy pockets. Outvoted by a landslide, the doctors swallowed their ideals and focused on improving the treatments and filing their IND (Investigational New Drug Application) with the FDA.

Acceptance of this first stage would open the door to begin testing on human candidates. The vote to use somatic therapy did little to quench their enthusiasm, even though they'd have to administer it to the human race one at a time.

Things appeared to finally be falling into place. But their troubles weren't over just yet. Not by a long shot.

∽

The doctors thrived on preclinical testing. Research was their forte but they were soon bombarded with the harsh realities of bringing a new drug to market. They'd simply been riding the silver lining of a dream, nursing an if-you-build-it-they-will-come mentality, thinking everything would merely work out once they'd proved their theories and offered their findings to the world. But the world was a tough place for a dream.

Though they'd seen the statistics, the doctors hadn't really *seen* them until they were about to become party to them. Where as details like the fact it costs a company approximately $359 million and twelve years to bring a new drug from laboratory to shelf were merely annoyances before, they now seemed staggering. Only five in 5,000 preclinical compounds made it to human testing. And out of the five that actually did, only one of those would ultimately be approved.

It was too much reality. Not only that, but they received one rejection after another when the IND was repeatedly denied, ironically being shut down by the same government that had funded their early research. As meticulous as they were in documenting their findings, passing the IND was supposed to be easy. It was at this point that the doctors had begun to suspect that more was going on behind closed doors in Washington than merely business as usual. Anti-aging drugs were a hotbed of controversy and they decided it would be a difficult road, all the way to clinical treatment.

Whereas Dr. Petrov had a great deal of patience, Dr. Hunter did not. As far as he was concerned, at the rate things were going, they'd be forced to administer the gene therapy on themselves in order to live long enough for the FDA to grant final approval.

Even though he was only attempting to make light of their predicament, the notion wasn't completely out of the question. At least from Dr. Hunter's perspective, that is.

"I'll be damned if I'm going to let the government invalidate our research with one sweep of the pen," Hunter had said. At the time, Petrov hadn't understood the implications. But over the weeks that followed, he began to observe a transformation in his colleague, starting with his suddenly beginning to stay late, accompanied by evidence that his stamina was on the rise. Before long, Hunter's nocturnal activities had become obvious. Petrov confirmed his suspicions when he found syringes that hadn't been used on the test rodents. The complete therapy involved a three-week regimen of alternating injections. Judging from the quantity of discarded syringes, Hunter was nearing completion of the treatments.

If the other obstacles were difficult to overcome, the genetics duo was about to face one that would be impassable. Decades of study, research, and visualizing a better world – one in which people regularly lived 200 years – was about to come to a piston-seizing halt. Hunter began losing focus, as well as making off-the-wall statements that puzzled Petrov. But it wasn't until the man strolled into his office one morning, closed the door and shades, removed a revolver from his desk, placed the barrel in his mouth and made jelly of the brilliant gray matter; in an instant, destroying half a team that might have been shoo-in candidates for the Nobel Prize.

Nobody had been sure whether the self-administered treatments from Project Methuselah were to blame or the man had simply become too discouraged over their inability to make it past the FDA's rigid first stage. Nobody cared. The FDA performed an investigation and shut the project down. That was that. All their research culminated into zilch. Nothing. Nada.

The investors had wanted blood and since Petrov was the only one left, his looked as good as anyone's. In a desperate attempt to salvage Albatross and save face, Petrov had pulled something he'd been keeping secret since the day they'd started raising venture capital, out of his sleeve.

Plan B.

Though it was light-years from the gift they'd hoped to give humanity, and though it could only benefit a select few, the project had helped to appease the investors and stood a marginal chance of turning a profit. Petrov scoured the world to find the best people – a lean but crack team of scientists – using the remaining funds earmarked for Methuselah to make Plan B a reality. Since the scheme didn't involve a new drug, FDA complications were avoided.

The new plan – named Project Alice, in honor of Petrov's daughter – had gone smoothly for over a year when the problems began. Because it was still in the early stages, Dr. Petrov didn't think he could live through another disaster such as that which had happened with Methuselah. Rather than following in the footsteps of his partner, he would simply deliver a letter to the board, offering his condolences to the years of fruitless efforts and bowing out as gracefully as possible. Let someone else take over and die young – an ironic side effect, given the mission.

The phone call was the last straw. Candidates weren't supposed to know he existed, that any of them existed. The team only watched from afar to make sure everything went smoothly. But they'd discovered that people who couldn't remember their past always sought it out. It was especially true when they sensed that their lives were a fabricated lie. Even though they weren't supposed to, they *just knew* something wasn't right.

Moments earlier, Mark Sweeney, the monitor's team leader, had reluctantly paid him a visit, explaining that their latest plan had only partially worked out. His team was continuing to work on it, but it appeared the subjects in question had become suspicious. Petrov was about to follow Sweeney to the observation pit when his phone rang.

He sighed and shook his head. "What now?" he said.

❧

"And…what do we expect to accomplish?" Kristen inquired, following Jack to the rack of phones.

"Your guess is as good as mine. Anything would be better than nothing."

He held the paper close to his face in the dim hallway, studying the area code. Though he couldn't place it, the number consisted of ten digits like a U.S. number. Picking up the receiver, Jack caught himself holding his breath as he keyed in his calling card number, followed by the digits Eli had scribbled down. Even Kristen seemed nervous as he listened to the *bdrrr…bdrrr…bdrrr* on the other end.

For all he knew he could be calling the devil or Santa Claus, so it failed to surprise Jack when a man with a distinct Russian accent answered.

"Petrov," the man said. "What is it?"

Jack didn't know what to say. He'd been so focused on his New York strip and trying not to think about the situation that he now felt unprepared. What would he ask? He felt like a contestant on *Who Wants To Be A Millionaire* with thirty seconds to ask a question.

"Hello? Who is this?" the man demanded, beginning to sound more than a little agitated.

"My name is Jack Stuart," he said. "I was told you could help."

A long pause.

"Who gave you this number?" he demanded. "This is unlisted."

"Please, if you'll let me explain."

But the man was more interested in finding out who'd violated his cherished phone number than in what Jack had to say. And he wasn't timid about saying as much.

"A name," he demanded. "Who gave you the number?"

Jack thought about mentioning Eli Houston, but decided he wouldn't violate the man's trust even though he hadn't made any promises.

"That's not important."

"I'll be the judge of that. Now who was it? I demand an answer this instant."

"Would you shut up about the damn number," Jack bellowed. "I need some help."

"I'm hanging up now," Petrov warned him. "And don't call me again."

"No, wait! Don't hang up," he pleaded. "Do you know anything about Albatross Life Corporation?" It was the only thing he could think of. Eli had spoken the name as if he should have known what it meant. Though he didn't, he suspected it was somehow important.

Another pause.

"What did you say your name was?"

"Jack Stuart."

"I know that name," the man said.

"From Atlanta. I was told you were someone who could help."

"No!" he heard the man say softly and told someone on the other end to leave and close the door, that he'd be with them shortly.

Seconds ticked by and Jack felt something very bad or very good was about to happen. He wasn't sure which but braced himself for either case. Kristen found her fingernails and was working them over, eyes big as cookies.

Finally. "Jack Stuart from Atlanta," the man said. "You have a girl with you." It was a statement. Not a question. As though the man were reading his plight from the glowing blue screen of a computer.

Jack looked at Kristen and slowly nodded. "That's right."

The man cursed although Jack couldn't understand the Russian words.

"Mr. Stuart," Petrov said unctuously. "Something has gone terribly wrong, sir. You should never have been given this number."

"It's a little late…"

"I agree. It's too late. So here you are," the Russian said.

"What can you tell me?"

"Nothing at the moment. I need to be briefed first. I'll have to get back to you."

Jack asked how long it would take. Should they give him the number to the payphone and wait for a call?

"No," Petrov said. "We'll phone but it may take some time."

"I don't know where we'll be," Jack told him hastily, afraid of sliding back down the slippery slope he'd just struggled up.

"After I check into a hotel I can phone you with the number. I don't want to miss your call."

"Don't worry, Mr. Stuart," the man said. "We'll know where you are and how to find you. You can be sure of that."

The line went dead and Jack felt unsatisfied, with more questions and no answers.

CHAPTER 26

He parked the pickup in an alley behind the hotel, tossed the revolver in the glove box no reason to alert security – and grabbed the briefcase full of cash. He'd soon acquire more suitable living arrangements, but first he needed to take care of some pressing business. Pay a visit to an old friend he never met.

As he slipped off the pickup's seat and pushed the door closed, he could feel the activity coming from inside the massive building, countless electrical pulses surging through every corridor and wall, culminating into a trunk of information that made its way out the back door where he stood. His senses were becoming more acute, as he became more in tune with his surroundings and increasingly felt exactly what was going on in any of the hundreds of rooms or at any of the many gambling stations. Only one pocket of space held a dark spot where no information was available and that was at the very top where he was headed.

They were no doubt hiding behind their own ability, having become more trained in its use. Whoever they were, they were fools. It was blatantly obvious to Jed where they were by their lack of exposure. They were trying to hide, but the very act of hiding made them as obvious as a child who'd pulled a sheet over a pair of chairs and crawled inside.

Slipping into a service entrance, he made his way down a narrow corridor where elevator doors lined one wall. Even if these elevators wouldn't take him to the penthouse, he could get closer. He pressed the up button but it didn't light.

It was then he noticed the keyhole. Nobody could use these elevators without authorization. He'd have to find another way. But even as he stood staring at the blank metal doors, he could sense the cab just on the other side, waiting for someone with the right touch to slide back the doors and step inside. Prying them apart never crossed his mind. But when he placed his hand on the cold metallic surface he sensed that access to the elevator wasn't hopeless. In fact, there was something odd about the way his mind scanned the electrical circuits just behind the panel. It was almost as if the wires and hardware were so close he could reach through and touch them. If not with hands then with his mind.

Jed attempted to visualize turning the lock's tumbler. His temples pusled as he strained to make it turn. Nothing happened. And for just a moment he felt silly for having attempted the feat. Bending spoons and levitating bodies were best left for gurus or stories in tabloids. He'd have to make progress the old-fashioned way.

Just as he was about to go in search of a stairwell, a man dressed in overalls appeared and inserted a key into the slot. The key was only one in a whole nest of keys, held together with a large ring. The man nodded but said nothing. When the doors opened, Jed stepped in behind him.

The man pressed the button to the fourth floor. "Where you headed?" he asked.

Jed looked at the bay of buttons, ranging from B all the way through the 32nd floor. "The top," he said.

"The penthouse suite?" the man asked. "You ought to be taking the elevator in the south wing. But you can get there from the thirty-second floor." He pushed the button.

"Thanks," Jed said, wondering why the man wasn't calling for security. Certainly casinos wouldn't let people roam freely around employee areas. The ride to the fourth floor was fast, but long enough for the man to glance at the briefcase. If the man so much as asked a question, Jed was prepared to deal with him accordingly.

But the man stepped off at the fourth floor without incident. Jed continued to the thirty-second floor where he exited and made his way toward the south wing.

❧

Jed decided the place was like the friggen Taj Mahal, featuring a degree of luxury he could easily get used to. Whoever lived here knew what it meant to spread out and enjoy the finer things in life. This would be his new home for the time being. It would serve as an adequate base for his search. He'd find those who knew something and then take them out of the equation.

He'd start with the one presently standing on the balcony, overlooking the city as dusk fell. He could see a man with his back toward a pair of sliding glass doors, hunched over the railing, scouring the city streets below. Maybe the man could sense that someone was coming. If it were true, the pathetic fool couldn't tell that his adversary was standing right behind him.

Tough luck.

Jed approached the open glass door. Stepping onto the balcony he took in the spacious landing with its garden-lined troughs and potted trees. It was deep and wide, easily taking up a third of the space on the west rooftop. The impressive penthouse he'd just come through covered the remainder of the roof. A brisk, warm wind blew across Jed's face as he walked toward the man.

From the back he appeared to be considerably older than Jed, about the same height, but clearly no physical match. When he was within ten feet of him, Jed stopped and set the briefcase down. Sensing someone was behind him, the man turned his head. His sad eyes appeared tired, apathetic. Then to Jed's surprise, he simply turned back to look at the city again.

"Who the hell are you?" he asked.

Jed put his hands together and cracked his knuckles. "I might ask you the same question."

"Difference is, you're in my house. Now get out." The sound of his words were carried partially away by the wind.

Jed had hoped he could read the man's thoughts. But although he tried desperately to sense something, there was nothing. Other people poured forth a plethora of information but this man was somehow different. Certainly this man must know something. His identity search would start here. Now.

"Tell me your name," he demanded.

Finally, the man turned and looked at Jed, smirking. He nonchalantly leaned an elbow against the railing as if taking a breather from an upscale party.

"Don't tell me," he said. "You're another lost lamb, trying to find your way through wonderland. I'm getting sick of this. Leave me the hell alone, already! This crap has to stop."

Jed didn't know what he was talking about and he didn't care. "Shut up," Jed said, approaching him threateningly. "I'll ask. You answer."

"You're some piece of work," the man said calmly. "Probably not your fault. What'd they do to you, anyway? The last ones were fed a line about the mob."

Jed frowned. Suddenly he had the gut feeling that the mob was what this was all about.

He took a step closer.

"What's going on here?" he demanded. "And don't bother lying to me. I'll know."

"If it makes any difference," the man told him, "the name's Eli Houston. I'm surprised they hadn't already told you. As for what's going on here…"

"Tell me."

"You don't want to know. Trust me."

Jed stepped closer.

"Try me," he seethed.

Eli looked at Jed while his hair blew to one side by the wind. "Go back to whatever box they put you in and forget about it. If not, you'll be sorry."

Suddenly Jed was furious. Nobody spoke to him that way and lived to take their next breath. "Is that some kind of threat," he said through clenched teeth, seizing Eli's neck with one hand. "You just said the wrong thing, buddy."

Eli's eyes looked defiant, unmoved by the forceful gesture, which infuriated Jed further.

"Not scared of me, huh?" Jed snarled. "We'll see about that."

Jed squeezed, and for the first time, Eli began to look uncomfortable. Jed kneaded the soft flesh of the man's throat between his fingers. It felt nice. The control he wielded felt even better. He'd get the information he needed and then dispose of this old fool. However Eli had managed to make it to a penthouse lifestyle, it would be a swift, humbling ride to the ground floor.

"Now, I'm going to ease up so you can explain to me exactly what's going on. Do you understand?"

As he eased his grip, Jed could feel Eli's throat muscles contract, trying to swallow.

"Go to Hell you son of a bitch!" he whispered.

Jed squeezed with rage and then shoved. Eli had no chance to grasp hold of the railing as he flipped over the side of the terrace like a rag doll. The last thing Jed saw was the shocked expression on his face as he tumbled over the edge.

Jed was still seething as he watched the body flail in midair, before smashing into the lobby rooftop below. Now he was back to where he'd started. If he couldn't glean information from his victims, he was doing nothing more than eliminating the competition. That was all.

He looked across the city, lights now coming on from the onset of darkness, and tried to locate the others. He could sense that there was one directly across the street in another building. Further out, there was another one. It was a small house at the edge of town. These two locations were silent while everything else in the city gushed information.

Jed decided to visit the house at the edge of town first. Then take his time with the one across the street to make sure he handled the interview more carefully.

Marilyn always insisted on having Drew tuck her in at night. He realized how strange it might seem for a grown man to pull the blanket up to a woman's chin, kiss her cheek and explain that she should keep careful watch over those pesky bedbugs to make sure they didn't nip at her toes during the night. But Drew treasured the occasion, regardless of how silly Marilyn accused him of being.

With the house settling down for the night, Drew went to the kitchen where he'd left the latest issue of the paper. Unlike most clergy, he wasn't the early morning type who liked to beat the sun up for prayer and study. His days started slow and gained momentum, culminating in a productive evening after Marilyn was asleep. That's when he would read the paper, open mail, and generally worry about their financial situation when such worrying was warranted.

On the anxiety scale, tonight he was off the charts. Though he attempted to push it to the back of his mind – an easier task when Marilyn was present – the nagging reality of their plight gnawed at him like a dog chewing its way through a fence. Little by little. From one relentless moment to the next.

He tried to console himself over the fact that God would provide as he always had, and even considered that perhaps another number would begin to appear. Even though he had promised himself that he wouldn't after what had happened the last time, God was God, and he'd obey to receive His provision.

As he unrolled the *Las Vegas Sun*, Jed half expected to see some numbers in the headlines, the beginning of a long string of numerical manifestations which would lead him back to the roulette wheel. But instead, the headliner for the day was, "Danger Zone."

The article went on to explain that the Las Vegas zoning committee had finally approved the construction of a shopping center adjacent to a housing tract. The builder, a local businessman by the name of Rob Danger, had been courting the city for months and had finally won their blessing. Citizens who lived nearby had mixed feelings about the decision. Some were happy at the prospect. Others were outraged, saying the decision would be a catalyst for dropping property values.

The article was of moderate interest to Drew, but what troubled him was the headline, itself. Though he didn't want to second guess the Sovereign Lord, what if it were another, more disheartening message. Struggling with his faith, he set the paper aside and turned on a small television mounted under the kitchen cabinet.

The eleven o'clock news was well underway and he was just in time for stories involving local interest. A pleasant-looking woman with medium brown hair was standing with her back to what looked like the Colorado River.

"Warning signs were posted along the riverbank today in the wake of the second consecutive drowning over the past month," she said. "Fortunately, the one that occurred here yesterday wasn't fatal."

She went on to explain how a boy had been swimming and was carried out into the current. When the parents realized he wasn't with them, they began searching.

But Drew had stopped listening. He was unnerved by the anchorwoman's initial piercing words.

Warning signs.

Danger zone.

He prayed it was only a coincidence but the first piece of junk mail he opened was headlined, "GET OUT," with a subheading that read, "The treasure buried in your equity." The ad was from a bank, offering the fulfillment of a dream and the promise of a second mortgage. Take a vacation, renovate the house, or put your oldest through college; all you had to do was sign on the dotted line. The flyer pictured a smiling couple, clearly happier, more productive people for having gone deeper into debt.

Drew suddenly had an overwhelming sense of dread. The message was becoming clear. It was a warning. There was danger and Marilyn and he should *get out*. Drew pushed aside the mail, turned off the TV, and sat thinking.

Maybe it was time to leave Sin City, the place he'd been called to minister to, although he couldn't remember such a calling. That had been before the fever and now he felt no attachment to the place. He'd read his own words written in a journal from before the illness, showing a passion to preach to the masses that were using the bright lights of Vegas as another form of narcotic to sooth ailing souls. But now those words seemed as foreign as if he were reading the scroll of a long dead saint. It was a calling he no longer felt. Perhaps the Lord was accommodating his new temperament and allowing him to leave.

The only problem was that he no longer had any means to do so. Relocating to a new city took money. Money he didn't have. As he stepped onto the porch, a gentle night breeze blew in random puffs, causing leaves to dance on the cypress he'd planted at a time he couldn't remember.

Even though Drew wanted to believe the messages were prophetic, a portent leading them to a different place, a different life, something else was stirring on the inside, causing him to shiver and look cautiously at dark shadows. Something was coming. He sensed it. Something unnaturally evil. And if he were smart, he'd pack a few belongings, wake Marilyn, and leave as fast as they could.

He shook off the feeling, went to his bedroom and tried to get some sleep.

CHAPTER 27

Jed sat motionless, deep in concentration, staring at a half-filled glass of whiskey on a nearby table. He licked his dry lips and tried to imagine the taste, unsure if he could make it happen again. Clinching his fist, he strained and willed the glass to obey. But it sat as motionless as a stubborn child, scorned and unwilling to comply.

Earlier, he'd watched the liquid's surface ripple on its own, some kind of vibration setting it off, occurring at the split second when he considered taking a sip. It was as if his brief desire had touched some telepathic region in his mind, causing the glass to move. The sensation was similar to what he felt while standing in front of the elevator, certain he could manipulate circuits with his mind.

But the harder he tried, the more frustratingly pointless it seemed.

Jed threw up his hands in frustration. He was a fool to have thought that he could bend matter to his will. He wanted to pick up the glass and smash it against the tile floor. Because he knew it was possible. He just wasn't tapping into the right mental current. His logical side impassively pointed out that he was entertaining a notion that violated the laws of physics. Kinetic energy would be the only thing that would move the glass.

Defeated, Jed leaned back in his chair. "Screw it!" he muttered to himself. "I've got better things to do with my time."

There was a sudden, sharp *plink* sound, coming from the table where the whisky in the glass now shimmered. Strangely, the liquid appeared to be evaporating before his eyes, as though time had suddenly sped up.

As Jed examined the glass more closely, a pool of whiskey was forming around the base of the glass, where it had no doubt sprung a sudden leak. Picking it up, he noticed a crack along one side that splintered all the way from the top to the bottom.

What had caused the crack? His anger? Or perhaps he was simply trying too hard. He relaxed and imagined the glass being shattered, and suddenly, it dissolved before his eyes, the tiny shards flying outward in all directions. Brushing the damp pieces from his body, Jed's heart pulsed with excitement. He could do it then! His mind could control things.

And then, in his inner eye, he saw them coming. They were in the elevator. Eli's shattered body had been found and his friends were coming to investigate.

Jed quickly formulated a plan and headed to greet them when they arrived.

*

The box was narrower than usual. But though she had begun to panic, she held herself in check, not wanting to scream and lose all control the way she normally did. *She'd endured a flight across the country*, Kristen attempted to console herself. Even though she'd been unconscious at the time, it was at least something that she'd lived to tell about. But the thought of the airplane only made her feel worse.

Her breaths were shallow, not only because of the confining restriction to her chest, but because the wooden box only had so much oxygen. If she weren't careful, she'd use it all up before Jack could find her. Surely he was looking. But then she remembered his saying something about going home to check on his family. *No!* He couldn't just leave her here to die. He'd come for her. She was certain of it.

Haunted by the ghosts of abandonment, she lay silent, motionless as the monster prowled about, trying to turn her into a zombie like everyone else except for Jack, her one connection to the living.

He'd come for her.

As she fell deeper into sleep, she heard its breathing – regular and deliberate – as it came closer. Somehow it just knew where she was. The quieter she was, the closer it came, digging its way through the earth toward her grave.

Hurry, Jack. Please, please hurry.

⁂

Instead of racing to her rescue, Jack was in the next room, having a dreamland chat with a man claiming to be himself. He shrugged, his eyebrows bristling with rebellious strands. "It's like I said. You don't want to believe me? That's your problem, not mine."

"But if I'm you…" Jack countered, and then shook his head. "This is insane. Why am I even talking to you?"

The man leaned forward. "Because you know it's true," he rasped. "That's why."

Jack considered the man's words. Even though he knew this was only a dream, it disturbed him to think he could look like the pathetic troll before him – that anyone should have to look like that. But the thing that frightened him most wasn't the way the man looked. It was something that he felt deep down when the man spoke. He'd seen this person before, but he couldn't remember where. And it was more than that. There actually was some personal connection.

Jack wondered how his mind had conjured up such an atrocious little man. Perhaps it was the result of some ugly childhood memory, trying desperately to push its way through the foggy amnesia.

The man let out a coarse laugh that started slow, and built into a torturous round of wheezing and coughing, tied together in a throat full of phlegm. Jack cringed.

"You know I'm right, don't you?" he asked when the disgusting exhibit was over. "Think your somethin' don't you. I got news, pal. You're as ugly as what you're lookin' at."

"I don't believe you," Jack shot back.

"Oh yeah? Then why are you looking in a mirror? Answer me that. Huh? Hm? Huh?"

Jack felt weak as he realized that he *was* looking into a mirror. It wasn't possible. It had to be a trick. He couldn't be this awful man staring back at him.

And then the man reached out through the glass and grabbed at him. Only instead of a hand, it was a giant red pincher, like a crab's. Jack stared at the claw in horror, clicking and snapping, trying to grasp his shirt. Suddenly the image was no longer a man. The skin was now red and covered with a crusty shell.

"Come on, bud," it said. "This side is where you belong. No sense lying to yourself. Don't worry. I know how you feel. I've been like this my whole damn life. It ain't fun. Trust me."

Jack tried to step away from the pincher, but realized he was standing in a room that was shrinking toward the mirror. It was presently no larger than a phone booth and growing smaller. He shook his head and stared at the creature-of-a-man trying to grab him. "No. This can't be happening. I won't go back," he heard himself say.

Just as the claw finally found Jack's shirt, he screamed and tried to hold onto the smooth walls around him. Where the room had been filled with furniture moments earlier, there was now nothing to grip.

"Say bye-bye, my friend. You're coming home," the giant crab-man chortled

❧

When Jed opened the door, five men stood in the narrow corridor that connected an elevator to the penthouse. A badge declared the one in front head of hotel security. With him were three police officers.

"Where the hell have you been?" Jed said, feigning agitation. "I phoned hours ago. That maniac tried to kill me."

The head of security looked confused and surprised. The officers glanced at each other.

One of the officers – a tall, muscular fellow with blond, crew cut hair – said, "Sir, a man fell from this penthouse earlier this evening. He was Eli Houston, the occupant of this penthouse. We need to inspect the place and ask you some questions."

"Don't be ridiculous," Jed said. "I live here. That man came here to rob me." He turned to security. "Tell them who I am," he demanded, all the while pushing his thoughts toward the man. He was getting through to him. He could see the sweat forming on the man's forehead as he struggled against the inexorable force entering his head.

"I, uh…of course. You're Mr. Houston," he said tentatively. "I'm terribly sorry for this inconvenience. I don't know why I thought…"

The officer with the crew cut glanced suspiciously at the head of security. "*This* is Eli Houston?"

"Yes. Yes, of course," the security officer told him. "Actually, I'm not feeling too well. This whole ordeal has left me a bit shaken."

"Can you explain why your wallet was found on the body of a man that fell, sir?" One of the officers asked Jed.

"It's like I told you," Jed replied angrily. "The man was trying to rob me. I can't put it any simpler than that. He took my wallet and forced me onto the balcony. I thought he was going to kill me. There was a struggle and he fell over the railing. That's it."

Jed wanted them to leave, to just go away. He pushed his thoughts toward them, fueled by anger, commanding them to leave him alone. Suddenly the confines of the corridor became surreal.

The officer opened his mouth to speak, but nothing came out. The whole group appeared like there were in some kind of stupor, standing motionless, not sure what to do next.

"Actually, I'm not feeling too well," the head of security finally said, and then looked confused at having repeated himself.

"Can you explain why your wallet was found on the body of…" the officer mimicked his earlier question but stopped in mid sentence. "Uh," he stammered. "I see. Okay, gentleman. I think we have what we need."

The elevator doors slid open behind them as if an invisible force had pressed the down button. When the doors slid closed, all five men were still facing the back of the cab.

Jed smiled to himself as he closed the penthouse door. Had he really done all that? The feeling of power surged through him, making him feel like a sorcerer who could rip the building from its foundation and float it among the clouds. And this, with a simple flex of his mind. Yet the results were still somewhat random. If he wanted better control, he'd need to practice.

That night, Jed fell asleep on Eli's massive bed. It was perched atop a platform, draped with gold and red silk fabric. The man clearly knew how to live. And sleep. Jed decided he'd take full advantage of his acquisition until moving on.

But the last thought that went through his mind as he fell asleep was taking a trip in the morning to a small house at the edge of town.

ఌ

Mark Sweeney called an emergency meeting in the morning. He'd been up all night with Ridley trying to unravel Jared's mess. His head ached, his clothes needed changing and – save for adrenaline being sustained by strong cups of black coffee – he was mentally and emotionally spent. The past twenty-four hours had been harrowing to say the least.

First there was Erin's debacle, which had led to a call placed directly to Petrov from one of the subjects. Subsequently, Mark had spent two hours in a closed-door session with Petrov, taking heat while they worked through a reasonable plan of action. He watched Erin now, entering his office surreptitiously behind Zack, taking a seat in the far corner, her bounciness gone, keeping her eyes low, being careful not to look in Mark's direction. That was okay. He had too much on his mind to consider the way she filled out her t-shirt and jeans, or to be captivated by her dripping sexuality.

As if that ordeal had not been enough, there was now Jared's mess, something Mark had yet to tell Petrov about. Ridley and he had desperately tried to override what Jared had done, but were without success. They'd even called in the services of Satish, from the systems group, but Jared was no dummy. They were unable to get anywhere. Now it was time for Mark to pull out all the stops, make the other monitors aware of what was going on and hopefully get some problem-solving feedback.

It angered Mark to think he'd been duped by one of Guerridelli's own family members, proving, in effect, that the man's demented legacy was alive and well. In spite of the thorough interview process, Jared had managed to deceive everyone.

"Here's the situation," Mark began, and went on to explain Jared's real identity, the fact that the other subjects were now vulnerable, and that Petrov wasn't aware of the problem yet, concluding with an expression of confidence that the group could solve the problem before Petrov needed to find out. It was intended to be a win-one-for-the-gipper speech to stir a fighting effort. But it somehow fell short, leaving the group pensive, rather than fired up. There was no figurative helmet banging or talk of storming the proverbial field.

As the last of the monitors shuffled out of his office, Mark realized that, by the end of the day, if no progress had been made, he'd have to confront Petrov; a prospect that seemed less desirable than a whole slew of other unpleasant activities on par with root canals and proctology exams.

If the analysts happened to show up right now, the bad timing would be disastrous. It would be better to make Petrov aware of the situation sooner than let him find out later from the analysts.

All he could do now was hope his group was up to the challenge.

CHAPTER 28

The moment Jack woke, the telephone on the nightstand began to ring. Using his fingers, he rubbed the sleep from his eyes. Even though his night had been filled with images of an ugly little man, he felt better, rested. And as he listened to the abrasive double ring of the phone, he decided that if they couldn't get anywhere with the Russian by the end of the day, he'd pay another visit to Eli Houston, using whatever means necessary to find out what the man knew.

After the third ring he lifted the receiver and offered a sleepy greeting, half expecting Kristen to be on the other end, complaining about the accommodations, or moaning about breakfast like a hungry child. But the voice he heard snapped him into an upright position.

"Mr. Stuart. This is Dr. Petrov. I trust your sleep was restful?"

"How did you know where I was?"

"That's not important. But I have some explaining to do. You must promise to keep it confidential. You weren't supposed to learn anything. Now that you have – let's just say some form of elucidation is in order."

Jack's heart quickened. Would it all come down to this? His accident? His life before? His sudden involvement with Kristen? He didn't know, but felt a great weight was about to either slide smoothly from his back, or crack it in two.

He waited.

"I work for a company that performs highly classified research," Petrov said. "You've obviously heard its name since you mentioned it to me yesterday. Albatross Life Corporation."

"Yes," Jack confirmed.

"Before I say more," the man paused. "I should tell you that you don't *need* to know what I'm about to say. I can assure you that you are not in danger, in spite of what you've been led to believe. It was an unfortunate mistake and I personally apologize."

"And just what do you think I've been led to believe?" Jack asked, though he suspected he already knew. The poker game. The mob. But he wanted to hear it from the Russian, himself. Eli had been a fraud. If Petrov really knew something, he should be able to accurately tell Jack what had been happening.

"Trust me. I know everything. But if I tell you the truth, you won't like it. Your life will never be the same. Do you understand?"

"What can you tell me about what's been going on?" Jack asked. "How do I know you're not just lying like Eli Houston?"

"I know you think the mob's after you," Petrov said after a pause. "I assure you it isn't true. You did not steal money from them in a poker game five years ago, nor at any time for that matter."

"Was it someone else? My partners?"

"No," Petrov said quickly. "There was no poker game."

Jack was both relieved and perturbed by this revelation. "Then why was I told there was?" he demanded.

"You must understand, Mr. Stuart, that we're dealing with sensitive information. Someone thought it would be better to have you think the mob was after you. You were growing restless. Your attempt to leave the country was a red flag and – one of my subordinates made up the story to keep you busy. And for that, Mr. Stuart, I sincerely apologize."

That was it. The man was legitimate. Jack hadn't told anyone about the airport. Bizarre notions began swirling through his head as he desperately tried to grasp the implications. Someone was watching him. Apparently they'd been watching his every move for some time. But why? And now he suspected that Kristen was part of this wacky conspiracy, whatever it was. After all she'd been the one who'd originally told him about the poker game. On the other hand, if that were the case, she deserved an Oscar. Her performance had been convincingly brilliant.

He wondered if she were even in the next room.

Then he remembered how she'd seen the trucker at the motel outside Panama City. If she'd been behind the conspiracy, certainly she wouldn't have reacted the way she did.

"What about Kristen?" Jack asked.

"Miss Bandy is another subject, just like you are," Petrov said. "She knows nothing. You were brought together deliberately as part of the distraction ploy. She was growing restless as well. We thought that bringing you together and giving you something else to think about would be enough. But I was never consulted on the approach and now it seems our organization has made a mess of things."

"Okay. Tell me this," Jack said. "Why are you playing us like puppets? What's all this about?"

"Are you sure you must know?"

"Yes. Tell me."

Reluctantly, Dr. Petrov began. "You're name is not Jack Stuart, although I'm not at liberty to discuss your true identity. The accident you were in that supposedly caused your amnesia never occurred. Your loss of memory was an unfortunate – but necessary – side effect of the research. After the research was complete, we placed you in a life that we believed was suitable to your personality. We gave you a career. A home. A family."

Jack was speechless. Even though he'd felt for months that something was wrong, here was a man confirming that his life, as he knew it, was nothing more than an illusion, a fabrication. No wonder he felt no real connection with the woman he'd supposedly married. And even his children – though sweet and entertaining – seemed more like angelic robots than the disorderly creatures kids were supposed to be.

And his job. It was all too easy.

Of course!

What the man was saying had to be true.

"But you saw through it, didn't you, Mr. Stuart?" Dr. Petrov said. "Sadly, most of the subjects do."

"What was the nature of the research?" Jack asked, so shocked that he was barely able to continue.

"I'm not at liberty to discuss that aspect of our business. Suffice it to say, we strive to make the subjects as comfortable as possible. But it seems it's never enough. If there's anything we can do to make your life more pleasant, I assure you we'll do what we can."

Make his life more comfortable? More pleasant? A stab at the truth would be a start. He didn't need another shiny new car, a big house on the hill, or another pretty young wife. He needed to know the truth or he might never be sane. It had to be what Eli meant when he'd said, *"Tell them what you want."*

Jack suddenly grew angry. "What gives you the right to toy with peoples lives? How do you get off playing God? Just who the hell do you people think you are? Who let you do this to us? To me?"

The silence on the other end was deafening. Finally, Petrov said, "You did."

If Jack was at a loss for words before, he was utterly speechless now. Certainly what the man was saying was possible. He couldn't remember. Then again, Petrov could be telling him another lie and he'd never know the difference.

"I don't believe you."

"That's your prerogative. I assure you it's true."

"Prove it." Jack's was growing increasingly agitated.

"Mr. Stuart, I have a signed agreement that states you waive all rights to knowledge of our research. And in exchange, we agreed to certain requests." Then he quickly added, "And we've provided everything you asked for."

A sick feeling was forming in his stomach. Even though this could merely be one more deception in a great big pack of lies, for the first time since his accident, Jack felt he was in the presence of the truth. As bizarre as the whole thing sounded, and even though he didn't want to believe it was true, he couldn't deny the man's candor; his genuineness.

"I want to see the contract," Jack said, defeated.

Another long pause. "I'm…sorry. I can't do that."

"What do you mean, you can't do that? Isn't an agreement supposed to be accessible by both parties? A meeting of the minds and all that? If you don't show it to me, the agreement's no good."

"I wish I could make it different, but I can't," Petrov said. "The agreement states that you relinquish all rights to knowledge of said agreement, the research, and everything from your past life. It's only by chance you became aware of anything. My hands are tied, Mr. Stuart. We had a deal."

"Prove it. Or I'm going to the…" But he stopped. Who could he go to? The police? FBI? CIA? An attorney?

"You may go to whomever you like, Mr. Stuart," Petrov said, confirming Jack's fears. "But you'll be laughed at all the way to an asylum. I don't exist. We've taken great pains to assure there are records showing you've been Jack Stuart since the day you were born in Escondido, California. You grew up like any other child, went to school, married, had children, moved to Atlanta, helped form a technology company, and met with an unfortunate accident that left you without memory. Attempting to prove otherwise will only be wasted effort."

"You bastard!" Jack seethed.

"Mr. Stuart –"

"Stop calling me that!"

Petrov paused. "Even though you think I'm the enemy, I'm on your side. Really."

"Then show me the agreement."

"That's impossible."

"Why?"

Petrov sighed. "Our policy dictates…"

"Screw policy. I'll come to you. Where are you?"

"You can't do that. You waived all rights to see the agreement."

"Then prove it. Just show me the damn signature. That's all."

"You don't know what you're asking."

"If you don't show it to me," Jack suddenly spoke softly with determination, "I'll spend the rest of the life you created for me hunting you down. And when I find you, remember that I stand to lose nothing."

"This conversation is over," Petrov said.

"Wait," Jack blurted. Suddenly he realized how important it was that he not lose his only source of information. "Can we at least meet somewhere? In a public place. That way I won't know where Albatross is. It's the least you can do."

"That's impossible. Seeing me is not an option."

"Why?"

"I told you. I don't exist."

"That's ludicrous. Nobody will know. I swear it."

"Mr...." Petrov said, but caught himself. "We appear to be going in circles. Leave it be. There's nothing more you need to know. I implore you to accept what I've told you and get on with your life; albeit not the life you expected. We'll be glad to make adjustments."

Tell them what you want.

Jack heard a soft rap on the door separating his room with Kristen's.

"Tell me where Albatross is. Please!"

"It won't do you any good," Petrov told him. "They'll deny the whole thing. Nobody in the front office knows about the research. They don't even know who I am."

"I know," Jack said. "You don't exist."

"Exactly."

"I don't care if they don't know. At least it'll prove something you've told me is true. Tell me," Jack pleaded, certain that if he found the company, he could get to Petrov.

"I can't do that," the Russian told him again, wearily. "I'm sorry. You won't be hearing from me again."

The phone went dead.

"Hello?" Jack began to panic.

There was a rap at the door. "Hey. Who you talkin' to?" Kristen called to him. "Let me in."

Defeated, Jack went to let her in. She stared at him in amusement as she glanced him over. In another circumstance he would have felt embarrassed for having let her in while still wearing only his boxer shorts. But at the moment, he didn't care.

"Nice," she said and strutted past. "So who you talkin' to?" she asked, plopping down on the half-used bed, stretching her arms out behind her.

"Petrov. The Russian."

"Really?"

"Yep. But I'm not sure you want to know what he said."

"Of course I do. Tell me," she demanded.

Sitting down on a chair opposite her, Jack slowly began explaining how they'd apparently been involved in some sort of research project, one that had wiped out all memories of their past. He explained how they'd made up the story about the mob and how they'd brought the two of them together; how Petrov had refused to explain the nature of the research.

"Wow!" she said when he had finished. "Just…WOW."

"Do you believe it?" Jack asked.

"Yeah. I think I do," she said, her dark eyes glistening with excitement. "That explains how I saw Randy, the trucker, still alive."

"Do you?" she asked.

Jack sighed. "Unfortunately. It's the first thing that makes any sense."

"And all along I thought it was Gerty and everyone else trying to push me into Harvard Law School." She laughed unconvincingly. "It was probably some secret fantasy I had…you know, before. The real ass-kicker is that I probably asked to go there and they were only doing what I told them." She grinned. "Can you imagine me being a lawyer?"

"Yeah, I can imagine it," Jack said. "You'd be a real pain in the ass in the courtroom."

"Defense or prosecution?" she suddenly asked.

"Prosecution. Definitely prosecution."

They sat quietly now, digesting the implications.

"He swore we'd never be able to prove it. The research I mean," Jack said. "They've wrapped up our new identities in a nice tight package that nobody can penetrate. Including us. He said everyone would think we're crazy if we try."

"Somebody knows the truth," Kristen offered. "If he's for real, that means people we know might be in on it. Unless they're just as deluded as we were."

"I don't think so," Jack said. "My wife is – well, perfect."

"Good for you," Kristen said sarcastically.

"No. You don't understand. She's *too* perfect. Knowing what I do now, I'd swear she was nothing more than an actress or a model in an unusual job that's going to last a lifetime."

"That's just crazy," Kristen retorted. "Who would give up their whole life for something like that."

"I don't know. But I've felt that way since I woke up from…" Jack caught himself. He'd started to say, since he woke up from the accident. But now that wouldn't do. He'd have to start rethinking what had happened. "Since the research," he said quietly.

"So, you mean Gerty, my grandmother, is a fake?"

"Possibly."

Kristen slumped forward, elbows on knees; her youthful face frowning. "This is so messed up. Isn't there anything we can do? I mean, if our lives seem screwed up now, how bad were they before? Who would agree to such a thing?"

"Until I see an agreement," Jack said, "I'm not convinced. I know there's probably some truth to what Petrov is saying, but he's not telling us everything. That's for damn sure. I know there's still some nasty little secrets in this whole mess."

"So what do we do?"

Jack looked at the piece of paper on the nightstand that Eli had given him. "We don't quit until we find out the *whole* truth. That's what."

"Where do you propose we start?" Kristen asked.

Jack leaned back in the chair. "You know some law. Isn't it true that an agreement has to be a meeting of the minds? Both parties have to be fully aware of the intent?"

"Yeah. Why?"

"Petrov claims we signed an agreement that says we gave up rights to even see the thing. Is that legal?"

Kristen thought about it. "The meeting of the minds has to happen when the contract is executed," she said slowly. "Even though we can't see the agreement now, it might still hold. It's the same thing when declaring a will. An ole guy may have gone senile, but as long as he was sane when executing the will, it stands," Kristen said, but added, "If we really signed it, that is."

"That's just it," Jack said. "We don't know. It has to be challengeable in a court of law. Otherwise, what's the point? We can't even remember having a meeting of the minds. How legal is that? It can't be right."

"I never finished law school," Kristen admitted. "And I sincerely doubt there would be precedence for something like this. We'd need better counsel than what I can offer."

"If we can even find Petrov," Jack said. "How do we take him to court if we can't find him? He says he doesn't exist."

"We have a phone number don't we?" Kristen said.

Jack snapped his fingers and grabbed the paper. It was a trick he'd learned in business when a company would inquire about their software products. In order to research the size of the outfit, he'd drop digits from the end of their personal phone number, adding zeros instead, and could usually reach the company switchboard. Receptionists were easy marks for information.

He punched the 'nine' button to get an outside line and then dialed the number Eli had given him for Petrov. Only instead of the last two digits, he replaced them with zeros.

"Crap!" he said, listening to the annoying mechanical operator, one he was becoming all too familiar with. "It's not a valid number. Okay. Then I'm going to contact Petrov directly again. I have no choice."

But Jack's mouth went dry when he heard the same mechanical voice, telling him the number was no longer in service.

"How can that be? It's not in service," Jack said in astonishment.

"Maybe he had it disconnected after you called yesterday."

Jack snapped his fingers again and picked up the receiver. Then he dialed '*69' to connect to the last caller. He didn't know if it would work on a phone system as complex as the one at the hotel, with its hundreds of extensions. But it was worth a try.

"We're sorry!" The voice said. "That function is not available. Please hang up –"

Jack slammed the receiver down in frustration. "We're back to square one."

"Someone knows," Kristen said. "What about your wife? Can't you get it out of her? She's a *fraud*, after all. She has to know who they are. Especially since they probably hired her."

Jack noticed her emphasis on the word 'fraud' and sensed that Kristen took great pleasure in pointing it out. She was right of course. He could contact Maggie, but it would be no good. He knew it. She'd merely deny everything, brushing it away just as she did anything unpleasant and then try to coax him back. She was a master at avoiding confrontation. Besides that, he'd feel foolish telling her about the conspiracy. Even though he suspected it was true, telling someone like Maggie would be demeaning, humiliating

"It's no good," Jack said. "She'll deny it. I'd have to confront her in person."

Kristen started to say something but stopped herself. Finally, she said, "Speaking of frauds, what about the guy we talked to yesterday? We *know* he could tell us something. He did give you Petrov's number, after all."

"That's exactly what I've been thinking," Jack said.

Kristen smiled and looked at Jack, giving him the once over. "We're starting to think alike."

Now, for the first time since she'd come into the room, he started feeling awkward about his attire – or lack thereof. "I still wish we knew where this Albatross company was," he said, all business. "While we grill Mr. Houston, I can have my marketing people check it out. You'd be amazed at what a good group of marketing folks can drum up on an organization. I can tell them it's a potential client. But we don't even know what state they're in."

"Yes we do," Kristen said, matter-of-factly. "Arizona. Scottsdale, Arizona."

A look of shock appeared on Jack's face. Suddenly he started questioning her involvement again. "How…did you know that?"

"Eli said it yesterday," she said. "Weren't you listening?"

Jack looked down and tried to remember. "He did?"

"Yep."

"Why didn't you say anything before?"

"You never asked."

Jack was elated. Now, at least, he could start the ball rolling. They'd get to the bottom of this. Oh yes.

"You're amazing," he told her. "I could kiss you."

"Why don't you?" she asked and grinned. "It's the least you can do to thank me."

"I might if I weren't in my underwear and you weren't practically a child."

"Chicken?" she said.

Their eyes met for a long moment that was a little too awkward. Jack suddenly felt conspicuous, his face flushing red. He stood. "I've got to take a shower. So if you don't mind…"

"I don't mind if you don't," Kristen said grinning as he walked past her toward the bathroom.

When he'd finally reached safe haven, he called from behind the bathroom door, "As soon as I'm finished here, I'll give the guys at the office a call. Later on, we'll pay a visit to our dear friend across the street."

"And…" he added. "Close the door on your way out."

Petrov pinched the bridge of his nose with his eyes clamped shut. The headache that had started when Jack Stuart phoned was growing worse. Even extra-strength Tylenol wouldn't be able to ease the pain for this kind of headache.

By attempting to smooth things over, he feared he had only made matters worse, more complicated. Well, what did he expect? How had he thought the man would respond when told he'd been part of a research project and that his life was nothing more than a laboratory experiment? Any sane individual would have to know more.

Besides, Jack Stuart was the least of his worries at the moment. A short time earlier he'd learned of another problem that had arisen in just the last twelve hours, and was presently in the process of turning into a full-blown catastrophe. Systems were breaking down and he could sense that his little empire was starting to crumble. He wasn't sure why Mark Sweeney hadn't come to him.

He'd had reservations about taking on Guerridelli as a client because of his connections to the mob. Albatross was supposed to be a clean operation. But somehow the man had weaseled his way into territories that threatened to destroy the whole project.

But how had it happened? Their security measures were impeccable.

He didn't have to wait long to find the answer.

Mark Sweeney appeared at his doorway with a somber face. The man looked so exhausted that Petrov repressed his first impulse to scold him for not coming to him immediately.

"I thought we could fix it before you found out." Sweeney answered the question without being asked. "I'm sorry."

"What in the hell is going on down there?" Petrov asked, keeping his voice low.

Mark shook his head, while Petrov waited for more bad news.

"The last technician we hired was Guerridelli's grandson."

"How could we have missed this? Is our security really that bad?"

There was no way Mark could answer that question.

"Well," Petrov said. "Has it been taken care of?"

"Yes, sir. He's gone. But…"

Petrov knew what Sweeney was going to say before he said it. Given the way things had been going, he would have been surprised if Sweeney hadn't told him such news.

"The damage has been done," he said. "It's spreading like an infection. And now – we're completely locked out."

CHAPTER 29

When he opened his eyes he'd hoped that, having had a good night's sleep, he would no longer feel the dread of the evening before. Drew had been sure it was only the result of fatigue from a day filled with financial worries. But the feeling was more intense now. He could sense the same message that had only been put on hold while he slept.

Danger. Warning. Get out.

Whereas at first he'd merely thought it was a sign to leave Las Vegas in the coming weeks or months, it now commanded his attention, refusing to be ignored. Something major was about to happen and he should take heed. His mind drifted to biblical heroes, trying to find an appropriate parallel like he often did.

The most obvious was Lot and how he'd been told by the Lord to leave Sodom. When he'd hesitated, two angels had taken him and his family by the hand and led them out just before the Lord rained down fire on the wicked city, telling them not to look back. If Drew hadn't known that humanity was presently blessed with an age of grace, he'd have sworn the same fate awaited Las Vegas. Sin City.

As his eyes began to focus, his pulse suddenly quickened. He threw back the covers and stood next to the bed, staring in astonishment at the ceiling. He walked slowly around the room, bumping into the dresser, studying the window with sunlight streaming in. His bedroom window faced east and the sun's rays shown through the branches of a tree in the backyard before finding their way into his window, projecting random silhouettes on the walls and ceiling.

At least normally they were random.

Whether the tree had shifted in the night or he'd simply never noticed it before, the shadows formed something that resembled letters.

N – O – W.

They weren't perfectly shaped, but plain enough. The 'O' was more like an oblique rectangle, and the crest of the 'N' extended beyond where it was supposed to, but the 'W' was nearly perfect. Not only that, but the letters were laid out sequentially the way they would read if written on paper. Drew waved a hand across the window and studied the way the light shown through the branches and then reflected off a mirror onto the ceiling to produce the effect.

What were the odds; especially in light of the messages he'd received the night before? But this message carried all the fears and immediacy he'd been harboring since he'd woken up. How much clearer could it be? They were to get out. Not in a few days. Not in a month or when they had enough money.

Now!

Suddenly Drew was aware of TV chatter coming from the other room. Marilyn was already up, which would make things easier. Throwing on some clothes, he found Marilyn in the family room watching cartoons, eyes transfixed.

"Marilyn," he said, trying desperately to sound calm. "I need you to get ready. We're going somewhere."

Bugs Bunny and Daffy Duck bickered about when Elmer Fudd should shoot the duck, it being hunting season and all. Marilyn did not respond.

"He doesn't have to shoot you now," Bugs said in complete control of the situation.

"If I say he has to shoot me now, then he shoots me now," Daffy countered.

"Marilyn? Sweetie, I need to you to get ready."

Daffy stomped up and down, demanding that Elmer Fudd shoot him this instant. Elmer Fudd complied by blasting the duck with his shotgun, sending his yellow beak spinning and leaving Daffy's head smoldering and charred to a crisp.

"Let's try that again."

Marilyn laughed.

"Marilyn!" Drew said sharply. "Turn off the TV. You need to get ready. We're going for a drive."

"We're not going back to the bad place again, are we?" she said, frowning. "I don't like it anymore."

"No, sweetie," Drew tried to reassure her. "Not there. But try to hurry or we might be late."

"Where're we going?"

"It's a surprise. Hurry and get ready," he said. "Oh, and bring a few extra clothes. Underwear. Socks. Pants. Shirts. That sort of thing. Use the small duffel bag in your closet."

She looked confused. "We're going for a long, long time?" she asked.

Drew fidgeted. He didn't know what to say. Should they leave the house and all their belongings the way Lot had, never to return? Or would the danger eventually go away so they could come home? Questions with no answers. They'd have to play it by ear. Live each day as the Lord led.

"Not too long," he lied. "Just be quick, sweetie. We need to get going."

When they were ready, Marilyn followed him out to the carport where a low-end, dated Hyundai sat – the best an out-of-work preacher could afford. Saying a silent prayer of protection, he started the engine and backed out of the driveway.

Something wasn't right. Jed could tell. As he inched the old pickup along, navigating according to his internal compass, the target seemed to be moving. Just as he turned onto a street where he knew the house was located, the dark spot would shift illusively to another street.

They were on the move.

He suspected that somehow whoever had lived there had sensed that he was coming and fled. He cruised slowly past the uninteresting house, a dump compared to the penthouse, and began feeling his way toward the moving vehicle.

He wasn't about to let another source of information slip away.

The morning was warm, dry and still, and Marilyn, seated in the passenger seat, closed her eyes to feel the sunlight on her face. "I like surprises," she said.

Drew didn't know what to say. He was trying to figure out where to go, intensely aware of a presence moving menacingly toward them. Closer and closer it came. He found himself wishing that he could be as innocent as Marilyn.

He pressed his foot down on the accelerator. Though he'd never encountered a major physical threat, he'd done his share of spiritual warfare, against the wiles of dark forces which seemed to be everywhere in Las Vegas. There were times when he'd have sworn these forces were as real as the people who filtered in and out of casinos. But something had changed. Whether it was one of those dark spirits that had somehow become manifest in the real world, or whether it was a madman who'd been possessed by one, he didn't know. But the enemy was the enemy, just the same, so he prayed fervently.

A metal trashcan bounced into the street ahead of the car, as though someone had tossed it deliberately. But nobody was around. Marilyn screamed and put her hands on the dash to brace herself as Drew mashed the brakes and swerved to avoid it. His heart was now racing, his senses alert.

"What happened?" Marilyn whimpered, clearly shaken.

"I don't know," was all Drew could offer. "Put on your seatbelt, sweetie."

She pulled the buckle over her breast and snapped it in place. "What about you?" she said, her voice still shaky.

As they passed a house with a white picket fence, something struck the side of the car hard. Marilyn screamed. "What's going on?" she said.

At the same moment, the white slats of the picket fence began popping off, one at a time, shooting like arrows at the side of the car. Terrified, Marilyn unfastened her seatbelt and clamored toward Drew, throwing her arms around his neck just as one slat struck the rear window, causing it to explode and glass fragments to spray the interior.

Marilyn was shrieking in Drew's ear now and crying hysterically. "What's happening? What's happening?" she was saying over and over. "Make it stop!"

If only he could. But it was as though the gates of Hell had suddenly been unleashed in all their fury against them, the dark lord, himself, paying a visit in the suburbs of Las Vegas. *For I am convinced,* Drew told himself, quoting from the book of

Romans, *that neither death nor life, neither angels nor demons, neither the present nor the future, nor any powers, neither height nor depth, nor anything else in all creation, will be able to separate us from the love of God that is in Christ Jesus.*

Clearly, the Hyundai couldn't hold out against this assault much longer. In the rearview mirror he could see an old brown pickup turn from a side street and begin to follow, speeding up as it came. For just a second he wavered between heading for a church or a police station.

The police would be useless against spiritual forces. Then again, what if nobody was around at a church to help. They could fall prey between pews and nobody would find them until Sunday morning. Not only that, but this threat might not have anything to do with spiritual forces. At least he couldn't rule it out.

Deciding on the police station, he tried to comfort Marilyn, and pushed the Hyundai as hard as he could, all the while checking the rearview mirror and watching the brown pickup as it came, inching closer.

ꕥ

Jed was having a hard time focusing on the moving vehicle. He needed to see it. If only he could channel his thoughts correctly, the engine would explode and that would be the end of their flight. But unlike the drug dealers he'd jacked the day before, the person in the fleeing car was savvy to him. All the more reason to exact information and then silence him forever.

Deciding that the car must be stopped by whatever means, he propelled a trashcan into the street ahead of the car and followed it with a rain of slats from a picket fence.

Shifting down into second gear he took a corner, tires squealing and hood rattling. Finally the car was just ahead. In it, he could see the silhouettes of two people, the one in the passenger seat clutching the driver. Seeing them allowed him to focus. He zeroed in on the engine and tried to will it to cease.

ෙ

As they left a residential neighborhood and entered an industrial area, lined with low, aluminum sided buildings, Drew gunned the accelerator. He knew this was a straightaway with little traffic and no stoplights and could only hope that the small engine would be enough. Marilyn was sobbing uncontrollably. It was all he could do to keep from scolding her.

"Please. Stop the car," she cried. "Stop the car!"

"I can't, sweetie."

The R.P.M. gauge approached redline. Glancing in the mirror, Drew could see he'd managed to put some distance between them and the truck. Maybe they could outrun their attacker, after all. He mentally mapped out a route to the nearest police station, one that would keep them on open stretches to outpace the pickup.

Marilyn turned to look behind them. "Who is it?" she asked. "What does he want?"

"I don't know, sweetie, but I need you to be brave. Sit back and put on your seatbelt."

She hesitated.

"*Now*, Marilyn," he said firmly.

She drew back, glancing apprehensively through the back window.

Just as they were getting to the end of the stretch where they would need to turn, something under the hood popped and started hissing. Steam poured around the hood and wisped up the windshield, making it hard to see. Glancing at the temperature gauge, he saw it begin moving toward red.

An overheated engine was all they needed.

Drew refused to consider what might happen if the pickup overtook them, perhaps a result of being broken down at the side of the road.

He strained to see through the steam. Halfway into the curve, he accelerated to hold onto the small lead he'd managed to pick up. The needle was nearly to the red and climbing.

Suddenly, the rear window exploded in a sickening sound of falling glass bits, causing Marilyn to scream in terror. As the temperature entered the red zone, the Hyundai started losing power, the exhausted cylinders gasping for breath. Drew watched in horror as the truck took the corner, sliding and then correcting as it aligned itself to move in for the kill.

He no longer had delusions of making it to a police station. All he wanted now was to reach the mini mart at the end of this stretch where Marilyn and he could run inside and the attendant could phone for help.

And then there was a sound like a gunshot, closely followed by a second. By the time they heard the third tire *pop*, the Hyundai had become difficult to control and the car slowed to a ridiculous crawl.

Noticing a small gap in a chain link fence, he pulled hard on the steering wheel, maneuvering the car up onto the sidewalk, just as the remaining windows exploded. Drew brought the car next to the gap in the fence, pulling ahead just enough so the passenger door could still open. In the rearview mirror he could see that the pickup was almost upon them.

He turned to Marilyn who appeared to be in shock, her eyes glazed. "There's a very bad man behind us," he told her. "I don't know what he wants, but we have to get out of here *right now*. Open your door, get out and run for that warehouse over there. Do it NOW, Marilyn!"

As soon as Marilyn squeezed through the opening, Drew threw his legs over the gearbox and pulled himself onto the passenger seat, out of the car and through the gap in the fence.

"Go," he shouted after Marilyn who was obediently jogging toward the warehouse, her awkward strides making her go too slow for comfort. "Don't look back." The man was out of the truck, holding a revolver, and aiming it in their direction. But seeing the weapon was nothing compared to what he saw next and the unnerving terror that followed as the Hyundai suddenly collapsed, crushed into a ball as though it were a crumbled piece of paper.

Drew gasped and stumbled forward, thankful to see Marilyn slip through a doorway and into the building.

⁂

Jed stood on the brakes to bring the truck to a screeching halt. They'd pulled up next to an opening in the fence and he knew exactly what they were attempting. Not because of any special insight, but because it was obvious. These people were somehow different. Just like the guy in the penthouse, he couldn't read them or get inside their heads.

They might be immune to his power, but certain that they weren't impervious to bullets, he scrambled for the revolver he'd left in the glove box. By the time he climbed out, the man was through the fence and racing after the girl.

He aimed the gun. It would be a clean shot. The guy's back would make an easy target. But he couldn't risk killing them just yet. He couldn't afford to waste another source of information. In order to follow, he crumpled up the car with his mind and shoved it aside, wielding the mental authority that was becoming easier with each use.

He'd have to follow them on foot, using whatever means he could to keep them from escaping completely. The gun would come in handy once he learned what he needed.

⁂

The inside of the warehouse was dark and uninviting, the only light coming from a row of skylights overhead. Pallets of boxes sat in marginally organized rows, while several forklifts were parked to one side. Though he wasn't sure why the place would be abandoned on a weekday, Drew suspected that someone must be around, if only in a back office. He caught up to Marilyn whose wide eyes looked ghostly in the dingy ambiance. Grabbing her by the hand, he led her down one of the rows toward the back of the building.

Somehow he knew the man with the gun would never quit until he caught them. His only hope now was to find someone – anyone – who could get word to authorities. But having seen what he'd witnessed moments earlier, he feared that no authority would be able to stop whatever force was pursuing them, save only the sovereign power of The Almighty.

"Please God. Help us," he prayed.

Suddenly he heard a voice coming from somewhere nearby, echoing off boxes and ceiling as though they were in a cavern, and he knew it was their pursuer.

"We can do this my way," the man chided, "or the hard way. All I want is to ask you some questions. That's all. I promise you'll be out of here in no time."

For all Drew knew, whoever it was would be standing there with the revolver when they rounded the next pallet. What could this man possibly want with them? He feared the answer to that question might be more than he could handle. Nothing could explain what he'd witnessed moments earlier, except that it had been a show of demonic power.

They came to the end of the row where an open space at the back of the building was darker than the rest, away from the skylights. Drew could just make out the empty blackness within the frame of a doorway, leading to another section that was devoid of all light. Marilyn gripped his hand to stay him when he began heading for it.

"I just want to check it out," he whispered.

But she was paralyzed with fear. Reluctantly, he released her hand and stuck his head into the room where darkness engulfed him. The air in the warehouse was beginning to warm up as the desert sun beat down on its metal roof, but inside the doorway, the air was cooler and he could sense it had a lower ceiling than the main part of the building they'd just come through. He felt along the wall for a switch but couldn't find one.

Entering these dark confines would be risky, but no more so than sneaking around pallets in the main section. Hoping that their predator would be unable to detect them in the darkness, Drew decided he must try to convince Marilyn to follow him through the doorway.

❧

Marilyn didn't want to breathe for fear the bad man would hear her. This wasn't like TV at all. It was very real and she knew the difference. Never in her life had she been so frightened. And yet she didn't know why the man was after them. Maybe it was somehow her fault. What if it was because she'd disobeyed Mr. Prescott and not stayed put where he'd left her that day. Now someone was coming for them. After all, she didn't really know what Mr. Prescott did at that place with the funny-sounding machines.

Because she'd disobeyed and wandered off, he hadn't been able to finish his 'busyness'. That's what he called it. That was why they were now being chased.

"Come on out," a voice called. "You're making this awfully difficult. I only want to ask some questions."

The voice sounded closer than before and the pitter-patter of Marilyn's heart wouldn't be quiet. She was afraid the man could hear it as loudly as she could and began to whimper.

Suddenly a sharp crack split the warehouse's still air and Marilyn felt a puff near her face. A wooden support column exploded near her, blossoming into a splintery flower. She screamed and ran for Drew who had disappeared into the dark place, running straight into him when she stepped through the doorway.

Even though she wasn't real smart like most people, Marilyn had watched enough TV to know that that had been the sound of a gun. As incredible as it seemed, someone was shooting at them. Oddly enough, she thought of Daffy Duck and how Elmer Fudd had blasted him with a shotgun. The funny animals in cartoons could never die. Even when they got shot. She decided she would just be like Daffy Duck. The person chasing them was nobody more important than Elmer J. Fudd with his harmless old shotgun.

It was the only thing she could hold on to, save for the strong arm of Mr. Prescott. It would have to be enough.

⁂

Jed watched as the girl ran through the doorway and into pitch darkness. He'd meant the shot to scare her, to make her freeze as if she were a deer caught in the headlights of an oncoming car. But now he'd have to follow them. He cursed and walked toward the doorway, knowing full well that no matter how they tried, they'd never be able to lose him – lights or no lights, it didn't matter.

⁂

Drew gripped Marilyn's hand as he led her deeper into the dark corridor, the only trace of light coming from behind them. A faint shift in what little light there was caused him to realize their pursuer was entering the hall. His heart pounded and he felt the walls spinning even though he couldn't see them. He prayed Marilyn wouldn't lose it now with the attacker just behind them. There would be no way to escape if she suddenly dropped to the floor in panic. Amazingly, she followed him silently.

"You can't get away." The voice said it casually, sounding too close for comfort. "I hope you realize that. I have cat eyes. You might as well come back so we can talk."

Drew glanced back just briefly enough to notice the silhouette of the man, still standing in the doorway. Obviously he was lying. If he'd been able to see them, he'd know they were less than thirty feet directly ahead and he'd have been upon them before they could take their next breath.

Suddenly his hand met with open space, a void in the side of the wall. He felt across to the other side and could tell it was a doorway. He stepped inside and gently tugged at Marilyn's arm to lead her through. Now there was no light at all, the last remaining trace no longer in sight. He felt for the door and prayed it wouldn't squeak when he closed it.

Fortunately it didn't. He pushed it carefully against the latch and left it, fearing it would make noise if he closed it all the way.

"Are you okay?" he whispered to Marilyn.

"Yes," she whispered without conviction.

He moved forward into the room and then immediately ran into something, which he quickly defined as a desk and then, all at once, there was light. Just like that, one of the overhead florescent lights hummed on. He had pulled the door closed behind them, but they were now trapped with no way out. No windows. Not even a closet. It was a small room with a desk and filing cabinet. Not much else. Marilyn's face looked ghostly pale as her big eyes stared frighteningly ahead.

The florescent tubes above them suddenly popped and glass fragments could be heard dropping onto the plastic covering above them. Then it was dark again.

Drew stood still, not sure what to do. In seconds the door would come open and a spray of bullets would no doubt fill the room, ending their flight without their ever knowing why all of this had happened.

"Get down," he whispered to Marilyn and pulled her to the floor. At least the desk separating them from the doorway would provide some protection.

Another light bulb flashed and exploded into fragments as though mortar cannons were being fired above their heads, embedding a sudden image of the room into Drew's retina. He saw a wall and a square shape, too small to be furniture. As the image began to fade, he scooted along the floor, pulling Marilyn by the hand, inching closer toward what he hoped he'd seen.

He reached the wall and began tracing thin strands of cold metal with his fingers. Praise God! Now if only it would come off and if the hole were large enough for them to fit through…

More popping lights could be heard as Drew gripped the metal grate.

ঌ৩

Jed was growing impatient. Though he could see the layout of the unlighted area with his mind, his eyes grappled with the darkness, causing a moiré of confusion. He still wrestled with his new abilities and walking in darkness was awkward and unnatural.

He willed the lights to turn on, but once again, his lack of control caused them to light and immediately burst. His agitation grew with each step.

Sensing a shadowy void shifting within a room to his left, he pushed the door open, certain there were no exits. He finally had them. But as he entered the small room, he could tell they were moving away again, on the other side of a wall. How was that possible?

"Fine," Jed seethed under his breath. "Don't want to do things my way? Then we'll do it the hard way."

He marched out of the building the way he'd come, bent on destroying the very place that concealed them. If he couldn't find out anything useful from them, then they would be destroyed.

CHAPTER 30

After his shower, Jack phoned CareSoft, hoping to find one of his marketing folks in. Almost anyone else who answered would be of little help. Software developers were notorious for coding into wee hours and then groping their way back into the office at around noon with dark circles under their eyes. They lived for the challenge of constructing substance out of nothing, virtually creating value from their minds as they typed in line upon line of code. Most of them were single. Those who weren't often had dysfunctional marriages. Their bodies usually suffered from malnutrition brought on by a vending-machine diet. These were the coal-miners of a modern era, digging out a living in spite of horrible working conditions and self-abuse.

The marketing folks, on the other hand, were always early to arrive and departed on schedule, going home to their perfect families and ordered lives. Being that there was two hours difference between Vegas and Atlanta meant there should be no problem reaching someone in marketing.

Initially, he asked for Lynchman, hoping to grill the man further about the poker game. He couldn't wait to hear what his supposed best friend and partner had to say now that he'd learned the whole thing never happened. Not that Jack was even sure how he'd handle himself or if he should reveal what he knew. But as it happened, Lynchman wasn't in, which didn't surprise Jack. The man had conveniently disappeared and probably for good reason. If he were a part of the conspiracy, the last thing he'd want is to confront Jack.

Fortunately, Claire put him through to Jillian Thomas next, a peppy young protégé with lots of marketing potential. Ever since he'd hired her straight out of college, the girl had proved to be a valuable asset to CareSoft and had already created numerous leads the company might have overlooked, being nothing short of tenacious when it came to digging up the goods on potential clients and the perfect person to do some detective work into Albatross Life Corporation.

Jack was careful to word his request in a way that would not alert her to his true reasons for wanting to learn about Albatross. He merely told her that he'd been on a flight with a man from the company and that it sounded like a good fit with their medical application software. It was a research organization and Jack felt their operations might benefit from CareSoft's patient-tracking module.

Technically, patient-tracking software was the last thing Albatross would need, since he'd witnessed firsthand how adeptly they kept tabs on their folks with Big Brother efficiency. He finished the conversation by telling her he thought they were headquartered in Scottsdale, Arizona, but that they might have other offices. Jillian seemed excited at the assignment and Jack was confident she'd sink her teeth into it quickly. If there were anything to be learned, the girl would find it.

"Since I'm out this way," Jack told her, "I'd like to swing by before coming back to Atlanta. If you could find something out within the next few hours, that would be outstanding."

"Absolutely," Jillian said. "Give me two hours and I'll give you the social security numbers and net worth of all the officers, their cousins, and the location of each of their dog's favorite fire hydrants."

"Good girl. But specifically, find out what they do. He was a little vague about that. But he gave me the idea it was patient-based, which is why I'm thinking the patient module."

"No problem, chief. If they've made a drug that'll cure the common cold, discovered a magic pill that'll lift women's breasts, or are secretly using spotted owls for guinea pigs, I'll find out."

Jack laughed. If he wasn't careful, she'd have his job – a job he was no longer sure he'd rightfully earned.

After hanging up he flipped on the TV, hoping for some distraction from his chaotic private affairs. Any news would do. Something that would make him feel as though the planet was continuing on, even though his own life was crumbling into pieces. Just as he found a suitably innocuous morning talk show, Kristen pushed through the adjoining door without knocking.

She looked different. For one thing she'd removed the chain from her neck. Apparently she had showered because her hair was damp. She wore a black midriff T-shirt that read The Mirage, Las Vegas. Her heavy makeup was gone and for the first time Jack could see her softer, more attractive features. She quipped something about the hotel shops not having any decent makeup and then ran fingers through her black, shiny hair.

For just a moment, he felt something for this strange girl who'd suddenly appeared in his life, forcing her way in like a stray kitten. Was it possible he was growing fond of her? She was, after all, a dozen years his junior. Not to mention the fact he was married. Or at least he had thought he was.

"What are you staring at?" she suddenly asked.

Jack turned away in embarrassment, trying to cover his obvious fascination. "Nothing. You just look different. That's all."

"Sorry to disappoint."

"No. It's not that," he said. "You should go without makeup more often."

She shrugged the corner of her lip and crinkled her nose. "Please!"

"Really. You look…nice." He quickly changed the subject. "I called the office and had someone do some research into Albatross. We should know something within a couple of hours. While we're waiting we can pay a visit to Mr. Houston – assuming he'll see us."

"What? We're going to ask?"

"Somehow I don't think we can get to the penthouse unannounced. They'll have security."

"I bet I could find a way up without anyone knowing," Kristen told him. "You really think he'd offer to see us after yesterday?"

Jack's attention was caught by a special bulletin that flashed across the screen beneath a live video being fed from a camera on a helicopter. It showed what looked like the jumbled remains of a structure made of metal sheeting and steel girders. An anchorman was describing the situation.

"Hello," Kristen said.

He put up a hand to keep her from speaking and stared at the TV.

"Less than an hour ago, this warehouse on West Sunset collapsed. Police have blocked off the area surrounding the building and investigators are on the scene to assess the situation. Currently we have no information as to the cause of the collapse or whether or not there were any people inside..."

Kristen seemed indifferent and even a little annoyed that Jack had ignored her.

"I don't think we can rule out terrorism," an on-the-scene man was saying. *"Although we don't have much to go on at this point."*

Jack stood and turned off the TV. "Bizarre. I guess stranger things have happened," he said. And meant it. If he needed proof, the circumstances of his own life were stranger than any building that had fallen apart for no reason. The truth of the matter was that Jack couldn't make room for any more unexplained peculiarities. It would have to remain a curious anomaly that held no bearing on their current dilemma.

"Let's go see Mr. Houston," he said.

⁂

Just as expected, the elevators they'd ridden on the day before were private, secured behind locked doors. Even though Kristen was sure she could find a way up, Jack insisted they go through the front desk. The last thing they needed was to be arrested by hotel security. Maybe Houston would agree to see them after all. If that didn't pan out he'd consider her way, a strategy she was quick to point out would be best executed if the staff hadn't been alerted to their presence. Nevertheless, they approached the concierge at the front desk.

A lone guest was standing at the long marble counter, staring blindly ahead and completely motionless while the concierge ignored him. After standing there for several minutes, thinking the man was waiting to be helped, Jack finally caught the attention of the concierge just as the guest turned and ambled away, looking confused.

"Wonder what his problem was," Kristen said under her breath and watched the man go.

The man now seemed attentive and ready to serve, so Jack asked if they could see Mr. Houston. A strange look appeared on the man's face. "I'm terribly sorry. Mr. Houston is no longer with us."

"He left?" Jack asked, glancing at Kristen. "Where did he go?"

The man looked nervous. "That is to say…he's departed."

"Departed?" Kristen said.

"Uh…he's deceased."

Jack couldn't believe it. "He's dead?" Jack asked incredulously. "What happened?"

The concierge was visibly shaken by the line of questioning. "Who did you say you were?" he asked, glancing at Kristen's Mirage T-shirt.

"I didn't. We met with him just yesterday. We are – were…" Jack said, pausing and looking to Kristen for help.

"Friends," Kristen said with a hint of urgency in her voice. "Close friends. Please tell us what happened."

"It was an unpleasant accident, I'm sorry to say," he told her in a low voice, eyes shifting left to right. "He – he fell."

"No!" Kristen exclaimed fearfully. "You mean from the Penthouse?"

"I'm afraid so," he told her. "It was an awful tragedy. Just awful."

Had the reality of their situation not been what it was – the only known source of information now gone – Jack might not have been able to hold himself back from cracking a smile at Kristen's superb acting.

"When did it happen?" Jack asked. "We saw him yesterday afternoon and everything seemed fine."

"It was an awful tragedy. Just awful," the man said again, with the same inflection; the same shake of his head.

Jack and Kristen exchanged a curious glance, wondering if the man had a screw lose.

"Around dusk." the man said, finally answering Jack's question.

"Could we…see his place?" Kristen asked, dabbing at her eyes. "Perhaps a moment alone in the penthouse would help. We were…very close. I just can't believe this has happened."

"Oh, I'm sorry. I can't allow that," the man apologized. "We have strict rules."

"It's just that…well, you see, I know it isn't the sort of thing to bring up at a time like this," Kristen said. "But I left my purse here yesterday. If it wouldn't be too much trouble…"

"Yes. Yes, of course," the man said. "Even though I can't let you in, I'll send someone up right away for the purse."

"I'd really like to go myself."

The man didn't respond, suddenly distracted by nothing in particular. He stared past them for a moment and then finally said, "I'm awfully sorry, miss. The best I can offer is to have someone try to find the purse for you."

"Oh, never mind," Kristen said impatiently. "Let's go, Jack."

But Jack wasn't finished. "Was it suicide," he asked, "or do the police suspect foul play?"

"They aren't sure," the man said. "Terrible thing. Just terrible."

"Is it just me or did you find that whole conversation really weird?" Kristen asked as they moved away. "It was like the guy was in la-la land."

"I know what you mean," Jack said, glancing back at the desk where the concierge now appeared to be busy behind the counter.

"So what do we do now?" Kristen asked.

Jack sighed and considered taking her up on her original idea. If investigators were no longer in the penthouse, maybe they could find out who Eli Houston really was and what role he played in all of this. But feeling it was too risky, he suggested they go back to the Mirage and wait for Jillian's call. After all, it might lead to something.

Kristen grudgingly agreed, but made Jack promise he'd let her take a stab at getting them into the penthouse that evening when the casino was in full tilt and security had their eye on other things.

It occurred to Jack, as they crossed the busy street, that Kristen wasn't acting skittish around automobiles the way she normally did. She was too busy glancing back over her shoulder.

"What's wrong?" he asked as they reached the other side.

"Slowly turn your head to the left," she said. "See the guy in the blue jeans and red shirt standing by that newspaper stand."

The man was around Jack's age, but shorter and more muscular. "What about him?"

"I've been noticing him since we left the building," Kristen said. "I'm pretty sure he's following us."

A black Cadillac DeVille cruised slowly up West Sunset toward a blockade where several police were turning away cars. Motorists looked perplexed and aggravated by the inconvenience of having to take another route. After all, it was their right to drive on the streets their tax dollars had paid for.

When it was the Cadillac's turn, an officer motioned it through without checking the occupants ID. Once passed the blockade, the car inched along while the passenger carefully scanned the ruins that had once been a warehouse. More officers stood alongside other officials, scratching their heads and wondering what had happened. A group of hardhats had begun to attack the ruins and were presently climbing onto the mess and peeking through gaps in the sheet metal. Two news vans with microwave dishes on top were parked along the side of the road.

The single passenger of the Cadillac told the driver to stop near a crumpled vehicle just outside of a chain link fence surrounding the grounds, where an officer stood, shining a flashlight through crevasses in the matted steel.

The passenger opened a door and told the driver to wait. He'd be right back.

Lying still in the dead silence, save for an occasional whimper coming from Marilyn, Drew wanted to give up. It had been the worst sound he'd ever heard. If the scraping of fingernails across a blackboard were nerve-wracking, the reverberation of twisting steel being ripped apart and shredded like paper had been enough to make Drew wish he hadn't been blessed with the ability to hear. Marilyn and he had mashed their ears as tightly as they could while everything around them came apart at the seams.

Marilyn had screamed in terror when it started, the intensity being exponentially worse because of the lightless cooling duct through which they were trying to crawl. The oily darkness was suffocating. Since Drew had gone into the duct first, and since it was too small to do anything but wriggle through as if they were human worms, it was impossible to comfort the poor girl. He'd felt her against his legs, crawling up as far as she could alongside.

The small shaft they were in had become even smaller as the structure around them quaked and convulsed in an ungodly manner until Drew feared they would be crushed under the weight of collapsing beams.

Finally. After several painfully long minutes, the noise and the motion had stopped.

He wanted to give up. If not for Marilyn gripping his legs and sobbing he might have merely lay still and waited for the Lord to come for his spirit.

But now that he was Marilyn's keeper, giving up was not an option.

Since there was no way to move backward through the duct, all they could do was press forward and hope the shaft hadn't been crushed beyond their ability to pass. He had no clue if it would lead them to safety. By the sound of things, they were lucky to be alive.

He called back to Marilyn, urging her to release his legs so he could move. The danger was over. The bad man was gone. It was time to get out of there. None of which he could be sure of.

After several minutes of coaxing, she let him go and they began inching along again. After spending the better part of an hour, sliding and squeezing, Drew began to doubt if they would make it out alive. But they finally turned a corner and he could see a pinpoint of light in the distance. It was sunlight. The phrase "light at the end of the tunnel" suddenly became real. The renewed hope brought new life to his limbs as he strained and pawed at the slick sides, pulling himself forward.

It was then that Drew thought he heard a voice. "Hey!" Drew shouted. "We're trapped in here."

All at once there was light. A man, dressed uncharacteristically well for digging around in ruble, pulled aside a large piece of metal sheeting. He reached in to grab Drew's hand and pull him out.

"Is the girl with you?" he asked while Drew pushed with his feet to free himself from the suffocating confines.

Later he would wonder who his rescuer was and how he had known about Marilyn. But for the time being, he was content to accept assistance without questioning it. Together they helped Marilyn out of the rubble. Her cheeks were streaked from tears running down her dirty face.

"Come with me," the man said.

"What's happening?" Drew asked. "Who are you?"

"No time to explain."

Drew grabbed Marilyn by the hand and followed the man past the rubble toward the street. Several people in the area glanced their way, but returned to the business of sorting through the mess. When he saw his crumpled car, still lying in a heap by the side of the road, Drew felt sick. He wanted to believe it had been nothing more than a bad dream. But here was living proof that it had happened, just the way he remembered.

They stepped through the same gap in the fence they'd come through earlier. The driver of a black Cadillac jumped out when he saw them coming and opened the rear door for Drew and Marilyn. The seats were covered with dark gray leather, soft to the touch when they slid in. The man who'd helped them out of the rubble got in on the passenger side.

"Where are you taking us?" Drew asked.

Marilyn, dazed from the ordeal, sat quietly beside him, hands in her lap. Her hair was tangled and the yellow top she'd been wearing was now soiled from having rubbed up against the cooling shaft.

"We need to make a stop and pick up two others," the strange man told him. "After that…we'll get word."

Drew didn't know what the man meant, but was satisfied to sit back, feeling marginally safe again. If there were forces out there like the man who'd been chasing them, perhaps there were angel-like people as well. Just like the man who pulled them out of the ruble.

CHAPTER 31

Jack had nearly become convinced that Kristen was right. The man in the red shirt followed them across the street, keeping enough distance so he wouldn't be obvious. Rather than seeing it as a threat, Jack decided it was good they were being followed. That meant there were still those around who knew what was going on, even if Houston had fallen to his death from the penthouse. And even though the man behind them might be dangerous, Jack was convinced the guy worked for Albatross and was assigned to keep track of the company's victims. That's how he thought of himself now. Whether or not he'd agreed to any of this at another time, he was a victim and certain Albatross's actions could be prosecuted in a court. Signed agreement or not.

But when he looked back before entering through the main door of the Mirage, the man had stopped a distance back and was engaged in a conversation with a young man wearing baggy clothes, carrying a boom box radio in one hand and a skateboard in his other. Was the kid just one more strand in their tightly knit web of deception, Jack wondered? Whatever the answer, the man in the red shirt no longer seemed interested in following.

When they reached Jack's room, the message light on the phone glowed red. Even though it had only been a half hour since he'd spoken with her, Jack wondered if Jillian had already found something out about Albatross. He picked up the phone to listen to the recorded message. There were three.

Kristen seemed preoccupied at the sink just outside the suite's bathroom, fidgeting first with the light switch and then with the faucet knob.

The first message was from the front desk, where there was a concern about his credit card, which had been rejected while trying to process the evening's charges. Jack sighed and shook his head.

"It's the front desk," Jack said. "They're saying my credit card doesn't work."

"A little maxed, are we?" Kristen said. "That's what happens when you use it to buy cars and unnecessary hotel rooms."

"No. I have plenty of credit. This happened before and it cleared itself up."

"Right!"

"What's that supposed to mean?"

"I dunno," Kristen said. "Maybe the wife decided to go shopping without telling you."

"Shhh!" Jack hissed, listening to the second message. He grabbed a pen and small pad and scribbled something down. He pressed a button on the keypad, listening to the message again to be sure he'd heard it correctly.

Kristen's curious eyes begged for an explanation. "What?" she said. "Who was it?"

"Jillian. The girl I had investigate Albatross," Jack said and gave a look of satisfaction. "We have an address."

Kristen grabbed the piece of paper and stared at it. "Cool. Scottsdale, like we thought."

"Funny thing is," Jack said, "there was no listing of an Albatross Life Corporation in Scottsdale, Arizona. In fact, she couldn't find a listing anywhere in the country. In any country for that matter."

Kristen looked up from the paper. "Then how'd she get it?"

"That's the odd thing. She looked on the Internet. The major search engines didn't have anything about Albatross. But Jillian likes using the more obscure engines and she happened upon a reference in a medical white paper, mentioning Albatross as a leading company in gene therapy. She said the article didn't give much information – at least as far as Albatross was concerned – but that the subject of the document was longevity."

"You mean like living longer?"

"That's right."

Kristen studied the address again. "She found out all that since you called her? This girl's good. How'd she get the address?"

"Once she knew what kind of research they do, she started digging in the right places. Medical websites and everything she could find on longevity. Said she didn't find much that mentioned Albatross, but came across some investor relation's stuff. It was some kind of online prospectus or business plan meant to attract deep pockets. Here's the really weird part. Jillian didn't think the thing was legit. Thought it was some kind of hoax. Either that or they made some serious typos. You wouldn't think they'd make that kind of mistake on a business plan."

"What was it?" Kristen asked.

"She said the date on the document was all wrong and their timeline was out of whack."

"What does she mean it was wrong? How could she know when it was written?"

Jack chuckled. "Well, it was dated eleven years from now."

Kristen scrunched her face. "Huh?"

"Yeah," Jack said. "I'm not even going to try to understand that one. But at least it had the company address. That much has to be true. And it was in Scottsdale, Arizona, just like you said."

"You mean, just like Eli Houston said," Kristen pointed out. "Who's now dead, I might add."

"True. His death may or may not be related."

"Pu-lease!" Kristen said. "You expect me to believe he just happened to commit suicide the day we came to visit? I don't think so."

"I honestly don't know," Jack said. "But I say we go to Scottsdale. Poke around and see what we can find."

"You like living dangerously," Kristen said, grinning. "I like that."

Jack ignored her and headed for the bathroom. "Get your things together. I'll need to take care of the problem at the front desk and then I think we should rent a car. Drive to Scottsdale."

Kristen shook her head. "You're incredible. You've maxed out your credit card and still you insist on renting a car. I'm surprised you don't want to find the nearest dealership and buy a new one. I could get us there and it wouldn't cost you a dime."

Jack had stopped at the door to the bathroom and looked back at her. "Thanks, but no thanks. I don't hitchhike."

Kristen brushed the nails of her fingers on her black shirt. "Your choice. Oh, by the way. The water isn't working. I tried it when we came in. Nothing's working."

Jack had flipped on the light switch to the bathroom and just realized it never came on. He lifted the silver handle to the faucet, but nothing came out. Not even a surviving drip. For a second he wondered if the hotel would have turned off service since his credit card hadn't worked. But then he decided the idea was ludicrous. Certainly they wouldn't do such a thing. In any event, he'd had enough bizarre circumstances over the past few days to last several painfully long life spans.

"Let's try your room," he said.

❧

Jed would wait to make his move until there weren't people around. Following his quarry back to a hotel room would be perfect. He could question them at leisure there and they wouldn't be able to get away like the members of his last party. Not only that, and unlike the others, they didn't seem to know he was following them.

He held up a hand, flexing his fingers, the feeling of power now growing stronger. He was pleased at how easily he'd turned the warehouse into a pile of useless rubble by merely exercising his anger toward the building. He was becoming invincible. Unstoppable.

It was only a matter of time until anything he desired would be his, merely by thinking it. Yet he wondered how he was able to wield this kind of supernatural authority and for what purpose. He'd never have believed such things were possible if he hadn't witnessed them firsthand. What eternal being had decided to step down from the cosmos and give him the unfathomable power of the gods? As the feeling of supremacy surged through his veins, his head filled with delusions of grandeur and immeasurable self-importance. Maybe he, himself, were a god.

Jed was beginning to believe that perhaps he was a gift to the world, a leader of nations, an invincible general who couldn't be defeated. His purpose was no doubt greater than he could imagine, his potential only now starting to be realized. Though solving world hunger and bringing about peace on earth weren't at the top of his list, something along the lines of aggressive leadership in a chaotic world were. This would serve society to a greater good. Left to themselves, people made a mishmash of convoluted ideals and principles. Ultimately, dictatorship was the only solution. People needed protection from themselves. And up until now there hadn't been anyone who could fill the lofty role on a global basis.

Though he wasn't sure from where he'd come, his obvious fate was slipping onto his hand like a well-fitting glove. These thoughts tickled his hungry ego while he fancied himself becoming the greatest figure in human history. By the time he was done they'd reset the yearly calendar to the day he woke up in that little clinic in Bootleg Hill, Nevada. It was only a matter of time, inevitable.

This made the others – those who were like him – more of a threat than he'd realized earlier. They must be dealt with according to plan. There was no room for compromise. He'd extract what they knew and then dispose of them.

But just after crossing the street while following the couple, he heard something that stopped him cold. It was the second time he'd heard it, his prior message coming from a radio. Only this time it was set to music.

A teenager was rolling slowly by on a skateboard, wearing baggy clothes and a baseball cap, the bill reversed to face backwards, a ghetto blaster held to his ear.

...allow me to introduce myself, the tremulous voice slithered through the music.

I'm a man of wealth and taste.

I've been around for a long, long year.

Stole many a man's soul and fate.

These were no less than the exact words he'd heard spilling over the pickup's aging radio. People on the sidewalk coming toward the boy stepped out of the way, leaving a wake of aggravated pedestrians. Jed stretched out his hand toward the skateboarder, which made the young man suddenly plant a braking foot on the ground, causing him to nearly lose his balance.

He glanced around in confusion, wondering what had happened.

...hope you guess my name.
But what's puzzling you, is the nature of my game.
Ooo, who. Ooo, who.

The song toyed with Jed, as if it spoke to him directly. *What's puzzling you, is the nature of my game,* it said. Just below the surface there was something entirely disturbing about it, evil. Meant specifically for him.

Jed beckoned the skateboarder with his mind. The teenager's mouth hung open as he turned his head with a puzzling gaze. When his eyes came to rest on Jed, he stomped the end of the skateboard, causing it to flip up so he could grab it, and walked toward Jed.

...when Blitzkrieg raged and the bodies sank.
Pleased to meet you. Hope you guess my name.
Ooo, who. Ooo, who.

The young man's face was expressionless as he stood, staring at Jed. "You say somethin', man?"

"That music," Jed said. "What is it? Where does it come from?"

"This music?" he asked and nodded toward the ghetto blaster. "The Stones, man. It's classic. What about it?"

The name meant nothing to Jed. "Who is this...'Stone' person?"

The kid's acned face suddenly cracked a grin. "You serious, man? You know. The Stones. As in *Rolling Stones*."

The fact that the stones were rolling or otherwise stationary didn't seem relevant. "Who's singing it? What's his name?"

"Jagger, man. As in Mick. Where've you been for the last forty years?"

Good question, Jed thought.

Clearly, this line of questioning was getting him nowhere. As far as the kid was concerned, it was merely a classic song, played by a forty-year-old band. Nothing more. If this Jagger person – *as in Mick* – were somehow linked to Jed's identity, he'd have to seek the man out. Find out what he knew. But somehow that wasn't right. It wasn't the musician that held the key he needed, but the words themselves, almost as if the band were merely being used as an instrument of delivery without knowing from whom the message came or where it was to be given.

But what's confusing you, is the nature of my game.

Ooo, who. Ooo, who.

Just as every cop's a criminal and all the sinners, saints.

And then the kid offered a tidbit of his own. And with it came the understanding Jed sought at exactly the moment the song, itself, revealing as it did the identity of the messenger.

"You never heard *Sympathy For The Devil*, man? It's a classic."

As I end this tale, just call me Lucifer, 'cause I'm in need of some restraint.

Jed fell back, shocked into speechlessness.

"That it?" the kid said and then waved a hand in front of Jed's face. "Hello!" Finally he dropped the skateboard, hopped on and pushed off with his free foot and disappeared into the crowd.

The last words he heard were, *Use all your well-learned qualities or I'll lay your soul to waste.* The only thing missing from the lyrics were the words given specifically to Jed over the truck's radio, his personal commission and purpose in the world.

You're here to do my bidding.

Where moments earlier he'd fancied himself becoming a central figure in human history, now he was faced with the possibility that perhaps his role was the antithesis of a great leader. His allegiance sided with destruction rather than salvation. Anarchy rather than order. Darkness rather than light.

No.

It couldn't possibly be.

Even though Jed could believe he'd been given the power of gods for the purpose of leading the world out of chaos, it was far more difficult to believe in devils. His mind grappled with a man in a red suit, holding a pitchfork and rejected the idea as ludicrous. There was no such thing. Unless, of course, Lucifer was a far more cunning adversary that hid behind a shroud of obscurity, selecting his vessels with great care and then equipping them with his dark powers.

He thought of how he'd brought down the warehouse with incredible destructive force. But that had been for *his* purpose.

Hadn't it? He wasn't acting on the whims of some underworld leader whose throne room rested amongst fire and brimstone. Was he?

A strange feeling came over him as he stood in the Las Vegas sunlight, the pavement heating up around his feet as if Hades were rising up to greet him from below. A bead of sweat trickled from his forehead. And for a moment he thought he could feel the darkness of Hell. Instead of rising up out of the earth, it was approaching from the west like a massive wall of destruction. It was as if everything were being engulfed in its suffocating grasp. And it was coming.

He was the messenger of darkness and the darkness was coming.

Could it be true? How else could he explain his abilities – *his well-learned qualities?* Though Jed wouldn't deny he was filled with selfish ambition, the idea that he'd been chosen by a being that was purely evil was repugnant, sickening.

Deep down he felt he could justify his actions for some greater good, even though he couldn't explain what it was. But to destroy and maim, purely for the sake of diabolical pleasure was unfathomable, unspeakable.

You're here to do my bidding.

Jed clasped his ears. Desperately, he tried to tell himself it wasn't so, attempted to ignore the slithering voice now chanting through his head. He wasn't evil. Manipulative, yes. But not evil. Not an instrument of pointless malevolence.

After several minutes struggling, his composure finally returned. The voice became a dull whisper. Ever present, but manageable. Jed wasn't sure how, but someone was messing with him, perhaps one of the others that possessed his abilities. It was all the more reason to hunt them down. Find out what they knew.

He resumed his trek toward the Mirage, quickly squelching any attempts by the voice inside his head to confuse him further.

Use all your well-learned qualities.

Or I'll lay your soul to waste.

It was absurd. He was in control. There was no reason to panic or hurry. No reason to fear something that didn't exist outside of the paper-thin speakers of a radio.

❧

After being fired, Jared Guerridelli had returned to Chicago, a place where he felt more comfortable. Coming back to his hometown offered Jared plenty of connections. And there was always the family business to fall back on.

As he purchased a girlie magazine from a newsstand, he reflected on the fact that he wasn't too upset about being let go. It had really only been a job within a job, after all. The family business had been paying for his technical abilities and they'd wanted to make sure gramps got the biggest bang for his buck. Collecting two paychecks for the same work had been sweet. And the job itself was a badass ride while it lasted. Then suddenly Sweeney had been on to him. Good things didn't last forever, and Jared was the first to realize he'd pushed too far, too fast. In hindsight he should have eased the old man into things, letting him grow slowly with the fantasy. In a way he felt a little sad he hadn't been able to stick with it longer. It would have been a hoot making gramps do things he only dreamed of. Loretta had been his idea, but the Viper hadn't bitten. Too bad. Loretta would have done the old man's heart muscle a world of good.

As for Albatross, he'd screwed them, for sure. Jared wondered if they'd discovered his little stunt yet. Once they did, it would take them months to recover. Nobody fired a Guerridelli and got away with it.

When he heard the voice yell, "Freeze!" he dropped the magazine along with a big warm pretzel. He turned around to face several dark uniformed men pointing revolvers at his torso.

"Shit!"

"Get your hands behind your head. Move it!"

He did as the agent said and was immediately rewarded with the cool hard feel of handcuffs being snapped around his wrists, all the while considering that the good folks at Albatross must have, indeed, found his departing gift. Tough luck.

Still he wondered how the FBI had caught up to him so quickly.

Of course, they couldn't arrest him for impersonating the prince of darkness. But he was charged on several other counts, including fraud, aggravated assault, conspiracy to commit murder – a charge they'd never make stick – and tampering with government research.

Jared wasn't worried. His old man would come to the rescue and he'd be out by the end of the day. It was just so damned inconvenient.

CHAPTER 32

Jack walked through the doorway separating the two hotel rooms, Kristen following behind, when he stopped and snapped his fingers. "I never listened to the third message," he said.

"There were three?" Kristen asked, sounding surprised. "My, my. Aren't we the popular one?"

"Cute," Jack said and tried to go back into his room. But Kristen blocked his path.

"You go do your business in my bathroom and I'll check the last message," she said. She turned and headed for the phone.

Jack shook his head in dismay as he glanced over her room. It was a mirror copy of his with a couple of differences. The strap to Kristen's purse was draped over a chair. But most noticeable was the bed. Whereas Jack barely made use of the one side, Kristen's bed was a jumbled mess with covers, blankets, pillows and sheets all twisted and thrown around. No one would have believed it was the resting place of one girl. Clearly she was no sleeping beauty.

He couldn't imagine trying to sleep while Hurricane Kristen raged in the next bed, now glad he'd insisted on two rooms. Being homeless, normally sleeping in malls and on park benches, she'd probably felt lost in a sea of covers and had been swimming for shore.

Walking to the sink, he flipped the light switch and it came on, lighting up the vanity. He lifted the silver faucet handle and water sprayed out, gushing copiously into the marble sink. The utility problems must have been isolated to his suite. Though he didn't dwell on the issue, it was curious that both the electrical and water would go out at the same time.

He shrugged it off and made use of Kristen's bathroom, his thoughts occupied by the results of Jillian's Albatross findings. Why hadn't the company been listed? Jillian had no doubt used more than one method to try and find them. Dun & Bradstreet was one route she'd probably followed. And the girl had several other methods that she used to cross reference and dig up the goods on virtually any company; whether they were unlisted or not, well known or obscure. The only way they could slip under Jillian's radar would be to deliberately hide themselves. Not a great marketing approach for any business, regardless of their product.

The only thing that made sense would be if the company was the property of the U.S. government, existing solely for performing classified research. Based on what he knew about Albatross and his own sketchy involvement, this was not only possible, but likely.

Putting together his conversation with Petrov, the information Jillian found on the web, and his own speculation, he decided that Albatross was conducting classified government research in the field of longevity, life extension, or whatever they called it. Kristen and he were part of that research, an arrangement they'd supposedly agreed to at one time. Apparently a side affect was amnesia, which made the agreement suspect; leaving them to go on faith it even existed. Once they'd poked and probed with their needles and did whatever the hell they did, Albatross placed them in make-believe lives, expecting them to take things at face value. He was a corporate V.P. She was a Harvard Law student. He'd been in an auto accident and she'd had a life-threatening fever. Now they had amnesia and wasn't it a shame.

This is your life.

But the thing that puzzled Jack, was why the company apparently followed their research candidates around. If the research was complete, why didn't they leave the 'victims' alone? They'd done their business, so why stick around? Unless, of course, they weren't finished yet. What if Kristen and he were essentially walking and breathing lab rats, meandering around life's maze, searching for a tasty morsel of understanding while proving some sort of longevity theory?

The idea was barely conceivable. But now as he thought about it, that was the only thing that rang true. Who knew how far Albatross had gone? He suspected that tapping phone lines and installing hidden cameras weren't out of the question. Not to mention surrounding them with people whose souls were bought and paid for by Albatross Life Corporation. Lynchman. Maggie. *Justin and Amanda, his kids?*

Jack flushed the toilet, zipped up, washed his hands and went to tell Kristen that the water and lights in her room were working. But when he came out of the bathroom, the place seemed unusually quiet. The door on this side was partially open and he could see through to the other room. Kristen wasn't at the phone. Instinctively, he didn't push through, but called to her instead, "Kris? You there?"

No reply.

"Hey," he called out. "Your lights and water work. I don't know why…"

He stepped into his room and noticed the light over his vanity was now glowing. But the room was empty. Kristen wasn't there. The bathroom was empty and dark, but the door to the hotel room as slightly ajar.

Though he wasn't sure why, a flutter went up his spine as he studied the open door. Had she left for some reason without saying anything? She'd been moaning about her lack of makeup. Maybe she went to find some. But certainly she'd say something. Especially since she was about to check the third message. He looked at the phone, but the message light was still lit.

Now he was growing worried. If she'd listened to the last message the light would have gone out. So either someone called while he was in the bathroom – unlikely since he would have heard the phone ring – or Kristen had never listened to it.

He stepped into the hall. It was eerily quiet. To the left the corridor seemed to stretch on forever. A newspaper lay in front of every door. Strange that no one had picked theirs up as late in the day as it was now. But that was beside the point. A dozen doors down, there was a break to one side where he knew a bay of elevators sat, though he couldn't see them from where he stood. There was a cleaning cart several doors down, which wasn't unusual given the time of day. To the right the hall ended abruptly at a vending machine alcove and a metal door with an exit sign above.

Even though hotel corridors could often be still and quiet – he'd stayed in his share during the eighteen months he could remember – this one seemed unnaturally so. It was as though all life had simply gone to sleep on the fifth floor of the Mirage.

And even though he hated to do it, he had to question Kristen's sincerity. Her act in front of the concierge had been flawless. Even though he wanted to believe she was truthful, he had his doubts. She could be a master of manipulation.

But deep down there was something else. It wasn't the indignation he'd feel if he discovered that she hadn't been completely honest with him. He was afraid something had happened to her. Days ago, he wouldn't have given her a second thought if he'd seen her sleeping on a park bench. But now she'd become a part of his life. There was an uncomfortable emptiness when he considered her absence.

Her purse.

If she'd left, her purse would be gone.

Jack hurried back into his room and went to the doorway separating the suites. He went through and glanced at where he'd seen her purse draped over the chair seconds earlier and was relieved to see it was still there.

Somewhere a door slammed shut.

"Everything come out alright?" a voice behind him said.

Jack jumped and wheeled around. Kristen stood there grinning.

"What's with you?" she said. "You look like you've just seen a ghost."

"Where were you?"

"Just down the hall. Don't have a heart attack."

Jack felt flustered. He didn't want to seem obvious, but he'd really been worried.

"I didn't know where you were. That's all."

"Miss me?"

He ignored her comment. "I thought you were going to listen to the message."

"I was. Just as I was about to, your light flickered on," she said. "It was like really freaky. It was kind of making these weird electrical snapping sounds." Kristen shivered as if she'd suddenly caught a chill. "I went to tell the cleaning woman to send someone to look at it."

Jack pushed past her and studied the lights. "Well, they seem to be working now. Are they sending someone?"

"I never found anyone. That's what's strange. I went into the room where a cart was parked and there was nobody there, even though the door was open."

"Maybe they ran out of supplies," Jack offered.

"Maybe. I don't know what they were cleaning, though. The room was empty."

"What do you mean, empty?"

"As in, no beds. No furniture. No bathroom fixtures. Nothing. White walls so bare it hurts your eyes to look at them."

"Really?"

"No. I'm lying. I've got nothing better to do than go around saying there's an empty hotel room down the hall."

"Just –" Jack held up a hand. "Never mind."

"It's kind of like it was when we went into that guy's house," she said.

"Hasselbaum?"

"Yeah."

"But his house had stuff in it."

"But. You know. We thought it was like a prop or something. I know it sounds crazy, but that's the same feeling I get about this place."

Jack couldn't help himself from laughing. "What? You think the whole Mirage is a big prop for our benefit. Somehow I don't think so."

"Oh, never mind."

"No. Go ahead. I'd love to hear it."

"I can't explain. It's just a feeling I have, all right?"

Even though he was teasing her now, he'd felt the same way moments earlier while staring down the hauntingly empty hallway.

"Well," Jack said. "All I know is we need to get moving if we hope to make it to Scottsdale today. I wonder how far it is." He went to the phone to listen to the third message.

Kristen crossed her arms and glared at him from across the room.

The first two messages were still there. When he listened to the third, he frowned. "Huh?" he said in puzzlement.

"What?"

Jack hung up the phone, frowning. "It was some guy. Didn't say who he was, but that we should get out of here right now. Go outside where there's lots of people, he said. Said someone's after us. They're trying to kill us."

"Lovely."

"Maybe we should do as he says."

"You believe it?"

"Last time this happened I made the mistake of thinking it was a joke. I've learned my lesson."

"You mean the rock through the condo window," Kristen observed.

They both turned their heads in unison when they heard three firm raps on the door.

"Maybe it's the management come to get credit card information," Kristen said.

"If we're lucky."

Jack peeked through the peephole.

"It's the guy that was following us," he hissed. "I wonder what he wants?"

"What if he's the one that killed Eli?" Kristen asked, whispering.

The two caught each other's frightened gaze.

∞

The bluish glow in the dimly lit observation pit caused their faces to look like undead creatures as they stared at their computer screens. One of them occasionally typed something on the keyboard, groaning.

Petrov looked on, watching his life dissolve before his eyes.

"How could this happen?" he demanded, shaking his head in disgust. "Didn't we take precautions? I don't understand."

"We did," Sweeney muttered. "It wasn't meant to keep out monitors. Jared knew everything we did. Who knew we'd be sabotaged from within?"

"This is a disaster. Is there nothing we can do?"

"I'm working on it," Ridley said, typing furiously.

"How long do we have before – well, before the end?" Petrov asked Sweeney.

"Three hours and…" Sweeney glanced at another screen. "Forty-seven minutes. But it's already begun. Collapse is coming from the perimeter and moving toward the center. Damn it!"

"We'll never make it," Petrov said softly. "We'd better alert the medical staff. Meltdown is imminent."

Ridley's fingers became a blur, creating one continuous symphony of clicking. "Wait. Wait. I'm close now. Just two more firewalls and I'll bypass Jared," he said, grinning with satisfaction. "One more and we're in."

The pit became deathly quiet, every eye glued to the screen. Suddenly Ridley stopped typing. "Shit!" he said.

"What?" Petrov demanded. "What happened? You were almost in."

"It's no good."

"A trap?" Sweeney asked.

"A trap," Ridley confirmed. "Covered his tracks pretty well." He looked up at Petrov and Sweeney, both oddly pale in the screen's glow. "There's not a damn thing we can do."

Petrov's heart sank. There had to be something. Anything.

"What about Satish's idea?" Sweeney asked. "What about the safe house?"

"It's not bad. Problem is, since all we have is voice comm, we won't be able to move them from here. They have to get there by themselves. And with under four hours before total meltdown…"

"Three hours and forty-one minutes," Sweeney said.

"I doubt they can make it."

"We have to try," Petrov said. "If we don't we're going to have one hell of a medical crisis on our hands. We don't need to worry about anyone who can make it. We'll just have to deal with the others on a case-by-case basis."

Petrov didn't relish going to family members and explaining what had happened.

"Let's get Satish in here ASAP. Work with him setting up the safe house," Sweeney said, then turned to Zack, standing to one side. "Better let everyone know. It's going to be a long night. We'll need to find a location immediately so they can start moving."

"There's only one logical place because of its proximity to the hub," Ridley said, typing again with passion. "Scottsdale. It'll buy them more time than anywhere else."

"Scottsdale it is," Sweeney said. "Let's move."

Petrov turned to Sweeney with a concerned look. "Will it work?" he asked.

"It better!"

Even though there were candidates as far away as New York, ones that would never make it on time, there were plenty who might. It was worth a try. The alternative was unspeakable.

Ridley sighed.

"What?" Petrov asked.

"Now he's coming for Jack and Kristen. If he gets to them," Ridley said, looking at Petrov, "it will complicate things. If we're all busy setting up the safe house, we may not have time to deal with it."

Petrov gritted his teeth. He wished he'd never heard the name Guerridelli. "Saving as many as possible has to be the priority."

"They'll have to fend for themselves for the time being," Sweeney said. "We're still having them picked up. Right?"

"Yeah," Zack replied. "I got a message to them to get in the open."

"If Guerridelli gets close that means five are at risk instead of two," Ridley pointed out. "Maybe we better have the others go on without Jack and Kristen."

Petrov turned away from the screen and put a hand to the back of his neck. He could no longer bear the burden alone. Why had Hunter taken the easy way out and left him to battle the world by himself?

"What should I tell them?" Ridley asked.

After several long seconds, each painful tick moving them closer to destruction, Sweeney said, "I think we still need to try and pick them up. If things get out of hand, we'll abort. All we can do is hope for the best."

Ridley stared blankly at the screen. Petrov wondered if Sweeney had made the right call. As it was, with Guerridelli in pursuit, Jack and Kristen didn't stand a chance.

ꕥ

Until that moment, Jack had felt reasonably safe. The fact that the guy following them was now in the hall was no reason to panic. They were securely behind a hotel's door, manufactured to withstand fire, noise, and break-ins. And if the guy didn't leave they could call hotel security.

And although this was a heartening thought, his pulse was pounding. When he heard the click coming from the lock, he instinctively reached up and moved the steel security latch over the nub and backed away. The door came open and caught the latch, separating them from the guy with nothing more than a small security device that looked far too inadequate.

Jack thought quickly and motioned for Kristen to go through to the other room. She went without speaking. Jack followed her and pulled the door on his side as far as he could and still remove his fingers. Then he pushed the door closed on her side. As he did so, he heard the sound of splintering wood, followed by a door slamming against a wall. The guy was in his room.

Kristen looked scared, standing between the bed and the vanity.

"Should I call for help?"

Jack looked at the phone and then at the door he'd just secured. Fortunately there was no handle on the other side, but he wasn't sure how long it would hold if the guy started kicking at it.

"Wait," he said. It was important that this man be well into his room before they slipped out. "Get ready to leave. When we go, make for the emergency exit to the right. We'll take the stairs down."

Jack put his ear to the door, just as it suddenly shuddered, causing the jamb to moan with fatigue and him to jump back in alarm. There had been no sound of impact that should have accompanied such an attack. Something strange was happening.

Now the doorjamb was vibrating as though under intense pressure. Jack pointed to Kristen. "Go."

She opened the door and disappeared to the right. Jack followed. Just before he entered the hall, an earsplitting crack came from behind. When he turned to flee toward the emergency exit, he caught sight of the door flying across the room. The whole building seemed to reverberate with the impact as it crashed into the opposite wall.

They flew into the stairwell and the world went from Technicolor to drab. The walls were gray cinderblock and the stairs were metal with raised crosshatches, so the soles of shoes wouldn't slip.

Jack and Kristen were down one flight when they heard the door above them open, echoing in the shaft. They continued their descent, breathless.

All around, something suddenly groaned, as though the place were alive. A hauntingly eerie sound ricocheted off the cinderblock walls. The whole shaft trembled and moaned.

Strangely dizzy, Jack managed to keep up with Kristen as she scrambled down the treads. Suddenly she stumbled and caught herself on the railing.

"AH!" she screamed. "It's hot."

She was right! He helped her up, feeling dizzy again. Above, methodical drumming footsteps grew closer.

The sound of groaning steel continued.

Ahead of Kristen now, Jack saw why she had stumbled. The gaps between the treads had become uneven, some two inches and others as much as a foot.

He gasped in disbelief. "Watch your step," he told Kristen and continued down, holding her hand so they could steady each other. Since the railing would scorch their skin, it made for a treacherous descent.

When they reached the second floor landing, it was all they could do to keep from falling. The stairs below were growing violent. The landing, itself, was now heaving and moaning. They'd have no choice but to exit and continue their flight through the hotel corridors. The last message had said to get to where people were. They had to get in the open.

When he tried to open the door it caught on the landing, now bending and convulsing out of shape. Though Jack pulled, the steel door was frozen, pinned by the floor. The sound in the shaft was growing unbearable. Suddenly the landing dipped downward, causing a furrow, and the door swung open. They scrambled through, once again on solid ground.

CHAPTER 33

Kristen's hand still throbbed from touching the railing. She glanced at the red burn marks as they ran down the hallway. Even though she knew that many of her fears were far from rational, she was aware that one more had been added to the list. Stairwells were now off limits. Even though an automobile had never actually attacked her, a bunch of wild stairs had.

She'd thought all along that seemingly harmless mechanical things really had minds of their own, filled with malice. Now there was proof. She even had a witness.

They reached a pair of elevators and Jack pushed the down button. It didn't light, but Kristen was grateful. If a stairwell was bad, an elevator was wicked bad.

"Great!" he said, and continued down the hall.

Kristen followed, wondering why there were no people. She tried to remember the last time she'd seen someone – anyone – and decided it had been when they'd passed through the lobby earlier. The thing pursuing them couldn't be human. Though she harbored the notion that inanimate objects were evil, the one chasing them was the puppet master that made them dance. He was evil incarnate, bringing all her nightmares to life.

The hall seemed to stretch on forever. Suddenly the walls were alive, curling inward from the ceiling and floor. The wallpaper peeled from the top and bottom, silently scrolling toward the center.

A chill ran up Kristen's spine and she could feel the panic beginning to spread.

Not now!

If she passed out, she'd never make it. The puppet master would be upon her in seconds. She remembered the dream: the monster digging toward her. The thing behind them was even more terrifying than that.

Jack was farther ahead and the gap was widening. She made the mistake of looking back. All the doors in the hall rattled violently in their jambs and she saw the puppet master emerge through the emergency exit. He walked slowly, methodically toward them, confident he'd catch up and there was nothing they could do to get away.

Maybe there wasn't.

Kristen froze, staring. Her dream now real. The monster coming for her.

She had to get away but her legs wouldn't move.

The darkness hovered over her. She pressed against the coffin lid. But she was awake. Wasn't she? Images of the grave were just a dream.

Something was grabbing her.

"Kris! What are you doing?" Jack yelled. "Come on."

She turned and saw that he'd come back for her. "I…don't know if I can make it," she stammered.

"Look at me," Jack demanded. "Right here." He made a V with his fingers and pointed to his eyes.

She tried to focus. She could feel the enemy approaching from behind. That mechanical breathing. Those sharp claws ready to rip through the aging wooden slats.

And then her eyes locked with his. The connection was made and she drew strength from his determination. A lifeline. He'd thrown it to her again. He was alive. Whatever everything else was in her life, Jack Stuart was alive.

He looked over her shoulder, breaking the gaze for a brief moment.

"Kris. We've got to go. Are you all right?"

She smiled and said, "Kiss me."

"Are you out of your mind."

"I don't move unless you kiss me."

She, herself, wasn't sure why she did it. It was almost as if to confirm that he was a living, breathing human who could have feelings for her. If he were nothing more than all the others in her life, then why struggle. Why bother running away from the inevitable end that awaits us all.

His lips touched hers, for the briefest moment. It was enough. She felt alive again, escaping the beckoning grave once more.

As they approached the end of the hall where a pair of glass doors separated the rooms from the common area, two side doors blew off their hinges, sucked across the exit, blocking their progress. Askew, the top corners rested against the overhang, while bottom corners caught on the aluminum sill.

When they reached the blockade, Jack grabbed a corner with both hands, his face contorted in strain. "What the hell?" he shouted.

They both saw it at once. One of the rooms where the door had blown off was empty just like the room she'd seen earlier. Pure white walls. No furniture. Not even carpeting. Nothing.

Kristen glanced down the hallway. For the first time it registered how normal the guy seemed. He strolled toward them as if heading for the casino, but he was now less than a hundred feet and closing.

Jack looked perplexed, turning his head frantically around, trying to figure out their next move.

Where Jack was at a loss, Kristen was now thinking clearly. She pushed on the glass door and it moved. "Hold it open," she said.

Jack did as she asked while Kristen dropped to her belly, pulling herself through. She stood and held it open.

"Now you."

Jack looked at the tight squeeze. "I don't think I'll fit." He turned around and stared up the hall. The guy was no more than fifty feet. Jack leaned his back against the door, frozen.

Kristen reached through and grabbed the back of his shirt. "You have to try," she screamed. "Look at me!"

He turned to face her. Their eyes met as she gave back the strength he'd given her moments earlier.

"Get down on the ground and try," she said, forcing her voice to remain calm. "And don't worry about bozo back there."

Jack dropped to the floor and poked his head through. His shoulders caught on the doors. He turned to the side, but his masculine frame was hopelessly large for the small gap. Kristen pushed with all her weight to make the door shift, but it was as futile as if she were attempting to lift a corner of the building.

Their stalker was twenty feet away now.

A crack.

It started in the center of one of the doors, a razor thin line that spread outward along the grain of wood.

"Get back," Jack yelled, then tucked his head inside.

Just as Kristen stepped away, the wooden door split in two. The bottom half, under intense pressure and no longer held in place by the overhang, flipped violently inward, thrusting through the glass door, which blew into an icy spray that blasted past Kristen and tingled like wind chimes as they struck concrete below. The top half of the door now slid to the floor, repositioning itself across the bottom of the doorway.

There was now a way out. Jack stepped over, free.

"This way," Kristen shouted and ran down an open flight of stairs.

There were people at last. In the lobby. Motionless and glassy eyed. At the exit, a doorman moved his arm back and forth as if opening the door like an animatronics device that had malfunctioned.

Outside, the sky had grayed over, the sun's rays seeping through at an angle, casting a yellowish hue over everything. The air was hot and still. Everywhere they looked, people were in a foggy haze, the yellow tint adding to the surreal ambiance. Animated bodies stammered along the sidewalk or stood motionless. Some cars had simply stopped in the middle of the street. A few others bumped into signs or drove onto curbs.

"What the hell?" Jack mumbled.

"Let's get out of here," Kristen said frantically, grabbing Jack's arm and pushing past a young man who turned toward them with a mindless grin. She screamed. One half of his head was missing, severed down the middle of his face; one half of his mouth turned up in comic bliss. She backed away in horror and revulsion.

"Kris?" Jack said, touching her shoulder.

She was too appalled to speak.

"Kris!"

She finally turned. A small, light-colored sedan sped toward them, hopped the curb and barreled along the sidewalk. A mannequin-like woman turned lazily to acknowledge the car, just before it struck her thighs. She bounced up and over the hood, limbs flailing, before crashing to the ground with a sickening *thwump*.

What was happening?

Nobody screamed or cried out. One man who'd been thrown over the hood and landed on his back, stood up, scratching his head as though puzzled. Jack tackled Kristen, pushed her out of the way as the car careened out of control past them.

As Kristen scrambled to her feet and helped Jack up, she saw the now familiar red shirt and jean-clad legs approaching.

It was the puppet master.

❧

"First you tell me one thing. Then you tell me another. Make up your damn mind." The man who had rescued them held a cell phone to his ear. "So now you want us to go back for them. Am I hearing you straight?"

Marilyn sat quietly while Drew attempted to formulate just the right question. But none seemed to materialize.

Just after they had left the collapsed warehouse, their host had received a call. By the man's responses, it sounded to Drew like the person on the other end was telling him to forget about the others. Don't pick them up. "He's gotten to them?" the man had asked. "Crap!"

Even though Drew was still in a state of confusion, he wasn't so naïve that he couldn't figure out who they were talking about. The demonic creature who had pursued them was now after someone else. Fortunately for Marilyn and him, the entity must have thought they were dead. Unfortunate for the others.

Minutes after the car had turned and was on its way out of town, the second call came through.

"I'm not a friggin yoyo. This better be it. Where the hell are they?"

Marilyn put a hand on Drew. "I'm thirsty," she whispered.

"Just hold on a little longer, sweetie. This'll all be over soon," he tried to reassure her.

"Uh huh. All right. You're sure he won't be around," the man said. He put a finger up so the driver could see and drew an imaginary circle in the air.

The driver pulled the car to the side of the road, looked carefully in the rearview mirror and then navigated the Cadillac around so they were heading in the opposite direction.

"…'cause if I so much as smell that bastard, we're out of there. Got it?"

⁂

Jack stumbled along with Kristen. *Get in the open where there's people*, the message had said. It was a futile warning, rooted in fantasy. For it was clear that people around or no, their pursuer would never stop. But who the hell was he? Why was he after them? How was he able to command metal stairs to twist out of shape or doors to fly off their hinges? Not to mention apparently possessing the bodies of hundreds of people.

And yet he couldn't be *all*-powerful. If that were the case, he'd have stopped them long ago. The fact they were still on the run gave Jack hope.

He was half tempted to simply stop to ask him what he wanted. What was the worst that could happen? If he'd wanted them dead, he could have accomplished it in the corridors of the hotel by simply causing heavy doors to crush them or steel steps to fold them into their maw.

But he had Kristen to think about now.

Her hand gripped his with the intensity of an arm-wrestling partner. Where could they run for safety? Jack feared even the police wouldn't be able to help.

Another car wove in and out of the aimless traffic, moving up the street toward them. If the car was setting up for another kamikaze run they would be cornered by a six-foot high concrete wall.

He was coming, walking methodically, unwavering.

Jack watched as the car swerved to avoid the others, rolling slowly along, as if the drivers were confused. He braced himself and was prepared evade the car if it angled toward them.

Thinking it would pass, he took his eyes off just long enough to hear the screeching of tires. Smoke was wisping up from angry treads as they slid abrasively across pavement. The car, a black sedan with tinted windows that made it difficult to see inside, squealed a full hundred-and-eighty degrees before slamming its right wheels against the curb next to where they stood.

A man wearing a black uniform stepped out and walked away with the élan of someone putting something distasteful behind him.

"Get in," a man's voice said.

Looking around for Kristen, he saw that she had backed against the concrete wall that surrounded a casino and was staring at the car with frightened eyes. He knew how she felt about automobiles, and even though he didn't fear them, the idea of climbing into an unknown vehicle just now, given all that had happened, was less than attractive. Even a little unnerving.

"What are you waiting for? Hurry up!" the man shouted.

The voice was somehow familiar, though Jack couldn't place it.

"I think it's okay," he told Kristen.

"I'm not waiting. You want to stay? Stay," the man said.

"Wait," Jack said. He grabbed Kristen by the arm and coaxed her to the car.

Something small flew by his head, just missing him, while he helped Kristen into the back seat.

Jack could see a swirl of loose objects floating in the air over the street and moving toward the car. Purses, newspapers, what looked like chunks of masonry, and pieces of cars, blew at them like a twister. He scrambled in on the front passenger side and slammed the door shut just as an onslaught hit them from every side.

The driver punched the gas and the sedan squealed to life, being chased by a fading barrage of loose objects as it sped away.

"Nice to see you again," the driver said sarcastically.

It was Eli Houston.

CHAPTER 34

"I thought you were dead," Jack stammered.

"What?" Kristen said, staring at the driver.

"For all intents and purposes," Eli told them, "I was."

Jack braced himself against the dashboard as the car swerved to the right of some cars. There was a clean-cut looking man in the back seat sitting beside, of all people, Marilyn Monroe.

One more anomaly to accompany their trip through Wonderland.

Eli turned onto another street and finally there was clear road ahead.

"What's going on?" Jack asked, coldly. He was tired and wanted answers.

Any answers.

"Tell me what you know and I'll try to fill in the blanks," Eli said.

"Not much. I called Petrov. From the number you gave us. He told me about the research. That we were part of it. Doing a little research of my own, I figured out it has something to do with life extension. That's about it."

"I don't mean to interrupt," the man in the back seat said, "But I know far less than that. If you want to fill in some blanks, you'd better start with an empty page."

There was something about him. In a strange way, despite everything that was going on, the man seemed at peace with the world, an unlikely partner of the blond who sat beside him.

"They part of it, too?" Jack asked Eli.

"That's right. We all are."

"So how come you know what's going on and we don't?" Kristen asked.

"Twist of fate," Eli said. "I wasn't supposed to remember. Unfortunately, I do."

"You mean you remember signing an agreement with Albatross?" Jack asked.

"Oh yeah. I remember the agreement. We all signed it."

Jack had been hoping to hear differently. Now that it seemed to be confirmed, it angered him even more that he'd been party to such a thing.

A cell phone rang and Eli hit the send button to answer. He listened briefly and then chuckled. "You're joking. If this is one of your sick attempts at humor…it's impossible. There's no way in hell we can make it to Scottsdale in three hours. It's over three hundred miles…YES I heard you, but did you hear ME? You'll have to find another way."

Eli pulled the car to the side of the road and slapped his palms against the steering wheel.

"What's wrong?" Jack asked. "Who was it?"

"Our friends at Albatross."

"What?" Kristen exclaimed. "You talk to them?"

Eli looked at his watch, ignoring her. "They say we have to be in Scottsdale in barely three hours. And I don't think we can make it."

"What happens in three hours?" Jack asked.

Eli stepped on the gas and the car swayed from side to side as he wheeled it around. All hell caves in," he said. "That's what."

"I thought the expression was, 'All hell breaks loose,'" Kristen said.

"Not in this case."

"Would somebody please explain what's going on," the man in the back said.

Eli didn't answer so Jack gave it a shot. "I doubt I know much more," Jack said. "But apparently we've been part of a research experiment performed by a company called Albatross Life Corporation. Even though none of us can remember – except Mr. Houston, that is – we apparently signed an agreement, allowing it. It has something to do with living longer. That's about all I know. I'm clueless about the rest of it. Like the guy chasing us."

"You mean my amnesia?" the man said.

"An effect of the research," Jack offered.

The man fell silent as the impact hit him. Beside him, Marilyn said, "Where are we going, Mr. Prescott?"

Jack ignored the strange way the girl had articulated. "Who is this guy that's after us?" Jack suddenly asked Eli.

"Believe it or not," Eli said. "He's part of it too. Like one of us."

"So why is he after us?" Kristen asked. "And how can he do those things?"

"They didn't tell me, so your guess is as good as mine. At first, I thought it was one of the monitors trying to be cute. Have a good laugh at our expense. Now I suspect the project got away from them. Something went wrong."

"Monitors?" Jack asked.

"They're the ones who watch us all the time to make sure everything's hunky dory. Sometimes I think they get bored. Wouldn't you?"

"So the research hasn't ended," Jack said. "We're still being observed."

Eli glanced over at him. "Where'd you get the idea this is all about research? It might interest you to know that we paid Albatross damn good money for this."

Jack was speechless. It was bad enough that they'd been subjected to a life of confusion, wondering who they were. Somehow he'd thought that if they'd agreed to such an ordeal, they must have been paid well to do it. But learning that they had paid Albatross was unfathomable, incomprehensible.

"What?" Kristen exclaimed. "Why would *we* pay *them*?"

"Do you have any idea how old you are?" Eli asked.

"What's that got to do with anything?" Kristen retorted. "I'm twenty-four."

Eli chuckled. "Right." Then said, "There's a hell of a lot of diversity in the world. I met a man once whose dream was to study fungus. Can you believe that? Who'd want to spend their life digging under rocks, searching by mossy streams for toadstools? Not me."

"What are you talking about?" Kristen demanded.

"But regardless of how weird and different people are, you know what it all boils down to?" Eli continued, bent over the wheel as the desert sped past them. "That one elusive dream that everybody wants. It's such a basic human desire that we've built religions and created gods to help us deal with it. We want to live forever."

"I take exception to that," Prescott said. "God is God. *He* created *us*. It's not the other way around."

"Believe what you want," Eli said. "But I guarantee you'd spend every penny you have at the chance to take a magic pill and live forever, rather than risk the possibility that the hereafter doesn't exist."

"Never," Prescott said emphatically.

"Truth is on my side, Mr. Prescott," Eli said. "I happen to know that you already paid up. Just like we all did."

Jack held up a hand. "Hold on. Wait just a second. You're saying that Albatross managed to pull off immortality?"

"In a very practical sense, you could say that."

"Is that why you're not dead?" Kristen asked. "Or was that another one of their lies."

"Oh, I fell from the penthouse, all right. That bastard pushed me off the balcony. But thanks to Albatross, I woke up safe and sound in a hospital bed without a scratch."

"So, if we can't be killed, then why are we running?" Jack asked, barely believing he was asking such a question in all sincerity.

"It's complicated," Eli said. "Besides, we're not just running from him anymore. There's far more at stake now."

"All hell caving in," Kristen observed.

"You learn quickly."

Eli slowed the car as he squinted ahead.

"Try explaining," Jack said.

"Can't right now. We may have company. See that police car?"

Jack saw the police car lurking under an overpass. "Can't they help us?" he asked.

"Unfortunately not," Eli assured him. "If we're lucky they'll ignore us."

At that moment, the cruiser's overhead lights began to flash.

Eli sighed. "This is going to be harder than I thought."

ঌ

Punching the brakes, he slid into a corner, and then hit the accelerator halfway through the curve, causing the car to fishtail and grapple with pavement. The chase had lasted ten minutes now and Jack had counted three cruisers behind them. There was also a helicopter hovering overhead.

"Why are police chasing us?" the Marilyn Monroe look-alike said.

Eli squealed around another corner.

"This is just insane," Kristen said. "Albatross has influence over the police, too?"

"The police are being controlled by Jed Pope, now," Eli said, "the man who's been following you. If you can call him a man."

"How is that possible?" Jack asked.

"Look," Eli said. "All I know is that if we're not at the safe house in Scottsdale in less than three hours, our little dream of living forever may come to an abrupt halt."

Two more cruisers suddenly pulled into the street ahead, blocking their path. Eli edged the car to the side, bouncing it up onto the sidewalk. The passenger side scraped a fence as the car sped forward, sending a tricycle airborne. The front left fender struck the back of the police cruiser as they passed, causing Marilyn to yelp and grip Mr. Prescott's arm.

"Have you got a plan?" Jack asked. "Or is this just a joy ride?"

"There's a small airport on the other side of town," Eli said through gritted teeth. "I keep a plane in a hangar there. If we can get in the air within the next half hour we might stand a chance."

"You fly?" Kristen asked, sounding both surprised and terrified.

"It's about the only thing I brought over from my previous life. Only thing worth hanging on to. It's a bit of an obsession."

Jack looked out the back window. The three cruisers made it past the blockade, which only briefly slowed them down. They were gaining on the Cadillac again.

"This is the Las Vegas police," a voice suddenly boomed over a loudspeaker. *"Please pull the car to the side of the road."*

Jack looked up at the hovering helicopter. “How do you propose we get your plane out of the hangar under these conditions?”

“Damn good question. Hadn’t thought that far ahead. Better start praying back there, preacher. We’re gonna need all the help we can get.”

Jack glanced back at Mr. Prescott. He could believe the man was a preacher just by his manner.

By the time they reached the entrance to the small airport, the place was swarming with police. Several rows of cruisers were parked at funny angles, blocking the entrance. The one helicopter was now joined with two of its friends, circling overhead like vultures. Eli accelerated and headed straight at the airport entrance and parked cruisers.

“Are you crazy,” Kristen screamed. “You can’t make it through there.”

But at the last second, he swerved and barreled to the side of the cars and through a chain link barrier with a sound of screeching metal as the car ripped through the fence, pulling the adjoining posts right out of the concrete. The Cadillac’s wheels spun in the sand, kicking up a cloud, and then worked feverishly, wheels spinning, to make progress across the mushy field. Eli kept easing off the accelerator and then re-engaging, hoping the wheels would somehow dig in and take hold, but without success.

“Put it in low,” Jack yelled. “Don’t try to go so fast.”

Eli followed his advice and eased off the accelerator. Dropping into low gear, he moved slowly forward. Even though the progress was painful, they were making headway.

“You’re surrounded. Stop the car and get out with your hands where we can see them.”

Even though he could no longer see them because of the cloud of dust, Jack knew that the cruisers had followed them through the gap in the fence. It was only a matter of time until they were caught. Even if they made it to the hangar, the police would box them in. They’d never be able to get off the ground.

Kristen clutched his shoulder, clearly panic-stricken. “Jack,” she said. “I can’t do it.”

"What do you mean?" he said, and then he realized that she'd passed out when she learned they'd come to Vegas by plane. Now she would be asked to climb aboard one of her own volition. Something she simply couldn't do.

Her eyes were huge, pleading with him to understand her predicament.

"I wouldn't worry," he said. "Chances are it won't be an option."

☙❧

Anything but flying in one of those metal winged creatures.

Over the last few days she'd managed to ride in cars and even allow herself to be hoisted by elevators. But never on her most reckless day would she willingly fly. The thought of it made her stomach churn, her head to go limp.

While Mr. Prescott was no doubt praying they'd make it to Eli's hangar, Kristen fought the urge to beg deity for the exact opposite. Maybe the police would catch them before they ever got near an airplane.

Finally the tires met with pavement and the Cadillac lurched forward, all its bottled energy released in a fury of screeching wheels.

"I have an idea," Eli said frantically to Jack. "Once we get behind those hangars I'll hop out and you take the wheel. You'll have to keep moving. Don't let them catch you. Drive out to the runway if you need to, but don't let them pin you in. If they do, it'll never work. Understand?"

"Okay," Jack said. "But then what?"

"Watch for a Cessna Golden Eagle. It's a private, twin-engine plane. Assuming they follow you and ignore me, I'll taxi out to the runway in a few minutes. It's a long shot but it just might work. When you see me coming, do your best to lose them and head for the plane. I'll leave the hatch open. You may only have a few seconds to get on board, so don't mess around. Once you're in you'll have to close the hatch. I'll punch it and we're out of here."

Kristen felt helpless. Her hands were already shaking and her heart seemed to skip whole beats in horrible anticipation. Marilyn reached over and patted her arm, somehow sensing her apprehension.

"It'll be okay," she said. "You can sit next to me."

Kristen swallowed but her mouth was dry.

Jack studied her face with concern.

"Uh," Jack finally said.

"Do you understand?" Eli demanded.

"Yeah. We may have a slight problem."

"We haven't got time for problems," Eli said. "What is it?"

"Kristen is petrified of airplanes."

The Cadillac squealed around the corner of a hangar where Eli brought it to an abrupt halt. He left the car idling and jumped out. "Deal with it," he said. "You're not at the end of the runway when I'm ready to go, then I go alone."

With that he disappeared into an open doorway.

Jack slid into the driver's seat, set to the music of sirens. The car took off again and Kristen felt her body sink into the leather seat. The wheel was in motion. She'd have to make a decision when the time came. Stay and face whatever horrors Jed Pope and company had in store or climb aboard the most horrific object of all her fears. But hadn't she already made up her mind? Shouldn't she tell Jack to stop the car so that she could get out and distract the police? With a little luck they'd stop. Buy the others a few extra minutes.

"Let me out," she said.

"Are you crazy? They'll catch you."

"I don't care. You know I'll never get on that plane. I might as well create a diversion and help you get away. They might stop for me. That'll buy you more time."

"I'm not stopping," Jack said. "You don't go? I don't go. We'll get these two to the Cessna and then you and I will fend for ourselves if we have to. But I'm not leaving you behind."

In addition to the paralyzing fear, Kristen felt a lump forming in her throat. Jack had come full circle, willing to possibly give up his own life to be with her, when just days earlier he'd tried to abandon her at a gas station. Somehow this man felt the same connection she did. Her eyes became moist with tears.

"Crap!" Jack exclaimed.

"What's the matter?" Mr. Prescott asked.

"Fuel gauge is on empty."

Everyone fell silent while Jack slung the car around another corner and headed for open tarmac.

CHAPTER 35

Jack glanced at the digital clock on the dash. It had been only three minutes since they'd dropped Eli off. He wasn't sure how much longer he could stay ahead of the cruisers. There were now at least six directly behind and a dozen more roaming around the tarmac, attempting to block them in. Several cruisers lined up at one corner like rooks on a chessboard, waiting to make their move.

Where the hell was Eli? Even though Jack knew preparing an aircraft for flight was more complicated than hopping in a car, every excruciating second brought them closer to capture.

Suddenly a cruiser appeared out of nowhere, just to the right of the car, slamming into the side of the Cadillac. Jack nearly lost control as they swerved to the left and Marilyn started blubbering. Jack glanced in the rearview mirror and could see the girl had comfort on both sides, sandwiched between a pair of emotional crutches. "It'll be all right," Kristen told her. "We're going to make it, sweetie," Mr. Prescott said.

But Jack had his doubts. He could see the cruisers starting to circle, setting up to close in for the kill.

He looked down at the fuel gauge as a chopper flew by, the dust on the tarmac licking up around the car's burning tires. It had dipped below empty and Jack wondered how much longer the engine would hold. *Hurry up, Eli. I can't keep this up much longer.*

The circling cars were moving closer, inching in. Jack slowed the Cadillac, glancing frantically around. Inside of a minute they'd have him boxed in, exactly what Eli had told him to avoid. Out of the corner of his eye, he saw the white fin of an airplane moving along behind a low wall near the hangars. It had to be Eli's Cessna.

Turning the car away from the hangars, he tromped the accelerator, praying the fuel would hold. Leading the cruisers away from the Cessna seemed like a logical choice. No sense in alerting them to the only means of escape.

Trying to gauge the distance to the circling cruisers and anticipate where he could slip through a gap, he steered the car into a wide arc. A cruiser sped up to counter his move and slammed into the passenger door. Glass exploded and the steel frame buckled inward. The car jolted to the left with such a force Jack's head bounced violently from side to side. A cruiser to the left had stopped and the Cadillac's side slammed into its trunk with a sickening crunch of metal. The leather on the driver's door bulged and pressed against Jack's leg.

Screaming and crying came from the back, mixed with the restrained utterances of a preacher in distress. "Ah! Uh. Oh my!"

The Cadillac was now pinned between two cruisers. One on each side. A third slid up behind them and a fourth was circling toward the front.

Checkmate.

But Jack wouldn't allow his king to be knocked over just yet. Slipping the car into low gear, he stepped on the accelerator. The engine groaned. The tires spun. He stayed the gas and the whole pack seemed to shift slowly to the left, almost as if on ice and a slight downward slope, strangely gliding.

"Cease and desist." The words blasted from the chopper PA as it circled overhead.

Jack gritted his teeth. The cars were shifting. The fourth cruiser now pinned them in at the front. Throwing the car into reverse, he jetted through the back, the new momentum created from forward pressure opening up space to the rear. The back of the car collided with the front of a cruiser, pushing it aside. They were free.

Staying in reverse, he put his right arm on the adjoining seatback, twisted his head around, and angled the Cadillac toward an open field next to the tarmac. At least nine cruisers stormed toward them.

The car jolted as it left asphalt and dipped into the dirt. Suddenly the cruisers disappeared in a cloud of flying dust. Jack went straight back for several more seconds and then made the transition to drive, cranking the wheel while braking, thrusting the shifter, and hitting the gas in one fluid motion.

Marilyn was still sobbing, but Prescott and Kristen seemed to have her under control. Thank goodness for that. It was already hard enough to concentrate.

Jack deliberately accelerated and then spun with locked brakes to kick up as much dirt as he could. The passenger side window was no longer there, and plumes of dirty smoke bellowed in, making it hard to breathe. Jack's eyes watered and his lungs instantly filled with dust.

"Oh God!" Kristen choked.

Even though the cloud hid them from the police, it was impossible for him to see anything. He nearly closed his eyes, and then drove straight ahead. Jack held his breath while the three passengers choked and coughed in the back. The speedometer said they were up to forty-miles-an-hour, but he wasn't sure if wheels spinning in dirt counted.

Dust plumes raced at them while the sound of tiny rocks and debris hit the windshield as the car plunged forward. They were lost in an infinite shroud of yellow-brown oblivion.

The scraping of steel was accompanied by a sharp jerk, as a cruiser brushed against the side of the Cadillac. Jack gasped, realizing it could have easily been a head-on collision.

The car sputtered and he suddenly remembered the fuel gauge. It was bad enough the end would come without reaching the Cessna. But now they were stuck in a dusty quagmire with no means of escape. The car's engine hiccupped again just as they broke free from the cloud. One split-second they were in oblivion and the next they were back in sunlight. Just like that.

Jack wiped his burning eyes and glanced quickly around, trying to ascertain where they'd emerged.

"There!" Prescott shouted. "To the left."

Jack looked and saw that the Cessna was waiting at the end of the runway. It was several hundred feet away and no cruisers were around. They were apparently all lost in the haze. But as he tried to stomp on the accelerator once more, the Cadillac finally gave up, sputtering to a halt.

"Out of the car," Jack shouted. "Run!"

Kristen's heart thumped against her ribcage, more from the idea of flying than anything else. In spite of the damage to the car's frame, her door pushed open and she slid out, finally being free from one of the lesser evils. She could help with Marilyn and then watch as the others climbed aboard the horrid thing, now sitting menacingly at the end of the runway.

Jack was slamming his shoulder hard against the door, trying to get it open. Mr. Prescott and Marilyn scrambled out their side and tried to help.

Kristen stood and stared at the beast, its sharp fangs whipping around, ready to chew her to bits. It started to move. Slowly at first, and then it screamed and began rolling forward. She stared, mesmerized.

Finally free, Jack grabbed her by the arm.

"What's it going to be?" he asked. "We stay or go?"

Kristen saw Mr. Prescott and Marilyn run toward the approaching Cessna.

"I don't know," she said apprehensively.

"Okay," he said. "Let's get out of here. Make for the hangars."

She was wrenched between her need to be with Jack and her desire to see him safely away.

Jack grabbed her hand and started toward a building.

"Wait. I'll…I'll try," she stuttered.

The Cessna was as close as it would get. It was now or never.

She tried to move her legs but they wouldn't budge. Somewhere in the back of her mind she registered the helicopters overhead. These were different beasts, talking to them with loud voices. Sirens emerged from the dust cloud behind them.

Then she was floating. Everything around her moved in slow motion as she hovered over the ground, gliding along like a winged fairy. She saw Jack. At least she thought it was Jack. But why was she seeing him like this? It was a side of him she wasn't familiar with. His backside. It was funny how his legs kept moving back and forth, back and forth.

The beast was upon her now, its sound screaming in her ears. And then it was dark. Peaceful.

ঌ

Jack scrambled up the steps of the Cessna, the veins in his neck bulging under the weight of Kristen slung over his shoulder. Mr. Prescott reached down and pulled him up. Kristen flopped to the floor. Prescott reached through her arms from behind and dragged her away from the hatch so Jack could pull it shut.

The last thing Jack saw before it closed was an old brown pickup, speeding toward them across the tarmac. He slammed the fuselage with the palm of his hand and said, "We're good to go."

Jack felt the props pull the plane forward, while the acceleration pulled him toward the rear of the aircraft. He and Prescott lifted Kristen into the seat next to him and buckled her in. Her head bobbled to one side, still out cold.

The sound of the engines grew as the Cessna built momentum for liftoff.

"AH!" Eli yelled and cut power.

The aircraft bolted to one side as Eli cranked the wheel. Jack glanced forward and saw a steel drum bounce by in front of the airplane.

"Where the hell did that come from?" Eli shouted. He turned the other way to center the plane. "We'll never make it now. There isn't enough runway."

"What are you going to do?" Jack asked.

"Go to the end and turn around. It's all I *can* do."

Jack looked back but the rear of the plane was windowless. It was probably for the best. He could only imagine what horrors lurked behind. It would make for an interesting trip back up the runway when Eli turned the Cessna around.

Eli throttled up again, but not all the way. He was clearly trying to outrun the cruisers and get to the end as quickly as possible. When they reached it, Eli eased off the throttle and applied the wheel brakes, preparing for a sharp u-turn.

"Brace yourself," he said. "This could get ugly."

When Eli turned the plane around, Jack expected to see – among other things – a caravan of police cruisers with lights blazing and sirens wailing. But astonishingly, the runway was clear. In the distance, off to one side, the cruisers sat lifeless. No lights flashing. The large brown cloud of dust was being carried slowly away by the wind, dissipating over the barren sand dunes just beyond the airport.

Opposite the cruisers sat the brown pickup Jack saw moments earlier. He could just make out a small figure standing next to the truck. Everything at the airport now seemed dead and still.

Suddenly Jack gasped. Straight ahead, on the horizon, was a band of darkness that stretched as far as he could see to either side. It met the ground below and the sky above. Though the strip of darkness was fixed in place, its fringes were alive with movement, creating the illusion of rain falling from the top and rising from the bottom. A billion tiny particles seemed to be dissolving as they moved from land and sky into the darkness, disappearing into oblivion.

He rubbed his eyes, thinking the anomaly must be the result of leftover dust and the strain of having to navigate through the cloud of dirt. But it wasn't going away.

"Do you see that?" Jack shouted.

"Yep," Eli said. "It's what I told you."

"What do you mean? What is it?"

"All hell caving in, my friend. Make sure you're buckled up. We're outta here."

Eli slid the throttle levers forward, causing the engines to grow loud. Gravity pressed Jack's back into the seat as the plane gathered speed. He glanced over at Kristen, peacefully avoiding all further confrontation, thank you. Jack didn't blame her one bit.

The cabin rattled so hard Jack was afraid the plane would start dropping pieces of itself before it ever got off the ground – *if* it got off the ground. Marilyn's head was buried in Mr. Prescott's arms as he attempted to console her.

The Cessna lifted off. Directly ahead was the darkness, eating up ground and sky, chomping away at the edge of the world like a hungry creature in a Stephen King novel.

As Eli angled the Cessna to the right, circling and heading toward Scottsdale, Jack wondered what he'd meant.

All hell.

Caving in.

*

Jed's anger fueled the heat now licking up and down the empty runway, as if he were finally starting to accept his role as the messenger of darkness.

The dead rattler hung around his neck as a reminder that he was in control. But every attempt at trying to trap these victims ended with their inevitable escape. He clamped down on his teeth in an effort to maintain composure.

His mind searched the confines of the tiny airplane cabin, at first in order to persuade the controls, force them into a freefall and make them pay for their insolence. Yet what he needed was information, a commodity that seemed harder and harder to come by. Sending them to a fiery grave over the barren desert wouldn't serve his purposes.

And then he saw the slip of paper. Though he couldn't identify its location, the hand-written message was clear. Jed committed the address to memory. A destination. Now all he needed was a way to follow. Even though the pickup had served him well, he needed something faster now. Scanning the hangars, he came across several lightweight crafts before finding what he was looking for.

He'd been attempting to ignore the wall of darkness but now felt it again, gnawing at his back, beckoning him to turn around and look. The gates of Hell were sweeping over the landscape, rising up from the horizon in the west, the antitheses of sunrise, not only in direction, but also in purpose, leaving the world in a perpetual state of midnight.

When he turned, Jed dropped to his knees and watched in horrible fascination. The darkness seemed to reach a mile into the sky and sucked up the earth below. The edges extended into infinity on either side. Though it should have made earsplitting sound as it came – pulling apart the very fabric of matter like a nuclear weapon detonated in slow motion – it was eerily silent, sweeping over Las Vegas as a massive thief. Quietly. Deliberately. Without warning.

CHAPTER 36

When she came to, she thought she'd been sleeping in a mall. But what was that sound? That awful noise. Kristen rubbed her burning eyes and blinked, attempting to understand what she was seeing.

She was staring through glass at something that looked like a transparent wall she'd once seen in a mall. It had been filled with liquid, while a purple light glowed through from behind. Bubbles floated up from the bottom, giving the viewer the impression of being underwater. But what she was seeing now had bubbles coming from both the bottom and the top, moving toward the center where it was black and lightless. It gave her a strange feeling to look at it.

She coughed and realized how thirsty she was. Her mouth and lips were dry and she felt as if she hadn't showered in weeks. It was her own fault, of course. If she hadn't left Gerty and taken to the road, she could be waking up in a comfortable bed, ready to step into a hot shower. But then she remembered those blank expressions and lifeless corpses hovering around like zombies and knew why she'd left.

Kristen groaned and turned her head, trying to determine what part of the mall would look like this. Would sound like this. This place had small, odd-shaped windows, and…

Oh no!

This wasn't right. And then it all came crashing back to her. Jack and her. Standing near a runway. Trying to make herself get onboard that creature. She vaguely remembered agreeing to try, but how had she gotten here in the belly of the thing?

The last thing she remembered before passing out again was Jack, grinning at her as if he somehow found the whole thing amusing.

What a sicko!

ॐ

Once they were safely out of harm's way, Jack fully intended to make his way to the front and have a chat with Eli. The man had more explaining to do. At the very least, he needed to fill in some of those blanks he'd promised earlier. But then he saw Kristen open her lazy eyes, acknowledge where she was and immediately pass out again, her head on his shoulder.

If he weren't being honest with himself he would say he didn't want to disturb her. Let the poor girl sleep. But the truth was that it felt nice and he didn't want to let the moment slip.

He barely considered Maggie any longer. Especially knowing she was merely a well-rehearsed actress, a thespian performing on his own private stage. Though she had often cuddled up to him, it had meant nothing, unlike the connection he now felt with Kristen. She was simply who she was. Fears and oddities. Far from perfect. To be near her was to accept her at face value. And she refused to be ignored.

Jack wondered why Eli had used the word 'unfortunately' when referring to the fact he could remember. There were times when Jack would have gladly taken a knife and sliced off several fingers in payment to regain the memories he'd lost. What had been so horrible that Eli didn't want to remember?

He feared he would soon learn everything, though he wasn't sure he wanted to know. But he'd simply have to deal with it like he'd dealt with everything else that had happened over the past few days.

For some reason his mind went back to when it had all begun. He thought of the girl at the airport, asking if he would rather take a trip to Hawaii instead of Europe. Maggie had also tried to keep them from going to Europe. He was sure of it. But why? So that the 'Monitors' could stay with him? Perhaps their surveillance tactics couldn't legally span international boundaries?

And then he considered the darkness he'd witnessed during takeoff. An engulfing behemoth was sweeping the world, and it all had something to do with reaching the safe house in Scottsdale in three hours – now probably closer to two. He rejected these ideas, growing sleepy. But if he thought he'd imagined the whole thing, all he had to do was look out the window since, although they were flying away from it at a tangent, the wall of darkness was moving toward them.

৩৩

Something jolted Jack awake. He blinked and then remembered where he was. The sound of the engines droned on. Looking out the window, he could see nothing but rich blue. The sky pressed against the edges of the small window. All traces of land had disappeared and there were only a few wisps of clouds like the white strokes of an artist's brush.

Just as he started to panic, thinking everything was now gone – the earth, itself, having been dissolved into nothing – he glanced across the cabin through a window on the opposite side and saw ground. The plane was turning.

The image below passed slowly across the window like a miniature diorama. The narrow line of a straight road. Infinitesimally small cars attached to it like motionless ants. Red-brown ravines that seemed flat from up here, but would likely be majestic when standing at the base. Countless years of water had formed them, receding slowly over a thousand years. A thin river snaked along the desert basin, giving striking contrast to man-made edifices that were so symmetrically neat.

"Hey!" Eli called. "Anybody awake? We're almost there."

The Cessna rolled back into the upright position.

"Yeah," Jack said. "I'm awake. How're we doing?"

Eli looked at his watch. "We should have time to spare. This puppy's pretty fast. Two hundred forty knots with a load."

Jack wasn't sure how fast that was in miles-per-hour, but judging from Eli's comment, they should make good time. He could see Mr. Prescott stirring and coming out of the altitude-induced sleep.

"I'll land at Scottsdale Municipal," Eli said. "It's on the north end of town. Once we're down we'll need to find a car. Oh, by the way, I spoke to one of the monitors. They said it would take about twenty minutes to get to the safe house from the airport."

Jack wondered how he'd managed to communicate with the folks at Albatross while in flight.

"Even though we're ahead of the clock," Eli said, "I don't know what we'll find when we touch down. We better be ready to move. I can't reach anyone in the control tower. I doubt we'll have trouble, but you never know."

"You can't reach anyone?" Jack asked. "Then how do you know the runway's clear to land?"

"I don't. But I expect it will be. The fact nobody's in the tower makes me think there won't be others trying to land or take off."

Everybody gone?

Just like the empty hotel corridors and the hotel lobby with animated mannequins. Even the streets of Las Vegas were filled with brain-dead zombies. Only the police had seemed alive. But Jack suspected that Jed Pope had been controlling them.

"Where are we?" Marilyn asked, stretching and looking around curiously.

Outside the window Jack watched the ground moving closer as the aircraft descended. He could see patches of yellow and blue flowers, scattered amongst cactuses that looked like soldiers standing at attention. A few more seconds and the arid vegetation was replaced with tarmac. The Cessna seemed to drift unsteadily from side to side like a kite caught in the wind, the nose angling up and the engines now calming to a dull roar.

When the wheels caught, the plane shuddered and began to slow. Jack peered out the windows and could tell the place was still and lifeless. Eli navigated the Cessna toward a group of buildings near the small tower where there were several parked vehicles.

When they finally came to a stop, Jack opened the hatch. He jostled Kristen's shoulders, calling her back to the land of the living while Eli helped Marilyn and the preacher exit the plane.

"Go away," Kristen groaned, pushing Jack's hand away. "I'm not bothering anyone."

"Kris," Jack said. "We're here. We're in Scottsdale."

Jack saw her alarm grow as she awakened to the realization that she was in a plane. Unbuckling her seatbelt with fumbling fingers, she made for the exit with him close behind her. Once on the tarmac, she pointed to the wall of darkness extending to the left and right for as far as they could see.

"I don't know," he said, anticipating her question. "Maybe we'll find out when we get to the safe house."

"Here's one," Mr. Prescott yelled.

Jack glanced over where Eli, Marilyn and the preacher had been trying the doors to cars and searching for an ignition key. Now Prescott held the door to a white van open, a key dangling from his hand.

It was a utility van with no windows or seats in the back. Jack offered to ride in the cargo area with Kristen and Marilyn while Eli drove and Mr. Prescott rode shotgun.

Jack could only see out the back where he could tell the streets were empty, other than a few cars that had stopped dead in the road.

"Why a safe house?" Jack finally asked.

"It's the only thing they could come up with on short notice," Eli said. "Not perfect, but effective. We're some of the fortunate ones. They said a lot of people won't make it."

"What happens to them?" Mr. Prescott asked.

"Depends on their condition," Eli said. "They may or may not survive. The ones with bad hearts will probably go into cardiac arrest. Handling one case wouldn't be hard. The problem is it'll happen all at once. A bunch of old folks having heart attacks and seizures with only so many hands to go around. I can see a hell of a lot of lawsuits coming Albatross's way. I don't envy Petrov right now."

Every word out of Eli's mouth seemed to spawn a hundred more questions. Though he heard what the man was saying, nothing made any sense.

"Are there doctors at the safe house?" Mr. Prescott asked.

Eli chuckled. "Not exactly."

"Then explain," Kristen said.

Eli slowed as they approached an intersection. He studied the street name and then turned left.

"Will Petrov be there?" Jack asked.

"'Fraid not."

"Why not? Where is he?" Kristen asked.

"He doesn't exist."

Jack and Kristen exchanged glances. There it was again. The man had said so, himself. Now Eli was reaffirming it. He wondered who the hell he'd spoken to on the phone then. Jack leaned against the side of the van as it rumbled through the abandoned streets of Scottsdale. Petrov clearly *did* exist, regardless of what he wanted others to believe. If the safe house was at Albatross headquarters – as he assumed it was – Jack figured Petrov would be there. Now he wasn't so sure.

"We're not out of the woods," Eli told them. "We won't be until we're at the safe house and this blows over."

Jack considered the implications. If Eli was correct that Petrov wouldn't be at the safe house, then the man could become nonexistent, indeed. The darkness was devouring everything in its path. That being the case, Jack might never discover the truth about himself, his true identity.

"We're almost there," Eli said. "It's just up this street."

The van turned a corner off of Roosevelt Street.

It was the name of the street Jillian had given him for Albatross Corporation. So the safe house wasn't at Albatross Headquarters after all. Petrov might not be at the safe house, but Jack was pretty sure he knew where to find the man.

"Here we are," Eli said, pulling the van to a stop. "With forty minutes to spare."

ꕥ

It was an old, gray shingled Victorian house, not very different from the others in the neighborhood, except that several cars were parked along the street and in the driveway, as if someone were throwing a party. And there was something else. It somehow seemed warm and inviting, protected from whatever had caused the rest of the world to grow cold and lifeless. Jack was eager to get inside and prove they were not alone.

The black wall now surrounded them on every side, its relentless vacuum silently sucking up all matter into the inky void, moving ever closer with each minute. Looking at the center gave him a lonely, empty feeling. It was blacker than black. Midnight so dark it was like peering into a cosmic rip in the fabric of the universe, seeing past stars and galaxies into the nothingness that lay beyond.

He abandoned his gaze to follow the group up concrete steps and onto a wide porch. Eli opened the door and walked in without knocking. Inside there were a dozen people, sitting on chairs, an old sofa, and several cross-legged on the hardwood floor, their backs to the wall.

An older gentleman stood and met Eli with a handshake.

"I'm Clarence," the man said. "Glad you could make it."

There was a young woman not much older than Kristen, with straight, medium length brown hair. She was seated on the floor and a young girl with red hair sat beside her, their hands clasped. A muscular fellow, standing in a doorway, nodded to Jack. A teenage kid, wearing baggy clothes and a toboggan cap, looked like he'd just been teleported off a mountain slope with his snowboard.

"Was it a phone call?" an attractive, middle-aged woman asked. "Most of us received phone calls. I didn't believe it until I looked out the window and saw the sky. I just got in my car and drove."

"Yeah," Eli said soberly. "It was a phone call."

Jack didn't blame him for not saying more. He'd just piloted a plane from Las Vegas and looked tired, worn. If they suspected he knew more, they'd assault him with questions.

Clarence came back from the kitchen with several folded chairs. "No sense standing," he said. "I'd offer you something to drink but the kitchen's empty. I don't expect we'll be here long."

"How do you know that?" the young woman sitting next to the girl said. "They didn't tell us what was going to happen. I left my condo, my job. I don't even know what's going on."

"It's the same with all of us," the muscular man said with a thick British accent.

"I don't like it," the woman said.

Eli thanked Clarence and took a chair.

"What happens now?" Jack asked Eli in a low voice, squatting next to him.

"We wait."

"And everything not in the safe house?" Jack asked, tipping his head toward the door.

"Gone."

"Everything?"

"Everything."

Jack suddenly felt dizzy. He wasn't sure why he should believe Eli, but he did. Everything gone. Just like that, his very identity notwithstanding. Somehow the only truth existed in a building not two blocks away, about to be dissolved.

Everything. Gone.

"I'll be back," Jack said as he headed for the front door. The others seemed alarmed but he couldn't just let the truth vanish. He'd rather welcome the approaching oblivion than face the remainder of his life not knowing who he really was.

"Make it fast," Eli said, glancing at his watch. "You're not back in thirty-four minutes, there won't be much we can do."

Jack ignored him and headed for the door.

"What do you think you're doing?" Kristen asked.

"I need to check something out. I'll be right back."

Once outside, he took a deep breath, trying to shake off the dizziness. Roosevelt Street was a short walk. He should be able to make it in five minutes. Even though he didn't know if Albatross would be near the intersection, he had to see. As he went, try tried to divert his attention away from the darkness.

"Wait!" a voice came from behind.

He turned and watched Kristen hurry to catch up.

"What are you doing?" he said. "You should be in the house."

She matched his pace and they walked side-by-side. "And you shouldn't?" she said. "Where do you think you're going?"

"I noticed that we passed Roosevelt on the way here. It's only a block or two away."

"So what."

Jack reached into his pocket and brought out the paper with Albatross's address on it, showing it to her.

"What do you plan to do? March in there and demand to know what's going on? There probably won't be anyone, anyway," she said and looked around the empty streets.

"Maybe," Jack said. "But I have to see."

"Okay," Kristen said. "But I'm going with you. Want to tell me how I ended up on the plane?"

Jack glanced at her sheepishly. "Well…"

"Well what? Fess up, nimble boy."

"I *had* to do something."

"Uh huh. You carried me, didn't you?"

"You were damn heavy, too."

The irony of bickering at a time like this wasn't lost on Jack. He suspected it was some sort of safety mechanism.

They walked quietly together before she finally said, "Thanks."

Coming from Kristen, at that moment, the single word spoke volumes.

When they reached the intersection, Jack could see that it was, indeed, Roosevelt. He studied the paper and looked at the brick building across the street on the corner.

"That's it," he said.

There was no name on the outside. A large white sign indicated that there were 40,000 square feet for lease, and that the contractor would build to suit.

"Must have moved," Kristen observed.

"Maybe," Jack said. He looked at his watch. He'd set the stopwatch before leaving the safe house and six minutes had passed, leaving enough time to do a little investigation.

"Let's go around back," he said and walked across the street. "Maybe there's an unlocked door."

"Why not the front?" Kristen asked.

"They wouldn't leave the front door unlocked."

"Worth a try," she said and angled toward the front of the building.

Jack sighed and followed her.

"Have it your way, but I don't think –"

She walked to the glass door and gave it a tug. It came open.

"See," she said and walked inside.

Jack shook his head. The girl had a knack for getting into places. Either that or she was incredibly lucky. She'd done the same thing at Hasselbaum's house and now here.

The desert sunlight outside was replaced by the dim interior of an unfinished foyer, where there was an opened set of double doors. Through the doors was an empty cavernous room with a concrete floor and cinderblock walls. Utilitarian stairs ascended to an area above the foyer.

"There's nothing here," Kristen said.

She'd been right again when she said there wouldn't be any people. Jack had at least expected to find empty offices with paper-strewn desks. If it had been Albatross Life Corporation's headquarters at one time, they'd made certain that nothing was left behind.

Jack looked at the vacant concrete floor and wondered what machinery or equipment had once filled the place. What had gone on here? He glanced at his watch. Ten minutes had passed. Twenty-four minutes to go.

"We better get back," he said.

They turned to leave just as the double doors through which they'd entered slammed shut.

CHAPTER 37

Kneeling on the runway, staring into the nothingness, Jed came face to face with the edge of his existence. As his world shrunk, he was forced to confront the truth about himself and he began to crumble under sanity's heavy burden. He could feel the madness sweeping toward him over the desert while the heat of Hell rose from beneath, beckoning him to accept his place in the kingdom of darkness.

You're here to do my bidding. Or I'll lay your soul to waste.

Was he losing his mind? He stood inside the empty building, cursing blank walls, feeling heat radiating from the floor, causing him to move to higher ground. Staggering up stairs, he mumbled to himself, mindlessly.

There is no Hell. There is no devil. He desperately clung to anything that would stave the determined madness from taking over completely while he paced back and forth across the floor.

Falling again to his knees, Jed was about to bring the building down – crushing cinderblocks, metal roofing, steel girders and all – when he heard voices. Was it the dark lord, himself, rising up to confront Jed's insolence? About to clutch his ears, deathly afraid of the ghostly utterances, Jed suddenly realized he was hearing the voices of people, talking to each other in the room below.

Then he saw them. The couple who'd managed to get away earlier were standing there, looking confused.

"There's nothing here," he heard the man say. "We better get back."

Instinctively, Jed closed the doors, slamming them shut against their escape.

ஐ

Jed Pope, the man who'd been chasing them in Las Vegas, was standing over them on a balcony above the foyer. He no longer seemed calm and in control.

"I'll give you ten seconds to start talking," Jed screamed, pacing back and forth. "What the hell's going on?"

Jack was speechless. How had this man appeared here? And there was something different about him. Whereas earlier he had commanded great composure and authority, he now seemed smaller, almost vulnerable. This was clearly a man on the edge of madness.

"I don't know," Jack said. "That's why we're here. To find out."

"Don't lie to me," Jed screamed, hopping over the railing and landing in front of them in a shock-absorbing crouch, a lifeless snake about his neck swaying limply from side to side.

"Tell me," Jed demanded.

The rage burning through the man's eyes were like fiery pits of molting lava.

"I swear I don't know," Jack said. "Much, anyway. If I did, I'd tell you."

Jed moved closer. Though he was a smaller man than Jack, his presence was far more intimidating, his eyes flashing wild. "You know more than I do. So start flapping that mouth of yours."

"I think this place used to be the headquarters of a company called Albatross Life Corporation," Jack said. "From what I've been told, they perform longevity research."

"What the hell is that?" Jed demanded.

"Making people live longer. Kristen and I were part of the research. I'm guessing you were too."

"How would you know that? How could you possibly know anything about me?"

"I don't, for sure. But people who participate in the research can't remember anything. They have amnesia. Supposedly it's part of…whatever they do. I'm guessing you can't remember. Just like the rest of us."

Jack watched Jed fight to understand. And fail.

"Who told you this?" he seethed. "And don't lie to me."

"A man named Petrov. Dr. Petrov," Jack said. "I've only talked to him by phone. He's apparently the one in charge."

Jack glanced at his watch. Fifteen minutes had passed. Nineteen minutes to go.

"Look. We have to get back to the safe house," Jack said. "Everything outside of that house will be destroyed. Soon. If you want to save yourself, I suggest you come."

Jed reached out and gripped the front of Jack's shirt. "Do you have powers?" he hissed. "Like me?"

"No."

"But you knew I was coming. At the hotel. How did you know?"

"Someone left a voicemail. They said we were in danger. They said that…"

"That what?"

"They said someone was trying to kill us. I think they were talking about you."

Jed released him, growling in rage. "What's happening out there?" he said and pointed toward the door.

Jack shook his head. "I swear to you I don't have a clue."

"It's Hell caving in," Kristen said flippantly.

Jed's eyes turned dark and wild. "NO!" he shouted. "There's no such thing as Hell. There *is* no devil."

"We need to leave *right now*," Jack said. "You can come if you want. It's your only hope."

They headed toward the door, still closed. Jed was muttering phrases that made no sense. When they reached the door, it wouldn't budge.

"We've got to find another way," Jack said. "We only have fourteen minutes."

"Leave me alone," Jed screamed, glaring down as if staring through a hole in the floor, directly into the fiery abyss of Hades. He ripped the snake from his neck and hurled it at the ground.

As they started toward a door at the back of the building, something struck Jack and all at once he was flying through the air. The walls of the room seemed to revolve around him. He was sliding, sliding, sliding. There was a bone-crunching thud and then he was staring up at the ceiling.

Jed grabbed Jack by the back of his shirt and hurled him into the cinderblock wall where he fell to the floor, his leg twisted at an unnatural angle.

"You can't control me," he shouted. "Nobody controls me. You'll do *my* bidding. How does that sound? Huh?"

Kneeling beside him, Kristen tried to shake Jack conscious. She had to maintain control of herself, be strong. It was time to help Jack now. If he didn't come out of his stupor they'd never make it to the safe house in time.

Jack groaned and rolled to one side. "What happened?"

"Get up," she said. "We've got to get out of here. We don't have much time."

Understanding suddenly came into his face and he looked at his watch. "Nine minutes."

When they had entered the place, it had seemed cool compared to the desert warmth outside. But Kristen now felt heat emanating from beneath them. As she supported Jack while heading for the exit, the floor began to shudder and a granite-splitting sound echoed off the walls. A gap, several inches wide, opened in the concrete, where a curious flame licked up to explore the room like a minion from Hell.

"*I'll* show *you*," Jed was screaming, now completely ignoring them. "I call the shots. You're nothing without *me*."

Cracks in the floor splintered out in all directions and flames leaped into the air.

Skirting around some of the fissures, they made it to the back exit door where Kristen braced herself. If it were as frozen as the other, there would be nothing they could do. They'd face the end alone. Even if the door did open, she wondered if, with Jack's injured leg, they'd make it back in time. Earlier, he'd been willing to stay behind with her. If necessary, she'd gladly return the favor.

She pushed the wide metal bar and the door swung open.

At once she gasped at the spectacle closing in on them.

Telephone poles and trees quietly dissolved at the tops, into a billion tiny particles, wisped away into darkness. The shingles of buildings a mere block away looked as if they were rising from rooftops, crumbling into oblivion.

Still leaning on Kristen and wincing in pain, Jack hobbled toward the street.

"Don't look back," she told him. "But go as fast as you can."

As they started up the street toward the safe house, it was all Kristen could do not to stop and behold the spectacle. The whole area was nothing more than a tiny island in a sea of darkness. On every side was the sad, vacant void that raced toward the center while everything in its path came apart at the seams. A small circle above was now the only blue that remained where the canopy of sky had once been. The building they'd just left was now dissolving at the back. It was coming too fast.

They'd never make it.

࿐

Jed split open the floor to confront Lucifer face to face. He forced the fissure to open wide, cinderblocks along the wall crumbling from stress. Anger manifested the flames, reinforcing his delusion that Hell existed just below the building's splintering concrete.

The entire back of the building was engulfed in darkness as it dissolved. Jed's mouth fell open. He turned to flee through the very door he'd frozen shut.

࿐

Kristen couldn't risk looking back. If they reached the safe house in time it would be a miracle. Groaning, Jack staggered along beside her, heavy against her shoulder.

"We're going to make it," Kristen said. "We have too."

She could see the house now, only a hundred feet away. The edge of darkness, straight ahead, was now unavoidable. From the front and sides it closed around them. A car that had stopped in the middle of the street was disintegrating; its molecules whisked away in a cosmic vacuum. She dared not look back for fear of having something similar happen to them.

They were one house away now. She could see the porch, the screen door. A frightened face peered out as they hobbled toward safety. The car ahead was now completely gone except the front bumper, which dropped to the asphalt with a *clank* before disintegrating like the frame it had clung to.

Kristen cut across the lawn and made for the steps of the house, which was now the only thing visible. Everything else was blackness. Nothingness. She hit the steps hard and pulled Jack up with every ounce of strength she had left. They were so close to safety now. They couldn't fail.

The screen door opened. Jack fell inside. And, at the same moment, Kristen felt iron fingers dig into her arms. It was Jed. She tried to pull away, but his grip was firm. His terror-filled eyes pleading for help as one of his legs disintegrated.

Grabbing his arm, Kristen fell in the direction of the open doorway, bringing all that was left of Jed with her. His upper body thumped heavily to the ground with his second leg gone. Someone grabbed her under the arms and pulled her inside just as the darkness reached the doorframe and silently stopped.

Kristen yelped as she stared in horror. Jed's torso was disappearing and then his head dropped to the floor, rolling to one side. The darkness ate away at the head while frantic eyes glared at her until they dissolved. His hand was still attached to her as if it had a mind of its own. Everything above the elbow was gone; tiny particles still coming apart and being wisped into the blackness through the doorway. Kristen clawed at the fingers, trying to pry them off her. It finally dropped to the floor, with a sickening *thud* of bone and flesh.

As the digits flailed helplessly – palm facing up – the hand continued to disappear until fingers dropped away unattached, now looking like five thick worms squirming to bury themselves in earth. Soon there was nothing left but fingernails as they manicured themselves into oblivion.

She collapsed onto the hardwood floor, exhausted. Everything was quiet and still now. The room seemed to be glowing red from some unknown source. Kristen struggled to keep her head off the floor as she turned to make sure Jack was okay.

They'd made it, which was the last thing she remembered before falling asleep.

"How long will they sleep?" Petrov asked.

"Just until we can repair the damage. A week. Maybe two," Sweeney replied.

Warning sirens shrieked as the medical staff work feverishly. Even with backup help from Scottsdale Memorial, they had already lost two patients to cardiac arrest. Several others were receiving treatment from defibrillators, paddles pressed to dying chests, causing them to heave with each discharge.

"I need that epinephrine *right now*," one doctor shouted.

"Grand mal on twelve," one of the interns yelled.

Another flatline alarm sounded from the far end of the room. "Cardiac arrest. Defib on twenty-eight. I need some help here."

Unit number twenty-eight was their latest addition and none other than Devon Guerridelli. As a scientist, Petrov would never show any trace of pleasure over the tiny bit of satisfaction he felt, knowing Guerridelli might not make it. It was small consolation, given the circumstances, but it was something.

"Dear Lord. What on earth do we do now?" he said, half to Sweeney and half to himself.

"I say we tell them everything, once the dust settles. Those who make it, anyway."

"Maybe you're right," Petrov said as he watched the chaos unfold around them. "But it's not as if we can merely sit down and have a chat with them."

"Maybe we can," Sweeney said. "You know what they say. A picture is worth a thousand words. I think we should just show them. My group could have it set up by the time things are running again."

Petrov was getting too old for this. After the situation was under control, he would prepare his resignation and deliver it to the chairman. If the government found him negligent, he could face criminal charges and prison. Should such a time come, he'd have to decide whether to follow in the footsteps of his comrade and fellow scientist, rather than face a life inside a different kind of cell than the one Albatross had provided for him all these years.

"Might as well," he said. "Might as well."

CHAPTER 38

When Jack opened his eyes, everything seemed different than it had moments earlier. Or had it been hours? Days? He wasn't sure. Sunlight streamed in from the windows. Earlier, the darkness had swallowed the subtle sounds that people hear but never pay attention to unless they're gone. But now he could hear the comforting purr of a car's engine passing the house. A warm breeze wafted in through the screen door with the sound of a neighborhood child at play.

Around the room, bodies lay strewn across chairs and sofas, slumped over like dolls. Several were sprawled on the floor, including Kristen. And they were all sound asleep. Somehow, Jack realized the world had righted itself while they slept.

Then he thought of the injury to his leg. Though he didn't feel it now, he was certain that the moment he tried to stand, the pain would come stabbing back in bone-twisting agony. He rolled to his knees and stood. Both legs felt equally fine.

His leg had been healed, restored.

A vague memory of Kristen, struggling to break free from Jed's grasp, drifted through his mind, but he couldn't remember if it was only a dream or something that had really happened. For that matter, had any of it happened, or had they all participated in a joint hallucination? Perhaps the result of Albatross's research project – if, indeed, he could call it research anymore.

Jack pushed open the screen door and stepped outside. Walking down the porch steps he felt the sun on his face, one more indication that things were back to normal – inasmuch as his life could ever be truly normal.

There were a multitude of questions to be answered, but perhaps the most important one would be left a mystery. That is, whether or not Petrov had made it.

His new sense of well-being was being replaced by a need to know, the peaceful morning turning into another quest to learn the truth. He began walking up the street. At first it was slowly, as he glanced at the houses that seemed awake with activity.

Several cars passed and a bicycler rolled by, cutting into a lawn to avoid him.

He walked faster, more purposefully now. The last time he'd come this way, all he could remember was the pain and panic, using Kristen as a human crutch and praying they'd make it to the safe house. He glanced at his watch, remembering he'd started the stopwatch when they'd left the house before. But it had somehow reset itself, just like everything else in the world.

When he reached the corner, he immediately saw large aluminum letters attached to the brick face with protruding posts. He wasn't a bit surprised. Perhaps it was because, over time, people adjusted to diverse circumstances, and he'd merely begun to accept that things could never be taken at face value again. Or maybe something inside had told him what he'd find. The fact of the matter was that Albatross Life Corporation was now right where Jillian had told him it should be.

Albatross's business plan had been dated eleven years into the future. What if he'd actually been sleeping for eleven years and now here it was, open and ready for business? How else could he explain it?

There was still no one about when he pulled open the glass door and walked into the lobby. But the concrete floors were now covered with beige tiles, and the walls with matching fabric. A reception desk and switchboard were to his right. The double doors that had led into the cavernous room were open and Jack could see a broad hallway leading deeper into the building. Seeing the yellow glow of a sign above one of the doors, Jack instantly knew that all the answers he needed were held behind that door; all of Albatross's secrets tucked neatly away so nobody could see. It was a feeling more than anything else, but a strong one.

Jack froze. This was the moment he'd been striving for. But could he face the truth? Behind that door was something so devastating that countless fantasies had been erected just to conceal it.

The lighted sign read, *Online*. It was a double door with small square windows, showing a dimly lit room with only the faint glow of ambient light seeping out. He could barely make out forms and shapes as he pushed open the door and stepped inside.

He heard the faint sound of beeps, like the hospital room of a critically ill patient; mechanical air, cycling through pressurized contraction and discharge; contraction and discharge. Now inside, as his eyes adjusted, he could see the room was far deeper than it was wide. Down the center was an aisle with neat, straight rows of large objects that looked like caskets. All of these were identical and finished with brushed-aluminum exteriors. The tops were transparent, convex domes.

Each unit had numerous cables protruding out of the head, attached to panels on the wall directly behind them. Above each panel was a plaque with a number and a name. Strange metallic grave markers.

Jack walked slowly toward the center aisle. When he reached the first row, he leaned down to glance through the transparent lid where a dim light illuminated the cavity within. He immediately jumped back, reeling in horror and disgust, for inside lay what appeared to be the corpse of a white-haired woman with fragile, wrinkly skin that looked thinner than tissue paper. Her mouth was slightly open and brown-stained teeth were partially obstructed by thin, colorless lips, while her hands rested over her abdomen with gaunt fingers.

Cables and tubes protruded from nearly every orifice of the cadaver, infusing artificial life into the body, as if the place were a high-tech production center of Frankenstein's reanimation laboratory. Her chest rose and fell with the sound of mechanical breathing, forcing air in and then letting it back out, effectively replicating what the woman's chest muscles could no longer accomplish.

Jack looked over at the opposite unit and found a similar view. What was going on here? He'd learned the company was conducting longevity research. It was as if they were keeping the bodies of people alive on machines, bodies that should have been buried and mourned long ago. Though the idea of preserving the life of a loved one was admirable, there was a time to let go;

release them back into the realm of the unseen. What possible good could be accomplished by forcing worn-out bodies to simply go through the motions?

When Jack grew this old, he wouldn't want some scientist forcing him to stay alive. No doubt they were in a state of limbo between life and the hereafter, not having any form of consciousness. Though he wasn't sure where his beliefs rested, to deprive these folks of whatever lay beyond death was a travesty against nature and borderlined abomination.

"We had to show you."

Jack jumped as the voice cut through the synthetic sound of medical equipment. He looked up and saw the silhouette of a person standing in a doorway at the far end of the room. It was a voice he'd heard before. One with a Russian accent.

"I feared you would never fully understand unless you saw."

"Saw what?" Jack asked. "That you're keeping people alive on machines? What do you stand to accomplish? What possible good could come from this kind of research?"

"We had great plans, Hunter and I," Petrov said, ignoring Jack's question, his voice sounding like the reminiscent utterances of an old man. "We honestly believed we could change the world; give people a better life by extending their time here. Double, possibly even triple their life spans. Project Methuselah was *this* close. It was a brilliant, ecumenical approach to gene therapy. The implications staggering," Petrov said, his strained inflections and over-exaggerated pronunciations giving away his passion. "But they shut it down. They had to shut it down."

Jack waited, deciding he'd learn more than he wanted by being patient and listening.

"I'll never forgive Hunter for what he did to me. To the project. We had it right here," Petrov said, grasping at air, "in the palm of our hands and he ruined it for everyone. For that I will never forgive him. Dear friend, yes. But a fool.

"I had to do something. The investors were threatening to sue," Petrov said. "It was far from the vision that Hunter and I shared, but somehow I justified it in my mind, thinking it was the next best thing. Who could reject the opportunity for a second chance? To do the things you've never done, but always dreamt of.

"You want to know what my biggest regret about Methuselah's failure was?" Petrov asked. "It was the fact we couldn't provide this great gift to every human. The new project was no substitute and left me playing political games designed better for capitalists than scientists. I was merely trying to salvage the company. Bring something useful out of all our work. But Project Alice would never be the global gift to humanity that we'd hoped for. It became a plaything for the rich. Sure, a second chance, but a grossly inferior alternative at best.

"Now I'm paying dearly for compromise. You tell me, Mr. Stuart. Or shall I call you by your real name, Howard Cochran, The King Crab – the man who made Crab Shack a household name. Was the second chance worth it? Would you do it again if you could?"

Jack's mouth went dry. All he could see was the awful little man that haunted his dreams, pinchers instead of hands, dressed in red...*like a crab*. He started walking slowly toward Petrov now. What the hell was going on here?

"I highly doubt it," Petrov continued, answering his own question. "In fact, I almost guarantee it. Even without the Guerridelli mishap, you were growing restless. You all were."

Jack finally found his voice. "What are you talking about?" he demanded. "What do you mean, a second chance?" He glanced to his right as he passed unit number six, where the name William Donald Stephenson was displayed.

"A second life, really," Petrov told him. "If you can call it a life. As flawed as it was, we sold you the concept that Project Alice was better than nothing. Than rotting in a grave. It was enough to spark the imagination of folks like yourself. People with lots of cash and nothing left to spend it on. In some ways I feel like a prostitute for taking your money just to save Albatross. Forgive me for misleading you, Mr. Stuart."

Jack walked past units eleven and twelve, not wanting to look at the withered bodies inside but unable to keep himself from doing so. "What exactly are you saying?" Jack asked. "I paid for a second chance?"

Petrov was silent now.

"Are you telling me that I used to be someone else," Jack said as he approached units fifteen and sixteen. Halfway through the room now, he stopped. "And that I paid you…I don't understand. How is that possible?"

"Our contingency plan was to keep people alive long after their natural lives had ended. Like what you see here. Through the use of modern medicine, we were able to simulate most of the body's functions with machines. Keep them running for twenty or thirty additional years – perhaps much longer."

"Why? What's the point?"

"Their brains are alive and well, I assure you. As yours is, Mr. Stuart."

Just as Petrov spoke, Jack's eyes fell on the plaque above unit number seventeen. He suddenly felt his heart pounding as his mind grappled with what he was seeing. For the name below the numerals read, "Jack Anthony Stuart."

No. Jack mouthed the silent word.

"There was no easy way to tell you," Petrov said. "While your body lies here, your mind has been fooled into thinking you're standing in this room talking to me. We've tied all brain sensory functions to a simulator using cybernetics. It's a lower profile science than genetics, but it held the means to salvage Albatross."

Jack was shaking his head, trying to reject the unfathomable notion. He felt as though he were staring at his own gravestone. Except that he could see the shrunken form beneath the transparent dome, more ghastly than the sarcophagus remains of an unwrapped mummy. It looked nothing like the wretched man in his dream, but hideous in its own way.

"It's you, Mr. Stuart. Like it or not."

"But how is this possible?" Jack stammered.

"Nothing that you've seen, touched, smelled, or encountered since you woke up in that hospital eighteen months ago has been real – except for the people at the safe house, people just like you who are being kept alive like you see here. We created a virtual world, Mr. Stuart, a simulated world designed and set in a period just after the turn of the twenty-first century."

Jack couldn't speak. He was having difficulty breathing – if he could even call it breathing.

"We've reconstructed Albatross's facilities in the life simulator. To show you. What you're now seeing is merely an emulated reflection of the real thing. When I said I didn't exist, it was true. Technically, I don't exist in the simulator. Right now I'm standing in a green room. My image is being projected into the simulator for your benefit while your image is being displayed to me on a computer screen."

Jack could barely register what the doctor was saying. Everything that had gone on over the past few days seemed common and ordinary compared to what Petrov was telling him now; a trucker coming back from the dead, the entire city of Las Vegas turning into a haunt of brainless zombies; even the darkness that had swallowed the world and everything with it. All of this was as commonplace as apples on the desks of teachers and the inevitability of junk mail.

"We should have told you," Petrov said. "From the beginning, when you awoke in the hospital. But our original intent was to hide the fact clients are in a simulator, make them believe they'd suffered an accident or contracted a high fever. It was the only way to explain away the amnesia. But we soon realized that wasn't good enough. Nor was the simulator. Computers can mimic the real world with incredible detail and accuracy. But the human mind is still far more advanced, able to detect slight nuances that computers can never imitate. Artificial lives leave clients with a shallow, unsatisfied feeling. Especially while interacting with simulated characters. That's why we started bringing clients together. It led to a more genuine experience, usually enough to convince them that everything was as it should be. You and Miss Bandy were an exception."

Petrov pointed to another unit where Jack could see a plaque with Kristen's name on it. Though he already knew what lay inside, he couldn't bear to look. Kristen was Kristen. Punk. Sassy. Full of youth. He couldn't stand to think of her as a decaying woman.

"Even though your life in the simulator was unsettled, there were signs you were beginning to bond with Miss Bandy," Petrov told him. "And that gave us hope that things could be salvaged. Now, of course, it's irrelevant."

Jack was trying to grapple with this new reality, attempting to make some shred of sense out of what Petrov was telling him.

"What went wrong?"

"Devon Guerridelli is what went wrong," Petrov said. "I shouldn't have agreed to take him on as a client, knowing his involvement with organized crime. He's the man you know as Jed Pope and our latest entry. We should have realized that he – or his family – would do something like this. His grandson came to work here as a monitor, under a different name. He was hired just before Guerridelli became a client. But he passed the background tests and polygraph without incident."

Petrov's voice seemed to drop in volume, growing older and more haggard with each sentence, as he explained how Jared had tampered with the simulator's baseline code, resetting Devon's security access to "god mode" and altering the way his grandfather interacted with the emulated environments, installing a loopback-on-demand feature that would deliver any information about the virtual world that he wanted to know.

In case he got caught – and as a clever precautionary measure – Jared built his own firewalls around his grandfather's processor that were like onionskin shells of security. At the innermost layer, he'd set a trap that would rebuild the security layers from scratch with all new passwords if anyone ever hacked in.

"When we discovered what was happening, we fired him, of course, naively thinking we could undo the damage. But we later learned that Jared had downloaded a virus into the simulator when he initially came to work for Albatross. It sat dormant so long as he fed it with a password every few days. When he was gone and wasn't able to regularly administer the antidote, the virus activated itself," Petrov said. "I suppose it was a sick form of insurance, knowing that if we fired him, all hell would break loose."

Petrov leaned against the doorframe, his voice growing wearier. "And it did," he said. "It did."

"The darkness," Jack said.

"Is that what it looked like? Darkness?" Petrov asked. "To us it was merely all the simulator data being erased, wiping out twenty terabytes of disk space. I suppose the fact it appeared like darkness was fitting."

"How come a safe house?" Jack asked.

"It was the only thing we could come up with in the short amount of time we had. The virus was erasing data sets from the highest numbered segments to the lowest. Each data set represents sixteen square miles of simulated space. Scottsdale was the first to be created and numbered segment zero. The rest spiraled out, created from the origin. So it erased from the perimeter and worked its way toward the center."

Being in the software marketing business, Jack understood some of what Petrov was saying. But he wasn't a programmer and was only marginally keeping up.

"Fortunately, I learned an important lesson from my first CS professor. He'd say, 'Always remember to backup.' But you don't simply reboot and restore with twenty-eight people attached. Our backup systems have backup systems. This computer can't go down or we risk sending a whole roomful of elderly folks into cardiac arrest. The strain of the cybernetic links being turned off and on would be enormous on a healthy person, let alone those who are barely hanging onto their lives.

"That's why we created the safe house. We hot-plugged a new processor with isolated memory and dedicated hard drive. It had triple redundant power to be sure nothing went wrong. One drive isn't much when you're dealing with this magnitude of data, but it was enough to hold the safe house. Since Jared's virus locked us out of our own system, we had to get those who could make it to the new processor before they were caught in empty sectors of deleted disk space. That meant reaching the access point we created, which was the house in Scottsdale. Once the virus ran its course we could reboot the simulator without affecting the stand-alone processor – the safe house, as it were.

"We restored from a backup just before Jared started working for Albatross. It was no easy task. The restore procedure, alone, took days to complete. Then the monitors had to reconstruct as much as they could of the several weeks leading up to the reboot. There will be many holes and inconsistencies, I'm certain, but it was better than losing everything.

"We were able to resuscitate some of those who didn't make it to the safe house, but sadly lost our fair share. Most to heart failure. In their condition, they simply couldn't withstand the strain."

Though he struggled with all of this, Jack was beginning to see that he hadn't been crazy; a thought that gave him marginal comfort. He'd felt he didn't fit with Maggie, the kids. In a life that didn't make sense and one that he hadn't created for himself. He thought of his attempt to flee his family and go to Europe and the strange circumstances, which had resulted in getting hooked up with Kristen. For some reason he pictured the woman outside of the grocery store asking him, *what exactly do you want?* The question had seemed strange at the time, but now made perfect sense. But this question was no less relevant now than it had been at the time. And still just as profound.

Before abandoning this strange link between the real world and the simulated, Jack said, "I have some questions."

As he hurried back to the safe house – realizing now that it was nothing more than a hard drive and processor – Jack glanced around. Though he tried, he couldn't tell that blades of grass were anything less than real, or that the pavement beneath his feet was not authentic. But now that he thought of it, something *was* missing. Subtle nuances, Petrov had called them. There was artificialness about everything as a whole that made him wonder why he hadn't noticed it before. Perhaps he had, but simply wasn't sure how to express it. Maybe that, along with the shallow, simulated relationships, had been the contributing factors to his angst.

He thought of Kristen and decided he couldn't wait to see her. All he wanted to do was stare at her until his virtual eyes hurt, knowing she was as real as anything he'd ever known before turning himself over to a machine.

Petrov had told Jack that she had once been a famous actress, perhaps the most famous of all time, grown tired of the spotlight, the glitter, the glory. Jack smiled to himself, remembering her brilliant performance in their encounter with the concierge.

Nearing the end of her life, she'd approached Albatross for a "second chance", hoping this time around, to lead the quieter life of an attorney. Since she'd dropped out of college to pursue acting, she'd chosen to attend the simulator's version of Harvard as a way to make up for not finishing school like her mother had wanted.

Interestingly, Kristen had rejected her fantasized role just as surely as the rest of them. Hearing about the others, it was obvious to Jack that the people who had been given the opportunity to tailor-pick their lot in life, had always chosen something different than what they had had before, an epitome of the greener-grass syndrome.

Jack learned from Petrov that he, himself, had never married or had a family, either because he was a work-alcoholic, relentlessly pushing out the boundaries of his Crab Shacks, or because no woman would have the ugly little crab-man that he had been, he wasn't sure. But given a blank check for a second chance, he'd chosen to be tall and good-looking, the antithesis of Howard Cochran, The King Crab, deciding also that he would be a family man in his prime with a pretty wife, a couple of well-behaved children, and an easy job with plenty of freedom.

As for Drew, his father had been a minister and had always wanted Drew to follow in his footsteps. Instead he had rebelled and gone into business, ultimately becoming the CEO of a major tobacco company.

While dying of cancer, however, Drew had decided to make his peace with God by following in his father's footsteps on a trip through cyberspace, only to find out that he wasn't cut out to be a small-time pastor. As for Marilyn, the less than attractive daughter of an auto industry mogul, teased while growing up because of her appearance, she had chosen to become a replica of the most glamorous woman of her time, Marilyn Monroe. The fact that her brain had been damaged during the interface procedure made her presence in the simulator a peculiar reminder of the American icon.

The irony that Kristen had abandoned the life of an actress while Marilyn had sought one was further proof that people, by nature, were never satisfied but were always fence-hopping to find that illusive greener grass.

The grass on Eli Houston's side of the fence had been justifiably brown and Jack couldn't blame him for wanting a drastic change. An investment banker who'd suffered and recovered through two market collapses, he had been traumatized by the suicide of his only son and unable to recover and, subsequently submerging himself in work, had lost his wife as well. The fact that he was the only client who had somehow managed to make it through the interface procedure with his memories intact added insult to injury, his second chance becoming nothing more than a bitter and angry existence.

Jack's sudden illness at the airport had been explained by the fact that the simulator contained massive amounts of data, requiring countless man-hours to define a single town, let alone a whole country. As a result, only the United States, Mexico, and the southern-most regions of Canada had been included. While they had to maintain the illusion that the rest of the world existed, there was no possible way they could allow one of the clients to leave the country. In such cases – actually, Jack's incident had been the only one to date – it was the monitor's responsibility to 'persuade' the client in another direction. Jack still felt queasy thinking about how persuasive his monitor had been.

When Kristen had seen her dead trucker, who'd seemingly come back to life, she was really seeing one of thousands of truckers who'd been created from the same template. Although the simulator was filled with millions of characters to emulate life in the United States, there was no way designers could tailor-make each and every one. To streamline the process, designers developed character templates. When automatically generating a new character, the simulator would start with a base template and then randomly choose properties like hair, eye-color, and numerous other attributes. There were a dozen templates, alone, for the trucker profession. Coupled with other attributes, this would allow for millions of combinations. The trucker she'd seen at the motel just happened to use the same template as that of Randy Longfellow.

Confirming Jack's suspicions, most people around him had been simulated characters; digital manifestations designed to fit carefully into the new life he'd chosen. The reason he'd felt nothing for Maggie was that she was little more than a glorified Barbie Doll, looking pretty and saying all the right things when he pulled her string. And no wonder Justin and Amanda had perfect dispositions. Even Peter Lynchman, his business partner, was a fake, along with the other folks at CareSoft.

Jillian in marketing was also a simulated character, but had strangely stumbled upon information about Albatross that wasn't supposed to be in the system. When systems designers had sought to recreate Internet content, they used real data taken from the Internet History Database. Though filters were used to weed out anything inappropriate, some information accidentally got included. One such item was Albatross's business plan, dated eleven years into the future relative to the simulator's calendar.

The anomalies they'd seen in Las Vegas were largely the result of Jared Guerridelli's tampering. Because of side effects from the virus, programmed characters were faulting and throwing exceptions, causing subtle to bizarre behavior. A few of the strange things they'd witnessed were a result of finding areas clients were never meant to see, such as the empty hotel rooms. With so much detail to create inside the simulator, designers hadn't filled in every nook and cranny, especially when it involved locations clients should never visit. Hasselbaum's house was one instance where monitors had had to quickly furnish the interior when Jack and Kristen decided to go inside.

As Jack neared the safe house, he could see someone moving inside. Unless Eli had already told them, he would have to and the thought of such a task filled him with dread. Jack took a deep breath and walked up the artificial steps and opened an imaginary screen door.

The first face he saw when he walked inside was that of Kristen. She looked both afraid and aggravated that he'd disappeared.

"Where've you been?" she asked.

But he could tell by the look in her dark eyes that she knew, somehow, that he had learned the truth.

"Folks," he said. "We need to talk."

CHAPTER 39

It came as no surprise when Dr. Malcolm Petrov delivered his letter of resignation to Albatross's board of directors. The time was right; in fact it had been for some time. In spite of Project Alice's many faults, it still proved to be their best hope for turning the company around. None of the board members blamed Petrov for the Guerridelli meltdown – which was the way they now referred to the incident – and, in fact, saw it as an opportunity to improve upon how the project was run.

Dr. William Hunter's son, Alex, became the general operating manager and made several immediate adjustments. First of all, he decided that there was no point in attempting to hide the fact that clients were in a simulator. When they woke up in the virtual world, they were already confused. Why not use that window of opportunity to acclimate them, rather than conceal the truth? Alex designed a program in which patients would be walked through a series of exercises to orient them into their new environment. Also, early in the orientation, they would be briefed on their prior involvement with Albatross and told the truth as gently as possible.

Various other changes were made as well. Most were intended to make life inside the simulator more tolerable and relevant. For one thing, clients no longer had to design the perfect life beforehand. Instead, they could choose their own path once they were connected and acclimated, often migrating from one situation to another during the course of their new life. Even changing their appearance wasn't out of the question. Having an extreme makeover took on new meaning, as they were given the opportunity to sample fuller lips, choose different eye and hair color combinations, or simply throw it all away for the body of their favorite super model. The best part about such creative body sculpting was that it was instant and painless.

But not all the changes were skin deep. Clearly, Albatross needed to improve the relational aspects, particularly since the computer-generated characters, while realistic and well-conceived, could never take the place of human interaction. Virtual conventions, of sorts, were created, where all clients could meet regularly and mingle. One of the system designers had also begun experimenting with interfaces to the real world. One day, it was their hope to allow regular interaction between those in the simulator and their loved ones. All in all, future clients would enjoy a far richer experience.

On the business side – something near and dear to Alex Hunter's heart and just what Project Alice needed – some marketing changes prompted new growth and two more life simulation rooms were added to the Scottsdale lab. Taped testimonials from inside the simulator were turned into television spots that showed happy retirees, young again and doing all the wild and crazy things they'd never done in real life. These bungee jumping, parasailing, scuba diving, snowboarding seniors had never looked happier.

In an attempt at the ultimate senior discount, Albatross arranged a deal whereby spouses could receive special rates when purchasing together, allowing them to share their lives beyond the natural world and into cyberspace, a far more meaningful experience, the commercials reasoned, than simply purchasing adjacent cemetery plots.

As new life breathed through the company, Albatross attracted the attention of a well-known pop artist who had an affinity with Peter Pan. Since money was no object they agreed to custom-develop his own environment, the costly endeavor pushing their books into the black for the first time. Geographically, they placed Neverland on Maganda Pulo, a small island in the South Pacific, and provided an alert mechanism in case anyone ventured near it. Coming upon the surreal island accidentally might prove to be disastrous.

Devon "The Viper" Guerridelli suffered from a major cardiovascular infarction when his world suddenly dissolved around him. The medical staff was unable to resuscitate him. Even though his sons tried to strong-arm the company for letting their father die, they ultimately realized that the real culprit was their own stupidity in allowing Jared to tamper with the technology. Had they simply let things be, Devon might have been able to find some shred of a second life, living out the remainder of his days in a dusty desert town called Bootleg Hill, Nevada.

Eventually, Petrov planned to enter the simulator himself, experiencing firsthand the fruits of Project Alice. Albatross's doctors, working together with cybernetic specialists, continued to refine their interfacing techniques with the hope that one day their clients' memories would remain intact. Petrov longed to spend his extended life, continuing to research gene therapy with a synthesized version of William Hunter.

❧

When Drew Prescott learned the truth, he was appalled that Eli had been right, that he had paid millions for a virtual fantasy rather than accepting his place in the hereafter, forced as well to grapple with the fact that much of what he had perceived as God's guidance had been nothing more than a monitor's handiwork. The result had been a depression, which Marilyn, in all her innocence, had snapped him out of. They'd gone on a trip to see Niagara Falls, somewhere he wanted to take Marilyn and think things through, and were peering at the spectacular wall of white water, spilling a million gallons every seven seconds, when Marilyn said, "It's awesome. Thank you for bringing me."

"It's not real," Drew told her coldly, unsure if the girl grasped what was happening, how their senses were merely being fed computer signals.

"I know," she said to Drew's surprise. "But it's still awesome. And I know that someplace is the real one."

Drew's throat had lumped up at that. Somewhere there was a real one, indeed. How else would they have been able to model such a spectacular display inside of a computer, had there not existed the original. And though his faith had been misplaced in the monitors, that shouldn't prevent him from having a genuine faith that circumvented the boundary between cyberspace and reality.

Drew eventually had a serious talk with Marilyn. It was time for him to accept what lay beyond, he told her, assured her that she would be cared for after he was gone. But Marilyn simply wanted what he wanted. Absolutely sure she understood the implications, he placed a call from a cell phone while they sat on a beach, enjoying the ocean's mild surf, and informed the attending monitor that the time had come.

Meanwhile, Eli Houston eventually decided to bring his simulated journey to a halt as well, but for far different reasons. Unable to bear the thought of spending eternity being tormented by all his past memories, he ended his journey with one final drunken orgy, his prearranged time clicking off his light at precisely two o'clock in the morning.

As for Albatross's other clients, most chose to remain in the simulator, waiting out their artificial lives until the machines could no longer sustain them. Had Kristen not come into his life, Jack wasn't sure which path he would have chosen.

But she had.

⁂

The blades of four Allison turboprop engines, mounted under the wings of a military C-130, currently being used for civilian purposes, cut through the air over Perris, California. In this particular world, military personnel had nothing better to do, anyway. Side benches lining the cargo hold could easily have accommodated dozens of troops, but on this September afternoon, there were only a couple of passengers, one of whom had her eyes open so wide she was in danger of having them remain permanently fixed in that position.

"You scared?"

"I'm not scared. I already told you."

Jack folded his arms and smiled. "Oh, you're scared all right."

"You don't know that."

"Just remember," Jack said. "The worst that can happen is your parachute won't open. You have a quick ride down and then wake up in the hospital without a single broken bone. It might actually be fun."

Kristen was clearly not amused by his remarks. "I'm not scared," she insisted, glaring at the fuselage as though it might suddenly give way to the air rushing by outside.

Jack was thoroughly enjoying this. For the first time since he'd met her, the girl didn't have a decent comeback. He remembered his first impressions of her, sitting there in his condo as if she owned the place. Now she looked terrified by what she was about to do.

In the days that had followed the Guerridelli meltdown, Kristen and he had spent most of their time together. Even though they were still just friends, Jack wondered if Kristen would ever want something more.

"It won't be that bad," he told her. "Really."

"I'm not scared."

"Of course you're not."

There was a sudden jolt, followed by the sound of groaning metal while the large, mechanical ramp at the back of the aircraft lowered. Kristen clutched Jack's arm as light poured into the cargo bay.

"I thought you weren't scared," Jack said, grinning.

"I'm not," she said and stood, pulling a leather cap over her head and fixing goggles in place. "It just startled me. That's all."

"Your head looks like half of a black and blue cantaloupe," Jack said.

"Very funny." Kristen turned to face the sky out the back of the plane.

Jack saw her flinch when a speaker crackled to life and the pilot announced that they were over the drop zone.

"Aren't you forgetting something?" Jack asked.

"Oh yeah," she said, turning. She grabbed the back of Jack's neck. Pulling his head down, she put her mouth to his in a long, sensuous kiss that lasted for what seemed like minutes.

"I…uh, meant your parachute," Jack stammered, red faced.

"It's right here, fly boy," she said, lifting it from the floor and strapping it on. "See you on the ground!"

And, giving a geronimo shout, she dropped quickly out of sight.

Mesmerized, Jack followed her. The valley below was breathtaking to behold even though he knew it was a fabrication of reality. When the wind sucked him into the plane's backwash, he suddenly realized his mistake and started to panic. The violent turbulence buffeted his body, giving him adrenalin rush. The ground below was racing toward him on a deadly collision course.

But it wasn't real, he told himself. He closed his eyes to regain composure while trying to remember where he was: not dropping from ten thousand feet over Perris, California, but inside a room at Albatross's headquarters. Finally he began to relax in spite of his blunder. Sure, it was a long way down, but so what?

He was alive. Free. The feeling of lightness was incredible. And now he also knew the truth. It was freeing.

So alive.

Kristen would tease him for not being more careful. Unless she was annoyed at the inconvenience of having to stop by the hospital to pick him up.

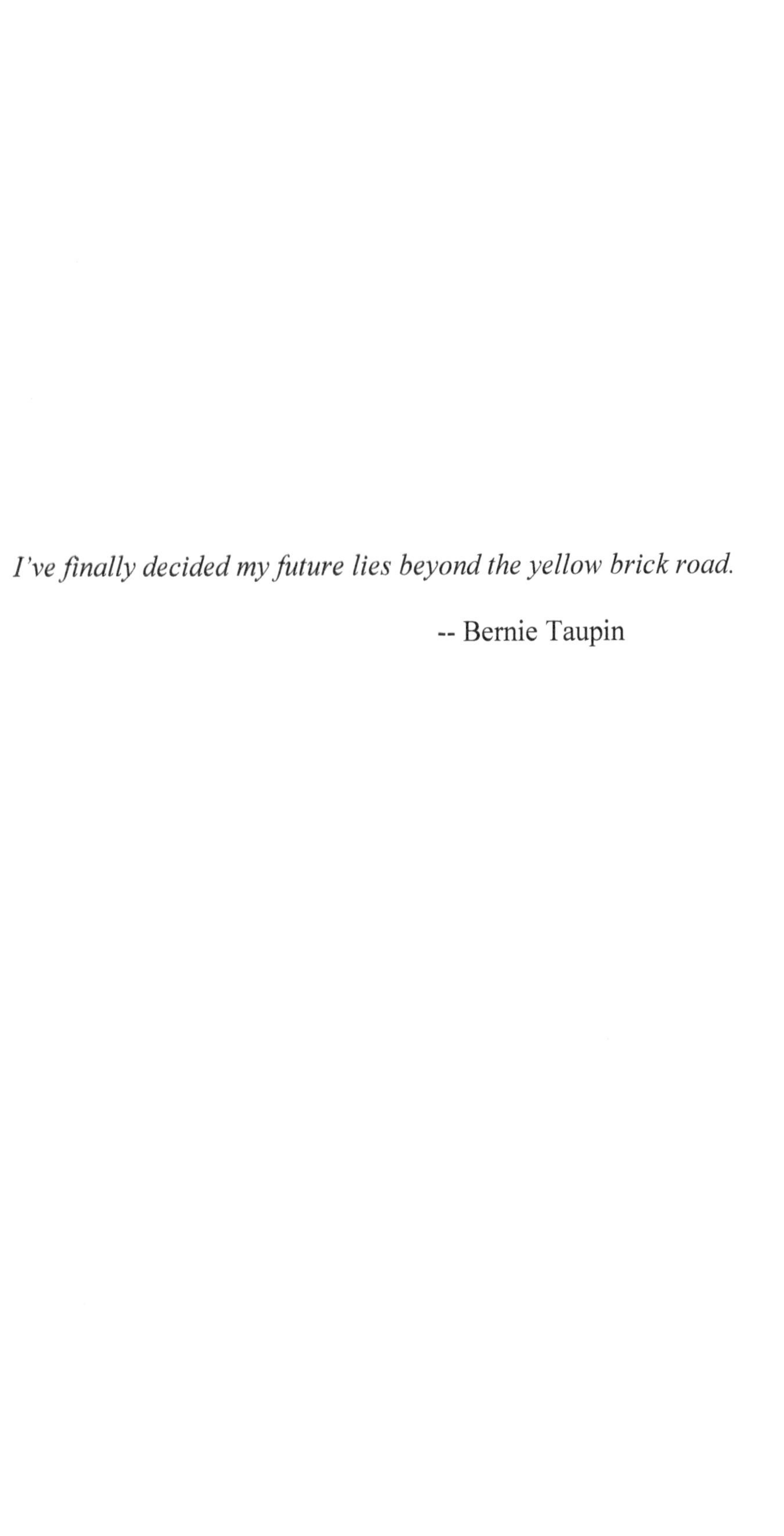

I've finally decided my future lies beyond the yellow brick road.

-- Bernie Taupin

www.ingramcontent.com/pod-product-compliance
Lightning Source LLC
Chambersburg PA
CBHW030422310726
48979CB00009B/1569/J
9780972076739